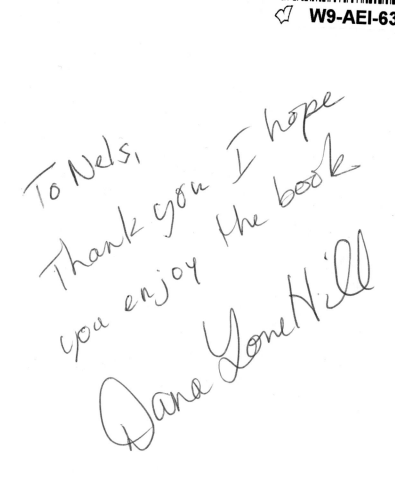

To Nels,
Thank you I hope
you enjoy the book

Dana LoneHill

Pointing With Lips

Early Praise for Pointing with Lips

"With so much literature out there attempting to portray authentic Native life, it is refreshing to have a work written from the perspective of someone who has actually lived it. This book is essential reading for those attempting to understand the life of Native people living in America."

- Brandon Ecoffey, editor, Native Sun News

"Dana Lone Hill is a powerful new voice from Lakota Country that has so often been confined to historical stereotype or painted in a contemporary setting with a one dimensional brush. Dana shatters those shackles and forms a deeply personal, raw and moving narrative that takes the reader deep into contemporary life on Pine Ridge Indian Reservation, one of the world's most complex and engaging societies."

-Steven Lewis Simpson director of the Native films *Rez Bomb, A Thunder-Being Nation & The Hub.*

"*Pointing with Lips* by Dana Lone Hill just might be one of the best books I've come across—if not the best. A beautiful, entertaining, relatable, inspirational, and so-much-more read, Lone Hill's poetic yet readable wording makes you feel as if you're sitting attentively across from her, gripping a cup a coffee waiting for more."

-Patricia Stein, Urban Native Magazine

"There are no lines to read between, no innuendos or creeds of illusion or clichés when *Pointing With Lips* has taken the breath our mothers, fathers and relations must breathe for each generation. Some say, "time has forgotten the Lakota," ... I don't think so. It has remembered us more so than any other nation borne out of living reality and not using reality."

-Tiokasin Ghost Horse, First Voices Indigenous Radio WBAI, NY

Pointing with Lips

A week in the life of a rez chick

DANA LONE HILL

Blue Hand Books
Greenfield, Massachusetts

Dana Lone Hill c/o Blue Hand Books
442 Main Street #1061
Greenfield, Massachusetts 10301/USA
www.bluehandbooks.org

Publisher's Note: This is a work of fiction. Names, characters, places, and incidents are a product of the author's imagination. Locales and public names are sometimes used for atmospheric purposes. Any resemblance to actual people, living or dead, or to businesses, companies, events, institutions, or locales is completely coincidental.

Book Layout/Editor: Trace A. DeMeyer
Book Cover: Kim Pitman, Firefly Inx.com with photography by Jaida Grey Eagle and Tom Swift Bird

Ordering Information:
Quantity sales. Special discounts are available on quantity purchases by corporations, associations, and others. For details, contact the "Special Sales Department" at the address above.

Pointing with Lips/Dana LoneHill. -- 1st ed.
ISBN 978-1495945298

Dedicated to the memory
of Grandma Dod with love and baseball.

I rolled on, the sky grew dark
I put the pedal down to make some time
There's something good, waitin' down this road
I'm picking up whatever is mine
I'm runnin' down a dream
That never would come to me
Workin' on a mystery, goin' wherever it leads
Runnin' down a dream
-Tom Petty

[one]

Friday

The pow wow grounds on my reservation are always dusty. Actually, the whole village of Pine Ridge, South Dakota is dusty. The pow wow grounds are in the center of town and are circular in shape, so everyone walks around and around the arena, making them the dustiest part of town in this dust bowl of a town—especially during a pow wow, which happens twice a year on these grounds. Our village is in the southwest corner of our reservation and in certain ways, on a certain part of any given day, it can be the most beautiful place on Earth, especially when the sun is shining on it just right. At other times, the heat and the wind kick up the old white clay dust that we all walk on and then it gets carried all over to layer everything in its path. The old folks around here call the white clay *gumbo*; they say you can't grow a blade of grass in it because it is clay. This may be why we have a lack of vegetation as grass and trees dot our town so sparsely. Then again, it could just be that people just don't care.

My grandma grew a huge lawn full of grass and surrounded the house I now live in with cottonwood trees and chokecherry bushes that she transplanted from the creek. Either way, it really sucks if you don't have air conditioning in your car at this time of the year, during the annual Oglala Nation Fair and Rodeo. Or as most people on the reservation like to shorten it to: the slang term known especially in our village of Pine Ridge as "Og Naysh."

This is when all the pow wow trail people come to town—not just them but tourists who are interested in pow wows and us. People from all over America and the world are fascinated with us, maybe because we are still here after all the bullshit America put us through. This late in the afternoon the sun is well on its way to the western side of the horizon, baking all the Indians a shade or two darker, and making our men congeal to that shine only an Indian man can possess. Somehow, we forgive them for their grease. Today, I am with my best friend and cousin, Boogie, and my six-year-old daughter, Jasmine. Boogie is circling and circling the pow wow grounds looking for the closest parking spot. I am not in a good mood. I'm a little hung-over from having a few beers the night before while I made some earrings and listened to Credence Clearwater Revival. I am hot, frustrated and running out of patience. I need to sell my artwork—absolutely need to—and here Boogie is acting like he is 138 years old.

My name is Sincere Strongheart, but almost everyone calls me Sis. I live on the Pine Ridge Indian Reservation in South Dakota, which is between the Sacred Black Hills and the Badlands. If the county we live on (Shannon) is not the poorest county at any given moment, then we are usually a close second to one of the counties of a neighboring reservation in South Dakota, and there are nine reservations in this state. Statistically, in the Western Hemisphere, we compare only to Haiti in poverty. The last time I checked our life expectancy rate, the average man on the Pine Ridge lives to be 48 with the average for a woman being 54, which means I passed my midlife crisis stage at 27. If I acted like some kind of midlife crazy-eyed bitch back then, I don't remember and I apologize.

I am a single mother of three and I get by. I really am not bitching, because I get to live in my grandparents' house, so I don't pay rent, but the house is old. My grandpa built it way back when my grandma first started making his heart skip a beat. I have been working at our town's only shopping center, the Great Sioux Shopping Center—an all-purpose variety store that includes everything from a hardware department to a toy department to a grocery department—for almost twelve years now, but I am still part-time. Part-time will cover any bills, which I usually avoid until I am threatened with a "shut off date," printed in CAPITAL LETTERS on brightly colored paper. I also do bead work and porcupine quill work. Quillwork is a more traditional and ancient art form, dating back to when our people didn't have beads and so they used porcupine quills for their design and adornment. The beadwork and quillwork help, especially in the summer time.

Anyway, to avoid getting the lights shut off, we are on a mission at the pow wow. I am hoping to sell the fifteen bracelets and six pairs of earrings I've been working on all week. I saved them to sell on the first Friday of our pow wow, so I can pay my light bill. Also, I want to go to the bar later with Boogie. We have had plans for a while now.

I taught Jasmine to string beads into simple necklaces, so she is going to try to hawk her goods at the pow wow, too. I had hoped she would never have to depend on her skills as an artist the way I did but, then again, maybe in the long run, it will come to be a blessing to her like it was to me because I never had to pawn anything. Not that I have much to pawn, but still I never lost anything to a pawnshop. When I was little, somehow my mom would luck out or get into some money and buy us a nice TV, an Atari, games, etc. Nice stuff. It would all eventually be lost in pawn in less than a month. And even though I'm poor, I never have to be broke. As long as I make and sell at least one thing a day, I am never broke. I just get tired of making and selling and working at my job all the while, still struggling. It is a hustle every day and relying on my artwork, while knowing I would always be poor, can be exhausting sometimes.

I sometimes wonder if I should have moved away to a city the way my little sister did as soon as she turned 18. What sucks about that is that this is my home and my people. Why should I have to leave the reservation to have a "better life and-or live longer?" What if I had married right away? What if I had gone to college like I had planned, instead of going through with a pregnancy that I didn't plan? That was the point when I went to work at the grocery store to put my "soul-mate-at-the-time" through college. I didn't plan on him dropping out and cheating on me, nor did I plan on having twins right off.

So, now here I sit in Boogie's van while he searches for a perfect parking spot. All so I can sell my art for the sake of electricity, and my daughter can sell hers for the sake of having carnival money for the weekend. Boogie finally finds a spot that suits him, thank God.

Stepping out of the car, the sounds and smells of the pow wow swirl around me like a shawl with its warmth and familiarity surrounding me, I immediately feel comfortable. This is my rez pow wow. The bells and jingles of the dancers, the beat of the drum, the pitch of the singers, the smell of the hot grease bubbling on the skillets, and the emcee booming over the loudspeakers, "Intertribal! Intertribal! Everybody, Pow Wow!" makes me immediately at ease with my surroundings.

Once upon a time, I snagged me a fancy dancer from another tribe from a galaxy far far away at an annual pow wow nearby. He was gorgeous with long shiny hair and perfect chiseled features. When I first saw him, I could seriously picture him in a loin cloth on a horse riding back to me after a war party. Boy, did I learn my lesson! Fancy dancers are bigger players than a whole drum group put together.

Never again in my life will I get romantically involved with someone on the pow wow trail, no matter how good the Indian Health Service dental clinic was to him or how much shit he could talk. Those types of men leave a trail of children and broken hearts behind on all the reservations and cities they visit. They put the "intertribal" in the pow wow circuit.

But that is the story of where my beautiful daughter Jasmine comes from, a result of my wanting to turn the pow wow trail into a fairytale. I will never let her know this, though, and her father will never know about her—something that Boogie to this day thinks I'm wrong for doing. But I just prefer it that way. I didn't want her to get her heart broken over and over the way he broke my heart over and over. He was never going to settle down and that was that. Especially after I found out she was his eleventh child and spread across seven reservations in three states. I can't deny that her height, her perfect nose, and her smile that's bright like the sunshine come from him though.

"Shhhh," Boogie turns to hush me with his finger to his lips. "I'm going to try and get us in for free." He giggles like a little bitch.

"Oh, shit, Boogie, just pay! It's too hot and I'll pay you back, I promise." I wipe a layer of sweat and dust from my forehead.

Next thing I know Jasmine is stage-whispering like Boogie. "Why doesn't he want to pay, Mom?"

"Because he's an idiot!" I tell her, crossing my arms, my Ziploc bag of quillwork tucking into my body.

Paying customers are making their way around us, and Boogie starts flirting with the young security guard as if he has a chance. I knew Boogie was gay back when we were three, although then we just called it "funny." Or, as my Grandma Pacific said, "He has a little sugar in his tank." He officially came out of the closet in kindergarten when we fought over the same dude, which scared him away from both of us. Everyone on our rez always knew Boogie was gay. Or, in our language, winkte.

Grandma said the word winkte comes from *winyan kte* and is shortened to winkte... it means to "be like a woman." She said that a long time ago, there was no homosexuality and a winkte had a purpose, which was to work with babies or children. Now it is just interpreted as being gay when that isn't the meaning. Some people now call it being two spirited, meaning that a person is like a male/female but liking the same sex. Grandma said, at one time, this person performed the roles of both male and female; they would do craft work and cook but also hunt and chop wood. Boogie likes to think being winkte means "two-spirited" so it gives him an excuse to have a bipolar breakdown and, after he's done flipping out, he will snivel, "Well, remember, I'm winkte—two spirited."

To me, being the modern rez chick I am, I just think it means being gay.

Boogie, despite his breakdowns, can be tough; he is 6'1" and 250 lbs. but he has already fought all the battles he was going to fight for being who he is, which made him into a tough-ass gay guy. My brothers tease me and say that I can't get a man because I substitute Boogie in so much and no dude would want to hang out with me and my gay cousin. But we're a package deal: hang with me, my gay cousin comes with—as long as the dude don't get all funny and "bi-curious" when we drink together. However, Boogie believes every guy is gay and just hiding in a straight closet.

"You see... there are people in there waiting for my niece's necklaces." He points to Jasmine with his lips. "Plus she's close to heat exhaustion, I think." He points with his lips again. Jasmine wipes her forehead and sighs. I roll my eyes.

Drama-queen-in-training.

"Excuse me?" Someone taps me on the shoulder. I turn to look and see that it is a tourist.

"You have those for sell?" ....A tourist with an accent. (Accents usually mean we can charge a higher price.) He was kind of cute in a British sort of way—or was he? Would he be cute with the same floppy hair, stubble, and arctic blue eyes, sans accent?

Boogie turns his attention to the tourist—who is actually one in a group of many—gets a whiff of money, along with musky foreign body odor, and gives up on hassling the security guard. Next thing I know, Boogie is doing what Boogie does best, telling stories. He guides them with his body language to follow him to his van where he says he will show them genuine artwork made by "real Lakota women" (his sister and his niece). I smile, he reminds me of a mother hen. We all follow Boogie to his van as he clucks away.

Since Boogie and I go way back to when we fought over Barbie dolls; we are like sisters, or brother and sister, or gay brother and sister. Whatever. Regardless, Indian way, he would be my sibling because we are cousins. At least, I think we are third cousins, I'm not sure. I give up trying to understand how people are related on the Rez. I just remember that if someone is not a blood relative, then we are related either through marriage or a "hunka."

A hunka is when you adopt someone into your family. It's a traditional ceremony that usually involves a feast and giveaway. I have a hunka brother and sister my dad adopted from the Winnebago tribe named Matt and Carrie. Matt became fluent in Lakota, putting me and my brother George to shame. Carrie and Matt both live in Wisconsin but they come down to our Rez for ceremonies and the pow wow, which means they should be pulling in right about now or they are already here camping at my dad and step-moms.

If you ever ask my Grandma Pacific though, she has a way we are related to everyone. She hunkas everyone left and right. Boogie said it's because she doesn't ever want to miss out on any wake, funeral, wedding, baby shower, graduation or memorial. She is one of the few select group of ladies related to everyone for "maximum wateca exposure." *Wateca* is a skill: it is when you gather leftovers after a feast. You know how when you go to a big dinner or feast and as soon as the dinner is over all the women start gathering leftovers to take home. Now, this may not sound like a skill, but then maybe you have never witnessed an Indian woman gather leftovers. We are able to produce makeshift tupperware out of thin air. My Grandma Pacific usually moves like syrup with her *sagye*, her cane, but when it's time to wateca, she moves as though she is a 20-year-old woman again. Most women get better at gathering leftovers with age. (I keep telling myself that is why I am not good at it. I'm not even young anymore, but I still get punked by my elders when I wateca.)

Anyway the "wateca queen," Grandma Pacific, even thinks she's related to Tom Brokaw and Bob Barker, just because they are from South Dakota. It's overwhelming to talk to her about all our relations, especially if you are dating; she will find a way you're related to your unsuspecting snag. The most horrifying moment I had in a new relationship with a cool-ass dude was her looking at both of us and looking away saying, "You two probably shouldn't be going out." How embarrassing! After he left, I went over the family tree with her trying to eliminate him, somehow. I mean, geez, he was from a district farther than our lips can point.

I ignore Boogie and Jasmine as they bullshit the tourists. The work can sell itself. They don't have to lie and tell sad-ass sob stories, but Boogie loves the drama and he drags Lil' Miss Drama Queen right along with him. I wanted to sell the work at a table in the pow wow to a vendor because it would be a one-shot deal: get rid of it and get out. I could almost taste the cold beer. But Boogie seems convinced that tourists are the way to go. You could make more money, but I'm just not that good of a story teller.

"Her dad is stationed in Iraq, she wants a phone card for her birthday so she can call him. Her birthday is tomorrow..." I hear Boogie; I watch the pow wow people walk in circles. I look even further away, beyond the present and into a place where I don't have to hear the lies being told to sell my work.

"I miss my dad," Jazzy sniffles. They are setting the bait. She is a better actress than Shirley Temple, the gall of her to pretend she knows her dad. I look away, not knowing if I want to smile or be embarrassed. I do both.

I look back over to see about twenty tourists all pawing over the stuff, pulling their money out. Boogie is snatching it and handing over items. Jazz is selling her necklaces for ten dollars each. Holy.

Boogie and Jazz are exchanging money, making change, and talking. I smile. My girl was going to be alright in this world. I have to admit they are getting great prices, better than I would have. If I had made more, we would have sold it today. Some tourists are walking away empty-handed as Boogie and Jazzy start counting up the money. Jazzy makes $150 for her necklaces, and I make $420. Boogie immediately takes $100 from Jazzy to put towards her school fund and then he takes us to put $250 towards my light bill. My smile fades slowly as he starts the van.

Boogie is no fun sometimes.

The trip through town takes forever, even though the pow wow grounds are about three city blocks and one stoplight away from the grocery store. There is so much traffic leaving from the pow wow and it is so hot. This is why I stopped going to the pow wows. Well, that and because of Jasmine's dad. The traffic is bumper-to-bumper and there are stands from local tribal members out on the street selling everything from delicious BBQ to arts and crafts to lemonade. (Most of our tribal members couldn't afford a booth inside the pow wow, so they started setting up on the sides of the streets.) The tribe started charging them, but it was still cheaper than having stands inside the pow wow arbor. It is kind of cool—a week of flea markets, fairs, and gypsies—almost. I have never seen gypsies; I've just read a lot of books. If it weren't for the heat and the traffic, I could go for this year round: the beat of the drum, the sound of the jingles and the food stands. Almost.

We pull in outside the Great Sioux Shopping Center. I peek back in at Jazz, "You coming or what?" She smiles and jumps out of the back of his van.

"Don't you dare pet Wahumpi!" Boogie yells at us. "I don't want any fleas in my van!"

Our Rez and our town is full of stray dogs, so many that PETA should really give a damn. Our human population on the reservation is about 16,000, but if you were to count the dogs it would be more like 32,870. We have so many strays, that they start to have names. This is where Wahumpi comes in. Wahumpi means "soup." Legend has it that Wahumpi was destined to be in a ceremonial pot of soup. He escaped the pot, but the name stuck. He's become almost the town dog. A huge St. Bernard-gone-wrong looking sort of thing. He hangs out at the grocery store all day and then heads out at night to sleep in different people's houses. He has spent a few nights at my house—and he makes a pretty good watch dog, if you ask me.

As we walk by Wahumpi and his gang of stray mutts, Jazz tries hard not to turn her head, only looking at him sideways because she knows Boogie is watching. He wags his tail twice as if to say, "Yes, I know you'd pet me, but your uncle is a bitch."

The blast of air conditioning hits me instantly, relief. Going to the store here is like a social event; you see people you really don't see anywhere else but here or on Facebook. I make small talk with the lady in the customer service desk as I pay my bill. I nod my head at her, agreeing to the horrible heat of this year, the traffic being bad, the jails being packed, and yes I'll tell my mom you said hi, since they did go to boarding school together way back in the day on the other side of the state.

After I'm done, I go off in search of my brother Raymond, or Misun, which means "little brother" in Lakota. He's 26 years old, he works part time in the hardware section, and takes his basic classes at our tribal college. He wants to be a teacher, I think. I kind of wish he would find a good woman, but we are all so protective of him, I don't know how he ever will. He definitely is good-looking with his dark complexion and easy smile. His last woman was scandalous, always cheating on him; I slapped the shit out of her, but that served the purpose only to make him mad at me. Anyway, he did get three beautiful daughters out of her. They've been broke up for a couple of years, but any new potential girlfriend usually has to put up with drama from his ex. She moves on (again and again), but she throws a fit if he does.

His three daughters are Jasmine's best friends and best cousins.

Cante Skuya, which means "sweetheart," is eight years old; Sahar is seven; and Winterblossom is six. Misun has his hands full for the next eighteen plus years with them. Jazz is going to the carnival with Misun and his daughters tonight, much to her delight. He lives just out of town on his grandparents' land in a three-bedroom trailer, and Jazz loves it because there are dogs to play with, a slip-and-slide, and sweet plum bushes.

Before I continue, I should explain my family structure a bit more.

My mom is Velma Rain-On-Shield. My mom used to be real pretty before she allowed all the drinking and partying to carry her looks away, slowly, like the wind takes fluffy dandelion seeds on a hot summer day. I have three brothers and three sisters. Well, now I have two sisters because Rita died of SIDS when she was 5 months old. In all, my mom had seven of us.

The eldest is my brother George Strongheart. He married my former best friend Chris, from the junior high days and they have two kids, George, Jr. and Georgette, as you can tell he is so full of himself by the names of his kids. He's 33 years old and a cop... a 33-year-old dickhead. He's pretty tough, but maybe I just can't forgive him for throwing me in jail a couple of times for drinking. We had been fighting all our lives, so one time I was drunk and tough and started pounding him, only to have him sign "assaulting an officer" charge on me. I had to sit in jail for two weeks. If Misun hadn't stayed at my house with my kids, social services would have become involved and it would have been a hot mess.

By the time George got around to dropping the charges, I wanted to kick his ass. But I maintained my cool and just anonymously batted the windshield of his cruiser out and spray-painted, "Fuck the Police" on the side of it with my brother Mark. Mark watched me go psycho on the cop car. All this happened while Misun took George out for target practice shooting prairie dogs. That is the secret we are carrying to our graves, because surely it is a federal charge.

Next in line is me, Sis. My full name is Sincere Charlie Strongheart. My dad wanted to name me Sincere, and since "Charlie" is his first name, they named me Sincere Charlie. Dad lives out by Denby Dam; I go to see him and my step mom once in great while. They make and sell tipis and star quilts online for a living. Rita, George and I all belong to Charlie Strongheart.

Then there are the twins, Mark and Misty, age 28. Misty left the Rez as soon as she could. She lives in St. Paul, Minnesota. She legally changed her name from Rain-On-Shield to Morris as soon as she could also. She really doesn't want anything to do with her culture, the heritage, or her people. In other words—us. We rarely hear from her. She wants to be white. She even wears blue contacts. Her and Mark have no problem passing for white, being iyeska (half white), they are both gigi or light skinned. She has no kids and is not married; she only wants to make money, save it, and count it to make herself happy. Our mom said that no man wants to marry a woman who isn't true to herself. And she must know—she isn't married. Neither am I, for that matter. I guess that analogy kind of sucks an egg.

Mark remains a Rain-On-Shield, even though he is a light-skinned Indian. Mark is an alcoholic who sometimes hangs out in Whiteclay, Nebraska (a Rez border town and the closest place to buy beer). He used to be really good-looking—still kind of is—but drinking has stretched his 28 years to look like a hard 40. He and Misty's dad died in a car accident when they were little.

Mark has one son that we call Yamni (or Yam) meaning "three" in our language, since Mark is a Jr. and his son was the third. Yam lives with his grandma on his mom's paternal side. He's a bit of a bad kid, running with gangs at age thirteen. But he is fiercely protective of his dad, Mark. Which is good because Mark drinks and doesn't care about much; we all have to keep an eye on him. At first we used to rush right up to Whiteclay and make him come home but, after a while, it got to be too much. He liked to stand up there like he had nowhere to go with a big can of malt in hand.

After Mark comes Raymond, or Misun—and I am closer to him than any of the others. I'm close to all of them but Misun has never stole from me. Well, George and Misty never have either but Misty is gone and George is, well, a cop.

Misun's full sister is Frieda. She is only 23, but the wildest of us all. She has four kids. She has John and Johnetta but she lost custody of them when they were two, and she was 18. She was arrested on a number of charges, which included a beat-down of the twins' dad's new girlfriend (that one almost went federal); she was remanded to tribal jail for a number of months. Their dad won custody of the kids and moved them off the Rez. His family more or less ran the tribal court, so they had a speedy trial while she was in jail. She stayed in jail until her baby, James, was born. A few years later, she had Wiconi which means "life." We all love Wiconi—she's a doll.

Frieda now is on housing assistance and lives in a tribal housing house that the federal government provides. It's the same program I am on the waiting list for. That kind of irks me, because I am living in my Grandma Pacific's old-ass house. I mean I am lucky: it has electricity and plumbing, although we can't get the kitchen sink to quit leaking so we have to keep an ice cream bucket under the sink and keep emptying it. And there is no heating system, except for a woodstove. Thank God I have two sons who are strong, because I don't split wood. I may be a rez chick, but that is going too far. Sometimes my brothers will split wood or my sons' dad or whoever my current snag is.

The youngest in our family is Shyla. She's 17 and is about to start her senior year of high school. She's trying hard for a scholarship off the rez somewhere because she doesn't want to go to the tribal college. She made us all proud by maintaining a 3.43 GPA and being on student council. She lives with our mom on the back road; they have no plumbing but they have electricity. They usually fill jugs of water up at my house to take them home, and Misun picks her up early in the morning to shower at either my place or his, and then he takes her to school. He doesn't have to do it, but he's cool like that.

We want Shyla to do better than us and not end up working at the Great Sioux. I've been working part-time there since I had my twin boys. It is better than being on welfare. I get medical and food stamps but no cash assistance. Misun keeps trying to make me enroll in the tribal college, but I already feel too old to go.

I walk over to the non-food half of the huge store that serves our reservation with just about everything we could need, without leaving the rez, but at triple the price anywhere off the reservation. You could save money buying off the reservation but you would pay the difference in gas. The store has evolved over the years but basically is your all-around general store from the Little House on the Prairie days. You can buy anything from limes to fish sticks to mothballs to beads to nails by the pound. And they, of all places, have the nerve to sell dream catchers made in China and no one protests. I hate complaining about it because I could protest myself, if I wasn't scared of losing my job.

I find Jazzy in the toy aisle being teased by her favorite uncle, Misun.

"Enit, Sis?" He winks at me. "Jazz is getting off with me now, huh? She's gonna stock shelves because that's the only way I will take her to the carnival. Enit?"

"Not uh!" Jazz, screams before I can embellish upon the lie. "There's such a thing as child labor laws, Uncle Misun!"

I have to laugh; she's gotten that line from her brothers. They all try to use it when we clean house on Sundays.

"What time are you done?" I ask him and look at my watch, which is really just my wrist because I lost my watch last time I went drinking with Boogie.

"Five o'clock. Will she be ready by then?" he asks.

"Yeah, Boogie and I still got to get ready. Shall I feed her?" I look at her looking at toys, "Jazz, you know you don't need a toy, they have stuff at the pow wow."

She glares at me. She's really good at glaring.

"Nah," he says, "Grandma Frieda is making all of us Indian tacos because she said she doesn't want us to buy any there, plus hers are better. She puts Hormel chili mix in the meat."

Yum. I had one of her Indian tacos before. They were delicious. Plus if you have a local taco, you are guaranteed commodity cheese.

Commodity cheese is the best thing the government has ever done for Indians. It was like their way of trying to make up for breaking treaties. Close but no cigar. Little slices of heaven, yes, but we would rather have our land back.

"Yippee!" Jasmine hollers at the prospect of an Indian taco and kicks out a quick fancy shawl dance move.

My girl's been wanting to dance at pow wows for a couple of years but I've been procrastinating. Every time I put energy into beadwork it is for sale and not for use, but maybe that is just my excuse. Maybe I am secretly scared of her dad, of her being like her dad, or of the potential of her meeting her dad.

"Hey, give your uncle your money so he can watch it for you," I tell her. She stops dancing and glares at me again. She knows it is pointless to argue with me, but I dread the time when she matures a little and gets all hormonal. She opens her little purple purse and hands Misun two twenties and a ten.

"Whoa, big bucks. Hey. Rich chick! I might need a loan from you, favorite niece," Misun says, which makes Jasmine giggle.

"I had more. I had $150 but Boogie took $100 for school clothes shopping." She gloats, "I sold all my necklaces."

"Good thing Boogie took it, so your mama don't spend it," Misun teased and ducks as I playfully take a swing at him.

"Speaking of Boogie, he's probably pissed. Let's go, little woman." I grab her hand and take her towards the front of the store.

On the way out the door, Jasmine talks me into buying Wahumpi a beef jerky because she feels guilty for not acknowledging him earlier. Then she wants to buy Boogie one for making him wait, then she wants one for herself for a "waiting snack" because she has to wait for her Uncle Misun to pick her up at five o'clock. That's when I decide I need a "just because snack" and buy myself a beef jerky as well.

As we walk out the door and back into the dusty, dry rez heat, Jasmine gives the dog his snack. Boogie sits in his van glaring at Wahumpi—seriously, who glares at dogs? What a loser.

An old rickety familiar van pulls up honking as steam comes up from under its hood. It's Ol' Albert High Road; he is maybe 60-years-old and a Vietnam Vet. Some people are scared of him because he is also six foot five and wears an eye patch. He's a hustler—then again we all are on the rez—but he's a pro at it and knows most of us artists don't have legitimate rides with insurance and updated tabs to go off the rez to sell our artwork. He buys quillwork and beadwork to sell online or in the Black Hills at tourist shops. He also always has quills, rawhide, beads, earring hooks, dyes, anything you need for crafts, all stuffed into his van. Albert's a good old guy—if the pow wow had not been during this weekend, I know he would have helped me with my light bill.

"There you are, Sis! Went by your moms and she said you'd been working on a bunch of bracelets. Let me look," he is hollering over his chugging engine.

"I just sold them, for twice what you would've gave me," I laughed.

"To who?" he demands.

I start to tell him about the tourists at the pow wow but his cell phone starts ringing. He proceeds to scream into his cell phone, "Where?! When?!"

He hangs up and tells me, "Gotta go. They said there is a big fat dead porcupine three miles west of here!" Then he spins out of the parking lot to go west. I swear he salivates at the thought of reusable road kill. I hate road kill and will never buy it from anyone ever again.

Jasmine and I get in Boog's van and she hands Boogie his beef jerky, who takes it, shoves it in his mouth and starts chomping like a cow.

Thank God, maybe she had something there. Keep him fed and you don't have to hear him bitching about how long you took. According to his dashboard clock, it is 4:15p.m. And we have exactly 45 minutes until Misun meets us at the house to take Jasmine to the pow wow. I remind Boogie about that and he finishes chewing on the beef jerky as if it were a struggle, then starts his van. I am grateful we are on the road again as he pulls out of the store's parking lot and turns south to make the two mile journey to Whiteclay, Nebraska. The breeze, although hot, at least dries my sweat. I am starting to feel like a piece of frybread.

Whiteclay is just two miles over the state line from our hometown of Pine Ridge and, being that the reservation bans alcohol and Whiteclay sells it, it is a very well-traveled road. Whiteclay is second to the city of Omaha in beer sales for the state of Nebraska, for the obvious reason that it is the closest town to us to buy alcohol. They sell almost five million cans a year and have a population of 12. How they justify that, I don't know. Who am I to even ponder that? I add to that grand sales total, also.

Boogie stops at the first bar where a hot, young guy with tattooed arms named Tony works. He gets out of the car, but is back quite quickly.

"Tony wasn't working," he explains, although he doesn't really need to. He hands me a six-pack of Budweiser and gives Jasmine a lime pop before he starts driving again. Traffic doesn't get thick until we hit town, and then it's like a New York City traffic jam. (Wait, do people in New York even drive?)

By the time we pull into my driveway at my house in the middle of town, Boogie has already finished one beer. We go in the house through the back door, which is the one we use the most. Boogie immediately turns on all the fans in the house, including the ceiling fan. He hates that I don't believe in air conditioning, but I like fresh air, not recycled. After spending two weeks in jail, recycled air makes me feel claustrophobic.

When my grandpa built this house for my grandma, he staked out a big yard. Then he transplanted baby trees from No Bottom Creek all around here, along with chokecherry bushes. Not only did that guarantee that my yard is enclosed with privacy, the shade keeps my house cool. The trees are huge now and I get more than enough chokecherries every year, which I sometimes sell, but most of the time, if anyone wants any, I tell them to come pick them themselves. Sometimes when I'm lounging out in the backyard, I look at the trees and think of how much my gramps must have loved my gram. And yet she seems so mean. She must not have always been mean to have a man do all this for her. Shoot, I'm amazed if a man makes me toast.

Jasmine starts packing an overnight bag. Boogie is digging in my fridge—because he's a pig like that—so I take the opportunity to jump in the shower before him. Boogie takes longer than a woman to get ready and he isn't even femme like that. Plus, I have more hair to dry.

I hear him start cursing as he hears me getting in the shower and I laugh to myself. His fault, plus he doesn't need to worry about hot water; it is so hot out a cool shower was just what we need. I don't know if I need to shave my legs, but I do anyway. You never know who you might meet.

I am sitting at the table putting my makeup on and Boogie is in the shower when Misun pulls up, still in his work shirt. He walks in the back door and makes a beeline for the fridge. I like how everyone heads for the fridge before they even say hi or tell me to fuck off. Sometimes, right before food stamps come out, there ain't shit in there and I want to laugh when they open the fridge and keep looking as if a Boston cream pie will appear out of nowhere. That's when I hustle on the beadwork or borrow food from someone. Since I used food stamps not that long ago, my fridge today is locked, stocked, and loaded.

"Who's watching the house?" Misun asks as he stuffs his face with a banana while making a ham sandwich with the other hand. What talent. He is noting the crumbs and syrup on the kitchen counter from this morning's breakfast.

"Man, quit putting your war paint on and clean this mess up. It's gross," he says while chewing his sandwich. His mouth is full while he talks, and he knows I hate that.

"What's gross is you talking with your mouth full. Grow up." I flip him off and go on applying what might be my 33rd coat of mascara with my mouth open. (It's impossible to put mascara on with your mouth closed.)

"Oh, and Craig and Creighton are watching the house, but they will be in late because of the baseball tournament."

"I'll check on the twins later," he says as he digs a Coke out of the fridge. After drinking it in one shot, he lets out a loud disgusting long burp that clearly came from the bottom of his soul.

"That sounded painful," I tell him.

"It was."

"You're gross; it's no wonder Tiff left you," I tease him. It was a low blow, but he is tough. He has to be: he is the little brother.

"No, she left me because she wanted to be a disgusting whore." He bombs his Coke can in the trash, then hollers for Jasmine, "Munchkin, you ready?"

She comes around the corner.

"Yes!" she says then she asks, "Uncle Misun, did Tiffany get her wish?"

"Huh? What?" He is all confused.

"Did she become a disgusting whore?" Jasmine asks him. I want to laugh, but I know better.

"Uh..." He doesn't seem to know how to answer that. I glare at him.

"Yes, she did and a damn good one at that," Boogie says as he appears, laughing, not a hair out of place and wearing enough cologne to suffocate a room of fifty.

Misun glares at Boogie. "C'mon Jazz, let's go eat Indian Tacos and go to the pow wow and let your mom and Auntie Boogie go pretend they're young and hot." He hurries out the door before I can throw something at him.

"Ready?" Boogie asks.

"Yah," I tell him and grab my purse.

"You got your overnight bag?" he asks. I grab the Wal-Mart shopping bag that has in it my change of clothes.

"Yah," I am ready.

"What about your wet wipes? Or baby wipes?" he asks.

"Really? I mean, really? Boogie, what the hell do I need those for?" I don't know what in the world he is talking about.

"You know to wipe it in the morning, in case you get lucky and don't have time to shower." Then he lets out his big, stupid Boogie laugh. I cuff him in the back of his head and mess his gay hair up. He pushes me away and straightens his hair.

Before we leave, I call the boys who are at their dad's to remind them that no one is going to be here but tell them that I will leave the TV and the lights on in the living room. Those were sort of our alarm system. (That and my neighbor Nam has great watchdogs that watch my house too.) I also tell them their Uncle Misun would check in on them.

Boogie grabs the four bottles of beer that are left along with a banana out of the fridge while I grab my purse and Wal Mart bag and then we are off: headed to a party at a bar in Rushville, Nebraska.

Or so we think. As we near Whiteclay, we see cops cars and flashing lights.

"Fuuuuuuuuuuuuck," we both say in unison. We always fail to get out of town in time for the roadblocks that go up every year during the pow wow. They also go up for New Year's Eve, Super Bowl Sunday, Christmas, Prom, Homecoming and Graduation. There are three different back roads, seven bootleggers in town, and a bar on every road leaving the reservation, but the pigs seem to think that a roadblock at this one stop will keep us from buying beer.

I see my brother's police cruiser parked to one side and George is pulling beer out of a washing machine that's in the back of a pickup. Man, you'd think that plan would have worked. It seemed brilliant enough. It probably would have but George thinks he's Super-Bacon. He's a hero dip wad cop like that. Boogie knows George would turn us in, even for just the four bottles of beer, so he turns in at the town's waste management site, aka town dump. He pulls up next to a row of dumpsters that are overflowing and immediately flies swarm the van and buzz inside his van. I start shoo-ing them away with disgust as Boogie surveys the roadblock. What a way to start the freaking night. He throws some trash from the floor of his van out into the dumpster. We both remember my brother

George taking us to jail before. Like I said, Super-Bacon. We start to head back into town.

"Damn!" Boogie hits the steering wheel, dramatically.

"I wanted at least another six pack of beer! Especially now that we have to go through Gordon or Chadron to get to Rushville!"

Rushville was a small town where the pool tournament was. It was only 23 miles away but to go through one of the other towns added another 30 miles on the trip, at least.

"Cruise by the pow wow grounds," I tell him. "I'll get you a lemonade—a good one." I try to convince him, because now he's pouting. He usually liked to have a buzz before we hit the bar.

He turns towards the pow wow grounds when we roll into town and cruise until he finds Aloysius Kick The Sky's stand.

"Two lemonades," Boogies says, handing him a ten spot. "With the kick," he says, in his stage whisper. We watch intently as Al grabs the ten, squeezes a lemon in each cup, with the whole lemon going in, then adds some sugar, and water from two different bottles—one of those really being vodka. After he puts ice in, he applies the lids and straws, and he tells us to have a nice day. Aloysius has been selling Kick the Sky Lemonades for years. I swear the cops have to know, but I bet he makes so much during the pow wow, he pays them off. He also buys a new car after each pow wow. We used to buy from him in high school even.

We sip our Kick the Sky Lemonades, and we head out East to the route that will take us through Gordon, Nebraska. We will go on through Gordon to Rushville to get a room and to meet our friend Zona. Zona is our third musketeer. We are supposed to meet her at the Watering Hole in Rushville, where she is in a pool tournament. We are going to be her cheering section.

Zona escaped from her abusive relationship and took her son with her to Alliance, Nebraska, to live and work off the rez. Alliance is a ways away from us, and we miss her terribly. She hates coming back because of the drama that she mostly created herself by carrying on with her high school sweetheart, which royally pissed off his wife and her husband.

"MMMMMMmmmm," Boogie is slurping his lemonade, and I swear snorting. I look over to make sure he isn't snorting. Nope, but he is sucking on the straw so hard his eyes are closed, while driving!

"Boogie!" I holler at him. He opens his eyes and laughs, adjusting the wheel to line up on the road better.

"Sorry. It's just so good."

I had to admit, the "kicker" lemonade never changes. You still couldn't taste the vodka, just like it was while we were in high school.

Boogie looks over at me with evil in his eyes, "Let's race?"

"Sure," I say, as if there was no question about it. And there was no question about it. I had worked for almost three weeks straight to guarantee these days off. I was ready and raring for that buzz.

Boogie stops at an approach and we start sucking through the straws; 40 seconds later, I have a killer ice-cream headache and Boogie is finished with a disgusting burp. I finished seven seconds later with what feels like an ice pick stuck in my right eyeball. Ouch... but, damn, it was worth it.

"You burp like a man, Boogie," I tease him.

"Sweetie," Boogie pats my shoulder, "at this moment, I am the only man in your life." Once again, his hurricane of laughter.

This pisses me off, because it is true. I rub my right eye until the ice pick is gone, then I grab two beers from the back of the car, open both of them, and hand one to the only man in my life. Sad.

He looks at me, "cheers to us," and drives on.

"You better fix your makeup again, Sis. It's all off your right eye." Then he laughs like what he said is so funny. He takes a long swig of his beer as we enter the sand hills of the state of Nebraska.

I get my makeup bag out of my Wal Mart bag and start to repair the damage the ice pick headache caused. Not only is Boogie the only man in my life, but he is a damn good one. What other man would tell me to fix my make up?

Of course, he probably doesn't want to walk into a bar with me looking all jacked up either. But in my lemonade-vodka buzzed moment, I truly appreciate him.

I might even forgive him one day for stealing my John Travolta *Saturday Night Fever* doll when we were five years old and drawing pubic hairs on it with a Sharpie marker.

Maybe.

Or, if he would ever admit to it, I would forgive him.

Dana Lone Hill

[two]

Moonlight

Boogie pulls his van in the small, dusty border town of Gordon, Nebraska. Most of the border towns around our reservation have a troubled history with our tribe due to racism, discrimination, hate crimes, etc., but I think Gordon might take the cake in that department. Back in 1972, an Indian man from our reservation was beaten, stripped, stuffed in a trunk, and publicly ridiculed, then left for dead. Out of the five people originally charged, only two were prosecuted on manslaughter charges with seven years served and a thousand dollar fine between the two.

Although times have changed, and we have to depend on border towns for such things as shopping, jobs and housing, relations are still and always will be strained. The racism around here is deep. It has not changed in over a hundred years, and I don't see it changing soon.

On the way up through the sand hills, Boogie bet me I couldn't hit one sign with the four bottles of beer we drank. And I missed, every single time.

Boogie looks at me with the same evil smile I know and detest. "Shall we stop at The Roost?"

"Boog! No!" I say. "Zona is waiting and probably already pissed."

"Pshh! Whatev!" He waves me off, already slowing down at the turn to The Roost. "We have a half hour to spare."

He pulls into the side parking lot and honks his horn twice as if they were expecting us. Boogie turns sideways in his seat, which is not an easy task with his chubby frame.

"Look Sissybug, we do have time. And you know damn well when we are spontaneous, it's when we have the most fun. When we go according to our plans, it never works out. Think of it as an adventure, Sissybug, a mission!" He pats my shoulder hard, in the way that he knows I hate and caused us to fist fight once.

"Ugh, don't call me that." I jerk my shoulder away, knowing full well that I lost before we even started.

"C'mon, I'll buy you a cherry," he sing-songs as he skips his way to the door. I hate it when he acts like that; it reminds me of Barney the Dinosaur. However, I brighten up a little bit. I do love the maraschino cherries soaked in cinnamon schnapps.

We walk into a really dark, dank bar that smells like dirty carpet, toilet and stale cigarette smoke. It takes a while for my eyes to adjust until I can clearly see the orange and brown paisley nightmare of carpeting. Every time I come here, I swear it will be the last time. Other than the smell, the town, and the carpet, I know that there is a life out there for me somewhere that this dive does not fit into.

I sit at the bar while Boogie orders a pitcher of beer. I stare at Jake the bartender, who is Native Hawaiian. A Native Hawaiian in Gordon, Nebraska. One time he explained to me how he ended up here but I forgot or was too drunk to remember. I am sure I hit on him too, with his tight, big build and huge exotic eyes. Boogie grabs the pitcher of beer and I grab the frosty mugs. He points with his lips to a table in the corner.

I shake my head, "I like it here." I glance at Jake, but he was already helping someone else. Definite eye candy.

"Nobody sits at the bar with a pitcher." He has one hand on his hip and pitcher in the other. I can be a pushover and I know that, but I don't care because I don't even want to be here. Although it pisses me off to no end that Boogie would even care what other people think, as if he is a star in his own reality TV series. I could care less, for Christ's sake, we are in our 30's.

Boogie leads us to a dark, inconspicuous corner. Boogie sits facing the whole bar, I sit with my back to the bar facing him. I turn and do a quick survey. No wonder he likes the dark corner; he can check the guys without them knowing. Real slick of him. There are a couple of rez boys at the far pool table, a couple of ranch hands at the table near us in tight Wranglers and cowboy hats. There is also an Indian couple dancing to Gary Stewart's sad ass song, *"Are We Dreaming the Same Dream."* The whole scene through the smoky neon lit beer signs makes me want to yawn. There is a bright blue sky outside and this is depressing as fuck. I think I need a shot of something. I guzzle my beer in the hopes that we can get the hell out of this place and at least maybe catch the sunset. The mug is frosty and the beer is ice cold. My buzz had been sitting in neutral but that ice cold beer kicked into high gear again. All of a sudden, The Roost didn't seem as hick as when we walked in a few minutes earlier.

I excuse myself to go to the bathroom. I put on more lip gloss and finger comb my hair real quick. My makeup and hair are surprisingly ok, since I had my head out the window on the way up, trying to bust a bottle off a sign. I smile remembering how Boogie laughed like crazy every time I missed. I owe that bitch four shots now. I look one more time at my hair. I had just cut ten inches off but it was still sort of long, just with layers. I had too much hair—I know that is a pure Indian girl complaint but it is true. I looked ok—I could stand to lose maybe 5, 10, 15, 27 lbs. or so. But I had a great sense of humor anyway, ha-ha, I always tell myself that when I start thinking of dieting. Seriously, I would have to drink light beer—ugh.

I get back to the table and there is a drink sitting in my spot. I look around, then pick up the glass and smell it.

"What the fuck, Boog—we are NOT staying!" I still drink it because it is a free drink.

"As if I would buy you a drink," he snorts and laughs at the same time. I notice I have a Crown and Coke and he has a Tequila Sunrise. Someone who knows us. I look at the hot bartender and point at him with my lips.

"Jake?" I stage whisper, as if he could hear us over Joan Jett in the jukebox.

Boogie laughs even harder. "Azzzzz IF! You wish! Here's a hint: he is a smoker."

They banned smoking in the bars here, so there is a deck outside for smokers. I grab my drink and walk towards the deck. There is different music playing on the deck, it's the familiar tune by Chumbawumba, "*Tubthumper.*" That is kind of cute for this town, even though it is an old song. I notice the beer tub bar out there and potted plants, as if they are trying to accommodate the smokers and try to make them feel better about smoking over an alley in a farm town over some dumpsters.

Then I look at the far end of the deck and I see him. I would recognize that big, hulking figure anywhere. The ever-present baseball cap, the way he holds his cigarette, his slight slouch. It was my on-again, off-again best straight guy friend, Ricky.

I run up behind him and squeeze him, though my arms don't go all the way around.

"Ricky!" I know that I have an ear to ear grin. Ricky has been in and out of my life since we were sixteen years old. I used to date his best friend, and Ricky's girlfriend and I were forced to be friends.

However, as drama goes with all rez relationships, when we were both dumped because my then boyfriend and his then girlfriend were in love, Ricky and I became best friends. I think our original intention was to date as a form of revenge, but we discovered something better. We both loved baseball. The only thing that ever kept us apart after that was when one of us was in a relationship; well, that and the one time we both got so drunk, we woke up in bed together in a hotel room. We both swore we would forget it and it wouldn't make us uncomfortable. Soon after, he went back to his drama queen, venom spitting woman, Lola. Since then, I haven't seen Ricky for about eight months.

"Did she kick you out again?" I ask.

He nodded and blew smoke out of his nose, "You know the deal. You going to be here for a while?"

"We're not even supposed to be here. You know how Boogie is. Anyways, Zona is in a pool tournament in Rushville at The Watering Hole. We're headed that way soon. Thanks for the drink, man."

He smiled and threw his cigarette in a tall ashtray. "Let's go in. Boogie's probably clucking like a chicken without you."

As we walk back into the dank darkness, I realize how much I miss Ricky when we don't talk. It's almost like life is, I don't know, more complete with him. I have been there through his stormy relationship with Lola. I have been there through the string of young girls he messed with while he was in college. We texted or instant messaged through a lot. So much so, that when he finally moved home, it was shocking we couldn't be together as much as when we were apart. But I understood he had his family with Lola. I had my kids. And when I was with the twins' father for those few years, we drifted apart. Nonetheless, instant messenger, email, and fantasy football brought us back together. Who else ever got drunk on instant messenger?

Ricky walks to the pool table and I go back to my seat across from Boogie.

"Talk about GLOWING!" Boogie says.

"Shh, whatev. He's just like a best friend." I take a sip of the Crown and Coke.

"No. He was like a best friend. Until you guys screwed. Now you entered a realm of friendship that you can't turn back from. No going back to the way it used to be. It's now called the *Twilight Zone.*" He laughs and starts humming the theme song from the old TV show.

Ricky comes over and sits in a chair between us. "So what have you two been up to? No good probably if you are getting along and out and about."

He knew us too well. Because even though Boogie was my first cousin, he is also my best friend and my heart. We may fight horribly once every two or three years that only resulted in a fist fight twice, we end up not talking for a couple of months but one of us usually gets over it and has to initiate the friendship back up again. Usually me, and the fight is usually over a guy. Not literally, like we are fighting over a guy, but as in he usually hates any guy I happen to fall in love with. And vice versa.

Truth is though, we can't live without each other. And Ricky has seen the turmoil, love, hate, and pure bitchiness that exists in our relationship and he saw us work through it many times.

"Oh, we're not up to a damn thing!" Boogie booms, "too many tourists, cops, traffic! Ugh, been there, done that! I can't afford to hang at the pow wow anymore! Who did you come with?" Boogie asks then slurps up his remaining Tequila Sunrise through the skinny straw, making a loud, rude, annoying slurpy noise.

Ricky points with his lips at the pool table. There stands Freddy, the Ernie to his Bert. They are neighbors, cousins, best friends and coworkers. Can't really get closer than unless they're bros, but they call each other bro anyway. Fred's a bus driver and Ricky is a kindergarten teacher.

"Lola has the kids all weekend for the pow wow, so I'm free of all obligations this weekend," Ricky tells me.

Boogie kicks me in the shin after he hears this and I try my best not to wince.

"Rick man, you're up!" Fred yells to Ricky and gives me the standard rez boy chin nod and I smile back. I don't know why, it just doesn't seem like a "chick" thing to do, to issue out chin nods.

"So you guys ain't staying?" Ricky asks as he gets up from the table.

I shake my head, "No, we have to go meet Zona at The Watering Hole."

He gives me a one-armed hug, "Maybe we'll meet up later."

I sigh as he walks over to the pool table; it sure is nice to know we are in each other's atmospheres again. The times we go without seeing each other are a void. I'll find something funny or something I want to make fun of, that only he would understand or get and I can't just pick up the phone and call him, or text him, or instant message him. Or even email him. All I could do is think—he would appreciate this.

Boogie lets out his horrendous, thundering laugh. "Girl, you got no game when it comes to that boy."

"Whatever Boog. I don't need game with Ricky, he's just like a.... best friend." I play with the ice cubes in my glass, stirring them around and around because I don't want to meet Boogie's eyes.

"No, I'm your best friend; he's your fuck buddy," Boogie laughs and laughs at that one. I hit him in the head with an ice cube and get up to leave.

"C'mon Boog, Zona is going to be pissed. We're already late." I grab the empties to take up to the bar.

I order a tall Captain Coke for Ricky and Boogie buys us each a cherry soaked in cinnamon schnapps. I walk over to Ricky and hand him the drink. He immediately starts sipping it.

"You heading out then?" he asks. He's looking at me over his glass and I let my heart race a little bit before I calm it down. I swallow the cherry and it's as if that makes my little racing scandalous heart calm down.

I nod. "Yah, you know where we will be. If not, we're getting a room over there anyway, so call me." I give the international signal for him to call me and put my thumb to my ear, pinky to my mouth and wiggle. Somehow this means call me. I look up at him one more time as we are walking out and he is watching me. I want to smile— instead I wave and raise my eyebrows. I feel silly and that is not how I am supposed to feel about him.

Boogie and I pull into Rushville after the supposedly eighteen-minute ride that took him about ten minutes and we get a room at The Wagon Wheel Inn. It is an old motel that has been in this town forever. It used to have a replica of a covered wagon out front, until some people from the reservation burned it, back when I was a kid. Rumor has it, it was my Uncle Shayne and his friends back in high school.

We settle in, claim our beds, pee check, mirror check and head out to The Watering Hole.

The Hole, as we call it, is one of my favorite bars ever. Not that I have been to that many bars, being that I am just a rez chick and I hardly ever leave the boundaries of our good old rez.

The Watering Hole is owned by Steve, whom I befriended when my brother Mark lived up here. Steve is a younger guy and lived in this town his whole life.

I see Zona as soon as we walk in. She is sitting at the bar, talking animatedly with the bartender and swigging from a bottle of Bud Light. She is dressed in one of her usual slutty low- cut shirts and tight jeans, but looks good because only she can pull that off. Zona is a big girl, but never scared to dress as sexy as she feels.

If that was me, there would have been too much of a muffin top showing for me to be comfortable with it. She has her long curly hair pulled up in one of her butt-whipping-time ponytails and has on her standard "rez girl hoop earrings."

She sees us in the reflection of the bar length mirror as she is guzzling her beer and screams at us.

"You're an hour late, you hookers!" She gets off her bar stool and gives us each a hug. She still wears vanilla body spray, I notice. We make our way to a table as she goes back to grab her purse.

"Tell him three beers, I got this first round!" I holler at her over the music and bar noise.

"Boogie had to check out the prey at The Roost first," I tell her as she settles in at our table. The bartender brings us our round of beers and I pay. I start sipping as Zona tells us how she whipped butt on her first round in the pool tournament.

"So were there any prospects at The Roost? Cause there sure as shit ain't none here," she asks as she eyeballs the people playing pool.

"Only for Sis, some big Indian guy bought her a drink," Boogie chuckled. I like how he emphasized big, especially being that he is bigger than Ricky. At 6' and 250 lbs., I thought Rick was "just right" for a guy. I like a guy to care about his looks and figure but not overly do it where he seems like a woman. I once went with a dude obsessed with himself; they have no time for anyone but themselves.

"Big Indian, huh? You know that's how Sis likes them. Big and greasy, just like her fry bread." We all laugh at that one, I can't even be mad.

"Shh whatever, it was just Ricky," I say.

Zona rolls her eyes, "Oh, your friend?" She sarcastically makes air quotes as she drags out the word "friend."

I didn't want to talk about him anymore. I can't explain our friendship to them. They think Ricky used me on our last go around. Zona even went so far as to say I was his mindfuck and then he messed with younger women, like I was the foreplay. That really pissed me off. I stayed mad at her for a week for that one, which is a long time to be mad at her because she will find a way to make you forgive her. Ricky and I get along great and when we feel the need to step out of each other's lives we just... do. That is all there is to it.

"Princess! You're up!" The bartender yells.

Zona swivels her way to the pool table; Boogie and I grab our beers to go watch. She is up against a cute guy; his wife is perched daintily on a barstool cheering him on. Zona starts talking her smack as usual because if anything gets her into the zone to whip some ass, it is a cute guy. I swear every shot she takes is either a cleavage shot or she is sticking her ass out. She moves slowly around the table like a cat in heat, using her cleavage to aim and even her hip one time, even when she knows there is no shot to take. She is a good pool player, mind you, she can whip up on anybody, even without the show, but she has been a show off all our lives.

Her opponents' eyes are bugging out of his head. His wife knows what's up and to make it worse, she tries to stand as close to him as possible, as if she is staking a claim. This only makes it harder for him to play—not only is she in his way, but also distracting him to the point where he is getting irritated with her. And it makes it easier for Zona to win.

Nobody is surprised when she easily defeats him while most of his balls are still on the table. Boogie lets out a *lili* (women's trill) like the winkte he is. I war hoop like his butch friend and we cheer her on. Zona goes to shake the poor guy's hand and he kisses it instead of shaking it. His wife grabs him by the shirt and drags him out the back door of the bar. A collective "Oohhhhh," goes up and Zona bows. She loves it and basks in it. She isn't known for her innocence, well none of us are, but let's just say Zona is known for treating men the way men usually treat women. That's one of the reasons she left the rez, too much drama with her relationships, since most of the men are recycled about as much as bacon grease. I'm not hating—it was just how it was at home. Men always went for younger women; younger women seem to be looking to be taken care of. It's never surprising to have a brother or sister younger than one's own children. My mom said, "Let them men take care of babies when they are old. We women can take care of ourselves."

So in a way, Zona's attitude was refreshing, even if she treats the male population badly. Then again, maybe too many abusive relationships made her that way. Either way I have her back, always. She's my girl.

She makes her way back to the table Boogie and I already settled at, then she made a detour to discuss the bracket with the bartender. I go up to her to buy the next round with a twenty dollar bill Boogie gave me when I notice the guy she just beat is walking towards here, alone.

"And that motherfucker didn't even buy me a drink!" she says with her hands on her hips. I point with my lips behind her. The guy is standing right there with a Bud Light in his hand. He looks at her like a puppy wagging his tail and waiting for praise.

Boogie comes up and buys a beer for both of us, snatching the twenty from my hand. I notice he takes advantage of taking his turn at buying a round when there are only two of us to buy for. That's Boogie.

The guy introduces himself to us. His name is Vern Seaver. I recognize the last name as one of the border reservation families that settled near the reservation eons ago. They grew up with our people over the generations. Eventually, as it became cool to be an Indian, it came out one day that one of the grandmas in the border families was from the reservation. I hear that story over and over, but it was not until movies like *"Dances With Wolves"* came out.

Vern asked if any of us were going towards Alliance. He lives there but his wife slapped him up and left him in the parking lot. Coincidentally, that is where Zona lives. I see her evil wheels spinning.

"Sure, I could, as soon as I win this tournament," she tells Vern.

With a $5 entry fee and winner-take-all pot, Zona could win $160. She has two wins down, and I don't know how many more to take it, but I have seen her do it before.

Boogie leans forward and squints at Vern. Geez, just what we need; Boogie has a way of getting mad at us about men.

"Aren't you the undertaker?" he asks Vern. He is eyeballing him up and down, probably trying to decide if Vern is gay and/or bi-sexual, and/or in the closet. Never once will it cross Boogie's mind that he might just be straight, period. And he was probably also trying to decide whether or not this guy was worthy of Zona or hanging out with us. He's oddly possessive of his friends like that.

"No, I'm not an undertaker or mortician. I just happen to work in my family's funeral home," he said.

"Yikes," I act like I move away from him a little bit and I am kind of a little bit freaked out for real. I hope he washes his hands and uses hand sanitizer and burns sage after each job.

"What?" He looks at me and laughs, "It's a job. I ain't carrying around any spirits with me."

Now that even freaked me out more. I am sure there were ancestors all around him.

"What exactly do you do there?" I ask and glance at Zona. The fact that he works with dead people doesn't change the looks she keeps giving him. She can't be serious! What the hell is wrong with this woman?

"Most of the time I drive them, sometimes I do their make-up and the setting up of the service," Vern boasts.

"Creepers," I look at Zona, who is still giving him her sexiest, most serious, come hither look. I elbow her, "Let's go pee... now!"

I know that Boogie will give him the ninth degree, pressuring him to find out everything about him, plus he will also look for any sign of gayness while we are gone. So I plan to talk to Zona about him, as if I have any say so in the matter anyways. We walk through a door labeled "Does," the other one is labeled "Bucks."

Zona walks into the one and only stall before me, which is annoying, since I am the one that needed to pee in the first place. I start pacing.

"He's cute," she says through the door.

"...And married," I remind her as I start crossing my legs to see if that make it easier to hold my pee in. Dammit, I could drink forever before I had kids. Now, it is like once I start, I constantly have to go pee. I better quit drinking before I get old. I can't be going out to the bar in diapers. I realize that crossing my legs doesn't work; the sound of her pissing like a racehorse makes it worse.

I pound on the stall wall, "For the love of baby Jesus, hurry!" I hear her laughing and flushing the toilet. What a bitch.

She walks out, zipping her pants up and laughing at me.

I plop down, relief at last. "Listen Zone, you know I don't judge anyone, hardly ever anyway, but he works with dead people."

She looks at me in the mirror as I am washing my hands. "Sis, that is the keyword, works. He works. He has a job, he is not some bum on the street or some hustler or someone sitting back waiting for an SSI check." She is applying more of her dark maroon lipstick.

"So he has a job and a wife, but who am I to judge morals? At least if you hook up, you can just play dead," I smile at her in the mirror as I finish with my lip gloss. She punches me on the arm and I laugh as we walk out to the bar.

"Shit, he might get off on that," I tell her. I'm laughing so hard, I almost bump into Mason Thomas. I stop short and hold my breath. I put my finger to my lips and motion for Zona to be quiet. This was Mason.

Mason Thomas.

Give me a minute to breathe. Mason is the reason I spent so much time in this dried up town when my brother Mark lived up here. He is the cutest white boy in this town. And I don't even like white boys, but he is the exception. In fact, he may be the cutest white boy in all border rez towns that exist. Maybe even the cutest white boy in the Nebraska panhandle. Shoot, he just might be the cutest white boy ever.

One time at my bros house, we bought a case to drink because we didn't have money to be going to the bar. We even spent quarters on that case of beer, so when we wanted to play quarter pitch, we didn't even have a quarter to pitch. So after arguing and a few beers later and realizing I will never beat Mark in Rock-Paper-Scissors or arm wrestling, I walked to Dad's Bar and Grill in the middle of town. Everything and everywhere in town was walking distance, for that matter. Anyway I walked down to Mason's family bar and explained to his dad why I need two quarters for four dimes and two nickels. Mase was playing pool and he came over to me, which was crazy because, although we kind of knew each other from the bar scene, we never talked. He slapped me on the back like I was one of the boys. So much for feeling dainty.

"Want a beer?" he asked. My heart took off—I remembered I was buzzed and how to flirt. After two more beers, my brother Mark comes bursting in the door pointing at me. I completely forgot about quarter pitch. Leave it to a brother to ruin any game I think I might have.

I'm looking at Mase's back and his awesome, awesome shoulders. I don't know what it is—I love a man with shoulders.

I mean a man without shoulders isn't even a man, right? I can smell whatever delicious cologne he is wearing.

I was just starting to feel like I was going to drool a little bit when Zona pushes me from behind and I bump into his back. I could feel my face turning red and hot as my lip gloss smears on his t-shirt. Thank God he was wearing black. Although I didn't pass up the opportunity to take another whiff—Oh my God, he smelled like heaven, if it were a man.

"Whoa!" He turns, smiles, and grabs me by the shoulders, as if to balance me. I notice he got a little bit of a beer gut but he is still sexy. My heart is going pitter-patter.

"Sorry, Zona pushed me," I turn to blame her but she is already at the table smiling at me like the evil wench she is. I also realize that I sound like a little girl on the playground, pointing fingers. God, why can't I just be a cool and classy bitch?

"So how's your Yankees doing?" he asked, smiling.

"I always have faith; you going to bet me this year?" I smile, Mason's a National League fan, which is good when you hate the Yankees I guess, because it will take a whole league. Redbone starts playing on the jukebox, *"Come and Get Your Love."*

He shook his head, "Not this year, Sincere."

"Fine be that way," I pout. I know he remembers my awesome betting skills.

I point with my lips to one of the four TV's above the bar. "How about a wager on tonight's game then?"

He looks up, I look at his eyelashes. My heart's skipping a beat.

"Against the Red Sox? Sure!"

We shake on it and bet a shot and a drink. Usually he likes the Chicago Cubs, but they're National League. He smiles and I feel as if 1,000 watts of pure love are shining directly at me. It might be the drinks and song, too, though.

I make my way back to our table and push Zona by her shoulder. "Oh my God, you are such a bitch," I hiss loudly at her, but I can't help smiling.

She laughs. "Just helping you out Sis, otherwise you would be sitting by the wall all night, giggling if he looks your way, like a damn squaw."

"Fuck you!" I tell her, taking a swig of my beer. "He's the squaw!" I point to Boogie.

He is displeased. He looks like a mad, wet cat without a tail whipping around, but if he had one, it would be whipping and snapping back and forth.

"Fuck you. You two are disgusting. You can be so derogatory and racist to your own kind, then jump in the face of someone as soon as they throw it back at you. Practice what you preach," Boogie snaps.

I ignore him, he's right.

The bartender yells at Zona that she is up and the married guy, Vern, follows her like a puppy.

"Well, there's her new cheering section, I guess we can watch our table now," I say.

"So what's up with you and Mason?" Boogie asks—he still has that wet cat look.

"Nothing," I say and point at the TV with my lips, "we just bet on that game right there."

"You guys always bet. Here's a hint, try flirting with him," Boogie says.

"But I always win the bets," I say matter of fact. "Besides, he likes skinny white chicks. I'm too chubby and dark for him probably."

Boogie rolls his eyes, "I was watching you guys tease each other up there, you look good together. Annnnd, not only that, he knows you have a flame for him, you lust him, you want to have his babies."

I sigh heavily, not wanting to remember. "Don't remind me, that is another reason I'm nervous around him."

One night, I was drinking at his dad's bar and confessed it all to his dad. Even told him Mase was eye candy. After that Mase knew, always gave me that knowing look, because he knew he can make me melt. That is when he bought me beers that time. Usually I have no problem maintaining my cool, but I slipped up there. Me and my drunk talk. Ugh.

All of a sudden and as always, I am craving a cigarette. Happens every time I go to a bar or hang out with my mom and I don't even smoke. I change the subject from Mason and my super crush to some petty gossip I overheard in the grocery store line the other day while checking people out. I knew Boogie would bite the bait.

He works at the waiting room, checking people in as an intake clerk at the IHS clinic and even though he has a cold half the year, it is the best place to hear gossip; my job being a close second on the rez for gossip. I zone Boog out and keep an eye on Mason over by the jukebox. I am half-listening to who broke whose windshield.

The gossip changes with the seasons. In the fall when the fiscal year ends, it is embezzlement season; in the spring, it is who bought what with their income tax. In the summer, it is who fucked up each other's income tax cars over snagging and cheating on each other.

I look out the window and see Ricky and Fred pull up. Nice.

I know Boogie never really liked Ricky. I never understood why, except that it probably has to do with me calling Ricky my best friend.

Ricky walks in, goes to the bar and orders a beer and starts looking around. He sees me waving and smiles. Boogie slides to the table next to ours to save seats for Zona and Vern. Ricky sits beside me and Fred sits across from me.

"What's the score?" Fred asks as he sees my eyes on the TV monitor.

"Yanks 4, Sox 5, top of the seventh," I say.

Ricky, Fred, and I are all in a Native Stars Fantasy Football League—that's the name of it. One year out of the past seven I won by dumb luck and I still talk smack about it.

Boogie detests sports talk so he saunters off to the bathroom.

We talk baseball, football then fantasy football, which of course brings up the subject of the live fantasy draft coming up at the end of the month. This was the first year of the live draft and I was nervous as heck about that. I hate pressure. This year, I have secret weapons for the draft and I told both guys so.

"Really?" Ricky raises an eyebrow in an adorable sort of way, "What are your secret weapons? This may be illegal."

"Whatever," I say, all loving his one eyebrow raised look. I am buzzed as hell on alcohol so I spill the beans. "Craig and Creighton," I beam proudly.

My twin sons have actually been fired up since I asked them. They have been researching and watching ESPN pre-season stats shows. They are more fired up than I have ever been. I don't know why I never thought of using them as consultants before. This pretty much guaranteed me in the championship round and not only that, but the chance to be the league's commissioner next year and more importantly, the chance to talk smack all year.

Ricky looks intrigued, "Really? I had no idea they would get into it?"

"Hell, yeah, they know what's up more than I do." I start concentrating more on the game because the score was tied.

I have been a Yankee fan all of my life. My grandma has always been into sports, so her household would be filled during post-season and championship games. My Uncle Shayne was in federal prison for a long time and would call home during a game to talk smack to my Grandma Pacific. She acted mean about it but she loved it. She can't for the life of her figure out how my Uncle Shayne first became a Yankees fan and then me. Truthfully, he was always my hero, so of course, I would like his team.

If I was at home, I would be sitting in front of my TV with a six-pack of Bud, screaming into the phone at whoever will listen to my shit talk.

My Grandma is a Red Sox fan, so if I am brave and tipsy enough, I will call her and talk smack then avoid her for a while after that—out of the pure fear Indians have of their grandmothers.

The game deserves full attention and no more bar chit chat. It was tied in the bottom of the 8th. At home I watch all nine innings like real baseball fans usually do. Tonight I was at the bar though and too busy socializing. But tied in the bottom of the 8th deserves my full attention.

"Let's Go Yanks!" I holler in my deep ass rez chick voice.

"Fuck the Yanks!" Ricky says.

"I would," I say quietly, but he hears me and shakes his head muttering, "Scandalous rez girl."

"Fuck the Braves," I tell him. He only cheers for the Braves because he spent a part of one summer in Atlanta on some Native American internship thing in college and fell in love with a Potawatomi girl. I would always tease him that she is from the "Pot of What Am I" tribe, just to get on his nerves.

It's the top of the 9th and the Sox have runners on 2nd and 3rd and they bunt and they score. Ugh. But I am not worried. I never doubt them until the last out.

"C'mon Yankees, one more strike!" I take a swig of the cold beer from the last round Fred bought. "Let's go Yankees!!" I yell loud enough for Fred and Ricky to hear me because they both hate the Yankees so much.

"Let's go Red Sox!" I hear someone yell, and I immediately know its Mason. I get up and walk over beside him. I grab his shoulder with my hand and say, "Get ready to pay up, boy!"

"You are three outs away from losing this bet," he says.

"Whatever, I don't ever doubt my boys, ever."

Jeter comes up to bat at the bottom of the 9th, he hits a single. Next up is Granderson, he gets walked. A-Rod comes up and I get nervous, but thank god there are no outs yet. A-Rod can never get out of a clutch and pull through. If there were two outs believe me, he would strike out. Surprise, surprise— no outs, so the dude hits a double and Jeter scores. Tied again. My throat is going to be so sore tomorrow and I am supposed to be cheering Zona on.

Finally Cano comes up and hits a homerun, like nothing. As if it is easy. I am screaming—this is why I love the Yankees. Yanks win by three in the bottom of the 9th.

I turn to Mase, "Pay up then, boy!" Wow, I must be drunk to be so brazen with him.

We stand at the bar and continue to talk shit about the game. Mason orders my drink, his drink and two lemon drop shots, one for each of us.

I hold up the shot to clink shot glasses and give him cheers, "Damn what is this? A bonus? Because the Yanks are that fucking awesome?"

He rolls his eyes and I notice his eyelashes.

Zona comes up to inform us she is in the championship with a "big ole Cornhusker." She has two men behind her, following her, one is that puppy dog of a man, Vern, whom she beat when we first got here and she may be causing him a divorce now. The other is some dude she just beat; he buys them both tequila shots.

At this point I notice everything is very fuzzy. I am far gone from just a buzz. I am having fun but all I hear is laughter and glasses clinking. Mason puts his arm around me and my heart goes into high speed. I can hear my heart above everything else, or maybe it is going along to the beat of the jukebox. Good Lord, I hope he don't hear it.

"Sincere, I have to ask you something." Damn, my heart is racing, I gulp. What is it about a man who uses my real name that is such a turn on? Seriously though, no woman wants her man to call her "sis." And what is even more of a turn on, he tells me that he is going to ask me something. That's some cool ass, old school rat pack kind of shit. He didn't say, "Can I ask you something?" He straight up told me.

"Did you tell my dad I was eye candy?" He is smiling. My face gets hot. "Was that you or some other 'pretty little rez chick they call Sis?' Huh? Because I only know you as Sincere but my dad swears it was you." He has a teasing look in his eyes but all the confidence and courage I just found in those two lemon drop shots all of a sudden had vanished.

I look in the mirror hanging behind the bar; I don't know why I looked but when I did, right there between the bottle of Grey Goose Vodka and Skyy Vodka, was Ricky's face. More importantly, his eyes. He was watching Mason and me and there I was with Mason's arm around me.

Our eyes meet and it seems like he is glaring. I hold his glare for a few seconds then break away and hear Zona laughing.

"She did!" Zona points at me.

"You wasn't even there!" I point back at her, and in doing so I realize that I just told on myself.

Mason throws his head back and laughs. "That's ok. Crushes are cute," then he kisses me on the cheek, all brotherly like.

I felt like a schoolgirl. I mean, they are the ones who get crushes, right? No single moms in their 30s get crushes or kissed on the cheek. What the hell. I feel dumb.

"This is my cue to go sit down." If it is at all possible to turn a deeper shade of red, I am sure I did. I am smiling ear to ear as Mason takes his arm off my shoulders. I stagger a little bit as I back away smiling at him. I bump into Zona. She is back to talking to the undertaker Vern. She looks at me and laughs as she breaks the stare down between Mason and I.

"C'mon!" She grabs my arm, "Come cheer me on and get those stars out of your eyes."

I high-step it to the pool table with her and notice the undertaker is gone.

"Where's your boy?" I ask.

Zona is cueing up and looks around, "I thought he was right on my ass. Maybe he's in the bathroom." She shrugs and gets her game face on.

When Zona gets in pool tournaments people buy her drinks and shots all the time; they think if they get her drunk they can beat her. What they don't know is that she has the drinking tolerance of a German at Oktoberfest and actually plays better when drunk. It doesn't take her long to beat the big ol' redneck, which I again wonder why they call themselves that—when all I ever see is pink. When she beats him easily, he sulks out the back door of the bar. She didn't even do any of her poses or play dirty like that—she went into what she calls her "Zona Zone." The bartender brings her over her pot, as she is kissing Vern.

"Let's get this party started!" she yells.

"Whatever, we're already all drunk," I laugh.

As we walk back over to our table, people are high fiving Zona and then I see two other girls standing there. One is short, so short that she makes all of my 5 foot 3 inches seem tall and the other is almost 6 feet tall making me feel short.

Zona whispers, "Who are these rez rats?"

"Quit being a hater," I whisper back. Then I arrive with my best glare, my best two-mile stare. I don't like the way the tall frog-looking one is leaning into my bff.

Boogie immediately starts making introductions, taking charge and showing off like he has been all his life. Which leads me to the theory that he invited these girls to our table. Which leads me to the theory that he did it to piss me off because of my boy Ricky. I was not in a sharing mood nor did I care what their names were. I saw them as Shorty and Froggy. I know I could be a miz Indian chick, but for real, c'mon. The dirty nerve of Boogie.

"And so I worked with her back in the day when we were youth supervisors for the summer youth program, and I worked with her when we both worked at the store in Whiteclay... and they also both went to high school with Ricky!" Boogie claps like a seal. Ugh, the more he drinks the more femme he gets and the more he gets on my nerves. Especially if I feel like he is doing something to annoy me on purpose, or booby trap me, or bamboozle me. I try to glare at him but he is avoiding my eyes. Neither Zona nor I say hi. Why should we? This is our table.

"It's Rick. Not Ricky," Ricky says coolly. This was the first time I heard that. I have always called him Ricky, but maybe because his mom calls him that, too.

"Well then, from now on I shall be known as Boog, not Boogie," Boogie says to the tune of his hellacious laugh and four Indian girls' bar cackles. He almost made me forget his real first name.

"Yeah, well whatever, I need to sit down. My feet are killing me and the next round is on me," Zona says, and flashes her winnings in everyone's faces, as if anyone would protest to buy their own drink. "Oh and Sis needs to sit down too. She was cheering me on and the Yankees on! Woot! Woot!"

We give high fives and I hear Ricky mutter, "That wasn't all she was cheering on."

Or maybe I didn't. I don't know. I am totally on my way to being wasted.

Zona buys a round of drinks and lemon drop shots and we all salute her victory. The lemon and vodka didn't taste as good as earlier, maybe it was because when I was with Mase, it was so good. Holy, here I am all crushing on a white boy. My Grandma Pacific would whack me with a broom. I am sure the shot was just more chilled earlier.

Boogie is chatting with Shorty and I have no desire to jump in. Zona and Vern are making out like horny teen-agers. Fred is watching Sports Center and drinking his beer. And Froggy is giggling and making hand movements and flirting with Ricky.

I watch them for a while. I admit, I am hating. But what the fuck is a giant frog doing trying to lean up on him like that? As if she is cute and dainty. I have such a hater status right now, I can't even watch them. I might puke.

I start talking to Fred about sports but he is boring as hell—everything I say trying to bait him into a debate—all he says is, "Rrrright!" And at the same time I can't help but notice Ricky being all entranced with Froggy's discussion about her shoe addiction. She is a dispatcher for the police department and talking about how she just bought herself a pair of Jimmy Choos. Yeah, she needs $700 shoes to work answering phones at the cop shop.

The fucked up thing is, Ricky was listening intently to a girl talking about all the things we—we as in 'he and I'—thought and deemed shallow. I could feel my temperature rising. I could feel my standard "rez girl" mad eyes going into place. Then I heard a gem... from her. I turned slowly to look at her and smile like the evil queen from Snow White and said, "Did you say you wear a size 14? In SHOES?"

I wanted to laugh but from the tone of my voice, you would think I was as sincere as my name. I couldn't even make eye contact with Boogie because he might call me out me for being evil.

"Well, that depends on the brand, sometimes a 13 and sometimes a 14 but some I can fit a 10 and a half," she said proudly. I am wondering, did she not read the fairy tale with the ugly stepsisters? Then I am wondering when God is going to send the lightning bolt through to me for being so evil minded.

I take a swig and look away but still retort, "Wow. That is the same size as you Ricky, if you were a woman."

I know I am evil, what can I say? I was raised this way. Boogie snickers. Zona laughs out loud and says, "ENIT!"

At this point, what's her name, Froggy says, "I thought it was just Rick, not Ricky?"

Ricky looks down as if embarrassed and depleted of charm. Before I feel sorry for him, I start talking to Fred about the game. Then Mase walks up and taps me on the shoulder.

"Hey cutie, I have a proposal for you. Why don't we bet on the whole season? The whole she-bang—and let's see who makes it the furthest, out of our teams."

I am a 32-year-old single rez chick, mother of three and he called me cutie. Ok, maybe he was drunker than two skunks. That is when I love to bet—that is rhyme-betting bait, right there. I get up and walk him to the bar, slightly pushing him and slightly giggling.

"A dartboard—electronic—with darts," I say, as if I have room for that anywhere in my house.

"That's boring," he says.

"A bar light to a good beer," I counteroffer.

Mase yawns, "How about a case and a jug, your choice—IF you win." He smiles and his one dimple shines at me.

I smile back and nod, "Your loss."

Mase laughs and walks away—he kind of staggers. Maybe he is drunker than three skunks. *"My Song"* by Aretha Franklin is playing and I feel like we should have slow-danced, but whatever. He looks back smiling and winks at me. Gross, I usually hate being winked at because it seems sleazy but he made me feel... all some kind of way.

"Shall we go smoke?" I hear Ricky ask. I was about to tell him I was craving a cig for some time when I see the amphibian nod her head and hop out the door after him.

Wow. That is all I could think. What just happened here? I make my way to the bathroom to take my hundredth piss of the night.

Pissing the night away. Didn't I hear that in a song somewhere earlier?

When I get back to the table, Ricky and his new chick are back. Boogie is making plans to party on. I was about to get fired up and say we did not rent a room at Hick Hotel to take the whole rez back to it when I hear Boogie mention something about a back road. It is a beautiful night with a full moon, so everyone is game. Boogie starts clucking around like a mother hen to remind us that everyone needs to remember to buy beer soon because they would quit off-sale soon. Zona buys a case, Ricky buys a case, and the two girls say they have beer but buy a bottle of Canadian whiskey anyway. Ricky asks me to ride with him since Fred's woman wouldn't stop blowing up his cell phone—he found someone from the same district and bailed with them before the bar had even called last call.

As we walk out of the bar, I wave bye to Mase and get in the passenger seat of Ricky's car. Mase is standing outside with some of his buddies. He nods and smiles at me and says, "See you later Sincere." My heart tries to not skip a beat and remain cool.

I immediately start fiddling with the radio knobs and when Ricky hears *"Brown Eyed Girl"* by Van Morrison, he grabs my hand and moves it out of the way. It wasn't like when he normally would have just swatted my hand away, he held it kind of gently and moved it so I couldn't turn it. I looked at him and he was smiling at me, except still holding onto my hand. Then he must have realized it. He pulled his hand away as if I shocked him.

"Remember that time we went to the city and all the bars were packed, all the cool ones where people our age hung out, so we ended up at that one bar with old people?" he laughs.

I laugh, "That VFW! Oh my god, that was the most fun night ever with all those old guys and they made you sing this!

That was a fun old man bar. We'll have to hang out there when you are an old man. Next year."

"Shhh whatevs," he said and handed me a small half pint of Crown Royal and a bottle of Coke.

"Badass! Where did this come from?" I open them and take a swig from each. "So Fred bailed on you?"

Ricky follows the little caravan and turns off the main road and onto the back road that eventually goes to the rez. He says, "Yeah. I knew he would. His cell phone was off the hook and his woman was pissed. Thought he was out with another girl so when he saw his cousin, he just decided to go home."

"That's why I asked you to ride with me, plus I had that Crown and Coke. I bought it for you," he said, quietly. I look at him but he is watching the road.

As we cruise through the glow of the moonlight looks awesome on the sunflower fields. I wonder how Van Gogh would paint this.

We pull up to a slow stop, brakes pads non-existent, metal screeching-stopping metal, tires crunching gravel. I see everyone getting out and snapping cans of beer open.

"Let's do a cheers?" I say as I find an empty water bottle on the floor of his car and pour a generous shot of whiskey in it for him. "To me, haaaawww!" I say. God, I am such a rez chick. I can never be some classy bitch—my rez accent is with me for life.

"As long as it ain't to the Yanks," he says and drops his shot before I could even drink mine. Damn, I didn't even say what we was doing a cheers to. I drink my shot quickly. Makes my throat and stomach constrict. Ugh, harsh. I look at the bottle to make sure it was Crown.

"What?" he asks.

"Just making sure it's Crown, went down like Black Velvet," I tease him. He hates Black Velvet. I used to love it but I upgraded over the years, or at least when someone is buying for me. I take away his water bottle and pour another shot in it.

"Anyways, do overs. For reals, this is to the sunflowers and moonlight. Van Gogh would chop his other ear off for this background." I hold my half pint in the air and Ricky busts out laughing before clinking his plastic water bottle to my glass whiskey bottle.

After we do the shot and I harshly give the standard whiskey exhale like in the Old West movies, Ricky is still laughing.

"Well, what is so funny?" I ask him.

"You! Sis, you can be such a fuckin cornball, sometimes. Who gives cheers to sunflowers and moonlight?"

"Whatever, Boogie would cheers that," I sort of pout, I was actually serious with that salute.

"Even that is too gay for Boogie," Ricky laughs.

"Well I just enjoy badass moments, OK. I am with three of my favorite people in the middle of a sunflower field and the moon is so pretty and bright. And above all that, the Yankees came from behind in the bottom of the 9th to win it for the millionth time in the history of baseball," I gloat.

Ricky smiled and his dimples have a little shadow in the moonlight that is adorable. He pours another shot to himself and hands me the half pint. "Well, here is to your badass, my badass, and to finally having a badass night together after many moons. Let's hope no one sees your moon tonight."

"Fuck you!" I laugh and act like I am going to punch him.

Just as we tip the shot, the Frog Lady is knocking on his window.

"Scary," I say.

"Be nice," he shushes me. I glare at him, but he isn't looking at me; he is rolling down his window and smiling his charming smile. I look at the sunflowers—they dance gently in that moonlight he was just laughing about a moment ago.

She immediately whines about him spending time with her, as if she is his wife of seven years. As if they are shopping and she wants him to hold her purse. As if she is one of those women that asks if a pair of jeans makes her ass look fat. And I immediately want to scream, NO bitch, you're Indian, your ass is flat not fat. Instead I roll my eyes, but I like to think it was in the most vicious and meanest of ways.

And Ricky, my Ricky, acts like a little bitch and soothes her, —Yes, yes, I will be right out—he says. This is seriously going against all the things we hate about relationships, but whatever. She walks away and I watch him watch her shaking her flat ass. Ugh.

Ricky glances at me, "Don't be too mean."

I open my door to get out. "Don't be too nice," I say and slam the door. We make our way towards the makeshift party. I walk over to Boogie and right then and there I notice my stagger. Ha, I had thought all that time it was a swivel. I laugh to myself.

I know I am totally wasted then. I have no idea when I crossed that line. Everything is happening so fast. It is the speed of drunkenness you see in movies sometimes, with the blur, the laughing, and the clinking glasses. Except there were no clinking glasses, only the snapping and smashing of beer cans. We are throwing the cans in some farmer's field. I am sure in the morning some fat farmer, riding his tractor will be raging and shaking his fist at the dear Lord in the sky, "These damn drunken Injuns!"

Fuck him, I think, as I throw a half full can into his field. This is our land!

Whoa, now I know I am shit faced. I hate littering. I really do, not to the point where I am the fake Indian letting a tear roll down my cheek. But I do care to the point where I do give a hoot to not pollute.

I snap another can of beer open and look at my people around me. I feel as if I am on a carousel and don't even know about the brass ring. Then I get this awful feeling of displacement that I get when I am really drunk. This feeling of loss of control, of loss of belonging. I am standing there, just... existing. I want to know that I belong here, not just that I am existing here. I feel as if I defied fate and somehow ended up here.

Fuck whatever, I am just blank, paranoid, and my friends are all ignoring me.

I look over at Zona, kissing that dude that acts like a puppy.

"Undertaker!" I scream. He stops kissing her and making the disgusting slurping noise and turns to look at me.

"Can you take your face of my friend so I can speak to her, PLEASE?" I had meant it as a joke, but it sort of sounded like I snapped and was a little bit on the possessive psycho side.

Vern moved away and sort of sent Zona my way. She gave me a hug, asked me if everything was okay. Which is what people ask psychos that snap.

"I'mmmmfine, IIIMmmmmffffffine," I slurred. "I juss wanna do ssssome cashing up withhh you." I am swaying. Wow. All that drinking from this afternoon on is catching up to me. My mouth isn't working right. Zona and I talk about old times, we talk about how much we miss each other, we laugh and we gossip a little bit. She is coddling me, I know, but I let her. I am beyond drunk and cannot hang.

Two cars pull in. Everyone gets quiet as we all look into the headlights. The license plates are obviously from the reservation but the car is coming from Nebraska. Boogie and Ricky walk over to the car as if they are sheriffs. Although, I am sure Boogie is doing inventory to see if there is anyone gay or potentially in the closet. I take this moment to go grab my bottle of Crown and bottle of Coke out of Ricky's car. I am only going to share it with Boogie, Ricky, and Zona, because I am a drunk, stingy bitch right now. And I am pretty sure I am mad, but I have no idea who I am mad at.

Boogie comes walking back all fast, tight lipped and trying to mouth some words to me, but I am drunk and squinting at him and holler, "HUH? WHAT?"

He grabs me by the elbow and puts his right hand up to my ear as if he is telling me the most awesome secret ever while he hauls me away, and I am trying to high step so I don't trip and fall.

"Don't look now!" He stage whispers, "But it's your ex, Will."

And because Boogie told me not to look, I do a double take. I see Will, talking with hand motions to Ricky. Ricky has his chest puffed out and is looking my way. He knows of my past with Will but he really has no business in it now, since it was nonexistent, anymore. I am a little bit mad. I decide to walk up.

I see Will as soon as I turn the corner of Zona's pick-up. He is smiling and shaking his head, talking to Ricky. Ricky is still trying to look all somehow.

"Hi Will," I say and smile. He smiles his hundred teeth at me. Now, I remember why I let him be the man on the first night, it was his smile. That beautiful smile always got to me, but all the drama with all his babies mamas turned me off. He has four babies with three women and can't seem to really break it off with any of them.

Will walks over to me defiantly to spite Ricky and gives me a hug. I reciprocate.

"Hey, Sis, how about those Yankees tonight?" He smiles again.

I smile like a goofball. "Whatever! You're a Twins fan!" I say accusingly. I remember every detail about giving him a spin for about a year. Only thing was, while I was giving this younger man a spin and thinking I was some kind of cool cougar, he was giving his three baby mamas a spin, too.

Despite that past, I make a failed, stupid ass attempt to look sexy by putting a hand on my hip and fake laughing. I could see myself as if I was having an out of body experience. No wonder my Grandpa used to warn us not to drink. He used to say our spirit would get ashamed and leave us while our body did stupid things. I don't know if I am my spirit right now, but I am pretty sure my spirit is ashamed of how I am acting. Who do I think I am?

Will does his thing, the thing he always got me with in the past. He starts talking old times. Like old times before he and I were ever anything. Old times like when he and my twins' dad were friends. I honestly don't think I am impressed but Boogie thinks otherwise. He grabs me by the elbow. Maybe my fake laugh was too much.

"Let's go pee!" he hisses.

I didn't think I needed to pee until halfway to his van, I felt the urge. I went on the other side of his van from him, because even though he can be a bitch, he was still a dude. Something about the fact that my cuz Boogie could still whip it out and pee with minimal damage, still kind of pissed me off.

The whole time we are peeing Boogie is preaching. He hates Will. Back when I was going out with Will and he was cheating on me, Boogie tried to tell me and it led to us not talking for awhile.

"Remember Sis, he was an ass to you, always showing up on your paydays, his baby mama trying to fight you at the store, he caused me and you not to talk.... oh and remember he slapped you," he says.

I am done peeing. I am standing, and making sure I am all zipped up at this point but as soon as Boogie reminds me about that incident, I grab my cheek as if I still felt the sting of the slap. In fact, it was that slap that led me and Boogie to be friends again. I went right over with a fifth of vodka I stole from Will and drank it with Boogie with whatever commod juice we could find. When we finished it we decided to go hunt down Will and gang him but all that happened was we both ended up in the drunk tank at the tribal jail.

"That's right, he did slap me and he slapped me hard." I am still holding my face. Boogie is nodding and pushing me along towards the party. "He slapped me like I was a little bitch and I never got to confront him about it," I say.

"Mmmhm," Boogie nods. His hand is on his hip.

"Nobody slaps me," I say, as we start high stepping back to the party.

"Yup," Boogie says, "You came from a stronger people than that to put up with that bullshit. A long line of strong Indian.... a strong line of Lakota women."

"You bet. I'll show him." The whole time I am on this victory march and Boogie is agreeing with me, it never crosses my mind once that this was five years ago. "The slap" should have been filed away as a loss and forgotten but Boogie brought it up and I have my game face on.

"Sis, just please be cool about this," Boogie says. "Don't trip or fall."

I march back, determined to slap Will for slapping me five years ago when I see something that makes me stop in my tracks for only a second. I gasp a little and start marching again, this time I forget about Will.

It was Ricky kissing the Frog woman. And not a peck or quick kiss, but a full on the end of a romantic comedy kind of kiss.

Kissing in the moonlight.

Among the sunflowers.

The same moonlight and sunflowers I just gave cheers to with Ricky. I need to leave. I look at Boogie. He sighs and gives me the silent message with his look, like, "Really?"

I grab his arm and act like I am hyperventilating, or maybe I am.

"I'm getting my purse out of your car!" I holler at Ricky and he stops kissing and looks at me confused, then the Frog grabs his face and starts kissing him again. I want to puke. I run to his car and grab my purse and then I grab Ricky's whole case of beer also. Fuck him.

Boogie pulls up as I throw my purse and stolen beer in the back of his van. As we pull away, I see them, in Boogie's headlights. Ricky has his arms around her and is holding her close. He watches us with a bewildered look.

I start crying as we pull away.

"Oh Jesus Christ! Not now!" Boogie says.

"Sh-sh-shut up B-B-oogie," I sniffle, trying not to cry. I wipe my eyes—my makeup is ok if it melts off now, it's just me and Boogie now. I hate how I start to stutter when I try to stop crying. I try to take a swig of beer because now I am hiccuping. As I drink, I hiccup and sniffle at the same time, causing the beer to go down the wrong pipe. So now I am crying, sniffling, hiccuping, and choking. Boogie pulls over and pounds my back until it hurts. He then hands me a tissue because now, to top it off, I am all snot-nosed.

"Girl, you are a hot mess. I would rather kiss a frog too, a real one at that. I know we are the only two in this van but maintain your cool please. I know for some reason you're hurt, but he ain't even your man. You have no right to be jealous."

"I'm not jealous," I sniffle and blow my nose, trying to get the most use out of that tissue.

"Whatever," Boogie says. "You're practically green with jealousy." He starts the van and gets back on the road.

I look out the window at the passing cornfields. The moon is still out but not as bright. Where the hell are all the sunflowers?

"I just think he can do better," I say quietly.

"Like you?" Boogie asks.

"No, just in general. She isn't his type." Sniffle-hiccup-snort. Did I fart too? If I did, it is only Boogie.

Boogie is looking at me with the same sideways look his Grandma uses and it is kind of a little bit scary. "Why can't you just admit you are jealous as hell? And did you just fart along with all that other mess coming out of you? Gross! I would definitely look for a frog to kiss, too!"

I only sniffle. No burping or farting or hiccupping or snorting. God, how am I ever even charming?

"I told you!" Boogie says, "This is where the relationship of fuck buddies goes wrong! I told you this a long time ago!"

I continue looking out as we pull into the small Podunk town and I watch the pale orange streetlights pass as Journey sings some song about city lights, ha—whatever.

"You m-make it sound cheap and shallow," I say.

"IT IS! That's why! You don't spend time or money on each other. You don't invest any feelings into a relationship with each other but jealousy and sports! You are only friends who have sex! All guys want that! And that my girl is cheap and shallow as a pond... wait, as a puddle."

Boogie pulls into the motel. I want so bad to tell him that Ricky bought me a half pint of whiskey and a coke and they were both name brand! Albeit, eight bucks altogether. But I don't.

As we walk into our room, I immediately smell the stale smell of shag carpeting and cheap bar soap. I carry in the confiscated beer.

Boogie lets out his thunderous, signature laugh. "Oh yeah, you stole his beer!" He laughs harder, "At least you are still evil. There is hope."

He strips down to his boxer-briefs as if he is a model and immediately flops in the one bed. I wasn't even tired yet. I lay on my side and my eyes won't close. I hate to admit even to myself that I am still pissed about that swamp-looking bitch so I stare at the wood paneling as if it will give me answers.

After 32 seconds of staring at it, I am convinced that I am evil and going to die soon. All I could see are devils and evil clowns and scary zombies in the patterns of the fake wood paneling. I hear Boogie snoring.

I try hard to remember if I smoked any weed and maybe that is why I am in a drama queen mode. I am pretty sure I didn't. I am kind of feeling evil and it is not from seeing all the evil patterns in the woodwork. I just keep thinking, "Do I really want one of my best friends to not experience happiness? Am I jealous of that? Or do I like him?"

I finally get up and turn the volume up. Boogie has to sleep with a TV on and the volume down. I turn it up and it is on the Food Network. Bad choice. I immediately want food. Ugh! I lay down again. The air conditioning sucks in here. It is damp and smells of musty shag carpeting. I lay by Boogie and kick him. He smacks his lips, farts loudly and finally rolls over as slow as a log in a still pond. Gross. If I have a gay friend—slash—cousin, I sure wish he wouldn't act so damn straight!

The fart immediately slaps me in the face and I sit up again. I need air. I open the door and look out at the dying small town. How these Podunk towns even exist, I have no idea. The air is cool and even though there is a stockyard nearby, it is fresher than the room with the musty carpet and farting queer.

I remember that Boogie has snacks in his van and my stomach growls. Duh! Of course! Boogie always has something to throw down, only in the most processed manner, since he doesn't cook, but the boy always has munchies.

I grab his keys and run through the summer insects to forage his van. I am still sniffling slightly as I guzzle my beer. The sky to the east is turning the faintest of blue from black. I dig in the console, in all the seat pockets, a back pack and a small cooler filled with water and melting ice slivers. I hear mourning doves cooing and robins tweeting. A dog barks in a nearby yard. I score. I find a Twix bar, a Chuckwagon sammy, a half-eaten bag of Funyons and a beef jerky.

Jackpot! I knew it.

I didn't even hit the way back of the van yet but my cell phone rings in my bra. Axyl Rose is screaming at me in my boobs. I need a more toned-down ringtone, for real.

"You got my beer? Or what?" It's Ricky, trying to sound as tough as the district he is from. Guess he forgot, I am from Lower Ridge.

"Yah. So?" I say, trying to put up a front that I know could melt like cotton candy in the rain.

"I want it back. What the fuck! I paid for it," he sounds all mean.

"Ok, fuck. Pick it up at my house tomorrow. I'm still in Rushville," I hold up my front well. My mama would be proud.

"I know you are, I am watching you rip Boogie off next," Ricky says and laughs. I look up from my scavenging and he is coming out of the office. Alone. He jingles a room key at me. I smile.

I hate him. I love him. Wait, I am indifferent. Right?

I get out of the van with my arms full of my confiscated goods.

"Come to my room?" he pleads. He has his hands in his pockets, one eyebrow raised and god fucking damn, the rez boy is adorable. I just nod.

I tighten my grip on the Funyuns because I feel them slipping and follow him. I hear him slip his key in and we enter his room. The layout is the same and the room is a little bit fresher than the one I just left.

"Are those Funyuns?" Ricky asks.

"Yah," I hand him the bag and he starts munching.

"Check this room out, it has a flyswatter with the name of the motel on it. That's tacky, huh?" He laughs as he swats the dirty fly swatter around like a sword.

"Yah," I say and put the chuckwagon sandwich in the microwave.

I don't know what to say all of a sudden. I'm ashamed for acting up. Why the hell was I jealous?

"Can I have half of that?" Ricky asks. We both watch the cheese melt in the microwave.

"Yah," I say as the microwave dings.

"Sis, you sound like Rainman. Talk to me and don't say 'Yah,' speak more than one word." He's looking at me, pissed. I get nervous. We never talk serious, really, hardly.

I take a deep breath and look at the ceiling. "It's just that she isn't your type. She's a scrub and I think you are too good for her," I exhale and grab the sandwich to start splitting it in two.

"While you left me at the table to go pay attention to a white boy all night!" He grabs his half and starts eating.

I laugh, "We were wheelin' and dealin', making bets. You know how I roll," I won't look at him as I look at my half of the sandwich.

"What was you guys betting? Kisses?" Ricky said in between bites.

"That was a peck, a little peck on the cheek," I say and finish my half of the sandwich off. Ricky is already opening the beef jerky, the empty Funyuns bag at our feet. One thing Ricky and I are good at together is eating, and we have no problem sharing food. We have almost a rhythm.

Ricky gives me half the beef jerky. "What are you guys? Chickens? Pecking each other? Or what?"

"Whatever!" I laugh, "You guys had your tongues down each other's throats like you was trying hard to turn the frog into a princess. I bet she had fly breath!" I'm such a bitch and then I laugh. An evil bitch to boot.

He smiles, despite that I am being snarky as hell. "That sounds like something Boogie would say."

"It is. Or it was. Or the first part is totally all Boogie. I take credit for the second part."

"You're both evil anyway," Ricky says. "So we still friends?" He offers his hand to shake on it.

"Yah," I say like Rainman and extend my hand. He bypasses my hand and shakes my left boob instead and laughs. I slap his hand. "Ricky! You asshole! Perv!"

We were done eating so we lay in bed together and stared at the ceiling talking for an hour about what has been going on in our lives, our kids' lives and what we missed out on for the last eight months. I spoon up next to him and it is just like the old days. Above the covers and fully clothed.

"Sis?" he whispers.

"What?" I whisper back.

"Do you think that food was okay? Boogie keeps shit forever. You don't think we'll get sick?"

"I hope not," I whisper back.

He puts his arm around me and holds me and that is how we fall asleep. My best friend was back in my life.

[three]

Saturday

I woke up the next morning with the sound of a bully-like mosquito buzzing by my ear. They don't buzz with a zzzz, they buzz like *neeeeeener neeeeeener,* as if they are teasing you. That is when I realized I had a mosquito bite by my eye, because half the world was bright and full of sunshine and the other half was as if the shade was pulled halfway down.

Then I heard Ricky let out a soft snore behind me. His arm was around me and one leg thrown over me. I went into panic mode. I have to sneak out without him seeing me looking like Cyclops. I don't know why, because he saw me have a food allergy attack once and my lips puffed up so big. We tried to keep hanging out but every time he looked at me he laughed. I pouted, although of course he couldn't tell I was pouting by my lips. So he just did a few shots of Crown Royal with me until I forgot I had fish lips. Then he would laugh at my mispronunciation of things. After a while I was laughing, too.

But for some reason, this was different. I slowly slid over, inching my way to the edge of the bed, until I could do some silent ninja-like roll off the bed, flop on my knees and then stand up. I tiptoed out the door and went to Boogie's room and knocked. I could hear him snoring. I knock again. He still snores. I bang on the door like a tribal cop. I hear him fart, choke and start coughing. God, he is disgusting. And here I am trying to be incognito with my one eye.

I hear him smacking his lips as he paddles to the door. He must peek out the peephole because I hear him laugh. He opens the door and laughs harder. I glare. He finally stops laughing and puts his hand on his hip.

"Girl! Did he hit you? Did he? Let's go fuck his car and then him up! I got a bat and a blade!" God, Boog is so overly dramatic. He was standing there huffing with his hand on his hip, just like our Grandma Pacific does when she gets fired up.

I shake my head and put my finger to my lips. "Shhhhhh. No, it was a fucking mosquito. Let's get outta here."

I go in the room and splash my mask. Ugh, I can't even look in the mirror. I take the quickest shower ever and change. The water wasn't even hot. Reminded me of jail.

"Boog, you got some extra shades?" I ask.

"I suppose. What the hell kind of shower was that? Did you even scrub it?" He laughs. I grab the sunglasses from him and we grab our goods and hit the road. I even stole Ricky's beer again, but he is supposed to stop by later anyway.

After we hit the road Boogie starts pouting. I say nothing. I am starting to hangover and don't want to deal with his shit. I have the worst headache and I start to feel as if I am not even human. I need to eat. I think all I ate was the cherry from the bar in Gordon. Thinking of that made my stomach turn and then growl.

"Boogie, stop at the gas station please, I'm hungry as hell," I plead. Boogie turns off at the Jump N Pump. I realize I hardly spent any money last night—that's the good thing about hanging out with friends that make more money than you. Not that I don't buy my share of rounds, they just buy more. I pitch in with Boogie on gas and go inside the convenience store. I buy a six-pack of the "ice cold beer" they advertise, some potato chips, dill pickle sunflower seeds, chicken gizzards, a corndog and some gum. Boogie comes in and buys a breakfast burrito from the taco bar on the other side of the store. I just can't make myself buy Mexican food from a gas station. However, I can buy deep fried gizzards from there.

We are quiet for the next seven miles. I am trying to eat my food but I can't seem to stomach it. I'm too *kuja,* or sick. I know I need a beer but I am really trying to not have one. I don't want to admit that I need one. I don't want to admit that I am like my mom, brother, sister, basically most of the other people I am related to. This is not me, this was never me. I was not the party girl, drinker; I always stayed home and took care of my kids, baked them cookies and all that. But, when I think about it, that was years ago. In fact, my daughter doesn't even know I bake great oatmeal chocolate chip cookies.

"Sister, I have some V-8—can you make me a red beer please? I bought a cup of ice," he pleads. I forget he was pouting but his favor also gives me the green light to snap open a can, too. He is hanging over just as bad as I am I realize, as I stir his drink with a straw. I hate the hair of the dog drink. I don't like tomato juice. I guzzle a beer as Boogie sucks on the straw to that drink as if it is his life support. By the time we make it to Whiteclay, we are both done with our second beers and feeling semi-human again. Boogie is singing along to Cyndi Lauper on his cassette deck. I swear he has had the same cassettes for twenty years but he said he buys them at the border town rummage sales he takes his grandma to. I told him it must be the same ones he buys his shirts from. I open the Big Red chewing gum and hand one to Boogie also, so we can cover the smell of alcohol as soon as we get to Whiteclay, or as people from Pine Ridge call it, Clay. I have no idea why we think gum covers the smell of alcohol, but we do. I guess we do it for the sake of the "dry reservation." He snaps his gum and slurps his red beer. I burp.

He looks at me sideways "Excuse you! Why do you have to act like a man sometimes?"

"Cuz you won't and don't!" I snap back.

"Whatever," he shakes his shaggy hair. That is a sign he is still pouting because he thinks I got lucky. Ugh. He can be such a bitch sometimes. Even if I DID get lucky, which I didn't, he should be happy for me. He should be happy because I wouldn't be as crabby as I am now. I would be shining like that big ol' sun in the sky that is beating down so hard I can hear my brains frying. Sometimes, I just want to slap him real hard. But I don't. Boogie is one of those gay guys that likes his boyfriends to have girlfriends and his girlfriend to not have boyfriends. In other words, he likes to be the only dude in anyone's life. He only dates in-the-closet guys and he also thinks that every guy is gay with the potential to be straight someday.

I'm thinking of why we have a dry reservation. All it seems to do is keep the police busy with throwing people who are drinking in jail and they don't go after the true criminals who are out there committing major crimes. Whiteclay, Nebraska makes millions of dollars a year on our broke asses. The bar-owners vacation in Jamaica while we live in a third world country. I look at all the people in the street, passed out, some are dancing, some are laughing, and once in a while you can catch a fistfight. Most of the time you see a relative, who will call you out because they know they can usually score a buck or some spare change off you. There is no honor and dignity—you get attacked by beggars for change so they can taper their livers off for another day. What scares the fuck out of me about that is I'm hoping that it's never me. I listen to Tom Petty sing about *running down a dream* and watch people who don't dream anymore. And then like the dumbass I am, I snap open the last two cans for Boogie and I as he pulls into one of the four bars.

"Get me a pickle," I order him as two guys knock at my window. Fuck. I shake my head but they keep knocking. They are lucky I am not hung over miserable anymore. I roll down my window. One is tall, gangly and wearing a bright orange hunting style stocking cap over his greasy hair (in August.) The other one is shorter, pudgy, has crooked eyes, crooked teeth, and crooked cut off blue jeans. He smiles at me, like he's a player.

"What?" I ask.

"Niece, do you have 31 cents we can borrow?" Once again I am amazed that the street people up here know exactly how much change they need. I look around Boog's console but only find a quarter. I drop the quarter in his grubby outstretched palm.

He looks at the quarter and drops his smile. "Is that all?"

"What the fuck! I can take it back!" I act like I am going to reach for it and they back off laughing at my anger. God! Why me?

"Wopila!" he yells and gives me the AIM fist in the air, protecting his prized quarter. Then they descend on Boogie as he walks out like vultures on road kill. I see him swatting at them and screaming around as if they are birds or flies and I laugh. God, he just may end up here someday himself.

"I don't have no six cents! And who the hell asks for six cents anyway! I need money too! Give me some money—shit, you probably have more than me!" Boogie brushes them off, walking with a bag of cherry berry malt liquors and gets in the van. He throws the pickle at me and peels out of there, spraying gravel everywhere.

"Damn, you didn't have to throw the pickle at me!" I tell him. I didn't even try to catch it because it bounced off my shoulder.

Boogie looks at me, "Oh please, quit acting brand new. I thought you was going to catch it with your mouth."

I am speechless and pissed. I glare at him. Then we both laugh. Finally, all is forgiven between us with a perverted, degrading thought.

"What the hell you yell at them so bad for? You on your period—damn, Boog." I put my shades on and look around to make sure I don't see any cops. I take a quick sip of my beer when I realize the coast is clear.

"Whatever! I get so sick of those people! They are ALWAYS helpless and ALWAYS begging," he complains.

"Well, they're still your people. And I gave them one of your quarters I found in your console," I laugh.

"The nerve! You owe me a quarter!" Boogie exclaims as he pulls into town. "Are you going to the parade?"

"Aw, fuck, yeah. I forgot. Eeez, Imma be hanging hard. Misun has it planned out anyways. I'll just follow his lead."

Boogie pulls into my driveway. He don't offer to help carry my shit in and I don't ask. Screw him, pout baby ass anyway. Not that I hooked up, but if it was him, I would have heard the story all the way back until I wanted to scream and choke him. I lug everything, well mostly my snacks, Ricky's beer and my bag of clothes to the house.

It is 8:30 in the morning and my house is a mess. A MESS! I want to get mad and scream at the boys but I don't. They are sprawled out on the sectional, snoring, uniforms on the floor. I know they probably played ball until two or three in the morning. That's just the way the tournaments roll here on the rez, especially during the fair and rodeo. I can't get mad at them. There are pop cans all over, wrappers from various burritos, chip bags, candy bars, etc. Sports Center is on TV and looks like it has been playing all night.

I walk over and turn off the TV and turn on my radio to the local tribal radio station. The house is filled with heavy rez accents, rez slang and country music. Many dub it the *hangover show*, but it's not. Indians just like their country music. I grew up with it, from my grandparents to my parents.

I grab a pack of bacon out of the freezer and throw it in the sink under some running water to thaw out. I'll make my sons their favorite breakfast ever. Bacon fried rice, and it goes a long way to feed a bunch of hungry mouths.

I guzzle a beer and get busy sweeping, mopping, walking around the living room with a grocery bag picking up the boys carnage. I throw their baseball uniforms in the washer and throw an extra cap full of softener in the wash cycle because I caught a whiff of them and whoof! I do my dishes and start sweeping my carpet because I never owned a vacuum in my life. By the time I am done, I am ready for another shower. I am all sweaty and feel refried, as if I never even showered earlier. I make sure all the windows are open and turn all the window fans on.

I feel brand new after a hot steaming half-hour shower. I smell fruity and feel 100%. Not only that, my house is clean and smells good, and I turn the burners on for the bacon and water for rice. I start the bacon sizzling and it is barely 9:30 a.m. I hear my front door slam so I go rushing in from the kitchen to the living room. I know the boys can't be up. And nobody uses my front door ever because the gate in the front is to damn hard to work.

It's Mark, my brother, one of the twins in our family. I go stand by the sink because Ricky's beer is under there and Mark can sniff out beer like an old bloodhound can sniff out a raccoon. He's all disheveled looking. Or wait. Disheveled is a compliment. He actually hurts my eyes and makes me start hanging over again.

"What the fuck happened to you?" I ask.

He smells, of course, like he always smells. An ashtray, stale beer, and three-day funk. He also smells like something sickeningly sweet and slightly familiar, but I can't place it. He has little blue fuzzball looking things all over him. I kind of don't know if I want to hear what happened to him. It looks like he was chewed up and vomited out. I notice he is shaking, from hanging over. He tells me he needs to use the bathroom and he will tell me what happens when he comes out. I get some of Ricky's beer from under the sink and put one on the table for him, and throw the four of them in the freezer. I turn back to the stove and Mark comes out and his face lights up when he sees the beer.

"Heeeey Sister, just what I needed. What makes me sick makes me better." He always says that and he isn't lying. What scares me about it is lately, that has been me, too. Buddy Red Bow's *Just Can't Take Anymore* starts playing on the radio. Mark lifts his can in respect to one of the most famous singers ever to come off our reservation.

While the bacon is cooling on paper towels and the rice steams, I grab an onion, a knife, and one of the beers that barely started to chill and go sit to listen to his story. Then I decide I want a red beer. I grab a glass of ice, can of commodity tomato juice and celery salt. As I walk back to the table, I take a whiff of Mark's matted-looking dreadlocks. He looks like our mom's old shaggy poodle, Bo Jangles, who never saw a groomer in his life. I know it was gross to take a whiff, but I know I can place that scent.... almost like a candle, except, wait—

"Corn Syrup! Commodity Corn Syrup!" I start laughing so hard, I sit down at the table and keep laughing. He drinks his beer looking at me.

"What the hell happened to you?"

I make my red beer as he starts his story.

"Fucking Tweaker! I was up on the hill at his mom's house. We was drinking wine from the bootleggers at sunrise this morning. Me, Tweaker, his bro Horndog, and Dan Shoots Twice. So we get fucking pickled, right? Drinking wine in the morning sun in August. Then someone passes a doobie around. I only took two hits, wasn't even 8 o'clock yet, right? Then I musta passed out."

He pauses to take a drink, so I take one with him. I start dicing onions for the rice. He finishes the can and gets up to throw it away. He checks my rice, turns it off, and then helps himself to a can from the freezer. I knew he was going to do that. He figures if he checks the rice, he is due another can. I bet he even snuck a peek under the sink. Gah, I need to start hiding stuff from him where he can't see them. He sits down, snaps the can and guzzles half. He's used to those big fortified malt liquor cans they have in Whiteclay. Crack in a can.

"So I come to and I can't move. I am rolled up like a joint in a blanket and its 110 fuckin degrees out already. I can't breathe, move, nothing, so I start screaming like a woman. I'm like a burrito. To make it worse, I have a blindfold on. I thought I was kidnapped for ransom, like by some KKK guys. So someone comes and pulls the blindfold off and its Tweaker's grandma; she's like 97 years old. She's screaming at me in Lakota and starts kicking me. I'm in a cocoon so I start screaming for the cops. Fuck it, I would rather sit in the drunk tank than have this 97-year-old grandma beat me up. That's when I look around and notice—they rolled me in a cheap fuzzy blue blanket. The kind the churches give out. Then they stapled me to the wooden deck in front of his house with a staple gun. Fuckin' Tweaker. I know it was his idea, the motherfucker is twisted. I could've died in this heat.

"Then Tweaker's grandma grabbed the cordless phone from inside and told me she was calling the cops. I told her please do, so I can charge her with kidnapping, assault, and other charges. So she goes back in. I'm waiting to go to jail and here she comes out with a switchblade. I thought I was going to die, but she cuts me out of the blanket. That's when I noticed they poured corn syrup on me first. Fuckin' Tweaker! Fuckin' full bloods! Oh, and his grandma told me to get away from her house and don't come back until I have a brand new blanket for her. As if! She is the one who cut it up!"

He guzzles the rest of the beer, proudly.

I suppose I'd grab him another coldie from the freezer. He deserves it for that story. I mean, my God, he still smelled of corn syrup and his hair was gathered in dreadlock-looking tufts. I am laughing so hard, I stop to double-over in laughter as I hold myself up with one hand on the counter.

I finally stand up to finish the bacon fried rice, scrambled some eggs in the bacon grease, then I sautéed some onions in some more of the grease. After making sure the rice was drained of all water, I throw it in the wok with the rest of the bacon grease, eggs, onions and stir fry it. Add soy sauce and it is done. Can feed an army with all this, and I usually do. I don't even have a drop of bacon grease to throw in my reserve of precious bacon grease on the back of the stove in an old Butternut coffee can. Man, if an Indian woman's worth was measured in her recycled bacon grease then damned if these rez boys don't know what a good woman I am.

Mark is still mumbling about full bloods so I thump him in the ear. Even his ear is sticky, gross. "Your mama is a full blood," I tell him.

"Oh yeah," he mutters and then guzzles the rest of the beer down. "That's what's wrong with her."

"I'm going to tell her you said that, too." I make him a plate, he tries to decline it. When he goes on long drunks he won't eat. I usually make him. Sometimes I will find him wasted in Whiteclay so I bring him home and feed him until he runs away again. I glare at him and nudge the plate towards him. I could tell he is pouting but he grabs the fork and starts eating, and pretty soon he is wolfing it down so much. I thank God he still has an appetite and smile to myself.

I feel satisfied but I grab his plate to get him seconds, and he doesn't object. I wonder sometimes if they know how hard it is to be the oldest sister. Half the time I worry about my siblings and the other half I want to be mad at them.

My cheeks hurt from laughing. This was a classical *Don't Pass out on the Rez* type of story. People are so cruel and messed up in the head. Geez. I grab the house phone and dial Misun. I am laughing so hard it takes me forever to tell him to bring a clean set of clothes for Mark. When he asks what happened, I laugh harder, and tell him it is worth it. "Just bring the clothes when you bring the girls for the parade."

"Geez, Tweaker's grandma better not try to act all somehow to me at the grocery store, either," I say and I dish him out more food and take it over. This time I sit and drink my beer.

He shook his head, "She won't. She better not, she agreed that if I didn't sign charges on her, she wouldn't turn me in for being drunk, but she kicked me as I was getting up. Screamed at me over and over, I owed her a blanket. Then I walked over here."

Mark stuffs a huge forkful in his mouth. I swear he didn't even chew—just washed it down with warm beer. I can't even be disgusted with him. Because here I am, on a Saturday morning, drinking a warm beer with my alcoholic brother, with the excuse of curing a hangover. I shake my head, geez. I must be getting buzzed—what the hell with these thoughts again, like I have no control. I never let myself be uncool, in my world, anyway.

"That bitch," he mutters.

I smile and shake my head. Oh, my little brother. I remember when he was little and would tell stories to make himself the victim. He never changed. I love him so much. I walk into the living room to wake my sons up to eat.

"GIDDUP!" I holler. My Grandpa used to holler like that and I hated it, but somehow, it is now my thing. "Kiktapo!" I holler and start turning the fans on high before it gets hot out.

Mark is looking at me and eating, smiling. "Sister, women don't say Kiktapo. That is a man's thing," he laughs.

Kiktapo means "get up."

"So, I don't give a shit. Putting a tipi up was a woman's thing too but I don't ever see women doing that now," I tell him.

He just mutters, "haun," and turns back to his plate, scraping rice off.

"Hey, speaking of women, where is Arlene?" I ask him. I shake my youngest twin's Craig's shoulder and he farts and gets up. Creighton, the older twin, is already slumbering to the table like a zombie and looking at Mark all funny with one eye open.

"That whore!" Mark guzzles the rest of his beer. "I heard she is partying with some Crow dudes. Traitor whore! She may as well stab me right here if she wants to party with them snakes." He points to his heart.

"She better not!" I say, remembering the last time she pulled a knife on him and I had to stalk her and beat the shit out of her. Not that I am that tough, because Boogie may have gotten a swing in, too, but she did slice and scar my little brother. I just had to beat her up because he is my little brother.

"Leksi, what the hell is wrong with you?" Creighton asks his uncle. I laugh and go to make their plates. Craig comes out of the bathroom and looks at his uncle and bursts out laughing.

He stops laughing and smells Mark's hair just to stop and say, "Ewwww!" then laughs again. I slap his shoulder playfully.

Mark glares at my twins. "I'm going to go take a shower!" he says.

"No!" I holler. "Hold up, Misun is coming over with a change of clothes. Plus I want Misun to see this dumb ass with all the blue fuzz balls glued on with commod syrup to him. I didn't care if he wanted to bitch up and pout now. This shit was classic.

My boys both start eating their bacon fried rice and Craig asks Mark what happened.

"No!" I say, "Wait until Misun gets here so you can all hear it, then he only has to tell his adventure once."

"Well, hell, sister, thanks for getting amusement out of my pain and suffering." Mark smiles and reveals the space where his tooth was knocked out by Arlene's brothers. So much drama in rez relationships and yet, everyone thrives on it. I don't get it. I suppose I don't help any; I am always the sister sticking her nose in their business, taking up for them, chasing whoever off and fighting. As if I am even a fighter.

I am grabbing both Mark and I another beer as Misun pulls up with Jasmine and his daughter Winterblossom; he must have left the two oldest with their grandparents. My hangover is gone, I am done being miserable and a little too happy for it being so early.

I give Misun a hug and he gives me a weird look. He knows I am buzzed up and it isn't even noon yet. He looks worried or scared; his eyebrows are drawn up as if in fear. I don't like my brothers and sisters to worry about me—that's my job for them. I look at my beer over by the fridge, kind of hidden. But everyone knows I am drinking. Well whatever, I am a grown ass woman and I can do what I want.

I grab some paper plates and start dishing out some rice for Misun, Jazz, and the girls. Misun is at the table, doubled over, laughing at Mark. Mark is already animatedly telling the story of literally being rolled. I smile to myself and drink my beer by the fridge, watching all the kids listen intently to their Uncle Mark. He is such a storyteller. Misun is shoveling food in his mouth from his plate, leaning against the counter, and laughing so hard, sometimes he has to put his plate down.

"And that is my pain, my suffering, and my story for this year's Great Oglala Nation Fair and Rodeo," he grabs his heart and looks far away as his eyes can go. Everyone is laughing as Mark takes a bow and holding onto his beer with one hand and the change of clothes Misun brought over with the other. He goes off to scrub all the syrup and blue fuzz balls off in the shower.

He turns around and comes back to Misun and me. We are standing in the kitchen, both leaning on the counter, Misun eating seconds and me nursing my beer. "Oh yeah, I went to Frieda's, before I came here. Man, she is in a bad way."

"What do you mean, bad way?" I ask. I already can feel heat rising to my face. She better not pull no bullshit. I will kick my sister's ass.

"I dunno, man. I thought she would have a hangover beer so I went there first. Don't even look like she was drinking. I mean there are empty cans all over, but there's foils all over too, man.

People passed out all over. I didn't see James or Wiconi, they must be at a babysitters, so I just left."

"Fuck," I say and look at Misun. Mark is already heading to the bathroom. "What the fuck, Misun?"

He puts his plate on the counter and goes to the twins, "Hey, can you guys watch the girls? We have to go get James and Wiconi. We will be right back."

Misun has Metallica blasting so loud, we don't have time to bitch about Frieda. And I am thankful for that. I am sick of her and her bullshit. She cares more about getting laid than anything and I hate to say it, but my sister is a whore. Not that I am a nun, but damn have some priorities.

Misun's minivan pulls into Frieda's dusty yard. She has had the same broken down car sitting in her driveway for the last three years, so we pull up in the yard. There are two flea-bitten runts laying on the porch. Misun shoos them away as we open the screen door with no screen and her door.

There are flies buzzing everywhere. Her house is hot. She must have sold her air conditioner, again. There is an ugly, greasy man passed out on the couch and empty cans on the end tables. Misun starts slapping the greasy guy up, he wakes up, and starts grabbing cans and shaking them. Misun slams his fist in the back of his head, cussing him up, and leads him to the door, throwing him out.

"James! Wiconi!" I holler. I hear their little footsteps running up the steps and my heart is instantly relieved. I take a little breathe to relax but instantly swallow it when I see them so dirty, and snot-nosed in the summer! I lean down and hug them. I want to cry but I don't.

"Where was you guys?" I ask and instantly try to spit shine the dirt off their cheeks but Wiconi says "gross" and moves away.

"We locked ourselves downstairs last night because mom told us to. She said they would be doing grown-up things, not to bother them."

Misun is shaking his head and his fists are clenched. He hits the wall and knocks a hole in the drywall. He makes a loud grunting noise that sounds like the "f" word when he does. Both kids start to cry.

"Shhhh," I hush them, "Don't cry, you did nothing wrong, we came to take you to the parade, OK?" I'm wiping their tears and they both smile at the chance to be a kid today and have fun. "I need you to wait in the car for us while I find you some clothes. OK?"

Misun is trying to not cry as he leads them out the door to the van. I know I drink, but I clean my house, and I hate the smell of beer, believe it or not. I have too many bad memories. I see the burnt foils by the stove. I go to the kids' room in the back of the house; there are no clothes, only a naked couple passed out with their clothes on the floor. I gather their clothes and throw them out the back door. I go down the steps to the basement, there was a huge dirty clothes pile and it smelled like it. I see the room Wiconi and James held themselves captive in. There were two open boxes of commodity cereal, the generic Rice Chex and the generic corn flakes, and an open box of raisins. There was also a pillow and one little blanket on the cracked linoleum floor. They slept on the floor. While all those assholes upstairs slept on beds and couches. I felt my face getting hot. I was pissed. My eyes were watering; memories of sneaking commodities to feed us kids came to mind as my mom held her parties. Jesus, did Frieda not remember that?

I gather anything that looks like it is James or Wiconi's in a laundry basket and go upstairs. I look in her fridge—some old butter, an empty pickle jar, and three beers. I walk to Frieda's room, and open the door. The urge to kick her face in is overwhelming. She is passed out next to some random dude. There were empty beer cans, burnt foils, and an open box of baking soda, lighters, and their clothes laying all over. I want to choke her, but instead I grab their clothes and throw them out the back door, too. I grab the laundry basket of dirty clothes and go out to Misun's van. Then I did what I try to avoid at all times— I called our brother George, the cop.

I am washing and drying clothes a half hour later. Misun is outside with all the kids, playing a game of tag. Frieda's kids ate the rest of the breakfast rice up, then they found my pickle, gizzards, corndog, and chips from my trip back with Boogie earlier and ate those, too. Now they are all full and happy running around outside, like all kids should be—instead of being kept in a basement. I am going to beat the shit out of Frieda when she gets out of jail. I don't care what anyone says.

I am wiping stray rice grains off the table cloth when I see George pull up in his cruiser. Fuck, I think as I grab Mark's hand, and lead him to my room. He was sort of passed out in the recliner, but at least he smelled and looked normal now.

I put my finger to my lip and whisper, "Shhh, George is outside." Before I can say anything else he drops and rolls under my bed. I follow suit, drop and roll in beside him, forcing him to inch over under the bed. That's when I remember my bed frame is broken. It is a very tight squeeze. I suck in my gut but it feels like a 500 lb. person is on the bed. Mark's head is pressed against the floor, ear first. I smile, despite my discomfort.

"Jesus, Sis! What the fuck is wrong with this bed?" he whispers.

"Shhh, the frame is broke," I whisper back.

"How the hell did you break it? You ol' whore!" he whispers but laughs out loud.

"Shhht!" I shush him... If I could hit him, I would. "If we don't go to jail, I'm going to beat you up." We hear the screen door slam and George's cop-like steps walking around the house. Misun is following him, explaining that we left. Mark is breathing hard out of his mouth but I can't tell him to close his mouth. I smell hot beer and toothpaste and I pray he didn't use my toothbrush. I want to laugh because the way his mouth is open, he looks like a trout. I hear the fridge open and a can snap.

"Hey bro, she charges fifty cents a pop."

I hear George take a big swig of the soda, then it sounds like he slaps Misun on the back. "Sis is my full sister. She would never charge me for a soda. I am not just a half-brother like you," he says in his over-confident, cocky ass-I-am-a-tribal-cop voice, instead of talking like we are family. He especially gets this voice during busy times of the year when the police have no days off. Ugh.

I hear him walking around my house. He is opening cupboards, as if I would hide my fat ass in a cupboard. Shit! I remember the beer under the sink. Now it is time for me to pray. I can't go to jail during the pow wow; everyone knows it takes forever to get out. *Please God, keep me safe and free and I won't do anything bad this year, **I PROMISE.***

"Man! George, does that badge make you feel that important?" I hear Misun asking him. I also hear someone pouring something in the sink.

"So if nothing is going on here, who was drinking this half of a beer?" George asks.

"I dunno, probably Mark, he left." I hear Misun stutter, slightly.

"Dammit!" Mark whispers.

"Haun," I shhhh him.

I see the cop flashlight shining all over the floor, even though it wasn't even noon yet. What the fuck, George thinks he is Robo-Cop!

"So, where did Mark go?" George asks as his flashlight shines in my room over the horrible pea green shag carpet.

Raymond sounds pissed. "I dunno! Why don't you check the pow wow George? Remember the women's jingle dress contest? Maybe he decided to go dance in that competition again, to make all the people laugh. And then when it's over, maybe his asshole cop of a brother can tackle him like he is a bank robber and break his collarbone again."

I hear George grunt. Then Raymond starts in again. Man! I want to tell him to shut up, but I don't want to go to jail.

"George, tell me one thing about being an officer of the tribal law, do you wear that uniform to be an asshole? Or were you an asshole already, so you get a job with a matching uniform?"

Now, I want to laugh. I can imagine Misun standing tall but thin compared to George, with his chin up. I can also imagine George pushing Raymond in the chest with his index finger.

"Careful boy, you are real close to assaulting an officer." I can hear George breathing out of his nostrils like he is a horse. I want to laugh. His nostril breathing caused many fights in our childhood. Sometimes, I think he was so easy to make fun of— that may be why he became a cop.

"Man, go direct traffic for the pow wow and throw more drunks in jail," Misun says.

I hear the screen door slam and more words, but I can't make them out. Then I hear George's unit start up and head out. He lets the siren do a quick squeal as he leaves. As if it was a warning.

A few minutes later, the screen door slams again and I hear Misun whistle, signaling to us that the coast is clear.

I can't move. Heck, I can barely breathe. Stupid broken bed frame.

I hear Misun whistle again that the coast is clear. "Where are you guys?"

"We're in here, under Jezebel's bed! Trapped!" Mark screams. I want to punch him but I can't move.

"Fuck you," I whisper.

"Misun, you have to lift the frame up. And call George and tell him to come back and get Mark, he's drunk," I said.

Misun lifts the bed frame up and as we roll out, the cat rolls out with us—as if he was going to jail, too. I hit Mark in the back three times as he walks away.

"Oh! Oh! Oh! Hey, watch it, Sis. Man, that ain't even cool anymore. We're grown up now, don't be hitting me. I might hit you back. Jesus, can't even tease you," Mark says, walking away.

I know what he says is true. I act like they are still under my watch at all times and not adults.

Misun is standing there laughing.

"What's so funny?" Both Mark and I ask at the same time.

"George's PBT thing was missing. He should know better than to leave his door open with all these wild Indian kids running around," Misun laughs.

So he wouldn't have been able to throw Mark or me in jail anyway—he would have had no proof we were drinking. That was funny, but George would have tossed us in anyway.

Mark and I look at each other and laugh. Mark goes walking to the back door. "I want them to PBT me," he says.

"Wait!" I holler and follow him. "I'm first. It's my house."

Mark blows way over the limit, but he is pickled all the time. One time they wouldn't let him out until he blew zeroes. He was in there for almost 46 hours without food. He drafted up a lawsuit and everything, had a tribal lawyer willing to represent him for cruel and unusual punishment—then when Mark got his money, instead of paying his lawyer, he went on a drunk with Arlene.

It was too bad he didn't follow through with the lawsuit,

I was mad at them for not feeding my brother for two days, but he couldn't stay sober long enough to sue them.

I blew just under the legal limit, but George would have thrown me in anyway. The new tribal law is liquor violation. If you have the smell on your breath, then you are legally violating by possession by ingestion. I've known people who went out drinking the night before, were thrown in the next day when cops came knocking on their door, smelled their breath and threw them in jail. That was Boogie, twice. And George that arrested him, twice. There is no love lost there. Boogie hates George for picking on him while growing up. George hates Boogie for being gay.

I take Wiconi and James inside to bathe them—they are filthy. Poor babies. I have them sing the *inkpata* song with me while sudsing their hair. I don't know why, but when we bathed, my grandma would always sing it to us.

"So is Frieda in jail, Misun?" I holler at him.

He walks up and stands in the doorway. "Yeah, she and all her scumbag friends are locked up. They went to jail with blankets on, George said. Since your evil ass threw their clothes outside," he laughs.

I didn't laugh. Well that was good for them, I thought. I dress James and Wiconi in nice clean warm, good smelling clothes from the dryer.

Wiconi takes a big whiff of her shirt as it slides over her head. "Mmmmm, smells so good. Thank you Auntie Sister." She gives me a big bear hug. My eyes tear up. Clean clothes should not be such a blessing in one's life.

"C'mon. Let's go show everyone my brand new shiny niece and nephew and go to the parade." I walk them to the kitchen and we grab plastic shopping bags so the kids can gather candy. I grab a bunch of water bottles, put them in my purse and we go out to the backyard. They still have the PBT contraption going. Jasmine is playing like she is her Uncle George, arresting her Uncle Mark for a DUI.

"You know what DUI really stands for, Jazz," Misun hollers at her. "A Damn Ugly Indian?"

All the kids get a kick out of that one.

Mark jumps up, "Whatever, hey! You kids go get your Leksi Mark some candy. I am going to go clean up all your messes inside."

I walk up to him and whisper, "Don't drink all that beer up either—it's not even mine, it belongs to this dude."

He raises an eyebrow at me, "Oh a dude, huh, and the bed frame is broke."

I punch his arm, playfully this time.

I went to a parade in a white town once. Parents and grandparents sit on the curbs, with kids in their laps and clap their hands to marching band music. A few pieces of candy are thrown here and there. It's all very patriotic and Yankee Doodle Dandy. It's not how we get down at a parade on the rez. Not even close.

Every kind of princess you can imagine goes by on cars on star quilts. I'm surprised there isn't a White Clay Dam Princess or Old Hospital Hill Princess. They play either gangster rap or pow wow music. If someone tells you their grandma was an Indian princess, chances are she rode on a make-shift float in Pine Ridge. All tribal programs have floats. An organization that provides outhouses throws out toilet paper. The diabetes prevention program throws out Frisbees. The alcohol prevention program throws out water bottles that say, "If you must drink... drink water." And every float throws out candy by the fistfuls, to future, toothless diabetics. One year, Planned Parenthood threw out condoms. They were banned for life from the annual parade, but they probably prevented hundreds of future parade grubbin' kids from being made that pow wow. Even at age 4, kids have to hustle down the candy and toys before other kids.

Now that is what I call a parade.

Misun and I sit in the shade by the church, where his Grandma Frieda and Grandpa Jim are selling chili dogs and raffle tickets for a star quilt. Misun's other two girls, Canté and Sahar, run over and jump on their dad's back.

"We thought you forgot us!" Sahar says.

"Never!" Misun said. "We had to get Baby Wiconi and Baby James. Take them to say hi to Grandma and Grandpa!"

The kids all run off. The thing about Misun, Mark, Shyla, and I, we all call each other brother and sister. There are no halves about it, like George, Frieda and Misty like to say.

George is my full brother but we don't get along and often fight. Frieda is Misun's full sister but they never got along—all that made Misun and me all the more closer.

All the kids come back with chili dogs.

"Hey, those things cost," Misun said.

"Grandpa Jim bought them," Jazz said. Misun's grandma and grandpa claimed all Misun and Frieda's nieces and nephews, too. They were awesome. I know that's how we have a shady spot for the parade, at their church's yard under a big ol' cottonwood tree.

"I better go explain Wiconi and James,"he gets up and hands me the grocery bags for candy.

"Tell them they're fine with me tonight, but Misun, her room has foil all over it. I think that's where her food stamps went," I remind him.

"Bitch," he says under his breath as he walks away. I don't know how many times we ended up coming to Frieda's rescue and truthfully it was getting tiring. I had left Mark with two beers and hid the rest. I hope he doesn't sniff them out. But I know he will. Misun walked back to me followed by eight kids, six of them skipping. I watch Baby James skip. Poor guy, he's the only boy amongst the younger ones in our family. Unless someone has more—and it isn't going to be me. It better not be Shyla either. If James ends up gay, he better remember auntie and take her shopping, cut my hair, do my nails, my eyebrows.

"Wow," I say.

"What?" Misun asks.

"Oh, it's nothing. I just hope Baby James ends up gay."

"Huh? What the hell? You're a sick woman," Misun says. "Who the hell says shit like that?"

"I am not sick," I explain. "I was just thinking of how it'd be nice to have him take me shopping, do my hair, eyebrows, nails.... you know?" I sip out of the water bottle, noticing my buzz was winding down. "He's around all chicks, all the time. All his boy cousins are older."

"I stand corrected. You're sick and selfish. You'll still have Boogie by then. Quit cursing Baby James, in fact from now on, call him Jim." My brother Raymond says this while picking lint off his shirt.

"Boogie don't do hair, or nails, or eyebrows, or take me shopping." I just realized that he didn't.

"Yeah, for real huh? What kind of gay guy is that?" Misun asks, then he takes a drink of water. "I bet he doesn't even listen to disco."

"That's what I'm thinking." I all of a sudden felt very short-changed in the gay friend department. Other girls with gay friends had highlights, free styling's, nice clothes, perfect nails they walked around the rez like they had the cash for all that.

But I had Boogie Shoes. He was a big, fat man who farts. It wasn't fair. I was going to have to do my own make-over on him to make him "more gay."

Two girls call Misun over. I drink my water and my instant "big sister" alarm goes off. Their hair's all piled on their heads, big hooker-hoop earrings, and ass cheeks almost hanging out of their shorts, cleavage as far as they can fake it with push-up bras. They're giggling like a school of dolphins.

No way.

Misun comes jogging back.

"Hell, no," I tell him.

"What?" he says all innocently.

"No more hoochies for you. Tiff was enough for a lifetime," I say.

"Geez Sis, I'm not looking to get married. I already have three little women in my life. Besides, Sarah Miles is okay. She was in my economics class. She isn't no hoochie. She's just, well, a few years younger."

I knit my brow. "Who's she?" I don't recollect the name. I pick apart a dandelion.

"She's a La Preaux... Or at least her mom is. She never lived here. She's been in California all her life," he said.

La Preaux is a big family here. But I really don't know any of them unless I went to school with them. Most of the time one of them is on tribal council.

"How old is she?" I ask.

"Ask her yourself when you meet her tomorrow," he says.

"When? Where?" I drink up the rest of my water.

"At 6:30 tomorrow night. There is a pot luck cookout—your house!" He smiles and then starts laughing. He must be laughing at how big my eyes get when he says we are having a cookout at my house. What the heck?

"You little rat!" I punch him and he laughs again. "Why are you so nervy? Who's cooking? Who did you invite? What if I had plans? What if I have a man coming over?" I would have more questions but he interrupts.

He starts making his point by counting on his fingers. "One, I'm not nervy, I'm your little brother. Two, I can get Mark to cook. Three, I want our whole family there, we never do anything together. Never. And that *includes* George. Four..."

He's thinking of my fourth question, then remembers, "Four, you never have plans. Five, you don't have a man and Boogie don't count."

"I could have a man," I say wistfully.

"Well, you don't. I want a big family cookout and your yard is perfect, private, and it's huge. We'll even go get Grandma Pacific."

"I guess," I say. I really was excited. I just didn't want to show it because it wasn't my idea. I am still shredding dandelions.

"I'll even have a beer," he says and smiles. He has perfect teeth. I bet the IHS dental clinic loves him. Him and his thousand teeth. A cookout does sound fun.

Mark can cook, if he's not too drunk.

Just then Spinners walks by. Spinners was around when I was a little girl. My kids love him. All kids loved him, he was a town character. He's walking on the sidewalk towards town, wearing a cowboy hat and leather vest. He's a permanent town fixture. When the kids see him, they all start yelling, "Spinners! Spinners!! Spin Spinners!"

He does what they've been waiting for. He jumps in the air and spins a perfect circle mid-air. The kids all laugh. Wiconi claps and Misun lets out a war hoop. All the way down the street you can hear kids hollering, "Spin Spinners!" He's spinning mid-air all the way down for the kids waiting for the parade. It's as if he's a little act before the parade.

"I wonder if other reservations have Spinners," Misun asks.

"We'll never know," I say.

"I will. I don't plan on living on this rez forever," Misun says. He's laying back on his elbows, staring through his shades at all the people gathered around.

"You got everything you could want right here, why leave?" I ask him as I get the shopping bags ready for the kids.

"Don't you ever want to see what's out there? See different people, different cultures, live some place where there's more to do than drink." He looks at me curiously.

"I never gave it much thought. How long you been feeling like this?" I ask.

"For all of my life Sis, all my life," he said. It was one of those times in life that he called me Sis and I knew he meant more than my nickname.

Misun rolls over on his stomach. "Sis, it's like Gibran says. 'And forget not that the earth delights to feel your bare feet and winds long to play with your hair.' That right there made me think how small I am, on this rez. Our people were always nomadic, following the buffalo to provide a better life for their families. Why can't I follow the buffalo to give my girls a better life? If I stay here, I'm stuck in a rut. See, I didn't tell anyone Sis, so you might as well be the first. I'm moving to Bismarck,

North Dakota, to go to school to be an X-ray technician, at the end of the month. They just had an opening in the student family housing all of a sudden, so I was next in line." He is smiling.

I am astounded. Sad—but happy.

"Wow, Misun," I gulp. "I'm proud of you, bro. I had no idea. I thought you were happy. And where did you learn of Gibran?"

He laughs, "Your books don't go to waste when I babysit. I'm happy. I'm just wanderlust, I guess."

"So this is the reason for the big cookout, then? You're leaving in three weeks? How long have you known?" I stand up to stretch my legs, plus the parade is coming. I can hear the pow wow music.

"I got my acceptance letter in June, but I wasn't sure I could accept until I was sure I had housing for me and the girls. I got the letter about the apartment last week. We have a three bedroom apartment waiting for us." He gets up and laughs at my shock.

I give him a congratulatory hug. The kids come running up for their bags.

"Watch them, chekpas!" I tell Craig and Creighton.

Chekpa means twin.

Boogie shows up out of nowhere with his big cup. I take a drink when he offers. It's his cherry-berry malt liquor. Uffda, it was sweet. We laugh as we watch the kids scramble for candy and prizes. Baby James has it down to where he gets on all fours as soon as candy is thrown and crawls around to gather as much candy as possible. He's a pure professional parade candy grubber. The twins help Wiconi since she is the slowest and youngest.

"Grab the toilet paper!!" Boogie yells.

The kids ignore him, so he walks over with authority and starts picking up the rolls of toilet paper on the street. The IHS float rolls by and they bomb Boogie with candy and scream, "Boogie Shoes," at him. The kids scramble over to Boogie to grab the candy. He laughs and kicks the candy away for the kids. I hear Jazzy tell him to leave his stinky toilet paper. He came back with seven rolls.

"I only need one for my van," he says and dumps the other six rolls on the blanket.

"Cool," I say and put them in an extra shopping bag. I will not act like I am too good to take free toilet paper; there are enough asses to wipe at my house.

Boogie takes his cup back from me. The parade is over but someone in a big green station wagon with no windows is at the tail-end. They are playing Keith Secola's *Indian Car* really loud. There are two big, greasy Indian guys driving with bandannas tied around their faces, like bandits. The guy in the passenger seat has a high powered squirt gun and is shooting people to cool off. That was great! We all laugh as we gather our things up. I tell Boogie about the cookout, and then I give him a hug goodbye. I'm still trying to think of a way to make him gayer. I am thinking, maybe hugging more?

"Hey Boogie!" I yell, "Come over early tomorrow, like 2 or 3, we'll watch a movie."

He nods as he backs out—he has no idea I am thinking chick flick.

We walk back to my house with the kids.

Baby James chomps on a tootsie roll and throws the wrapper on the ground. "Baby James!" I say. The other kids know what's coming, "Pick up your wrapper, son."

"But Auntie, there's trash everywhere anyway." He spins around, showing me with one arm.

"I know James, but that's because nobody cares. Just think, if everyone cared, there would be no trash on the streets. One candy wrapper means it could be more and more. Put it in your pocket and we'll throw it in my trash can, okay?"

I hate trash with a passion. I wish the rez would get a recycling program. I used to make the boys pick trash up for punishment.

We walk into my little house. Mark's watching *Law and Order* on TV. The kids all start throwing their trash away. My twins don't play their game until late because they are still undefeated, so they can hang out with the family until later when their dad picks them up. I tell Mark he's staying the weekend to chef it up.

"No problem, Sis. Just buy me beer," he says.

"I'll buy you beer," Misun says. "Sis, wanna ride with me? I got to run the girls to their other grandma's house. We'll stop and see Pacific real quick."

"I'll call her and tell her we'll pick her up tomorrow. She can watch the game here. Plus she's after me to go see my Grandma Dorie. There's no quickness about that," I say as I get in the van.

My Grandma Dorie was my dad's aunt. She lives at the nursing home, too. She's kind of senile because every time she sees me, she still tries to cut my hair. I used to let her until age 9 or 10 and one time at age 12 when she punked me out. But I have since learned to dodge her gigantic silver scissors and boarding school hair-do's. But at age 32, I just feel horrible telling her no, having to duck and dip out to avoid her chop shop. Although her butterscotch candies always look tempting, they are not worth the bangs.

As we make our way to Misun's ex in-laws, my cell phone rings; it's Ricky, cancelling.

"Good, I drank your beer up anyway. Josh." (Josh is our slang for just teasing or just joshing you). I inform him of the cookout tomorrow. He offers to bring pop and chips. After I hang up, I call Grandma Pacific.

"What!" she answers.

"Grandma." I'm kinda scared; my buzz must be wearing off.

"What!"

"This is Sis."

"I know!" She's hollering at me so the game must be on and turned up loud.

"I'll pick you up tomorrow for the game okay?" I say sweetly. "We'll watch it at my house."

"Why?" She gets suspicious.

"Just cause Misun wants to have a cookout," I say.

"Come early, your Grandma Dorie wants to visit you. Screw the Yankees." She hangs up. The nerve of that woman. She had to get the last word in there, about the Yankees to boot.

We cruise past Pizza Hut and pull up to a little house on a hill. There is lady there that makes pizzas cheaper and better than Pizza Hut, because they use commodity cheese.

Misun runs in and comes out with two pizzas for lunch.

"That'll do, because I noticed Mark had hamburger thawing out. He was planning on spending the night anyway."

We go to the grocery store in Whiteclay. I buy stuff for a salad, cat food, and dish soap. I did need toilet paper but not after the parade.

As I walk out the little grocery store through the door with a cowbell on it, someone says, "You stop!"

I didn't even steal anything this time. Not even deli condiments. I turn around and it's the frog chick from last night.

"Can you tell Ricky to call me? He said he was going to but he never did." She hands me a piece of paper.

I act dumbfounded. "Oh yeah, you mean Rick?" I tell her, "Sure, I'm going to see him tomorrow at a cookout anyway... at **my** house."

If Velma Rain on Shield taught me one thing about being a woman, it's how to turn "bitch" on and off and even to control the volume. I can be a bitch when in need.

Misun's on the phone telling someone about the cookout.

"Go to the bar," I tell him. "I need to replace Ricky's case of beer."

He pulls into the bar next to the grocery store. I go into the bar. They are not actually bars. What they are is beer stores, as liquor isn't even sold there. You have to drive 20 miles south to Rushville, Nebraska to get hard liquor. In this particular bar, everything was behind the counter. I buy Mark a pig's foot, just for being good. He hasn't been hanging out up here like a homeless person.

There are four bars and with the exception of two selling lottery tickets, they all sell basically the same stuff: beer, cigarettes, single cigarettes for a quarter, sodas, chips, ice, beef jerky, candy, cigars, chewing tobacco and hangover food.

Hangover food is like pigs feet, hot mamas, pickles, big daddys, pickled eggs, and so on.

I'm making small talk with Jen, who works in there. She's from a border family from between Rushville and Gordon, but she lives in Rushville now. She has a crush on Misun, so I'm teasing her that he's outside. As I'm saying this, he walks in the door. She looks mortified. I smile slyly at her.

"Good," I tell Misun. "You can carry my case."

"Geez, hold on," he smiles at her. "Hey, Jen."

She's blushing, "Hi."

"I'll take a twelve-pack of Bud Light," he says. "Oh and can I get two big cans of whatever malt Mark drinks?"

By the time we get back, Mark has the lawn mower going and he set up Jazz's swimming pool. Misun puts the pop and pizzas on the table and everyone eats. When Mark's semi-sober, he eats a lot and I like seeing that. I know he loves Arlene but I like it when they're on the outs. He is so much more human-like and not zombie-like.

"You need to stain your picnic table, Sis. Or paint it. It's going to start rotting," Mark says.

"I know," I say. "I knew it last summer. It's just one of those things in life. Do I paint my picnic table on my day off or enjoy my day off?"

"Good point," he says. "Just get a man, then."

"I don't need a man," I tell him.

"Yeah, sure you do." He actually drank a pop instead, but as soon as he was done, he grabs a big can of malt that Misun bought him. He is wearing a bandana, looking rez boy spiffy. My buzz is gone. I wonder what my PBT is now. I clear off the pizza boxes and grab Misun a Bud Light and one for me, too.

Misun's not a big drinker, but when he does, it's always Bud Light. I kind of thought he bought it for tomorrow and I was surprised when he opened it.

"This is bad ass," he said while looking around the yard.

"What is?" Mark asks, all kicked back.

"This," Misun said. "Just this."

Mark didn't get it, but I did. It was the fact that the three of us were sitting at the picnic table in the backyard. We were in the shade of the cottonwood trees, the yards was surrounded by lilac bushes and choke cherry trees. We were listening to a Red Hot Chili Peppers CD but you could still hear the pow wow going on. It was hot enough for the kids to splash around in the pool, but cool enough for us to sit in the shade and have a beer. It was a beautiful moment in life. Anthony Kiedis singing about scar tissue made it all the more beautiful.

Mark grilled burgers, I made a salad, and Misun was daughter-less for the night so he had another beer. We sat out in the fading sunlight with the Yankee-Red Sox game turned up on the TV. Every once in a while I would run in when a cute Yankee was up to bat. The boys' war hooped when the Red Sox scored. Eventually, the Yankees lost.

As it started getting dark out, we could hear the traffic and noises from the pow wow. I don't like going to the pow wow, sometimes because it is so busy; it's like being in WalMart when food stamps come out, and I just get too frustrated, but I do love being able to sit in my backyard and enjoy the drumming and singing. I could hear the announcer and bells even.

It was relaxing to sit and watch my brothers and my kids, nephew, and niece all running around catching fireflies to make a lantern. Times like these, I love being from the reservation. The kids knew they could get their uncle to tell a story if they got enough fireflies. Mark was great at making up stories off the top of his head. It was definitely very interesting to have a hand in raising him, which always falls in the hands of the oldest sister, no matter what.

When Uncle Mark measured the firefly light and he determined that that was definitely enough light for storytelling, he gathered all the kids around.

He takes a swig of his beer and puts it down, "OK, kids, today I am going to tell you of a contest, an event that happens in the district of Two Left Feet."

He looks around all slow and ninja-like, for drama's sake.

"Where's that at?" One of the kids interrupts and gets shushed from the other kids. They all know Uncle Mark tends to pout when interrupted.

Mark goes on, "This is the story of **Chepa Big Buffalo and the Mr. Commod Bod championship.**"

One of the kids said, "Nay-oh," but everyone else remained quiet to hear the story.

Mark gets his glazed look that could be from the storytelling or from the beer and his voice changes to that of a woman's.

"Would you like more to eat, Chepa?"

Chepa's mom, Verna, is standing above him with a skillet full of scrambled powdered eggs and a spatula. There was also fried potatoes and onions simmering in oil in a skillet on the stove. In another skillet the luncheon meat was slowing to a sizzle since Verna had just turned it off.

Chepa was still chewing, but he motioned for seconds with his hand. He nodded his head and shoved the plate towards his mom. He knew his mom turned commods into heaven. He has been living at home for all of his 33 years, well, except for a couple of stints in JDC and one time when he tried to go to job corps, but that didn't work out and Verna had to drive all night to pick him up.

One day, when his rap career got the jumpstart it needed, he would buy his mom a house with a brand new six burner stove—he only imagined what she could cook with a six burner stove. The chefs on Food TV had nothing on his mama. Even though he was almost full, his stomach growled.

She was made for breeding commod bods. She was also the manager and trainer for his dad, Chepa Big Buffalo, Sr. who had won the 4th, 5th, and 6th annual Mr. Commod Bod Championship.

Chepa was always proud seeing his dad grab the Golden Brick trophy and a hundred dollars cash. (Now the prize was up to $1,000.) After his dad would win, he wouldn't come home for a couple of days, when he did there would be a royal fight between his dad and mom. That always resulted in a shiner on his dad for a few days and hickeys on his mom as they enjoyed the Golden Brick Trophy, because it was always all he had left when he came back.

Now that his dad was no longer here, it was Chepa's turn to take over reign as Mr. Commod Bod; he only placed a close 2nd last year, and third the year before. Each time he lost to Lorenzo Belly Fat. Now that Mr. Belly Fat lost a toe in in a cat fishing accident—the title was up for grabs, as Lorenzo sans little toe, lost that Commod Bod swag that won him the title for 10 years straight. He no longer had that, "I just killed two buffalo and walked off the rez" look. That same look that gets Skins into fights when they move to cities.

So this year Chepa was ready. He was ready to avenge his dad and take back the title to bring it home to his mama. The same title his father received 17 years earlier and held onto for three straight years. He would do his father proud, because this year there was no Lorenzo Belly Fat.

Today was the big day, and despite hanging over, Chepa was ready. He had a few big cans of fortified malt liquor to help him through the hangover, plus he knew if he drank them, he would get that "just right shine" that was required only of Mr. Olympia's and Mr. Commod Bod's.

As fast as Chepa ate, Verna was there to dish out more. He ate faster than someone with a full set of teeth. "More Mama, more of the fried luncheon meat," he growled in between the forkfuls. The USDA approved can of luncheon meat gave a good gleam to his dark skin and it tasted better than SPAM. But the contestants from the body building competitions and weight lifting contests had to buy their shine. Mr. Olympia himself couldn't shine the way Chepa did when he was hanging over and ate a huge commod breakfast. It also helped right now that there was no air conditioning—the one in the window quit working two summers ago.

Finally after his fourth helping of everything, Chepa let out a long, loud belch that sounded like a herd of buffalo running. Then he drank the rest of his big can of malt and let out another loud belch. Buffalo again, running. He rubs his belly for luck and walks out to the clothesline full of white tank tops or "beaters."

"Chepa!" his mom yells out the window. "You're going to town shirts are at the other end of the clothesline, those are the whiter ones."

Sure enough, when Chepa looked, his dingiest, most yellowed tank tops were at the end he was standing at. These were the ones he did his hustling in, cutting wood, gathering cans, tearing the copper out of wires, all in the name of a dollar and a dream, a hustle and a scheme. He walked along the clothesline, letting his hand trail through all his beaters. The next set of beaters were not so dingy-kind of white, wearing around the house kind of beaters. The next set were the ones he snagged in, his around the rez, spittin' rhymes at a party kind of beaters. Finally the last set that he walked up to—the brightest white, almost torn from the package of three-white, fresh off the WalMart shelf-white. These were Chepa's going to town beaters. They were whiter than the tourists that came to the rez in the summer time to "hippy" it up, or the ones that came to "save" the souls of the skins rez-wide.

Chepa slipped the beater over his head and savored the smell of bleach that came with it. He pulled this over his tezi (belly) and went back in the house.

Once inside, he walked over to the full length mirror and started tying his bandana over his head; representation was everything. If he represented himself right, he might score an agent today. His mom was watching him down the hallway.

"You're so handsome; I don't know why I don't have any takojas (grand-kids) yet," she said to him.

"Don't worry Ma, once I win this, I'm going to use the money to get my rap cd cut, then you will be complaining that you have too many takojas, in every district!"

She smiled as she was folding a basket full of his tank tops.

Cheap took one more look in the mirror before he left. His shine was in full force—you would be able to find him on the darkest night in a blackout. His tank top hugged every roll and stretched tight over his belly like a drum. His jeans hung onto his body for dear life, hanging low where he should have had an ass and no matter how much he hiked 'em up, his butt crack always managed to peek out and give the world a sideways smile. He gave his jeans one more tug.

"I'm ready Ma," he said as he made his way to the front door.

Verna followed him out and handed him his sunglasses, aviators-AIM Movement style. He should have had an earring, dammit, he thought.

"Thanks Ma." He gets in the passenger seat of his mom's car and pulls the mirror down to check himself out with the shades on. He wished he had thick hair to be able to grow braids, maybe he'll try again. After all, he not only plans on winning this title, but hanging onto it for a few years. This contest was on his 10-year plan. The air conditioner in the car didn't work either and even though the breeze from the window was cooling

him off, he didn't worry about losing his shine, it clung to him always. He knew once he got on that stage, the sun beating down on him would simmer him and make him shine up like a new penny.

The parking lot was crowded. This was the last day of the fourth annual end of summer competitions. The first held a couple of days ago were the Commodity Cook Off.

Chepa had meant to go, but got lost on his way, hence the hangover. The second one, Miss Chokecherry Eyes was held last night, crowning the winyan (woman) with the most outstanding eyes, and ability to remember the traditions of the use of canpos - chokecherries, food of the Lakota. Earlier that day they had the frybread eating contest, using the wojapi from the Miss Chokecherry Eyes competition. And the best was saved for last: Mr. Commod Bod.

Chepa took his place in the Mr. Commod Bod line; he could already feel his pores emitting the sweat needed to keep the Indian man shine going. Other contestants were already taking their strut around the stage; you could hear some getting booed and some getting cheered on.

Chepa noticed the frybread leftover from the Frybread eating contest, along with big bowls of chokecherry wojapi used for dipping, on a table behind the stage. His stomach growled, even though he was full. He was getting sun drunk from the hot sun and the beers he had for breakfast. He couldn't resist, after all.... it WAS fry bread. He started dipping and dunking and growling and mauling the fry bread and wojapi until he felt a tap on his shoulder.

"You're up, man. They're calling you."

Chepa wiped his mouth on the back of his hand, pulled down his tank top because it had rolled up and walked out on the stage. This contest was his. He walked out with both hands over his head, half eaten-forgotten fry breads clenched in his fists.

"Here he is! The son of the man who won the 4th, 5th, and 6th Mr. Commod Bods! He is back to try it again this year, give it up for Chepa Big Buffalo, Jr!"

The crowd mostly boos, except you can hear his mother cheering wildly. Chepa leans into the mic, "Soon to be known by my rapper handle, Skillet! Skillet in da house, woot woot! Look for my new cd up and coming 'Big Greasy' to be at the pawn shop soon, and email me at skilletgotrhymes@rez.com..!"

He walks away from the emcee and does his strut around the stage with his fortified malt glaze, showboating in front of the judges table—yeah he was sun drunk. After they announced all the runner ups, Chepa had hope that he would win; $1,000 would let him party hard tonight and probably get him a girlfriend. He knew for sure his mom would let him party in his room in the basement, if he won.

"And the winner is......... (drum roll from the drum group)..... Chepa Big Buffalo, Jr., also known as Skillet!" The drum group beats hard on the drum. Chepa goes to do a round on the stage, remembers he still has frybread in his hands—he takes a bite of one of the breads, walks like a rooster across the stage and winks at Miss Chokecherry Eyes. He decides to show off for her, after all she may want to party later in the basement. He stuffs the whole frybread in his mouth, then realizes he can't chew it. It's too much—it feels like dough is rising from his insides. He can't even open his mouth, he was dying! His eyes were bulging!

"He's choking! He's choking!" He heard his mom yell. Oh lord, mama come get me... he thought in his head. One of the other contestants pushed on his gut to attempt the Heimlich maneuver but instead this happened: Chepa exploded on stage, kleppa (vomit) everywhere. Everything he ate and drank that

morning and maybe yesterday, too (when he staggered home in the middle of the night and started a small kitchen fire cooking dog food,) exploded everywhere on the stage...

He spewed like no one ever saw before.

"Disqualified!" one judge yelled.

"Noooo!" his mom screamed. All the runners up threw up. The judges threw up. The drum group threw up on the drum. Miss Chokecherry Eyes threw up, well, chokecherries. Everyone there threw up, barfed, puked, and kleppa-ed until they could no more. Eventually Lester Pretty On Top was the only one in the contest who didn't puke. He was 102 pounds soaking wet, 6 foot 4 and braids like a mouse's tail but he won. He was the new Mr. Commod Bod.

But nobody will ever remember who won that year, nobody will remember who won the cook off, Miss Chokecherry Eyes, or the frybread eating contest. All they will remember is the year everyone kleppa-ed."

Mark finished his story with a flair. I love how dramatic he is when he is storytelling. Our little brother Misun let out a war-hoop. I gave out a lee lee. Mark gave us high fives.

"NAY-OH!" All the kids chime in, at the same time.

Creighton started in, "Nay Uncle, that's from that movie, that old movie mom likes, *Stand By Me.*"

"No it's not, it's a true story," Mark says, as he is done giving high fives and sits at the picnic table.

"There is no sucha place as the district of Two Left Feet!" one of the kids chimes in.

"Sure!" Mark says, "It's over there." He points in no specific direction with his lips.

[four]

Sunday

I wake up in my bed the next morning with Jasmine, Baby James and Wiconi. I smell bacon frying and coffee percolating. I stretch and yawn; if I didn't smell bacon, I would go back to sleep. I go to the bathroom and then look at my reflection in the mirror. Egads! (Words like Egads were invented for reflections like the one looking back at me.) Jesus, who could love this?

I walk through the living room. Misun's passed out on the floor snoring. There's a fly crawling on his eyelid like he's a "Save the Children" famine victim.

"Sister!" Mark's in the kitchen, of course.

"What?" I walk in the kitchen.

He's got an assortment of veggies cut, some commod cheese shredded, bacon draining on a paper towel, and eggs.

"Do you still like bacon-avocado omelets?"

"Yes!" I pour a cup of coffee. "You're so sweet. Doesn't it feel good to wake up somewhere besides Whiteclay or jail?" I ask him.

Shit, it felt good to me just to wake up to a clean house and someone else cooking.

Misun lumbers in next, wiping the *pa'cli* or crust out of his eyes. His hair is sticking up from all the Brylcreem he uses to slick it back.

"Morning, Sunshine," Mark says.

I just noticed that at some point Mark washed his syrupy clothes and he had them on again. I remember a long time ago when he tried to be normal. He had a job at the packing plant in Gordon, lived in Rushville, and even kept his son, Anpo. Then when Anpo's mom Arlene moved back in, everything fell apart from there. Anpo moved back to his grandma's. Mark got fired, his lights got shut off, and he got evicted. All of that happened because of Arlene. That hooker.

"Mark, I asked you a question. Aren't you glad you woke up here and not in Clay or jail?" I say, as he sets an omelet in front of me.

"Shoot Sis, I'm thankful I have a beer on Sunday morning," he says.

I laugh. I forgot Whiteclay is closed until noon on Sundays. Many people suffer until then, through hangovers, especially at pow wow time. The bootleggers are busy on a Sunday morning.

"Here, here," Misun says as he cracks a Bud Light. "Where's my omelet?"

"Holy shit! It's going to snow!" Mark proclaims.

"No shit." I'm looking at Misun in amazement. "Beer plus Misun plus Morning equals no explanation."

"Shit. I'm grown," Misun says. "Where's my omelet?"

My omelet tastes like heaven and I tell Mark exactly that. Mark can out cook all of us—if he wanted, he could work in a restaurant.

I wished that he could move away, be straight, get a job as a chef or go to culinary school. It would be good for Anpo.

As it is, I think it might be too late for Anpo. He's one of those Indian youth that lost his identity and identifies with the black culture of gangster rap and movies. It's all about money, pimping, drugs, bling-bling, and sex. Youth hear that and think everything is about money. They think that there are no consequences to their actions as to how they get money. Gangster rappers are kind of fucking with a whole generation, in my humble opinion. They sold out their own fans for a dollar and a dream, leaving their own with only a hustle and a scheme. Anyways, I'm probably just biased. I just wished our own youth would be "real" about themselves, who they are and their own culture.

"What kind of omelet do you want?" Mark asks Misun, bringing me back to reality. He grabs a beer as if it's his first, but I know he's buzzed.

I'm the oldest sister and they can't get anything past me. Plus, I know he showered but he already has that three beer shine. Nothing shines like an Indian man with a buzz, not even a pair of brand new beaded moccasins.

"I want an 'everything' omelet," Misun says, sounding like a little boy.

I put my plate and coffee cup in the sink and burp loudly. The only men I can burp in front of are my brothers and Boogie. I don't have to sneak it out of my nose.

I grab a pen and paper.

"Now, who's bringing what?" I say. "Number one- Ricky- chips and pop, number two- Grandma Pacific- a bad attitude," I say and write.

"Number Three - Me - ice," Mark says.

"Number Four - Me - burgers, brats, and steaks," Misun says.

"Number five - Me - pasta salad," I add and write.

"Shyla's bringing potato salad." Mark explains to us that he called our little sis last night. She was at the pow-wow, and then went on to a 49.

"That was number six and number seven— Sarah said she'll bring watermelon," Misun said. "Oh and George is bringing baked beans," as he finishes off his Bud Light. "You guys hurry and drink yours up. I want to race you pros."

We both are shocked, "George?" We holler at him, but I am not sure if we are asking a question or complaining.

"Yeah, I know he's an asshole but he's still our brother. Be cool with him, he'll be cool with you," Misun says as he finishes his omelet and goes to put the plate in the sink.

"I'm not kissing his ass, Misun. I won't kiss his ass just so I don't get thrown in jail," Mark says and starts eating his own 'everything omelet' with hot sauce.

"You guys, let's make this work," Misun says. "George has problems and issues, too. At some point in time we need to be a family." Misun starts running the dish water.

"Don't compare my problems and issues with George's bullshit, ok? He has issues alright— BIG ISSUES," Mark pauses and with a fork in one hand and holding his other hand up, motioning that George has a big head.

I giggle under my breath.

"I'm done," Mark takes his plate and fork to the sink after wolfing down his omelet, where Misun is starting to wash dishes.

"Compliments to the chef. Who's ready for a beer race?" Misun asks.

"Hold on, let me burp again," as I toss my empty can at the trash can and miss. Then I burp and sigh.

"You're disgusting. No wonder you're single," Marks says laughing at me.

"Nervy, whatever... I thought you said I was a slut yesterday," I'm trying to pout at him.

"Oh yeah, that's another reason you're single." Now both of my brothers laugh. And I fail, too, because I also laugh.

I hit Mark but not Misun, because he's baby brother. But they both know those rules.

We all stand around the table anticipating the beer race rules from Misun. We only listen to him because he never drinks with us. I look at the sun shining off the lilac bushes and I get ready to guzzle my beer.

"One can race only, Mark, and then we start getting shit together for the cookout," Misun says.

Mark and I agree with Misun.

We give "cheers to Misun" and the move. Mark counts down. We snap our cans and the race is on. Mark, of course, wins. I'm, of course, second. Misun is, of course, last. We all burp simultaneously.

"You're all sick, sick sick!" Creighton is standing in the little hallway from the living room, sleep in his eyes.

"Morning, Buttercup," I kiss him.

"Mom, I'm twelve."

He hates it when I call him that.

"Hey, neph. I heard you got second place last night, good job," Misun pats him on the back. "We're having a big cookout this evening, so we're going to be gone a couple of hours, getting supplies and things ready. Can you hold down the fort?"

"Sure, I'm twelve. What's for breakfast?" He's sniffing the air like a rabbit.

"Oh yeah," Mark tells him. "There's a stack of bacon and cheese omelets in the oven in a cake pan. Use pot holders because they're on low to keep warm. And feed everyone."

"Cool, cool." Creighton's already making a plate.

Mark and Misun grab all my trash bags in the back porch area and load them in the back of the blazer. Instead of going towards the dump, Misun goes towards our mom's trailer on the back road.

"I got a buzz," Misun said. "I want Shyla to drive."

We pull into my mom's dilapidated trailer. She had sort of inherited it from a white man she was with for a couple of years. His family didn't want it, so now it's hers. There are two cars on blocks in her can strewn yard. The only other things in the yard are an outhouse, a tree, her grill made out of a tire rim and rack, and her mangy dog, Hota. There's an old car parked on the road. Hota barks at us as if he doesn't know us.

"Hey, shut up mutt!" a man yells—It's Uncle Shayne, my mom's twin. I haven't seen him for months. We walk up the three steps and walk in. Waylon Jennings' *"Are You Sure Hank Done It This Way"* came on. Misun danced in to our mom's house to the song, rolling his arms, snapping his fingers, moving his shoulders side to side, and bouncing. Instantly, me and Mark laugh. Misun *was* buzzed. We all were—but it was funnier that it was Misun.

"It's my babies!" Mom exclaims.

We all take turns giving her a kiss. I kiss Uncle Shayne and the boys shake his hand. He informed us he had been in the V.A. hospital for two months.

"We came to get lil sis. Shyla's going to help us cook. Come over and eat Mom. You and Leksi," Mark said. "About 6:30, I should be done."

Mom looked at Snitzy, who was her sometime snag and like fourth or fifth cousin. We all hated him. I hoped she didn't think Mark was referring to him as uncle.

"I'll come over early," Uncle Shayne said. "I have my horseshoes in the back of the car."

"You're on." Mark and Misun both smile. Indian boys love those horseshoes. The only time I ever tried to play, I broke a horseshoe and am kind of banned. For life. Everywhere.

I go to the back room. Shyla's still asleep. I shake her gently until she opens her eyes. "Let's go," I whisper.

"To where?" She whispers back, "You smell like beer."

"You have to drive, Misun's buzzed," I put a finger to my lips.

"Misun? What? What did you guys do to him?" Her eyes are wide as she gets up.

I watch a cockroach crawl up the wall. Gross. I just want to leave.

"He did it himself!" I grab her hoody. "Bring a change of clothes; you can shower at the house. You still going to make pasta salad?"

She nods yes and rubs her eyes.

"Well I have everything at the house except a bowl, but if you bring one, wash it out good." Shyla nods again, "I know."

We go out, say our byes, and situate ourselves in the blazer. I sit in the back seat with Misun. Mark's in front with Shyla. The trash is really starting to stink. Uff da.

Our first stop is the dump. Since I don't live in a HUD house, I have to dump my own trash.

After the boys get out and dump it, Misun tells Shyla to go for a cruise. KILI radio, the voice of the Lakota Nation, is playing old country music and Mark turns up Buck Owens' *"Made in Japan."*

"Yee-haw!" Misun yells as he passes beer to me and Mark.

Shyla takes us out to the dam on the Nebraska side. We park by the water and get out.

"Remember when we were kids, we used to swim out here?" Mark asks us.

"Yah," I remembered. My eye was on the corpse of a drowned Barbie floating in the water.

"I wonder if it was any cleaner back then. It didn't seem so polluted," Mark says.

Misun throws a stick in the water.

I watch the rippling where the stick landed. "I think it was cleaner, not a lot, but definitely cleaner than now. People don't give a crap anymore. It's too bad it's not maintained out here." I lean on the hood by my baby sister; she's drinking a Red Bull energy drink.

"Misun, why are you drinking?" Shy quietly asks him. She seems disappointed.

"I'm moving away. Don't worry, lil sis, I'm not going to start. I'm just celebrating with my family the *only way they* know how." He takes a drink of his beer.

"Where you moving to?" She has a worried look on her face.

"I got accepted to a college up in Bismarck, North Dakota."

We all give cheers to him by raising our beer cans.

"Congratulations," she says, but still looks worried. "Are you ever coming *back*?"

"Let me get through with college first," Misun laughed. "I didn't even leave yet."

"So is there a possibility you might not come back?" She looks at him imploringly.

I never thought of this being a possibility. And then when Misun paused momentarily, I panicked a little bit.

I took a drink of my beer and started counting all the cans that were strewn all over the ground, in the weeds, on the shore... 16, 17, 18...

"I don't know Shy. I have to think of the girls, what's good for them." He's looking out at the water.

I'm still counting. I'm in the thirties.

Mark's at a nearby snake berry bush taking a piss. 36, 37, 38, 39, 40...41, 42, 43...

"Why isn't the Rez good enough for them? What's wrong with this being home?" Shyla guzzled her Red Bull as if it was a beer. She drops the can at her feet, 48. I add that to my count.

"There's nothing wrong with it Shyla. It just feels hopeless sometimes. I don't want my girls thinking like that. Who knows what might happen. They might end up in White Clay," he snaps another beer.

52, 53, 54...

"You sound like Aunt Misty. Correction, you sound like that apple, Misty in Minnesota who once upon a time was from the Rez, but now hates everything about it," Shyla said.

Then she jumps in the car and turned up Merle Haggard's *"Sing Me Back Home."*

I stop at 68 cans. If I want to count more, I would have to take about 20 paces to the east... in the buck bush, and I don't trust buck bushes for fear of snakes.

"Wait!" Mark holds up a hand. "First off, I want to say, I stand in Whiteclay because I want to drink. Not because of hopelessness." He still has his hand in the air.

Misun whispers, "Same difference."

"And second off, Misty is not here to defend herself so don't call her an apple, whatever that means." Mark defended his twin, even though she was ashamed of him. He threw a beer can down. 69 beer cans.

"An apple, Mark, is red on the outside and white on the inside, like Misty. She was Misty Rain on Shield, just like all of us, well except George and Sis, but she moves away and changes it to Misty Morris. As if she's embarrassed of being a Rain on Shield. I hate that shit. I wanted a scholarship so I wouldn't have to go to our tribal college. Now I want to. If I leave, I'm taking political science. I want a law degree. I want to be a politician and come back and make changes here. We need change on our reservation. And the first thing we need to change is this pissing attitude about hopelessness and this "nothing's ever gonna change" shit. The only way to change is to stop these damn two-year seats. A tribal president cannot make change in two years. That's why there's no change or progress. When I'm tribal president, it will be four years and as a Rain On Shield. Bet on It. Let's go," Shyla finishes and starts the blazer, but we all stare at her wide-eyed as we jump in.

Damn, I knew she was in school politics, but I didn't know about all that. She starts to drive slowly out of the dam.

"I didn't know you felt all that, Shyla. I'm not ashamed of where I'm from; I'm just tired of it," Misun says.

"Did you go to a 49 or a campaign rally last night?" Mark asks her.

"Fuck off, Mark. I'll dump you off in Clay." Shyla slowly takes us around the dam, the south side of the dam, so we can finish our beers.

"Don't threaten me with a good time," Mark tells her. Pretty soon he hollers, "STOP!" and scares the shit out of all of us.

Shyla slams on the brake right when I'm taking a drink, beer spills on my blue T-shirt.

"Jesus, Mark! What the hell?" She turns and glares at him.

"Chokecherries! And plums!" He jumps out.

I get out after him and go pick a plum. Oh god, it was sweet. Heaven is on our rez.

"Let's pick some for the cookout!" Mark's still hollering, spitting chokecherry seeds out like he's an automatic weapon.

I go rummage in the back of Misun's blazer for something to put them in.

"How you going to have chokecherries and plums at a cookout? And Sis has chokecherry trees in her yard," Shyla says.

I find the bowl we grabbed from moms and a grocery bag.

Somehow the day just plays itself out. No one plans it, but suddenly, as a family we are all picking plums and chokecherries together. This would never happen if we planned it.

"The chokecherries in Sister's yard aren't ripe yet. They grow in the shade. They won't be ready for another month," Mark says.

We are all picking the chokecherries by the clusters and emptying them in the bowl. Misun's putting plums in the shopping bag.

"Yeah, I know," I say. "Jasmine ate some like three weeks ago, when they just turned red. She was on the toilet all night, still trying to boss us around."

They all laugh; they know how bossy their niece is.

"I know when the chokecherries are ripe," Misun says. "When they resemble the eyes of my sisters, daughters, nieces..." He sounds all dramatic.

Shyla and I look at each other; her eyes do look like chokecherries. We both bust out laughing at the same time. Misun's always been a cornball.

"We'll just put the chokecherries and plums in bowls," Mark says. "Put 'em in bowls with water and salt. Put a little tradition in our cookout. What do you young kids call it, Shy? Native? Let's Native it up."

She looks up at him and grimaces. "Native? You're using the word wrong, Mark. Native it up? Don't make sense."

"Hmph," Mark says as he pulls another cluster of chokecherries. "I'm using the word.... wrong? The word Native? I think all you Native Pride-wearing fools are using the word wrong."

He looks at Misun and me as if we are in on this. "Little Miss Political Ambitions and Dreams here, Little Miss Next Vice President of Our Tribe, tells me I am using the word wrong, while she wears a baby T-shirt with the saying Native Pride, with a dreamcatcher and sparkly feathers on it. HA!"

She stops picking chokecherries, puts a hand on her hip and glares at Mark. Great Spirit help us, she looks just like our mama. That's Velma Rain on Shield, about to give a beating.

"Can you please elaborate?" Shyla asks him.

"Yes. I can Shy, I can eee-lab-o-rate," Mark stops picking and takes a drink of his beer.

I do the same. My beer's warm. Acht. I drink the rest and get us some cold ones from the cooler in Misun's backseat. We all take drinks and await Mark's speech. Picking plums and listening because I know it will probably be a good one, I just hope he doesn't ramble into one of those stories that don't make sense, but he isn't "beer wasted" yet.

"See Shyla, I don't claim to know everything. I'm not smart, but I can read and I have a memory. I might not be Vice Prez of our tribe someday, I might not be shit, but the brother you ignore, standing in Whiteclay someday. Sometimes you might give me the seventeen cents I need for the next drink or a cigarette because it will make you feel better about whom you are. But who are you? Native? Native what? All you natives claim you don't like the term Indian. Well I'm an Indian. Indian is what the South Americans call themselves. It derives from the word Indios, meaning God's people. I'm fine with that. Columbus didn't name us. Shit, back then India wasn't even India, it was Kazzy Macky Razzistania or something like that. You and your generation might have a problem with the word Indian, Shy, but I'm Indian and I'm okay with it. Heck, I'm even proud of it. That Native Pride shirt you're wearing Shyla, heck ol' Hockenbach at the pawn shop could wear that—he's a Native from Germany. The Eggman could wear it, he's a Native Nebraskan. Ol' Bootsy McLane at the junkyard could wear that, he's native to.... junk? Don't go around representin' shit you can't back up, little sister. You're smart as fuck at seventeen but there's a whole lotta shit you don't know shit about. And be happy for Misun, he's a single dad and trying for his daughters. More than your dad does. I'm Lakota. Lakota Indian, the ones that defeated the U.S. Government on this soil, took their flag, and damn proud of it!" With that Mark war hoops.

Misun follows suit, "Indian Territory!" He yells with his fist in the air.

I giggle at both of them. My brothers are just off sometimes.

Shyla doesn't say anything. She was staring past the chokecherry bush to the water. I could tell she was thinking about her dad.

His name is Reed. Reed Burns Camp. He just goes by Reed Burns. Our mom calls him Reed Burns Bridges. He's on the tribal council. He knows Shyla exists. My mom sued him for child support. He was so scared of his wife, Bertha; he went in for DNA testing and lost. Shyla has been getting $250 a month since she was three. Mom has to give her the whole amount, though. Ever since Shyla was twelve she threatened her with emancipation. She pays the light bill, though.

I just thought of something as Shyla stood there. I wonder if she wants to go into tribal politics to prove something to her dad. He can never seem to win the election for tribal president. For the past twelve years, he's been a council representative. Maybe she wants to prove something. Maybe she wants to follow in his footsteps, or maybe it's just in her blood.

We finish filling up the bowl and grocery bag with gorgeous plums and chokecherries. Mark puts tobacco out on the ground, as a thanks. I guess none of us thought of that except him.

"Well, let's go home and get this started," I tell them.

As we pass through Whiteclay, Mark said he needs cigarettes. We all dig around for quarters for him. He only buys the cheap cigarettes they sell singly by the quarter. He claims he don't smoke enough to justify buying a whole pack of cigarettes. The cheap ones he buys are so cheap, they glow and burn down like someone's smoking them even when they sit in the ash tray, untouched.

We pull up to a bar. Mark and Shyla go in. Misun and I are enjoying the air conditioning and the music of Bob Seger. All of a sudden, Mark runs out with four bags of ice, throws them in at Misun, and runs back in.

"That fucker stole 'em," Misun says as he puts the ice in the back of his blazer. "How much you want to bet?"

"Cripes," I said. I look around for cops.

Mark and Shyla walk out. Mark has a fistful of cigs. Shyla has another Red Bull and a new T-shirt over her old Native Pride one. It says, "White Clay, Nebraska. We don't sell beer, we sell cans of courage." Everyone notices her new shirt. Nobody said anything to her about it. But we all knew that even at the age of seventeen, with her future all planned out ahead of her, she listened and heard what Mark had to say. She'd make a good politician, maybe.

We pull back into the house to chaos.

Jazz, Wiconi, and Baby James are screaming and pounding on the door in my room. Craig and Creighton are gathering sheets and towels to the washing machine. The house is a mess. My cat, Sapa, is on the table eating the rest of someone's omelet and my neighbor Nam's dog is scratching and barking at the back porch door because he hears the kids scream, so he thinks the kids are in trouble.

"What the hell's going on?" I yell and turn the cartoons off that are blasting on TV.

Craig's starting the washing machine. Creighton's spraying the sheets with OFF!

"Jazz caught bugs from Wiconi and Baby James. They all have cooties!" Craig yells "cooties" loud so they can hear through the door. I can hear Jazz fake crying louder.

"We quarantined them, Mom. For the sake of all of us," Creighton is still spraying the OFF can.

I start choking, "Gimme that, Jesus Christ. That don't work on nits." I take the can away and choke through the haze. "Craig don't overload that washer. Why don't you two go rake the yard for the cookout."

My brothers and sister are laughing.

"I'm glad you all find humor in this," I tell them. "Now I can't cook. Shyla, I'll instruct you. You can make both salads," I tell her.

"Mark, you do what you gotta do. You know what it is." He needs no instruction in the kitchen, but I am the oldest and had to say something.

"Misun, there's a clippers in the bathroom closet. Cut James' hair off. All of it and throw him in the tub. Fuckin' Frieda, is she still in jail?" I ask.

"She got out yesterday," Shyla yells from the kitchen.

"That bitch didn't even check on her kids or look for them." I pull the chair out from the door knob that was blocking them in. They run out like a herd of buffalo.

"That's because she knows you and Misun will come to the rescue," Mark says.

I ignore him, I know it's true. I just don't like to see them go through what we went through as kids. Plus, I'm scared they'll get taken away like their brother and sister, John and Johnetta, and we'll never see them again.

I take James to the bathroom and his Uncle Misun's running a bath and getting a garbage bag ready to tie around James' little body.

"Oh crap," Misun said. "Now I gotta check my girls."

I check Jazz's head first. She doesn't have that much, not enough to warrant a haircut, but enough to be in need of a good scrub with RID shampoo and a fine comb. There isn't a household on the reservation that doesn't have a bottle of RID and a fine tooth comb. If there is not, then just know that at one time or another, it did. Not saying there is an infestation on the rez, but the clinic gives it out for free, and you never know who your kids might get it from. The schools don't really care.

I look in Wiconi's hair. She is loaded. I'm going to have to have Misun give her a bob haircut before her bath. Misun can cut hair like Mark can cook. Frieda, when sober, could clean. George was the builder. I was the artist. Shyla was/is political. Misty, I don't know what she was. Depressing? Hypocritical? White?

I'm pulling nits out of Wiconi's head like a monkey on crack. Too many years, little brothers, little sisters, nephews and nieces, kids, they made me quick at it. Or maybe I inherited the nit-picking skill from my mom. And she inherited from her mom. I don't know. But I know that if an Indian woman is worth her ability to nit-pick, then them Indian boys are missing out.

Baby James comes out bald-headed. Oh, he looks like a refugee. I give him his clothes. Poor thing.

"Get dressed. You can go help the boys clean the yard. We're having a cookout today," I tell him. James gets dressed quickly and runs outside. "Don't clean up yet, Misun. Wiconi needs a new "do", too."

"Gunkle Ray, I don't want to be bald-headed," she tells him, halfway crying.

"Baby girl, that's the only hairdo I know how to do," he tells her with a worried look on his face, clippers in hand.

"Nooo," Wiconi howls.

"Get, *Hanta*," I tell her to move. "He's teasing you."

"Yeah, Chonie, he knows how to give Dora Explorer hairdos," Jasmine says.

"Don't call me Chonie!" She pouts and follows her Uncle Misun.

Jasmine squeezes her way in to wash out the tub and run bathwater for both of them. I start cleaning up.

After seeing how lousy they were, my head itches. I need a hot shower anyway. I go in the kitchen to check on the progress.

"Go away!" Mark says, "You have cooties."

"Whatever," I look in the fridge and grab a beer.

"Gimme one?" Mark tells me from over his shoulder. He's helping dice the stuff for the two salads.

Shyla has potatoes and eggs on the stove top. Mark has the brats in the slow-cooker. I hand him a beer and itch my head.

"Ugh, go away. You have cooties," he says again.

I hit him in the arm for like the hundredth time this weekend.

Misun walks in with the trash bag of hair. "I cleaned it all up, Sis." He throws it all away, itches his head, and grabs a beer.

"You have cooties, too," I tease him. "Ugh, seeing all that lice makes my head itch."

"Fucking Frieda," he says, taking a drink of his beer.

"I know."

I go to the bathroom to finish cleaning their heads.

As I'm washing their heads with RID then I use regular Suave for Kids Awesome Apple Shampoo. I hear my mom and Uncle Shayne show up. I strain my ears but I don't hear Snitzy. Thank fucking God.

My mom comes to the door. "Need help?" she asks.

"Hell yeah," I tell her. We go to sit on the front porch with a couple of fine combs and clean the girls' heads. We did this in silence until my mom said we were done. The girls took off playing.

"I'm thinking of putting an involuntary commitment hold on Frieda," Mom said then took a drink of her beer in a big cup. I silently wondered if beer in a big cup was in my future, too.

"I don't know, Mom. I think about it and think about her kids. I don't know what to do. I know I'm enabling her, but I still don't know what to do. She's out and didn't even call me to ask about them. I don't know, Mom." I take her cigarette and take a puff. I don't smoke unless I sit and visit with my mom or my dad.

"Well, I want to put the hold on her, but I won't. Who am I but another alcoholic?" she says.

"Yeah, I know, me, too." When I said that, I think it was the first time that I heard myself ever sort of admit that I was or am. But I was sort of in half denial, too.

Truthfully, I don't know where I was, except always buzzed.

I heard the horseshoes clang in the back yard. That was my signal that Misun was out of the shower and I was next.

Mom gets up to go help Shyla. I jump in the shower. Misun left me about four minutes of hot water but the cold water woke me up. After I felt non-itchy, I got out and put on some jean shorts, a Yankees T-shirt, and put my hair in a high ponytail for my Yankees cap. I grabbed my lotion and my flip-flops and went out to the living room. Boogie was there laughing. The TV was on the pre-game for the final Yankee-Red Sox game of the three-day series in Yankee Stadium. Boogie's got a big cup of something so I ask for a drink. It's whiskey and coke mixed, but not very strong. I put lotion on my legs as I sit on the sectional. I notice I missed like a line of hairs on my shin, but no one's looking.

"You missed a spot!" Boogie says to me and laughs.

Okay, Boogie was looking. That reminded me of my idea of gay makeover.

"Boogie, can you do my eyebrows?" I ask him.

"What do you want me to do?' He's sipping and raises one eyebrow. "Shave them? Or connect them with a Sharpie?" He laughs again.

What an ass. Why can't he be gayer?

I start getting frustrated. "Well, can you do my nails?" I ask.

"No," he says, "Boogie doesn't do nails."

"Well what the fuck does Boogie do?" I plead, sounding exasperated.

"Boogie does tire changes, Boogie puts oil in your beast of a car, Boogie takes care of all the things his Spinster girlfriends with no men need taken care of." He stops and puts a finger in air. "Except that thing. I don't need any women falling in love with me. Unless she has a cute man who's bi-curious or has a drinking problem. And she tends to pass out easily."

"God! Why can't you be gayer?" I ask.

"I don't know what that means or how to answer that. I am as gay as they come, my girl," as he hands over the soda mix.

I pause from putting eyeliner on, and say, "Remember when we were younger and I found out you like boys?" I ask with eyeliner in right hand, compact in my left. I had to put the compact down to take the Taco Johns cup from him and take a sip.

"You mean when I was three?" He's watching TV as if he likes baseball.

"Well, yeah, I guess. But didn't you fix my hair back then?" I swear to god he did.

"No. Never. I pulled it because you kissed my brother behind the shed." He seems like he's sort of glaring at me.

"Oh yeah," I smile. "Where is Eli nowadays?" I knew that would fire him up.

"Eli lives off the Rez, and he's married, and he's still your cousin, too," he says all matter of fact.

I kissed Eli when I was six and again when I was twenty-nine. Boogie knows we kissed but we both denied it. It was at a bar and Boogie went to the bathroom. I don't believe we're related. Neither does Eli. So it doesn't count.

"Well anyway, I was just wishing you'd act gayer," I tell him. It was about ten minutes until the game starts. "We should go get Grandma Pacific," I say and get up from my seat.

Boogie goes to the freezer and adds more ice. When we walk outside, my brother George pulls up with Grandma Pacific.

That saves me from having to go after her and see my Grandma Dorie. As horrible as that sounds, I just don't want to have her chase me with her scissors insisting I need a haircut today. I go up and kiss her, while Boogie goes to his van to make another mix.

My Grandma Pacific was born on the reservation back in the days when boarding school really wasn't an option. She was abused by Catholic priests and nuns to the point where she isn't religious at all. Or I can't say that she isn't religious because she is spiritual in our Lakota way of life, but she detests

Catholics and other organized religions that believe their ways are the only way.

Pacific married Ray Rain on Shield and after many years of trying—they had late in life twins, Velma and Shayne.

Velma had seven of us. Shayne only has one son he claims. His name is Shayne Jr., but everyone calls him Two Times. Because all the women, single or married, went out with him two times and all the men fought him at least two times. Okay, that's just the Rez legend. That's how cousin Two Times wants it to go down in history.

The true story? Uncle Shayne said when he was potty training, he used to get scared to poop. When he finally pooped, my uncle asked him, "Did you take a shit now?"

Shayne put two fingers up and said, "Two times, two times." He said it just like that—two times.

So that's the true story of Little Shayne "Two Times" Rain on Shield. Believe that.

"Grandma, everyone's in the backyard already," I tell her.

"Three Little Birds" by Bob Marley is playing and you could smell *peji*, or weed. That's how you know my Uncle Shayne is around—if you smell weed and hear Bob Marley.

"I came to watch the Red Sox kick ass!" Grandma Pacific says and walks with her *sagye* (cane) to the back porch. George is trying to help her but she shoos him away. Even at 5'4" and about 120 pounds, grandma walked like a tall, proud Indian woman. And everyone, every one of us, was scared to death of her. That's why they were all huddled in the back. They were getting high and she would have chewed them out for it.

"Boogie Shoes!" Grandma yells from inside the house. Indian way, she was his grandma, too. We were closely related enough he was scared of her, too. He comes back out looking dejected and pouting.

"What happened?" I ask him.

"She took my drink away," Boogie said.

George and I laughed. "I'll make you another one. Mark brought ice and I have Cokes."

George gives me the baked beans out of the back of his car. He also pulls out a twelve-pack of Budweiser and a twelve-pack of grape pop. Just then, we hear a yelp of a siren.

"Oh fuck!" He hands the two twelve-packs to Boogie. "Hold onto these," he says then walks to my front yard—just past the fence and lilac hedges sat a cop cruiser.

"Fuck," Boogie says. "Fuck, that's some fucked up shit, just like a cop."

We hustle inside. Boogie puts the beer under the sink. I'm standing at the window by the front door, near the TV, peeking out the curtain as slyly as I can. I see George talking to the cop in the unit. They're laughing and joking around.

"Phew," I let out a breath of relief.

Not that my brother George was drinking, but he pulled the beer out of his car. An arrest for liquor violation doesn't mean you just consume it, it means also having it in your possession. Any kind of arrest for my brother meant he was out of a job.

"Who is it?" Grandma Pacific says while slurping on Boogie's drink. Boogie's standing behind her shooting icicles into her back with his eyes.

"Nobody," I say and close my peeping spot with the curtain.

"Well, get the hell outta the way, *winyan*," she shoos me next. One thing is certain; she will shoo or shush everyone before the night is over.

I throw George's beans in the oven, on low, and notice the steaks were still marinating. Boogie tells me there's a bunch of hamburger patties and buns in the cooler in his van.

"Let's go see how far they are on putting it all together," I tell him.

It's about 3:20. We agreed not until 6:00 p.m. But it looks for once that the Rain on Shield family would be early—maybe it would be peaceful, too. I go to the backyard. They are throwing horseshoes. They are playing doubles, Uncle Shayne and Misun against Mark and George.

I notice two tents are set up.

"Where did the tents come from?" I ask.

The kids, including Misun's girls who must have been dropped off, are running in and out of the tents. My boys are watching their uncles throw shoes, probably trying to learn their secrets. My mom's buzzed and high and laughing at nothing in particular. Shyla's reading a book. I didn't think our family could have a peaceful cookout, but here it is. So far.

I know that George's kids and Anpo would show up later. I wished his wife, Kris, would come over, but they've been having problems in their marriage lately. Or so my mom says. But sometimes, I kind of miss my sister-in-law. She was my friend first from fourth through ninth grade. Once she got contacts and grew boobs, George took her away from me. We still were friendly after all these years, but you know, you just don't have friends like that "coming of age" time in your life ever again. Maybe it's because that "coming of age" time is a time in your life that you are in a limbo. Your hormones are raging, you don't know whether to hate or love, whether you want to play or act grown up. All you know is everything that happens—it all happens for one reason and always one reason: You.

"Where did these tents come from?" I ask again. Everyone's in their own world and ignoring me.

"Mine," Uncle Shayne says, then takes a hit off his joint. "I'm gonna camp here tonight. If that's okay with you? All the kids want to camp, too. I was gonna set up at the pow wow but all the reservation is there." I nod at him that it's okay.

George was watching the joint like he was starving and it was a ham sandwich. "I don't understand why people who live in town camp down there. Camping is a pain in the ass, if you don't have to do it," George said.

"I love camping," Mark says. "I love to know how it felt for my ancestors to be at one with nature. Every day you get to honor the sun, the moon, the Earth, and the four directions. It's the circle of life, man." Mark is stoned as he talks about the four directions and he stands in all four directions and makes a circle with his hand.

Uncle Shayne chokes on his smoke and starts coughing.

Everyone else busts out laughing.

"Haa Simba," Misun said, taking a hit of the joint. "Your circle of life is hangover, buzz, drunk. And camping doesn't include sleeping in an abandoned building in Whiteclay, man."

I notice they've taken the liberty to dig a fire pit. They have wood burning there and charcoal's burning on the grill.

"Mark, do you want the steaks now?" I ask him.

"Not yet, Sis." He crushes a can. "Let the fire on the wood burn down. I want the heat to cook them, not the flame. Bring everything out in about a half-hour."

"Alrighty." That kind of meant Boogie and I were stuck with Grandma Pacific. We walk back into the coolness of the house. The temperature was hot but it felt just right. Boogie wanted to sit in the kitchen or my room so Pacific wouldn't detect he had more whiskey.

"Will you paint my toenails?" I ask him, sitting at the table.

"Ugh," he said while looking at my toes. "I'm too shaky. And what the hell did you mean you want me to be more 'gay'? You hurt my feelers."

Ugh. I don't know what he referred to as his "feelers" and didn't want to know.

"Well, it's just that all them other girls with gay friends; they get their hair done, their eyebrows, and their nails. They go clothes shopping. I feel like I'm missing out or something. And I am the only one in town all jacked up looking," I pout.

"Oh, you poor thing," he rubs my head trying to mess my hat and hair up.

My hat falls off.

"There. Big Improvement," he says and laughs raucously. He takes a drink of his drink, which is his last; because his bottle was empty with Grandma Pacific getting the most of the half pint of whiskey he bought for $7.75 at the bootleggers. I don't know why they just don't raise it to a cool eight bucks. Rip offs, anyway.

"Listen Sis. I yams who I yams. Love me or leave me. Don't try to change me into one of those femme muhfuggers out there. Or I might try to change you into one of their friends that *need* their makeup and their hair-did. You're you, I'm me. You don't look all plastic and fake like those girls frontin' like they are Kardashians but deep down we know they're just dirty rez chicks. That's that. Let's take these steaks and meat out to your brothers." He hiccups. Then he burps. I guess sometimes men will always be men, no matter what.

We take the steaks, brats, veggie packs, hamburger patties, and hot dogs out to Mark. He arranges everything as he wants it and tells everyone to back off. The Iron Chef is here, or as he calls it, Maza Chef.

Misun and George are teaching my twins to play horseshoes. Leksi Shayne is playing Buck Owens from his car, but he and my mom are actually in my neighbor's yard. His name is Viet Nam or Nam. He never served in Vietnam or anything, he just looked Vietnamese. His wife's name Wilberta or Berta and they scheme and hustle every day for drink. It looks like my uncle took his case to their yard to drink it with them. They all drank large cans of malt liquor and called our cans of Budweiser "squeeze-its."

"Fishin' in the Dark" by Nitty Gritty Dirt Band started playing. Mom, Uncle Shayne, Nam and Berta started dancing.

Shyla's playing a game of "red-rover" with the younger kids.

I look around and think nothing could ruin this. Then, just because I thought that, and right after that thought—Frieda walks into the backyard with two other men and another woman.

Correction: They stagger into the backyard.

"Fuuuck!" Misun and I say in unison. Just when all was peaceful.

"Let's get this party started!" Frieda whoops. She's clapping her hands above her head and dancing in circles as if she's sexy, even though the song stopped.

"Oh, hell no!" Mom starts to get up. She and Frieda have gone rounds many times, always with our mom holding the title and kicking ass.

George walks towards Frieda and her bums and tells mom to sit down, he'll handle it. He takes her to the front of the house and they have a heated discussion. He comes back dragging Frieda by the hand. Her "friends" are draggin' ass elsewhere.

George cleans his throat, "Frieda here has promised to behave if she can stay. If she goes, the kids stay here." Frieda is rolling her eyes.

"Woo-hoo! She goes and we stay!" Baby James prances around in victory. "She goes! We stay!"

I watch him dance and feel sad, even though it is cute. Frieda better clean up her act, or her kids will grow up hating her.

Boogie and I start bringing out the foil covered dishes, since Mark gave us the signal. On one of the trips, Grandma Pacific gives me a toothless smile to inform me that Yankees lost 6-0. She demands I take my hat off.

"Bullshit, we didn't bet!" I say as I gather paper plates, plasticware, and whatever condiments I can gather.

Boogie's carrying the salads. "Better come out Grandma. It will be done in about half-hour."

"Take me 'bout that long to get out there," she hollers at him.

"I'll tell George to come get you," I say over my shoulder.

"Bullshit. I can walk myself!" I hear her behind me.

We pass Frieda on the way out. She better not steal anything. I'm trying to do a mental inventory of what's pawnable in my house, but I hear her coming behind us. She's shaking a can of something. I wonder what she's up to. She walks ahead of us and sprays something in the air above all the food.

Everybody jumps up and hollers at her.

"What the fuck!"

"Hey!"

"Are you retarded?"

"Don't you guys care that there are flies over the food?" Freida says as if she saved the world. She's wearing too short of cut-offs and a tight stained T-shirt that hugs her three rolls.

"I care that you just sprayed toxic shit all above the food for the cookout. You're damn lucky everything's foil wrapped!" George yells.

"At least there are no flies. Where's the beers?" she asks.

"That's because the flies are all dead over the table!" Misun slaps her in the back of the head. "And no beers for you!" He slaps her again. I hold back laughter.

She jumps up and slaps him back. Pretty soon it's a fist to cuffs episode. As siblings, nobody jumps in, at least not right away. We let them go at it for about 3 to 4 minutes. Maybe six minutes. The kids are taking bets, betting ice cream. We all laugh, watching them roll on the ground and punch each other out. Frieda's shirt is rolled up from being over her round beer gut and her belly is all white—it's pretty funny.

Finally, Velma comes over from Nam's yard with his water hose and sprays them down.

"Knock it off you idiots! You're grown! You're parents! Christ sakes!"

They both jump up dripping water and blood and hair all over.

Boogie and I start changing the cling wrap on all the food. George is flicking dead flies off the table. Then we notice there were three other spectators to the rumble. Ricky holding a cooler with chips on top, and the little hoochie Misun invited, Sarah, is holding a carved half of watermelon filled with cubes of fresh fruit, and Grandma Pacific.

Grandma Pacific was making her way with her cane. "Don't stop the fight on account of me," she said. "Let's see round two!"

"Grandma!" George said, "Don't encourage them!"

Misun and Frieda both have bloody noses and blood and dead grass all over their shirts. They're standing, glaring, and heaving at each other. Then Wiconi starts to cry.

That breaks up all the hostility. Sad to say, this is not the first cookout in our family that has involved blood. Mom is holding Wiconi soothing her, walking around the yard with her. Finally, Jasmine brings out a bowl of really soapy water to rub her hand together with it. She blows through her fingers to blow bubbles. I just know she probably used all of the dish soap.

I made a mental note to get mad at her tomorrow for the ghetto bubbles. For now they shut Wiconi up, so I say nothing.

Misun notices his little friend standing there with the watermelon. His hair is wet and plastered down from the hose; he has blood and dead grass plastered all over him, too. He brings Sarah over to the table to introduce her to us. The first thing our mom does is ask who her family is. She and Grandma Pacific start their wheels spinning and calculating the ever-many-ways that Misun and the girl, Sarah, could and could not be related. Through a process of elimination and after many "No, those ain't our people," the only slim chance Misun and Sarah could even remotely be related would be like thrice-removed, through marriage by way of the Cheyenne's a hundred or less years ago that settled out at Cheyenne Creek. If an Indian women's worth is finding out a way you're related to her, then the women in my family are priceless.

That's when I notice Frieda is eyeballing Ricky. She has the slow blink and is tugging at her shirt seductively. GOD!

"Frieda," I whisper at her. "Go wash the blood off your face and comb your hair."

She swishes inside like a cat in heat, looking at Ricky. I smile at him.

"Yikes!" he said, "I'm kind of scared."

"Just set everything down. Help me go get more chairs," I tell him.

"K. The Yankees lost you know. You should take the hat off," he teases.

"You sound like my grandma," I tell him.

"She's a smart woman," he quips and pushes the bill of my hat.

Boogie's bringing George's beer, pop, and the ice outside. We grab the kitchen chairs and the couple of camp chairs and milk crates I have. By the time we get out, Misun and his friend are making plates for all the kids. Misun washed up and put on the shirt he had brought over for Mark yesterday. Next, we feed the elders: Grandma Pacific, Mom, and Uncle Shayne. Then we all make plates.

The food is good. Mark even grilled tomatoes, peppers and potatoes. We feed Nam and Wilberta. They hardly ever eat. George gives cheers to Misun and wishes him the best of luck. Tupac's *"Keep ya' head up"* is playing. Frieda comes around the corner with two Mormon elder boys.

"You guys, look what I found. Let's feed them," she says as if they are stray dogs.

One is cherubic and blonde. The other is tall and red headed.

"Really, you don't have to feed us. We don't want to be any trouble to you," the red head stammers. His face turns redder than his hair.

"Bullshit. Sit. Eat. I know that church you work for don't give you beans to eat. Dang Mormons, want to convert everyone to their religion. Then want people to pay membership to be a part of it, then they want donations. Richest church in America. Then they send these poor, rich boys out to the reservation and jungles with hardly anything to eat on. Call it a mission! Hmph! Eat you poor boys. Pretend you're pilgrims and eat."

The whole time Grandma Pacific was saying this, she was pointing at no one in particular with a gnawed on steak. Now she went back to gnawing the steak with both hands and her gums. She never wears her false teeth and I don't know how she does it. She loves steak, well done, and swear to god, she can eat an apple, too. She almost made herself out to sound anti-Mormon, or atheist, or even antagonistic. Truthfully, she was just anti-organized religion. In her opinion, the white man came here and banned our religion, then forced theirs on us.

Now they come to our reservation seeking the Lakota way of life, paying to sweat and participate in sundance. And some of our people sell it. It's atrocious and hypocritical.

We all ate. Frieda made the Mormon boys plates. My brothers questioned them as to where they're from. Frieda slinked around them like they were fresh meat and she was in heat. I think she's been in perpetual heat since the age of eighteen, though.

George's kids, George and Georgette pulled in and made plates. They gave everyone a kiss and left bumpin' some kind of rap music. It was rumored they were slinging dope, but I left it at that, a rumor. If they are, I do not want to know.

Somehow, on the Rez, even when you don't announce you're having a cookout, people show up and wateca (meaning to take food with you. Mostly grandmas are good at this but the younger generation, as greedy as they are, excel, too.)

Next, Anpo, Mark's son, shows up. He woofs down a plate, grabs two pops to go, and a bratwurst. He looks high.

Next the cops pull up. Everyone throws their full cans of beer in the bushes, behind the wood pile. Nam runs behind a junked car in his yard and Wilberta runs into their trailer. Their front yard faces my backyard. They must have warrants. George laughs and gets up with his beer. He brings the two cops over. We all say hi. He tells them we all tossed our full beers away. They had only come over to make plates. That was their payment for assuring us that our cookout would be peaceful, in case anybody tried to call the cops. So far, it was peaceful. I guess everyone was still at the pow wow. Or it was peaceful until Frieda showed up.

"Hey Frieda," the cop named Tim turned to her, "you ready to check in and do your eight hours yet?"

She rolls her eyes at him, "Whatever."

The cops wrap their plates and leave. Next, some young gangster guy shows up and Boogie makes him a plate and pranced it over. He must be his newbie. Lastly, my cousin Two Times shows up to make a plate. I feel like I haven't seen him forever. Apparently, everyone else felt the same way. He got hugs all the way around, except from George.

"Where you been, man?" Mark gave him the shake-bro-hug combo.

"He's shacking up!" Uncle Shayne yelled.

"With whoooo?" Mom asked, raising one eyebrow.

"Nobody!" Two Times said hurriedly, but everyone noticed he made two plates and scrambled back to his truck. He had kids all over the place, but never stayed long enough to be called Daddy. After he left, he was the subject of gossip as everyone contemplated who his new woman was. Whoever she was, he sure kept her secret and he was one to flaunt about his women. The main guess was that she was either older, married, ugly, or all of those.

The Mormon's shake hands, thank us and leave. They ate a lot, so they must be starving, like Grandma says.

Another joint was lit and passed around. I took a hit (I don't smoke weed, not like I used to before I had kids. But I have been known to take a puff once in a blue corn moon. One hit wonder.) I passed it to Ricky. I blew my smoke at George. I knew he couldn't get high but he would appreciate the contact high. Some Stevie Ray Vaughn was playing and the shadows were getting long.

"Well, I better go!" Boogie fake yawned and stretched. I knew that meant the little gangster guy was probably going to be picking him up. I hated his taste in boys. They used him and he let them, but it was none of my business.

"Call me tomorrow!" Boog says, "Not the house, call me on my cell."

I nod and he leaves. Everyone is full and sitting in the evening air. You could still hear the pow wow was going full blast. The faint sounds of the bells, the jingles, the rides at the carnival, and the announcer floated in the air along with horns honking and dogs barking.

I looked around. Misun and Sarah were talking quietly on a blanket on the lawn near the fire. Uncle Shayne and George started a game of horseshoes with the twins. Mark sat on the other side of the fire and was telling stories to the kids. Shyla had taken Grandma Pacific home in George's car and Frieda was passed out at the picnic table and already hit the ground. Mom was partying at Nam's.

I turned to Ricky, "Help me take everything inside?"

He nods and we carry everything in. When we get inside, I start covering food and putting it in the fridge.

"Sis?"

I look up.

Ricky's standing by the fridge and says, "It's really over with her, with Lola. I told her today. I'm sick of her games. Can I smoke in here?"

"Outside," I point with my lips. "Let's sit on the front porch."

We sit and he lights up a cigarette. "It's never going to work." He repeats, "Never."

I nod and don't say anything, except take his cigarette away and take a puff. I hand it back.

What can I say, we have been through this before. I heard it all before. I used to wait for the day they would break up because I thought we were perfect for each other. Usually when they did, he would find an eighteen-year-old girl to replace her and I would go on being the best friend.

"She has hickeys from the powwow," he tells me, then he looks at me. "Go ahead and say 'I told you so!' I know you want to."

I look away, "No, no, geez Ricky no. You never told me that. We been though a lot of shit together, enit?"

"I told you that you were moving too fast with that fancy dancer," he said.

"Well, yeah, shit I was!" I remembered, and said, "I got Jasmine out of the deal, though. I guess. So it was all good."

"Enet!" He says looking far away at nothing. "Sometimes I wonder how things would've been different, if well, I mean anything different could've happened... all those years ago. If I never met Lola at that bar and well, I just always think 'what if?' You know?" He looked at me in a way that made me nervous.

"Yeah, I know," I can't even look at him in the eye. "*Chunli wanji maku*?" I ask him for a cigarette to change the subject.

He lights a cigarette and hands it to me. "Umm... you do know I'm talking about us?" He's still looking at me. I can see his eyes in my peripheral vision. I feel like a bird looking sideways. Finally I turn and look at him.

"Ricky. Seriously, I'm not your type. I'm not skinny and between the ages of 18-23. I have an I.Q." I laugh at that one. "You like them the way MTV likes them, and I am more VH1."

"But you're funny," he says smiling. "Come on, Sis. You're my best friend. We'll go slow or whatever. Can we just try to next step?"

How come I am hearing this, now? I think. My whole world was our emails, chats, phone calls, but they were always about other girls. I always wondered if he ever talked to anyone, anyone at all about me.

I leaned in and kissed him one time on the lips.

That was my answer.

I think.

[five]

Monday - At the Dam

I woke up the next morning with a wicked hangover.

This was getting old, it wasn't even cute. It wasn't like the days when I went out of Fridays and knew I would hang over Saturday. This hangover was consistent...chills, headache, nausea. It was Monday and I realized I had to work and I felt like crap. Ricky left about an hour before I got up. We actually were able to sleep in my room, being that everyone camped outside. I think Misun and that little Sarah slept in the twins' room. And for sure one of my brothers was snoring in the living room.

After Ricky and I talked last night, we joined the party again. At first I tried to play it cool and not sit too close to him. But he scooted close to me and grabbed my hand. So we sat holding hands and acting brand new. We all stayed up until about 4 a.m. with my brothers singing 49 songs. My brothers were teasing Ricky that because I was "spoiled goods" (single with kids, they said) all they wanted in trade for me was three chickens, a donkey and a fifth of whiskey. They even had it down to six commodity chickens, two dogs, one pint of "green lizard" wine and a sharpened pencil. What asses! I have to admit, though, it was nice to enjoy myself with Ricky—as his sort of girlfriend. Weird, but nice. I can admit to myself now, I knew—I always knew—we would be perfect for one another. Now for the convincing.

I look at my watch, it's 8 a.m. Only four "sort-of" hours of sleep. Holy, my head was pounding. I get up to go to the bathroom and start to feel the room spin. Fuck. It was one of *those* kind of hangovers. I make it to the bathroom and swallow two aspirin. Then proceed to throw up the two aspirin, the water, and dry heave. Oh my God. Did I really drink that much? I jump in the shower, thinking that should make me feel human. I can't believe I have to go to work as a sub-human.

By the time I dry heaved four more times and finish getting dressed, I smell coffee perking.

It's George and Mark.

"Shit. Sis, I woke up under the picnic table and freaked out at first. All the little girls were all peeking at me. I thought I was a P.O.W. at the refugee camp. Flashbacks of Nam," Mark said laughing.

He found a full twelve-pack of beer on the back porch. With quick negotiation, we agreed that he'd watch and clean my house, cook for the kids, and he can have the twelve-pack. It was one of those regardless situations. Regardless, he would have cleaned and cooked anyway. Regardless, he would have drank the twelve-pack anyway. I grab one of the beers, regardless. It takes me about less than thirty seconds to drink it with a shaky hand.

"Sister!" George exclaims. "Really, fuck, is it that bad?" he asks.

"What?" I turn to glare at him.

George is looking at me like he's pissed. "For fuck's sake, do you *need* that beer?" He's disgusted, slurping his coffee.

"No," I turn away to get my makeup bag. I can do my makeup now that I'm not shaking.

"Sis, seriously, maybe you need help," George tells me as he gets up.

"George, please don't fuckin' preach to me just because you're older and you're a pig," I tell him as I put my makeup on. "Other people in this family drink, too."

"You have kids you take care of, Sis. Mark don't. Mom doesn't, because Shyla takes care of herself. Frieda's a lost cause. You," he points at me, "you should know better."

"George, please mind your own fucking business. It's too early. Besides, don't you have a family to take care of too?" I tell him but he's already slamming out the back door and getting into his car.

"What the fuck crawled up his ass?" I ask Mark as he hands me another beer. He knows I'm still hanging over. One more couldn't hurt.

"Um, last night, after you all went to bed, he almost cried. He thinks Kris is cheating on him. You probably shouldn't have said that about his family," Mark says as he starts on the dishes.

I watch him add water to my last two drops of dish soap and shake it. Old Indian trick.

"With who?" I ask in disbelief. George's wife Kris was always so in love with him even though he cheated on her and treated her bad for years. Maybe that explains her recent weight loss.

"I dunno," he shrugged. "None of my business... or yours."

"That's true," I say as I drink up the rest of the second can.

I go in the bathroom to brush and rinse my teeth. I could steal a pack of gum at work if they ask if I was drinking. I would say last night, which was true. It started out as last night.

I grab my purse, cell phone and red vest.

"Okay Mark, I'm out to work. Don't let the kids wreck the house. Cereal for breakfast and cook out leftovers for lunch," I tell him.

"Sis, we ate all the leftovers last night at our 49, remember?" he says.

"Aw shit, well cook whatever. I get off at five. Bye," I wave.

I walk to work, which I immediately regretted. I didn't fire up my "Beast," my 1980 Ford LTD. I never use it for work unless the weathers calls for it. Instantly, the August sun beats down on the back of my head and neck. My buzz turn quickly into a sun-drenched drunk. It makes me woozy. I can do this. I can handle it. I sweat. I ignore my slight stagger.

I get to work and the air-conditioning feels so good as the ice cold air hugs me as soon as I walk in. I grab a pack of gum and go to the office to get my cash drawer.

"Why do you still have your sunglasses on?" Charlene, one of the clerk supervisors, asks.

"Shit, forgot," I tell her and put them on my head.

"Are you okay?" she eyes me suspiciously.

"Yeah, fine," I looks sideways, grab my drawer and go to my assigned register. I don't know what the hell her problem was.

My first few customers are OK, then I get Alice. Everyone hates getting Alice. She watches you scan her items, treats all clerks like crap, and tries to get a discount whenever possible. This time, it was a block of mozzarella cheese. She wanted half off because there was a hole in the packaging. I wouldn't give it to her because the hole was obviously freshly made. None of the cheese by the hole had hardened, it was still soft and fresh. We argued over this for about three minutes, but it felt like ten.

Then she said, "I don't know why I'm trying to talk sense into you. The apple clearly doesn't fall far from the tree."

"What the fuck does that mean?" I reach for her across the counter, but she's too quick for my claws. "Mind your own business, Alice, and your man wouldn't have to screw his co-worker." I yell behind her as she makes her way to the office.

Shit, I'm fired. I know it already. I won't give them the satisfaction. I dig in my purse and pull out a five dollar bill and head for Tawny, the other cashier, with the cheese. I see my boss, Walt, coming over as I'm taking off my vest. I give the cheese to Tawny to ring up and pay for it. She bags it and hands me my change. By the time my boss and Alice get to me, I want my dignity.

"Here," I hand him my vest. "I quit. And I *fuckin' bought* the cheese for her so she don't have to be making holes in stuff for a discount." I throw the bag at her and walk out. I was able to keep my glare until I got to the door.

As soon as I get outside, my tears welled up and the parking lot became blurry. I couldn't go home. I was now unemployed. I knew what I had to do and where I had to go. I turned to walk towards Boogie's. He lived directly behind the store with his Grandma and Grandpa. I hit the number one on my speed dial and hold my cell to my ear as I march like a Nazi, trying to high step.

"Are you home?" I sniffle into my cell phone when I hear him grunt hello.

"Yeah. Are you crying?" It sounds like I woke him up.

"No. I'll be there in a minute." I hang up and walk the rest of the hundred or so yards it takes to get to his house. I wipe away the tears. I knock and walk in. I wave to Boogie's Grandpa Earl as he sits at the kitchen table and head to the basement to see Boogie.

Boogie is such a big spoiled brat. His grandma and grandpa are the only retired drug dealers I knew that never got caught and knew when to quit. They even had an ice cream truck they used to deal out of. Boogie's big dream is to get that old truck going one of these days and sell ice cream out of it. He thinks he can fix it himself, but, well.... he's gay. If it needed an oil change, yeah he could do it.

I walk in his room. He's in bed. I fall on his bed.

"Ugh, you really meant it when you said a minute, huh?" He rolls over.

"Yah. I quit... before they fired me," I tell him. I still want to cry.

"Why?" he asks.

"Over mozzarella cheese," I say and sniffle again.

"Oh dear, sounds like a day of Boogie, beer and a blanket," then he got up and says, "Let me get ready."

I lay on his bed and close my eyes. I just want... what do I want? World peace. Or self-peace? Naw, I ain't no damn beauty queen. I close my eyes and drift off. I start seeing trailer house walls from my childhood when I feel Boogie slap my leg.

"Ready, Princess?" Boogie jangles his keys at me.

"Yes, my Queen," I say and I follow him out to his minivan.

We get in his van and I rehash the morning events to him. I'm all dramatic as I describe how I almost grabbed at Alice but she ran away.

"What a bitch," he says of Alice. "And who is her man screwing?"

"Nobody, I don't think. But it can't hurt to plant that in her head, though," I say.

"Ohh... you are sooo evil." He pulls into a bar in Whiteclay.

We buy nine Hype beers, a bag of seeds, four Slim Jims and a pack of pork rinds. Boogie buys a pack of cigarettes as an afterthought. When we walk out, we notice it's peaceful. No panhandlers. As we drive south, we see why. We see these people down the road with cameras. We pull under this spot called *Iyeska* Tree, which some people say means half-breed tree and others say it means interpreter.

"What's going on?" Boogie asks Crackers.

Crackers is my Grandma Pacific's "hunka" son—he bides his time between Whiteclay and the nut hut. I start searching my purse for change, because I know he's going to ask.

"Those *wasicus* over there are German. They're making a movie about Whiteclay," as he points with his lips. "Five bucks just to talk to them. Hey niece, you got any *maza* for *leksi*?" He smiles a jack o' lantern smile.

"Didn't you just get five bucks off the Germans?" I ask.

"Aye, hell no! No pictures of Crackers. I'm not letting that white man's camera capture my spirit for any amount!" he proclaims.

"Haa!" Boogie and I both say.

"Sister, my niece, you got any *mazaska* for your Uncle Crackers, then, or what?" He looks at me with the eyes of a bloodhound. I hand him two old wrinkled up dollar bills.

"*Hau!*" he says, "*Toksa, Paha Sapa!*"

And with that he walks off as if I was not his favorite niece, stumbling his way to the first bar in his path. The nerve of that old man.

What he meant by *Toksa, Paha Sapa* was that we have a huge settlement waiting for us with the government. They are willing to pay our people from the treaty they broke promising us our sacred Black Hills, or *Paha Sapa*, a set amount of money for stealing that land because of Black Hills Gold. This settlement has gained so much interest it would bankrupt the government. Yet, our people won't sign it. And the United States will never admit to being dirty like that. Instead, they want to pay us off with hush money and sweep the wrongdoing under the rug. Dirty bastards. I know I'll never see the Black Hills money as long as I'm alive and neither will my children.

As my dad put it, "We should be enjoying our Black Hills and riches. Like all those fat property owners up there. Instead, our people suffer in poverty."

Right now I was suffering; I was starting to hang over. Boogie turns on the backroad to the south side of the dam. Thank god he doesn't have to work today.

"What we gonna do?" I ask.

"Just lay on a blanket and see how these nine new beers taste." He turns back north towards the dam and hits every got damn bump and dip on the dirt road he can find. Every bump I let out a groan. I fake like I am going to throw up. I look sideways at him and he is quietly laughing. I sideswipe him with my fist and he laughs out loud. I pretend to dry heave. Finally, he finds a shady spot under a tree and parks. I get out to help him spread the blanket under a nice shady spot under the big cottonwood. As I am throwing the blanket up and down in the air, fluffing it, Boogies gives me a blank stare. He looks past me and his eyes get big.

"SNAKE!" he screams.

I scream and run towards him then I notice he is laughing.

"You asshole!" I hit him in the arm, "That was really fucked up Boog. You know I'm a chicken shit."

He just continues to laugh as we spread our food and only brings two beer out. The rest are in his cooler.

"Turn some music on, oh yeah, wait my antenna's broke, and the CD player is too."

He opens a Hype and slurps from it.

"There's some cassette tapes in there though," he says as I walk back to his van. I open the door and smell the sour from his seat in the heat. What the hell, he needs to scrub his "family truckster."

I switch his keys to the alternator and pop a tape in. The Bangles start singing *"Manic Monday."* What a fitting song for today. Boogie starts swaying and singing the song. What a queen.

"I swear this is your tape," I sit on the blanket across from him and grab the open beer from him. I take a drink and it is really sweet and cold, in a pleasing sort of way. I feel it race to my heart and behind my eyelids. I am instantly not as tired as I was when we were bouncing over that dirt road.

I read the ingredients—Malt liquor, 9.9% alcohol, enhanced with caffeine, taurine, ginseng and guarana. Holy crap, it was like an energy drink with alcohol. Ten percent alcohol.

We each take a drink, passing the huge can between us a few times without talking. The flavor Boogie bought was Blue Passion which tasted like a blue raspberry popsicle.

"Oh shitters," Boogie said. "Wait until the little kiddies get a kick out of this."

"Yeah, no shit," I say.

I drink some more because I noticed my hangover was coming back. Boogie does the same. I take a bigger drink each time and feel a little better, so he does, too. In fact, we drink as far as we can without having to stop for air each time and then we both burp.

"This was the fourth day in a row I woke up with a hangover," Boogie says. "I said to myself this morning, 'This is it Boogie. Today, you're going to end it all and kill yourself drinking!'"

Then he lets out his loud Boogie laugh—as if that was funny.

"Geez, whatever." I drink the rest of the Hype down. It goes down too smoothly and I feel the buzz. Big time buzz.

"That's how I like it Boog. Coast from the hangover to the buzz—smooth and swift." I make one fluid sweeping motion with my hand, like a wave.

Boogie laughs, "Shit, you ain't buzzed girlfriend, you junk!"

I guess I was. I lost track of time and didn't care as Boogie and I drank the Hypes. It seemed as if that time on that blanket went by so fast. The weather was perfect, the cans snapped, there was a slight breeze, and we passed can after can back and forth between us. The time didn't even matter to me as we listened to The Bangles over and over until on one of my peeing expeditions, I found a curtain rod. Don't ask me what the hell a curtain rod was doing way out here, but we rigged Boogie's antennae right up so we could listen to the radio.

"Ah, anything but The Bangles," I said as *"Margaritaville"* came on. "By the way Boogie, I know that Bangles tape is really yours."

"I can't help it if I don't throw anything away," as he snaps open our fifth can.

Damn, we're already drunk and just now at the halfway point of our beer. I make a point of this to Boogie and look at the sky.

"It's gotta just now be noon or so and this beer has me this drunk." I hiccup and take a drink.

"Yup," Boogie says as he grabs the can back and raises it in the air. "Those white muhfuggahs have the combination here that will kill our people off. Finally."

He tips it and drinks. "Smallpox in a can," he says.

"Damn, no shit and to boot it's sweet." I sat thinking about it until *"Cotton Fields"* by Creedence Clearwater Revival started playing.

"Sing with me, Sis," Boogie says and I do. We are sitting singing the chorus and rocking back and forth. I have to admit

I'm having fun. When we get through with karaoke at the dam, we notice Boogie's phone ringing.

"Sssh... I'm not here," I say and he swats at me like I'm a fly.

"Yeah, me and Sis," I hear him say.

What a dip.

"I said I'm not here!" I slap at his arm.

Carly Simon's *"You're So Vain"* starts to play and I sing it to Boogie but I substitute the word gay for vain.

I take another drink of the Hype and realize I need to pee again. I walk—stagger—to my spot by the bushes about thirty yards from our blanket and by the water. Men are so lucky they can whip it out but ugh, they have to have a "thing" between their legs and they have to touch it to pee, I think as I squat in the weeds. I try not to think about the weeds poking at my ass and that a snake could very well be there also.

I get through peeing and look at the water. Damn, I should be at the store working. Twelve years, I think, and I quit over mozzarella cheese. Or was it really because of the hangover? I don't want to think about it. I turn to walk towards the blanket and van.

Boogie grabs me by the shoulders and screams. I jump and scream back. I slap him and he laughs and then he slaps me back.

"You asshole!" I hit him as he laughs. My heart's pounding and I know part of it is the Hypes—all that caffeine, ginseng, and crap. Then Boogie scaring me was an adrenaline rush.

"Fucker," I walk back to the blanket. Boogie's on the phone again.

"It's my mom," he says and signals for me to open another can.

"Dammit," I say. All of a sudden, I'm very tired. I must be crashing from all the caffeine. I hand him his can and lay down.

"Tell your mom I said hi," I say and I roll on my back. The sky is so blue. I see the trees dancing. The leaves in the trees make music. I feel as if this tree was meant for me to be here to sleep. I feel like this tree will protect me. The breeze just feels so good, after awhile even Boogie's loud annoying laughter is nothing. My eyes close and damn, I didn't realize how dry my eyeballs were. How desperately they needed to close. I feel peace. I drift off to sleep.... it feels so good to close my eyes.

All of a sudden, I am nine years old.

I'm hiding in the back bedroom of our two-bedroom trailer house in the trailer park in the middle of town. My mom is having a big party, again. I could hear music playing, people laughing, beer cans snapping open, and smell the cigarette smoke seeping in under the door.

George and I are playing Rock-Paper-Scissors to see who has to venture out to go get food for us to eat and who gets to sit and watch the babies. George wins. I am pissed because I'm scared. George immediately starts coaching me, "Cereal, powdered milk, syrup. One big bowl, we can all eat out of it. If there's sugar, get the sugar, leave the syrup. Oh and water... be quick." He pats me on the back like I'm going into a football game to save the team on a fourth down and I am the quarterback. My legs are shaking. I hate it when my mom has people over to party. I hate all her weirdo boyfriends. I hate the way some of them look at me or try to tickle me. I hate hiding in closets from these men, only to have them find me and tickle too hard. Who said I like that? Why does my mom laugh? I don't even want them touching me. Usually George stops it. I could always depend on that.

I begin to imagine it like one of my favorite shows on Saturday mornings. I am the hero and it is my mission to bring food to the starving village people. In fact, I am even wearing my Wonder Woman Under-Roos that my Grandma Pacific bought me for Christmas.

I run out and do a quick sweep of the kitchen, throwing everything I was on a mission for into one big bowl. Then, somehow in the middle of my rush, my mom grabs me around the waist.

"Here's one of my babies!" She exclaims with her hot beer breath all up in my face. I turn my cheek. I learned to hate that smell at a young age, detest it even. "Go around and shake hands, this is my oldest girl Sincere."

I look around the table at a bunch of old greasy men. Scary old men. I wondered where my Uncle Shayne was. I don't see him anywhere. I thought he was here. Oh, no, I thought he was here.

"Mama, I don't want to," I say. "We're hungry."

"Don't be dis'spekful, Sister." She spits. I hate when she drinks and spits. Or just when she drinks period.

"Mama, we're hungry..." I plead.

I just want to go back with my brothers and sisters. One of the men are leering at me and smiling. I'm scared of him, he has only one eye.

"I made you all some powdered eggs. Put them in that big bowl you have," she says.

I spoon the all the eggs out of the pan and into the mixing bowl. I throw in a half of loaf of bread and a can of evaporated milk for baby Frieda's bottle. Frieda was almost one year, Misun was four and the twins were six years old.

"Shake hands Sincere Charlie!" she yells. I put the bowl down as my stomach growls. I want to cry. But I have to be brave, after all I am wearing Wonder Woman's panties. I walk around with my head down, shaking cold hands of the cold souls *of men who sat in my family's house not caring that there were so many scared and hungry kids in the back room. The man with one eye pulled me towards him and I pulled my hand away as if he were a hot rock. I let out a hiss, like a cat. He giggled under his breath and his one eye looked at me in a way that made me want even more clothes on than my little polyester pants and t-shirt.*

I look at my mom for help and she is drunk, blank. Head already nodding and mumbling about how she loves me. I grab the bowl and turn away from her. I was so disappointed she was not there for me right then.

I run back in the room with the bowl of eggs. Wonder Woman has returned to feed the hungry villagers. I want to put my arms up in triumph, but I am too shaky from fear.

"There's mold on the bread, dummy!" George slaps me on the back of the head. The hero status instantly deflated.

"Pull it off dummy!" I retort. "Not like you've never done it before!" I start making eggs sandwiches for the little ones, pulling off a few moldy spots here and there. It wasn't my fault, I thought, not like I could bake a new loaf of bread. Even Wonder Woman couldn't do that.

I pass the sandwiches out to the starving villagers, they scramble back in front of the TV that sits on the floor in the room. The antenna was all wrapped in tinfoil and even with all the adjusting in the world, the picture barely came in. Yet it was all we had.

"You're the stupid one! You forgot to get a knife or something to open the can with and plus we need water! We can't just give her the milk from the can, she'll crap all over." He punches me in the arm.

I ignore the pain; Wonder Woman wouldn't have even felt that; I rub his Charlie horse off my arm. I try to continue to eat my sandwich but the bread keeps falling apart.

"You go get it," I tell him through my chewing. Our bedroom (all five of us kids shared) consisted of an old queen sized bed. We all slept on it with the exception of George, who slept on a twin mattress on the floor. Mattresses and blankets— no sheets—because they were our curtains.

"Poor Baby Frieda," George tickles her. "She's hungry, too."

"Too!" she gurgles and laughs. I look at her chubby cheeks as she lays on the dirty mattress. Well, if I go, at least George will have to be the one to change the diaper later when that canned milk comes out of her not-so-cute end. I sigh and watch a fly irritate George as he slaps around the air for it. I smile, way to go fly. You are on my team.

"You can eat eggs, too, huh Frieda?" I say to her, eating my last bite.

"Too!" she screams and throws her bottle at me. She's too cute with her huge chokecherry eyes. I can't resist her. I pick up her bottle and decide it needs to be washed out anyway. It has some cottage cheese looking crud all over it and a thick white film, how gross.

I walk slowly out to the living room, then run to the kitchen. Everyone is passed out, except for the scary one-eyed guy.

"HEY!" he screams as I go flying past him.

Ignore, ignore, ignore, I tell myself over and over as I furiously wash out the bottle. I fill it up halfway with cold water and open the silverware drawer. There are only two knives—a flimsy steak knife or a butcher knife that's way too big. The kind that I'm scared of because they are always in scary movies. I have no choice but to grab the scary knife, only because I remembered trying to open a can with a steak knife once before and it broke.

I try to quietly walk past "One Eye" because he looks passed out, then he reaches out as I pass him and grabs my butt. I jump away and turn and point the knife at him. My body instantly goes into an attack mode but on the inside, I feel sick. Scared. I want to throw up the cold eggs I just ate. I glare and continue to point the knife at him as I walk backwards. I give him my best "Indian glare."

George says it should always work, just act mad and like you are staring five miles out. The one-eyed man lets out a wheezing laugh as I hurriedly try to walk through all the passed out bodies. I get to the hallway and hear him coming. His steps are loud and he is wheezing behind me. I think I need to scream now. I turn to threaten him with the knife again and he is closer than I thought. He pushes me into my mom's room. I lose my grip on Frieda's bottle—it goes flying in the hallway and spins. I am terrified as I watch it spin and spin, half full of water, so it's spinning in a wobbly sort of way. A ray of sunlight is shining through the water sloshing in the bottle until it stopped spinning, water slowly stops sloshing. It is making slow, wobbly reflections on the wood paneling in the hallway.

I feel as if this moment in my life is not real. I start to scream and he hits me in the eye. I am not sure if I passed out. If I did, it was only for seconds. I feel hot blood gush out of my eye and I try to cry but I feel as if all that is inside me and everything I am, at that moment, is frozen somewhere in the world. He pushes me down on a pile of dirty clothes and has one hand over my mouth so I can't make a noise—even if his hand wasn't there, I would still be frozen. That is how scared I was. I start gagging and trying to throw up; that was all I could do. I feel him pull my elastic waist pants and Wonder Woman panties down, then his fingers are up inside me and it hurts.

"That's what I want." He growls, suddenly my tears come down all hot and I am still trying to throw up my eggs. Then he pulls his hand away from me and I hear him unzipping his pants.

I want to be Wonder Woman again.

I want her to save me.

Save me, Wonder Woman, please.

I think of Wonder Woman over and over.

Die! I think and stare death daggers into him. I try to move and then I feel the knife in my hand.

The knife. The scary movie knife. He is struggling with his pants with one hand and his other hand over my mouth as I tighten the grip on the scary movie knife as tight as my nine-year-old hand could go.

Then I plunge it in his side as far as it can go. His skin offers a bit of resistance and then a small pop, then a whoosh. I don't look but I feel hot sticky blood and other stuff come out. He looks down in disbelief, takes his hand off my mouth and hits me again in the same eye. Half of my vision is gone as my eye swells shut. I pull the knife out and stab him again in another spot, this time it is easier and I start choking at the same time. He has to be over 250 pounds and laying on me. I feel his hot blood cover me all sticky and metallic smelling and slimy things fall out of him. I throw up all over myself and choke on my own puke.

"What the fuck is going on??" I hear someone holler. It's my Uncle Shayne; he was passed out on the bed.

I finally start screaming and screaming and don't stop. Shayne pulls this man off me. All of a sudden I am not frozen anymore. I sit up on a pile of clothes, my eye is cut open and swollen shut, pants pulled down, I am full of blood and puke and some man's guts, and I have a knife in my hand. I scream as loud as I can. I throw my head back and scream.

One Eye tries to talk but blood is coming out of his mouth and nose. All I could make out is, "Lil' bitch stabbed me... get help," and he's choking and gurgling on his blood. It comes out of his eyes and he is trying to put his guts back in his body. I see that and throw up again.

My Uncle stands me up. I am pulling my pants up and dry heaving. I am ashamed to have my pants down like that in front of my uncle.

"Ssssshhhh," he touches my eye—he is holding tears in his eyes as he takes the knife away from me and brushes my hair out of my face. "Did he touch you?"

I nod. "But I stabbed him, before he could do anything else, he hit me and... and...," I start wailing and choking on my sobs.

The man is holding his guts in his hand, laying on the floor "C-c-c-call cops," he begs as his eyes roll back.

Uncle Shayne kicks him in the head. "You fuckin 'perverted bastard!" He kicks over and over.

He stops kicking him and starts stabbing him, screaming the whole time. I was standing in the corner, pulling my pants up as far as I can and watching the fury in my uncle as blood flies everywhere. This can't be happening. This can't be happening. This can't be happening.

He had to be dead... finally Shayne stops stabbing and kicking and screaming.

He looks mad, so mad, his fear isn't showing but I know he is scared. He is breathing so hard, his eyes are wild. He has more blood on him than I do. In fact when I look, it is on the walls. I start crying harder. I knew I would never see my uncle again.

"Shhhhh.... Go get all your brothers and sisters and your mama, too. You need to go to Grandma and Grandpa's quick."

He has his hands on my shoulders. "Everything is going to be OK, Sister. Tell your grandma to call the cops and tell them to bring the feds. Tell her I stabbed a man. Tell her I love her. **Remember Sincere, I stabbed this man all by myself."**

He is pointing at the dead man as he spits on him and kicks him in the head again. If he wasn't my Uncle, I would have been scared of the look in his eyes. I run to the back room. My eye is throbbing, it is hot, it feels like it has its own heart.

I bust in the door, "George! We have to go to Grandma and Grandpa's now!"

He looks at me all weird because my eye is swollen shut, I have blood all over me, and I'm crying with my one good eye, hot tears are pouring out of it.

"Sister?" he says with a shaky voice, but he doesn't say anything else. He wants to cry, I can tell, but he is trying to be brave. He whimpers but says nothing. Then I hear my mom let out a scream in the hallway. She is crying, "NOOOOO NOOOO" over and over. We gather up all the babies and I try and gather whatever clothes I can see as I walk out the bedroom door.

As we walk past that room, Uncle Shayne is blocking the door but you can see the dead man's by his feet. I see George taking it all in. I see George taking it in like a crime scene and like he is a cop.

We make it outside and our mom is too hysterical to drive, so George takes the keys from her and walks out to Shayne's car like a man. He never really drove before but he knew he had to. He knew he had to do what he had to do—both he and I knew this. We moved about without even talking to each other. Getting our mom to shut up and putting all the kids in the backseat with her. George started the car and my mom wailed. She was still screaming.

George turned the car off and turned around.

"Mom, I love you but shut the fuck up! Something bad happened and it didn't happen to you. It happened because of you, so shut the fuck up!" He glared at her and I started crying. He rubbed my head and started the car again. Our mom whimpered in the back seat.

He could barely see over the steering wheel but he drives us to our grandparent's house. Our mom runs inside as we all unload out of the car; my shirt and pants are sticky with blood.

My Grandma runs out and puts her arm around me as I am helping the kids get out of the backseat. She tells my Grandpa to take over with the kids and feed them some soup and she hurries me in the house. We make a beeline for the bathroom and she immediately starts undressing me and running a hot bubble bath. She leaves to go make sure Grandpa Ray is feeding everyone the hamburger soup and skillet bread she made earlier for them to enjoy for a few days, then she comes back with a shopping bag for my old clothes and a change of clothes for me. I notice they are George's pajama bottoms, but I am so tired, I don't dare ask for mine.

"Baby girl, I want you to tell me what happened. I want you to tell me everything. And when you are done, you never have to speak of this again for the rest of your life," she says as she rubs my back. She is gently sponging my swollen eye. She is washing blood off me with a gentle baby shampoo from an Avon bottle with a picture of Bambi on it. It smells so good; my water and bubbles turn pink.

I tell her everything. Just like she asked. When I am done I cry and I cry hard. I pull my knees close to me and hug them and sob so hard, I start choking and trying to throw up.

"Shhhh, that's ok. You cry and you let it out. You did nothing wrong baby girl, nothing. You just remember what

your Uncle Shayne said, if anyone asks, **he is the one** *who stabbed that man. Your Uncle Shayne is Lakota, Sincere, like you are. He is a warrior, still in this day and age, he is a warrior. He don't go around and fight to look tough or be mean. But he will do what he has to to protect his own family. That is what a Lakota man does, you remember that. Kiksuye," she says the Lakota word for remember.*

She pours the water over my hair to wash it and starts singing an Indian song that she used to sing me when I was a baby and she would bathe me. It was about a woman standing on a hill waving her red shawl. Inkpata.

When I am done with my bath, I feel better, but I still feel dirty. A little more refreshed, but still sore. My eye still hurts. My privates hurt from where he touched me, too. My grandma gives me the bloody clothes in the shopping bag and tells me to take them out to my grandpa in the backyard.

They are all in the backyard—the kids are playing but looking at my face. George won't look at me, but he puts his arm around my shoulders and walks with me over to my Grandpa Ray where they had built a fire.

It was a really nice, crisp, day out and I hated that this happened because otherwise it was so beautiful. There were even bright fluffy clouds out.

Grandpa looks at me, "Put those clothes in the fire, Sister."

I throw them in the fire and watch them start to burn. They slowly take the flame off the logs as the plastic bag starts to curl and disappear. The Wonder Woman panties start to turn to ash and little pieces start to float up to the sky.

Grandpa starts to smudge us all with sage and then cedar, me first as he starts to sing the four directions song, first singing to the West where the sun sets, singing to the Grandfather sitting there watching us, singing that we need to pray to Him.

"Cekiya Yo Cekiya Yo..." I hear my Grandpa and George singing to all the directions. As they sing, I hear the police sirens, so many of them cut through town towards the trailer park. I see the tears fall from my Grandpas eyes as he sings. I see the tears fall from George's eyes as he sings, and I cry silently.

I cry hot tears.

"Sis! Sis!" I feel Boogie's foot nudging me. "Get up, you're crying, my girl."

"Wake up!" he snaps.

I open my eyes and see clouds; I feel tears on the sides of my face and wipe them with the backs of my hands. I look at the blue, blue sky through the branches and say a small prayer, thankful that I don't have to live through all of that again, but in a way I do. Every time I dream about it.

"Oh, she was just crying in her sleep, better not be over that dead end job, either," I hear him say. "I would have walked years ago, oh wait I did," then he laughs.

It all hits me. I quit work today. Shit. As if I could afford to do that.

I roll onto my belly. "How long was I sleep?" I ask Boogie.

"Shit, she's up, better go pay attention to her now. I know. Love you too mom." Boogie shuts his cell phone.

He looks at me and sighs.

"Really?" He says it more like a statement than a question.

"What?" I ask.

"You know there are some wet wipes in the console... and a brush too," he tells me.

"You was passed out for almost an hour. Zona should be here soon."

"Really?"

I jump in the van and look in the mirror. Yikes! No shit, he wasn't lying, I could scare five rez dogs. I open the console and get the wet wipes out to wash my face. I really don't want to know why this man with no kids has wet wipes. After washing my scary zombie look away, I find a brush, comb my hair and put it up in a ponytail. I grab a beer from his cooler and jump out.

Boogie's giving me a worried look. "You OK, my girl?"

"Yeah," I say as I snap the can. "Just the same bad dream about Uncle Shayne..."

I take a drink and pass it to Boogie.

"How many of these do we have left?" he asks.

I hold up two fingers.

"Perfect, Zona's coming with more beer." He takes a drink, "Was it the dream that you have about that time he killed that dude?"

I nod and pull at some weeds. I stare out in the distance and throw the weeds in the distance, too. No one knows the real story but my Uncle Shayne, my Grandma and Grandpa, and me. I knew but never said anything, that I really killed that man. I knew when my Uncle Shayne was locked up for all those years that he didn't do it. I did, I started it. I put the knife in that man. Shayne just finished it. I think George may have figured it out, but he never asked. My stab was the fatal one; he would've died from it eventually.

"Yeah, that dream," I say as I grab the beer and take a swig.

"How many years did he do for that again?" Boogie asks.

"Twelve altogether—ten and then two more on violations," I answer, thinking how my uncle did that for me. He only had one kid because he spent so much time locked up in the joint.

Grandpa Ray knew and took it to the grave. Grandma Pacific knows but she told me to never speak of it again, and when you're Indian, you don't ever, ever, for any reason go against what your Grandma says. It all went up in flames and disappeared with ashes like my Wonder Woman panties. We see a car approach and I hide my beer at first, because I always assume it's a cop. I hate going to jail, even if it's only for eight hours. It's always the longest eight hours in your life.

It's not cops, though, just an Indian family out for fishing. They nod at us as they drive by. Boogie hands me a Slim Jim and opens the bag of pork rinds. We start munching away. I hadn't realized that I didn't eat all day and they were delicious.

"I think my grandma's getting senile, like she might need a nursing home, but Grandpa would never," he says as he chews on his Slim Jim, deep in thought.

"Why do you *think* she is?" I ask. I study my toes. I really should not neglect my feet. They're getting pretty rough and I use the excuse that I'm in my thirties now and it doesn't matter. But they may be the one reason I am always single.

Boogie says, "Every time someone knocks she answers the door and asks them what size bag of weed they want." We both laugh. "It pisses my grandpa off. She even asked the Home Healthcare nurse the other day. And she always swears we still have weed somewhere in the house. She keeps looking for it."

"Oh Boogie, that's too funny," I shake my head. His poor Grandma Victoria doesn't know she's no longer a drug dealer. "Maybe you all should just sell again?"

"I wish!" Boogie says.

When his grandpa was done building the house eight years ago, he retired from selling weed. He forced Boogie into the workforce, which pissed Boog off royally. He had to work to keep up with his line of young dudes, being that he could no longer support their pot habits.

We pass the can back and forth a few times then I decide to tell him. "Ricky spent the night last night."

"So..." he says, then sighs, "That's not new, even if you guys did it, it's not new."

He hands me the beer. I take a swallow.

"Yeah, but this time he said wants to be boyfriend-girlfriend." I hand the beer back.

"He asked you that?" He drinks the rest of the beer and tosses it in with the other empty cans in the weeds. Since the price of aluminum went down, hardly anyone picks cans anymore. There was a time when you couldn't find a can to pick. My grandpa used to say soon as you threw one away, somebody would come by and pick it up.

"Yeah, he said it was really over with Lola. I guess she had hickeys. And... well, we're already like best friends. Like I said, we're perfect for one another. We always was, you know. He makes me laugh," I smile, remembering last night.

"Well, I'm not trying to burst your bubble, girl. I just don't want him to hurt you, or I'll hurt him. If you want to laugh, watch a funny movie, ...fuck," he says defiantly.

"How you going to hurt him?" I ask.

"I'll think of something. Hey, look there's Zona. Good, we're almost out of beer," he jumps up and starts waving his arms.

He didn't want to talk about Ricky.

Off in the distance, I see Zona's dual-cab pickup bouncing on the dirt road towards us, a cloud of dust behind her. Somebody is in the truck with her and we can hear her music bumping before she pulls in. *"Beast of Burden"* by the Stones is playing. She pulls up with the Undertaker. Boogie turns his music off as Zona and Vern jump out, Bud Lights in hand.

"Well, I got rid of my Fruitloop for a few days," she said. Fruitloop is what she called her on-again, off-again man, Jimmy.

"Where'd he go?" I ask.

"I took him to Rapid City for surgery on his leg. We got in a fight last week and I kicked him in the leg— it bent his rod. As it is, his family already blames **me** for *the rod*," she says and grimaces.

"Wait... what?" Vern says. "First off, you *have* a man? And what about his *rod?*"

Boogie and I laugh. This was always a funny story, no matter how many times you hear it... funny and disturbing.

"First off, he's my boy-toy. Second off, about two years ago, I got into an argument with him. I dumped him off on the back road by Northridge. Somebody did a hit-and-run on him and it wasn't me, although everyone thinks it was. Anyway, when they hit him, it was in his right leg and they hit him so hard, his leg bone flew out of his leg!"

"No shit?" Vern asks.

"No shit, and the fuckin' starving rez dogs took off with his leg bone. Now he has a rod in his leg and he socked me the other day so I kicked him and it bent. That's why I had to take him to surgery." Zona's all done telling the story and Boogie and I are laughing and Vern is looking skeptical.

"That doesn't even sound real," he says and takes a swig of his beer.

"Don't believe it, then. I don't care. I wish it wasn't true." She guzzles the rest of the beer and tosses it in the weeds.

"Well, you blanket Indians ready to go?" Zona asks.

"Yah." We gather up the blanket. There's no more snacks left. Boogie throws the wrappers in the weeds. I look at them for a minute and all the other trash. It's a lost cause. No matter how much I pick trash, my friends don't care, no one cares.

I jump in with Boogie. Zona decides to follow us to my house so I can let Mark know what's going on. We stop at Whiteclay and I buy him six of his malt liquors. Boogie's listening to rap. I hate rap.

"Boogie, can't you turn the station? Somehow that curtain rod's hanging in there and if you don't turn it, I will tear it off." As soon as I say this, the curtain rod flies off and the station turns to static. We both laugh.

"Well, there goes that little threat! Flew right away from you!" he laughs at me.

What the hell, I push the Bangles cassette back in. It's a short ride to my house anyway. One stop light and 8 waves and 2 chin nods later.

We pull into my driveway. "I'll be right out," I tell Boogie. He's already peeing in the driveway.

I run in. The house is quiet.

"Hi mom," Jazzy says. I kiss her on the forehead. She's getting a popsicle out of the freezer.

"Where is everyone?" I ask her, grabbing my makeup bag.

"Twins went with their dad to practice. Uncle Mark and grandma are smoking cigarettes on the front porch." She goes back to watching cartoons.

I open the front screen door and peek out.

"Hi, mom. Mark, I brought you some beers," I say.

"Alright. I better check that meat loaf. Misun and the girls went home and big surprise—Frieda took her kids home."

He slides past me to go in the kitchen, no doubt to get himself a beer. My mom's looking at me all funny, smoke exhaling out of her mouth and she breathes it back up in her nose. She thinks that looks classy because she heard they do that in France. It always got on my nerves. Something about the way she is looking at me makes me nervous. I look away.

"I came over to warn you about your brother George, he heard about you getting fired today. Said he knows you're with Boogie and probably drunk—he wants to throw you in jail and teach you a lesson." She takes another long drag of her cheap cigarette.

"Bullshit! I quit! I didn't get fired," I tell her.

"Well, anyway, he wants me to put an involuntary commitment hold on you, since I am your mom, and I can do that once you're in jail." She is still looking at me funny and I feel myself getting mad.

"What the fuck! You can't do that! After all the shit you put me through?" I immediately get on the defense. The nerve of this woman, thinking she can run my life when I practically raised my brothers and sisters.

She started laughing her raspy laugh that comes from too many generic cigarettes. "Don't worry, my girl. I won't put a hold on you. If someone wants to quit drinking it has to come from within them self. I did it once."

"When?" I ask her, because I surely don't remember.

"When I was married to your father," she exhales her smoke, looking off in the distance, as if she could see the past. "Anyway, just thought I would warn you; your brother knows your hangout spots. So be careful."

"We're with Zona—we're going to leave Boogie's van here and I have no idea where we are going."

"Can I spend the night?" she asks. "Shyla is gone and the house is too lonely without her. I'll pick quills for you—maybe we can do some earrings tomorrow. The pow wow is over but there are still tons of white people in town, all the church groups," she takes a drink of her beer in the plastic cup. Ever since I could remember, she has a plastic cup of beer in one hand and a cigarette in the other.

"Sure, sleep on the bed with Jazzy. I'll climb in with you two when I get back." I open the screen to let Sapa in the house. Fat old tomcat.

My mom points with her lips at the truck, "They're waiting for you."

"I know, thanks." I hug her and walk through the house. Something about her demeanor tonight made me want to stay. I wanted to tell Zona and Boogie to go without me. I freshen up in the bathroom, spray some fruity body spray on, and comb my hair again. Somehow, I just want to stay home.

I walk out and kiss Jazzy on the head.

"Are you leaving again?" and she sounds exasperated. She is setting up her Connect Four game, probably to play her uncle and grandma for pennies all night. They taught her how to gamble already. I remember when my Uncle Shayne used to gamble with me and George before he was locked up.

"I'll stay home tomorrow OK? Watch your Grandma and Uncle Mark for me," I tell her.

"Oh yeah, you better not stay here. Uncle George wants to toss you in the clink," she said.

I look at Mark and he shrugs his shoulders and laughs, "Dang, little girl has big ears."

She just reminded me, as much as I want to stay home, I better not.

"Love you," I tell her as I walk out.

"I love you, too Mom." Last words I hear when I walk out the back door to the driveway.

I walk out the door and jump in with Zona. Buddy Holly is playing full blast, singing *"Crying, Waiting, Hoping"* and we are on our way to cruise the night away without any real plans. Like when we were young.

"Sis, you smell like peaches," Boogie says. "No one wants your peach so you spray on fake peach spray stuff, or what?"

I ignore him as he laughs. I still have an overwhelming urge to stay home, not that he isn't already getting on my nerves. Because I realize how much alcohol has taken me from my home. And I feel really lonesome.

Boogie hands me an ice cold Budweiser and says, "Let's race."

We snap our cans and guzzle. Boogie intent on winning, me intent on forgetting my loneliness for the family sitting at the table playing Connect Four for pennies.

[six]

Tuesday

"Rise and Shine! This ain't no rest home!" My mom is screaming at me and I don't want to hear it. I don't even want to open my eyes. I pull the blanket over my head but I am roasting hot. So I kick it off me. The insides of my eyelids turn bright orange as I hear her open my curtains.

"Rise and Shine, this ain't no rest home!" I hear Jazzy scream at me next, repeating what her grandmother said, like a parrot in a pet shop that wanted a home. I can smell Pine Sol and bleach so they are cleaning the house the way that my mom cleans house. She scrubs everything and disinfects everything, even the ceilings and baseboards. It's kind of nice to have her around once a season.

The other curtain opens up, making it impossible for me to leave my eyes closed. I pull a pillow over my face.

"Ma, don't," I am blinking against the mega wattage pouring in the window. What the hell, where was my shady yard? The sun must be straight up to hit my windows. Damn, it must be noon.

"Please close the curtains. I am hung over, broke, unemployed... and maybe even heartbroken," I whine and think of every excuse to stay in bed. I curl up in a fetal position but she just slaps me on the ass with no sympathy and a harsh sting on the right butt cheek.

"Get up, my girl! Make hay while the sun shines! Don't you get tired of these old Dracula drapes on your windows, sheesh! Do you need them so you can hangover in peace? Or what?" Mom starts vacuuming. My cat jumps off the bed and runs away at the sound of her vacuum. Good idea.

I get up and stagger into the living room, it was nice and cool in here. With the windows all open, it smelled good. *The Price is Right* was on but hardly audible and the radio was blasting the rez radio station and some song by Conway Twitty. I didn't want to hear her reason for my drapes being so dark. I probably did get them to make the hangover easier. I found them at the church rummage sale and remember thinking, 'Yes, I can sleep forever with these.' But my subconscious screamed, 'HANGOVER!' Since that was the case, they proved to be worth the three bucks I paid for them. Who the hell was I to be decorating my house with even the thought of hanging over? I was sick, that's what I was.

I lay on the couch like I am dying and don't want to think about my stupid dark blue drapes. I grab the afghan on the back of the couch to cover up. I am hanging over so bad—it is as if I have the flu. I was just roasting and now I am shivering.

"Where's Mark?" I ask. He might still have some beer left. She puts her vacuum by the door and starts watering my poor neglected plants.

"He couldn't handle the hangover, Sister. He walked to Whiteclay." She looked away. None of us liked the fact that Mark hung out in Whiteclay. We used to go pick him up. We would try to shame him out and tell him he was too young to act like he is a homeless drunk. We used to tell him to come home and we would feed him. We didn't like him standing up there begging for money for beer, when in reality we were no better off. We drank at home. We went to bars.

The only difference between his alcoholism and my own was that he was out in the open about it and I hid mine because I didn't want people to know I drank as much as I did. Sometimes we still bring him home. Sometimes George will act like he is going to bring him to one of our houses and then he throws him in jail. No matter what we do though, he still ends up standing in Whiteclay.

As I watched my mom straighten up, I noticed her hands were not shaking. In fact, she was rather hyper and happy for all the beer I knew she drank with Mark yesterday. I mean it was almost to the point where I wondered if she wasn't lonely but rather she came over and then stayed because Mark had the six big cans I bought him. Fuck, whatever. It was none of my business. She respects my business. I watch her bring me a cup of ice water. Nope, definitely no shaking at all in her hands. I wanted to respect her business, but I wanted to be cured of my hangover, too.

"How come you're not hanging over?" I ask her, getting all up into her business anyway.

"I scored a pint of grapes," she says. That is her word for wine. Grapes. Some people call it "green lizard." It used to be the main drink from bootleggers long time ago. Now they sell whiskey, vodka, etc. And now that Whiteclay sells pretty potent, high in alcohol, malt liquor—it seems as if the sighting of a bottle of wine is rare now. I remember when I was a kid, instead of green grass, there was green glass everywhere. I used to pick the glass in hopes of recycling it.

After many cuts, three stitches on my right foot, I realized no one recycles glass like they do cans. Usually, it's the old timers you see with them. Which, in essence, I guess, is what my mom is, although, I would never tell her that.

"Do you think we can make some earrings today? Quilled and beaded? I picked a bunch of your quills last night, so did Mark, we took turns with that and playing Jazzy her Connect 4 game. What do you think? We work really fast when we do it together." She looks at me. I know she needs money. Shoot, I do too.

"Mom, I can't. I want to but I am so sick." I know for a fact I won't even be able to eat. Fuckin' alcohol, I don't even remember coming home. I have a faint recollection of being at a bar? Somehow, I remember the sounds of a bar. Oh wow, I hope I didn't act up.

"Did Zona bring me back?" I stretch out on the couch and instantly get a leg cramp. I jump up and start walking the leg cramp off and trip over the coffee table. I fall back on the other side of the sectional couch and land on the cat. He screams and jumps on the coffee table knocking over my cup of ice water. My mom starts laughing her raspy laugh and Jasmine is hooting away with laughter, too. I am so thankful my suffering can provide them some entertainment.

"Your boyfriend brought you back, I guess," mom tells me and laughs, but she won't look at me. What the hell did she mean boyfriend?

"Who?" I ask. My mind is racing. Please, Baby Jesus, don't let me have made a fool with some complete stranger, or worse yet, a junior high snag.

"Rick," she tells me and I let out a sigh of relief. Then a second wave of panic washed over me. Holy crap. Now, how did I act in front of him? I am sure I made a fool of myself. I don't want to ask or know. Eventually someone will tell me. I curl up and pull the afghan over my pounding head.

My mom comes over and sits on the armrest of the couch. She pulls the afghan down and starts rubbing my head, the way I remember her doing it when I was a toddler and it makes me want to cry to be this pitiful. This isn't even who I am, this isn't me. I fight back my tears. Swallow my pity. It sits like a big lump in my throat.

"Sister, I can get us beer to make you well, then we have to get some artwork done. We both need money and there are tour buses going to be at the church tomorrow. OK?"

I nod, because I feel like if I talk, I will cry. I want the old me back who was in control of my life. Never in my life, did I think I would be powerless... to a drink.

"Go shower, my girl. We'll get some beer and I will make some hangover soup and skillet bread." She goes back to the recliner and starts folding clothes. I love when she is here and in the mood to clean and do laundry. I don't even fold, I hate folding. I obey her immediately and walk to the bathroom to take a hot shower. Trying to wash away my shame—I suds up big time trying to scrub the hangover away. I almost feel brand new when I step out of the steamy bathroom. I don't even get a chance to put on makeup; they are ready to go, car keys in hand. Just because I don't have makeup on, I know I will see a cute guy. I put my sunglasses on.

We fire up "The Beast" and my mom drives very slowly to Whiteclay. I watch my hometown pass by. Lynyrd Skynrd's *"Things Goin' On"* is playing on the radio. Things sure are: dogs running in packs, kids playing in the streets, missionaries out to save the Indians, tourists driving through our rez slowly, aghast at the poverty, and then there is us, not seeing the poverty as we drive two miles away to cure my hangover.

Jasmine has 83 cents she won playing Connect 4 last night and wants to stop at Hockenback's Pawn Shop, the only place and last place to still sell penny candy, except it was now a nickel. I admit as much as Hock rips people off, I do love the store. It is a variety store-pawn shop. You can find almost anything in there you need. It's like opening a huge junk drawer. There are tools, old books, DVD's, farm stuff, clothing, pots, pans, beadwork, quillwork, jewelry. And if your house was ever robbed, you might find your stuff at Hock's. Good luck getting it back though, because he is on the other side of the state line; it makes it difficult to deal with him.

My mom is talking in hushed words in the corner to Hock. I hate it when she talks to old white men, always secretive like that. I don't know what they are talking about but she always dates guys like this and it brings back memories from long time ago. "This is your new dad" kind of memories, that made me realize in my later years she was hooking up with them to get her beer and to get us food. It was so embarrassing when she would show up at a school function with one of these guys. I turn away from touching the pots and pans so I don't have to look at them as I try not to remember those days. It brings up an ugly feeling in the pit of my stomach because I knew she was selling herself.

Jasmine is counting out candy pieces with Hitler, Hock's son. I don't know if I ever knew his real name, he just has a moustache like Hitler, so that is what everyone calls him. I walk up to the counter so Jazz knows to hurry. I love the store but it gives me the creeps the way my mom and Hock are talking.

"You about done?" I ask Jasmine. She nods as Hitler bags up her candy. I grab a bottle of water from the cooler by the door. I should have enough for it in the bottom of my purse. Damn Boogie, making me pay my bills.

I am shuffling around the crumbs of my purse, old gum wrappers and sticky coins and some sparkly makeup crud when

Hitler pushes the water back at me. I look up and he smiles a real slow creepy smile. Maybe it was meant to be sincere, but it creeped me out a little bit. Plus he has one fang tooth that hung down in the corner further than the others.

I said a quick thanks and shuffle on out the door with Jazz, pushing her along. I get out in the dry heat of Whiteclay and see all the homeless people. Our people, our relatives. How come no one cares for them? They are dying up here and no one cares. I guzzle the water. My body must need it. My mom comes out a few minutes later with $30, a twenty dollar bill and a ten dollar bill.

"I pawned my two rings," she says. I notice they are gone. Thank God she pawned them instead of making some shady deal date! The last thing I want is Hock turning up as my "new dad." She loved those Black Hills gold rings; she has had them forever except they spend more time in pawn shops than on her fingers. I felt bad she pawned them for me this time so I could cure my hangover. When did I become the type of person that needed to cure it? I should just get over it and move on. Party is over. I am not my mother. I didn't feel bad about her pawning her gold. I have issues with Black Hills gold and will not wear it. My boy's dad bought me a necklace once made of the stuff and I gave it to his mom. I told him never to do that again. I feel very strongly about it. That is why the government stole our land. And if you ever go to the Black Hills, it is so breathtaking gorgeous, you can see why they are sacred to us, why we never cared about the gold but about the land. But they were stolen from us over that yellow metal.

My mom starts the car and pulls over to the next lot, a red prefabricated bar with about twenty people standing around, milling about. She pulls up to the gas tanks; it is the only bar with gas tanks. She goes in. I see Crackers and his gang on the other side of the street panhandling. I wonder where Mark is. I scanned the homeless but didn't see him. I wonder if he knows we worry about him; if I see him, I am taking him back home. It's not like he doesn't have family. And too many times they have found our people shot in the head up there and the feds or state cops don't care to solve crimes on our reservation, unless it sends one of our own to prison. I am still scanning the transients when my mom comes out. Everyone is on their hustle for a drink—including my mother and me.

For those of us with addictions, I guess that is how the rez is. Every day is a scam and a scheme, a hustle and a dream. The rez isn't like that for everyone, though. There are plenty of "normal" people who don't drink. Some people may drink but only on weekends. I used to be both of those people. Somehow, I slipped from that world of normal and I don't know when. I wonder if that is how Mark feels when he stands in Whiteclay? I scan the homeless and hope to see him. Maybe he is barely hanging on to his family life with us but his addiction beckons him to this lonely street to beg for money for beer.

Someone taps me on the shoulder—it is Burt, green-eyed Burt. Green-eyed Burt who I kissed up on the way back from a football game once in high school in the team bus, then I had to fight his girlfriend the next day in school. He came to pump the gas. He works at this bar and has ever since he dropped out of college. He winks at me and smiles. He is still cute despite the grease and extra 30 lbs. from high school. He is still with the girl who gave me a shiner over him. She still would give me a shiner if she saw me smile back at him in my side mirror. His kisses back then were worth the suspension from school, my shiner, her split lip and the tufts of hair we managed to pull from each other's heads. Somehow, he always knows that— when he sees me he gives me a knowing look, unless he is with her and he won't look at me. I smile at the memory as he walks back in the bar and my mom comes out. I shake my head. Oh, to be a single girl on the rez, it's not easy. Everyone thinks you are after their man—rumors have you sleeping with everyone— even if you stay home.

My mom carries a twelve-pack of beer out, along with a pack of cigarettes and a small bag of Hot Cheetos and a strawberry pop for Jasmine. She rips the box of Budweiser open and hands me one. "Here, take a drink. I don't like to see you like this, this isn't you."

I grab the can and take a swig. It goes down hard, but I keep drinking it. I am glad I have my gigantic sunglasses on because she can't see the tears in my eyes. I'm finally done swigging and put the can down. Over half of it is gone. I put my head back and let out a silent burp.

"I don't like being like this, Ma," I say quietly. "It's never ending."

I don't even like being pitiful. Who does? I take another drink. This self-pity shit is getting to me. I look out my dirty windshield. My giant boat of a car comes to life as my mom turns the worn, beaded keychain that is missing beads. My niece Georgette made it for me in her Lakota class. I used to be close to her, too, until she discovered boys.

My mom puffs on her cigarette and looks at me.

"It's never ending for some people, like me. It will probably be the end of me. But, you... you're strong Sincere. We knew it the minute you were born, and whatever it is you need or are looking for, I know you will find it. You won't always be like this. I know you won't. Find yourself."

I feel the beer hitting my system and I am thankful. Because I am tired of trying to cry over something I should have control over. My mom telling me to find myself makes me wonder why she doesn't find herself.

Damn guilt of a hangover.

We start driving through Whiteclay on our way back to Pine Ridge. I give one more look around and hope to see Mark. I see two women fighting as if in slow motion and several people pulled over to watch them as if it were a boxing match. I don't see my little brother anywhere. Nowhere at all.

We pull into Pine Ridge as I finish the first can. I ask my mom to take a cruise around town so I can look at it through different eyes. I open another can of beer and take a drink, then close my eyes for a second.

When I open them, I am not me. I pretend I am looking at my hometown through the eyes of someone who grew up very privileged. I pretend I grew up in the suburbs with a full fridge and I never had to worry about hot weather because I never lived without central air. I pretend I came to this reservation from college to help people. I pretend I am shocked by the poverty. I see dogs everywhere I look. Some have only three legs, some have no fur, and most look hungry. As we drive through the terrible roads in one of the housing projects, kids are playing football and basketball in the street, stopping when a car goes through and resuming the game when it passes. I see trash everywhere. I see plastic shopping bags stuck and fluttering in trees, waiting for that one brisk breeze to give them freedom and take them away from the rez. I see the dilapidated trailer houses and the worn cluster housing.

We drive down Main Street. I saw the graffiti and the fast food places. I saw the vendors who set up on the rez to sell their goods at high prices because they knew some people didn't leave the rez. They sold everything from blankets to Native Pride t-shirts, made in China.

And I saw the "street bangers." The artists who go out in the streets to sell what they sat around their kitchen table making all day to get what they need to get through to the next day. Since there are so few jobs and we are very artistic people anyway—the summer months are good to the artist. Our culture is expressed through art in many different forms and mediums and sometimes sold on the streets because there is no other place to sell it. Whatever it takes for people to get food on the table, diapers, gas money, pay a light bill, and/or buy whatever fix they need to get through to the next day.

Some people need weed, some people need cocaine, and some people need beer. And some people didn't need anything at all. Unfortunately, I was now one of the ones who needed something to get through the day and onto the next. I felt my hand tighten around the can and I tried not to think about it.

I come from people stronger than this, I know I do. We have been through so much destruction and suffering, yet we are still here. This was my home, these were my people. I will not be needy. I am tired of being needy; tired of being a victim and a statistic. We cause our own suffering now. I need to quit drinking. Soon.

"Mom, let's go home and make some money," I tell her. She is coming down from the hill north of town where the old hospital was shut down for asbestos. We pass the old bridge on the creek—me and my siblings used to play in it when we were kids. The water is contaminated now. Maybe it was back then. Who knows, but we had fun. Then she takes a left and pulls into the driveway of my grandma's old house in the center of town. I open the back screen door and go in to make something pretty.

I see my boys were home from their dad's and made a mess in the kitchen; there was burrito wrappers on the counter and it looks like they attempted to make scrambled eggs in the worst pan I own—I never use it, and I don't know why I still have it. Burnt eggs are stuck all over the pan and in the air. Now the boys were happily watching cartoons at full volume, and the living room smelled worse than the burnt eggs. It smelled like burnt eggs, butt and feet. They were at that age where they didn't care if they stunk. I pray for the day they start noticing girls and care about how they smell.

"Woof, what did you guys do in here?" I ask. "It smells like butt n' feet."

"What the heck is a button foot?" Craig asks me.

I look at him for a minute confused then laugh at his mistake. "BUTT.... and FEET, not button feet."

We all laugh and Jasmine calls Craig a dummy, so he starts teasing her.

I was going to get after them for their mess in the kitchen also, but my mom gave me a shush signal and started cleaning up their mess. Well, they are lucky their grandma is around. However, if that was me when I was their age, I would have caught an ass chewing for making a mess in the house she just cleaned. I guess it is different with grandchildren.

"Mom, what colors of quills did you pick?" I ask.

"All of them," she tells me. She is wiping down the counters, sets the pan in hot water to soak, and she already has hamburger on the counter. Damn, she is quick. "They're all in your trays, the ones we picked. But we didn't cut any designs out."

"I am going to have to take Mark hunting for a porcupine again," I say as I look at my depleted supply of quills that I store

{ 195 }

in the little room that serves as a "back porch." It is unheated so we keep a deep freezer in there, my art supplies, and when I have them, porcupine carcasses.

"Hunt them?" Jasmine asks as I come back to the kitchen table with my supplies. "Uncle Mark told me he just puts a blanket over them and pulls it off and the quills come off, then the porcupine runs away happy."

"Yeah, right!" Creighton says. He walks up to her and pushed her in the back of the head. "As if—that's just like pulling all your hair out at once—shall we try that with you?"

"Uncle Mark hits them in the face with a baseball bat," Craig chimes in from the living room as he takes a swing in the air with an imaginary bat.

Jasmine lets out a gasp and gives me a watery-eyes pitiful look.

"Boys, quit lying and shut up. Go shower, you guys stink," I scold them and reassure Jasmine that they were lying. I kind of want to laugh because it all seems so ridiculous and morbid. I'm not sure how Mark gets them, I don't watch. We just cruise late at night on the country roads, and when he yells stop, I stop. He goes out and gets something out of the trunk while I read and listen to music real loud. I know he always brings tobacco to put down and he always says a prayer. Next thing I know, we have one or two in the trunk. My brother is like magic.

Jasmine is watching me with her eyebrows raised, "Does he, Mom?"

I look away because I might laugh.

My mom looks up from chopping her onion, "Jazzy, no, he doesn't. He tells them to drop dead and they do."

Jasmine runs to watch cartoons since the boys retreated to their bedroom. She must want to forget it all.

My mom continues cutting potatoes for her hangover soup. She usually throws in hamburger, potatoes, onion, carrots, corn and tomato paste. When I try it, it sure doesn't taste like hers.

I turn the old radio on in the corner to KILI. *"Fortunate Son"* by Creedence Clearwater Revival is playing and my mom lets out a yelp as she snaps a beer can open. I look up from cutting patterns out of the rawhide with my Xacto knife.

She is trying to make Craig dance with her. He entertains her and two steps with her a little bit before he spins her around, then goes onto the fridge. They are both laughing. I smile. It lasted maybe ten or twenty seconds but that small amount of time made three of us happy. This is what life is about.

"Go shower up, you smell like a boy," my mom tells him. She is looking through all the cupboards until she finds the flour.

"I am a boy—besides Creighton's in there." He grabs the commodity orange juice out of the fridge and pours himself a cup. Then he thinks for a second and pours a second cup. He walks in the living room and gives his little sister the second cup. She drinks as they both watch cartoons—all the teasing forgotten.

I take a break to get a beer. My mom is making the *gabooboo* bread, or skillet bread. I grab a beer from under the sink and watch her. She makes the bread with such methodic motions—sifting all the ingredients together, not too fast and not too slow. I know that is why her bread is always perfect. I tend to rush my bread and it never turns out like hers. It is mesmerizing to watch her make bread. I almost forget my beer. I open the can and take a slow drink. I am not hanging over anymore. My stupid body got what my addiction tricked it into thinking it needed, so I wasn't gulping it down anymore. Mom lets the bread sit a minute and comes to the table with me, since the soup had to cook a while.

She watches me cut out earrings, then goes outside to smoke a cigarette. I follow her. I don't know why, I'm not in the mood to smoke. It just feels good to have my mom around. We both sit on the porch in the front and enjoy the afternoon air. The weather was not so hot today and a thunderhead was off in the far west. I can hear the reservation life going on beyond the lilac and chokecherry bushes that surround the house. Cars cruising, playing music a little too loud, a siren, dogs barking, and kids playing. We sit in silence. Finally she speaks.

"When your Uncle Shayne and I were teenagers, we would sneak and pick those chokecherries at night, when your grandma and grandpa were asleep. They never knew. We would fill up a five gallon bucket and go sell them to ol' Susie Boots. Then we would go to the bootleggers and get a pint of whiskey and Shayne would buy his nickel bag of weed and we would come home and try to quietly party in the tree fort. Sometimes we got caught."

We both laugh at the memory. "Why did you guys do that, especially if you had to quietly party or risk getting caught?" I ask her.

"We were young and dumb and thinking we were cool. Shayne cooked the dishwater one time because he thought it was soup and ate it. He was so sick the next day. I don't know if your Grandma Pacific ever knew, but she used to say, 'We hardly got any chokecherries this year, we must not be getting snow.' Then one day, Susie Boots asked her if we had anymore to sell. Man, we got in trouble for that."

We both laugh again. She stubs her cigarette out and we walk inside back to the kitchen table. For the next hour we are busy tracing and cutting patterns. Since I only have one Xacto knife, she cuts the patterns that are straight edged and she can use a scissors. When we feel we have enough, we soak the quills until they are pliable enough to wrap and start quilling. We only break for beer, when the soup needs to be stirred, and when I get a big quill stuck in my thumb between the thumbnail and flesh under it. I scream and every time, she tries to help me get it out.

"Hold still, you big baby." She gets the boys to come hold my arm while she cuts the end of the quill off. Cutting the end off makes it easier to pull out. I close my eyes. I feel her tug at the quill as the boys pull my arm the other way, then I scream. Jasmine screams along with me. My thumb is bleeding and the ache of a quill with all its little barbs ripping through, it is like a dull toothache. I sniff a little and my mom and the boys laugh at me. Jasmine comes running around the corner with a washcloth and a band aid.

"At least someone cares," I sniff again.

My mom hands me a beer. "Damn drama queen! Bleed on those quills, that way we sell everything."

That was a superstition started by my grandma, that if you get hurt and bleed or cry while doing art, you had to make sure either your blood or tears fall into your work. Then you are guaranteed everything will sell. So far, over the years, she has been right. I let a drop of blood fall on the quills. When I was a little girl, I used to ask her why.

"Because we put our blood, sweat, and tears into our work," she would say.

"Well isn't it enough to just sweat on them?" I asked her, confused.

"When we sweat on them, something will sell. But if you want it all to sell, you know it will when you put your all into it," she would tell me, and she would tell me that it had to be an accident because if you tried to purposefully put blood or tears in your work, you cursed yourself. I tested this theory out when I grew older and once again, my grandma was right.

We take a break while my mother finished frying her bread and then we all eat our late lunch outside on the picnic table because the kitchen table is full of quills. Only Indians cook and eat hot soup and hot bread on a hot summer day. I am thankful she made a big pot to last us all day. As we sit there eating, Zona and her little boy toy, Vern, pull up.

They look horrible, both drinking Bud Lights, and they look as hurt as I did earlier. They even look like they have a slight green tint to their complexion. Apparently, they had just gotten out of jail.

"Are you guys done eating? I want to drink my six-pack but not out here," she looks around suspiciously.

I knew that meant gossip. The kids and my mom start clearing off the picnic table and we all go inside. She sends Vern out to her truck to get the six-pack—well I guess it is actually a four-pack now of Bud Light bottles.

The boys inform me they are walking the block to the church to go to vacation bible school. They want a snow cone. All three of them leave.

I knew Zona would fill me in on the blanks of what happened the night before, as my mom and I resume our jewelry making.

"So are you and Vern a "thing" now?" I ask her.

"Shit, I'm just passing time, girl." She changes the subject to the night before as Vern walks in with her beer.

Apparently Boogie and I got in an argument over my so-called "relationship" with Ricky, which I wasn't even sure it was. But somehow, I guess I made a blubbering fool of myself telling Boogie I loved him. So Boogie left us all at Sully's Bar, which is right off the rez border but still in South Dakota. He took off with Zona's keys and took her truck home. She interrupts her story to look at the quillwork.

"Is this going to be a bracelet?" she asks my mom because it is on her side of the table. My mom nods with her mouth full of pink quills. "If it's for sale, I want it. I love the color purple. I will get it ready for you. Just buy me and Sis some beer. Our twelve-pack is almost gone. That way we can just stay up and quill," my mom says and resumes with the pink bracelet.

"Deal," Zona says. She looks at Vern and gives him her keys. "You want to go get these two ladies an 18-pack of beer?"

"Sure," Vern says.

I notice she doesn't give him any money. Man, how does she always find guys that do everything for her? Then again, I don't think I would want a man with puppet strings. I kind of like them a bit arrogant and funny and they have to be able to debate me, which is probably why I am single. Or am I?

"Don't buy me no damn cheerleader beer!" my mom says through her quills.

"Get them Budweiser," Zona tells him as he goes out the door.

"Since you two don't have cheerleader bodies," mom says and laughs.

"Haa!" my mom and I both say at the same time. I don't know why she drinks the stuff—it made her lose her cheerleader body and all it does it make you pee more. Pointless beer. I know my mother and I still had beer left—she was just trying to guarantee enough beer for tomorrow—which is when I am scheduled to quit drinking—again. This time though, for real.

Just as I think that, *"This Time"* by Waylon Jennings plays. Back to Zona's story.

"Well, finish the story, Boogie left us and then what?" I ask as I take a swig of my beer. It had turned warm. Gross. I get up and guzzle what's left and grab another cold one from under the kitchen sink. Somehow they stay cold under there. Not ice cold, but drinkable. I never keep them in the fridge because that is the first place cops look if they should invade. I stop quilling to listen.

"Well, you kept drunk dialing Ricky. You were mad at him for something. Anyway, he showed up in about an hour and you were acting all somehow. He wasn't even drinking. Then you started arguing with him, so he took you outside. He looked pissed—have you talked to him?" I shake my head and she continues. She loves telling a story.

"Yeah, he marched you right out of there. He was mad about something you said. So I told you guys not to leave, to come get us because we didn't have my ride because of that fuckhead Boogie. So anyway we grab some beer to go and go outside and you guys are gone. So these people say they were going to give us a ride for ten dollars, then on the way into town, your dickhead brother stopped us and took us all in. He kept askin' where you were and I told him to mind his own business because you were grown. So when he wrote my charges out, he got me for assaulting an officer. That's why I sat in there so long. Vern had to bond me out."

"Damn!" I am shaking my head. When will I learn a night out with her and Boogie is always drama. "He got you for assault just for that?"

"Well, I probably said it with more cuss words, but yeah," Zona finishes her beer and gets another.

"And then he brought you home," my mom said, finishing her last bracelet and putting it on the pile with the others. She then picks up the bracelet Zona wanted, to finish punching holes and tying it off with leather.

"Jesus, now I gotta call him and make sure we're still cool. Fuck." I start quilling again.

"What about Boogie?" I ask her.

"I'm pissed at him and he knows it. Me and Vern had to walk from the jail to his house to get my keys because he wouldn't answer his cell phone. He barely opened his bedroom door and threw them at me. He knows I am pissed, or maybe he has some scrub laying in there. Dirty Ol' Man, anyway," she looks mad all over again, then we both burst out laughing.

Vern pulls in. He's bought us a case.

Zona puts her new bracelet on and gets off her chair, "Well we're gonna bounce back to Nebraskee, you guys be good. Good luck with that phone call, Sis." She gives us good bye hugs, then goes to the living room to hug the kids. They have always known her as Aunty Zona and she has always been there for them.

I groan, already dreading how I acted like a fool. "Mom, I think I am done. I finished eight pairs of earrings. I am going to go outside and call Ricky. We can put the earrings together tomorrow. And the bracelets."

She continues working on the one she started and I grab my cell phone off the charger and go outside. I hadn't noticed that my phone didn't ring all day—now I know why. I pissed off the two men in my life. The only two who care to call me.

I sit on an old kitchen chair that has to be from the 60's and is probably worth money anywhere else. I dial Ricky's number and immediately get nervous. Geez, I have never been nervous to talk to him. I don't remember seeing him at all, just bits and flashes of his face in the night. I shake my head of the bits and flashes. I cross my legs and watch the sun as it paints the sky in brilliant colors.

"Hullo," he answers. Damn, I was hoping to just leave a message.

"Um, Ricky?" Soon as I say that I feel stupid. I knew it was him. I dialed him.

"Yah?" he says.

"Um, this is Sis," I tell him.

"I know," he says.

Of course he knows. He knew before he answered it. I was in his phone contacts. Geez, I was feeling pretty dumb. What the hell is wrong with me, this was usually the guy I could talk to about anything.

"Oh well, um, I just wanted to say, uh sorry about last night. I kind of barely can recollect, I mean I was blank, shit. I'm sorry. Seriously, man, I have no idea what happened, if I mizzed out on you, flipped out, or if I was just weird. That's not me." I get it all out at once.

"Yah, I know," he says. He is eating something, like potato chips. Or nacho chips. Or something so loud, it is so annoying. How could he do that in my ear? He knows I am listening? Ugh. How can I be serious about him, he clearly didn't care about me?

He lets out a loud laugh after he is done chewing, swallowing probably a pop, and burping. I sigh. Seriously, how do I let him make me nervous? I would have put a checkmark by him a long time ago in the "no" category.

"Sis, don't worry about it. Jesus, remember that time I threw up all over that cab and that cab driver wanted to kick us out but you took up for me? Got us back to our room, took care of me." He burps again. Charming.

"Oh my god! Did I throw up?" I ask.

"Don't worry, it was on the side of the bar. That is when I knew I had to take you home—after you fought me for a good twenty minutes." He breathes heavy and he chomps on more chips. This is really grossing me out. Breathing and chomping hard. Wow, I am wondering if he always chewed like this and if he also would breathe so hard simultaneously as he chewed?

"Oh and on the side of the road about 3 miles down," he says as he swigs his soda again.

"Geez, sorry," I apologize.

I feel like a fool. We talk a few more minutes. Ricky tells me not to get drunk and that he will be over later to see me.

It kind of pissed me off when he told me what to do. Seriously, I have been single for nine years, maybe eight because I still fooled around with the boys' dad while he was married for that first year—but nobody tells me what to do.

I watch the ants running around my feet in a hurry to rebuild whatever we destroyed during the day by not regarding their homes as we came out to sit on the front porch. They work hard... I wonder if they get raises, benefits. Then I smile at my silliness. Humans are the only creatures who care about money. The rest care about living.

I try to cope with my embarrassment because I still was not really sure what Ricky meant to me. How many times had I wished it were more, but now it was kind of annoying to have him be more than a friend? I pushed for this, he abandoned our friendship because I pushed and now it just felt strange. Or was it me? Am I so incapable of loving a man, like Boogie says, that even the man I always wanted was all of a sudden not good enough? Or not the right one?

I am such a failure at girlfriend status. And human status. I blow on the ant pile until the round little dust pile they so carefully rebuilt blows away with a few ants hauling materials. One even had a bead. That better be from my house and not some hidden graveyard my house was built on, I thought. Sorry ants, I am a bitch. I get up and go inside.

I feel a little relief in the fact that Ricky is not mad at me. But at the same time I feel kind of mad at him.

I sit on the couch to drink the rest of my beer and a sad commercial about homeless animals comes on. It makes me want to tear up. I think about all the animals that wander around stray, sometimes people just run over them, and leave them on the road. Sometimes the housing department hires the cops to round up all the stray dogs up in a horse trailer and they take them out and shoot them. My sister Frieda lost her beloved dog Ruby that way. How can they kill them? Look them in the eyes and shoot them? And the cops know who everyone in town is, so they know who the family pets are. Ruthless world. Like me to those ants.

I realize I must be drunk. I try not to cry for whatever the hell reason I am trying to cry for. I walk around the living room looking for something to straighten up but it's already clean. I kick my flip-flops off and pick them up to take to my room.

"Hey!" My mom is screaming at me, just as I am looking at my bed like it is heaven. "Get in here and finish some more! We're going to find your brother tomorrow and make him sell every single thing we make."

I hear her snap open another beer and pour it in a cup as I walk back in the room. A Michael Jackson song starts playing and she gets up and dances her funky moves. I laugh at her and sit to start making earrings again. My mom is still dancing like she is at a dance. I get back to work and let her dance as Michael Jackson sings about some chick blaming him for her baby.

Jasmine and the boys walk in the back door and the boys head right for the fridge. Jasmine is carrying a cross made out of burnt matches. My mom snatches it from her hands and sits down from her dancing routine. She is breathing hard and sweating. I smile—all my life my mom loved to dance, even if she was dancing alone.

"Oh, can I have this? It is so pretty." She is looking at the cross, all its burnt matches and heavy glue that dried in mid-drip. "I know just where I can hang it."

"Sure, grandma. I was going to hang it up here but mom never goes to church anyway," Jasmine says and leans down to give her grandma a hug.

"I do too go to church," I protest. "I went to a funeral a couple months ago, and I go when they have their rummage sale."

Jasmine glares at me. "That is NOT church."

"Did you burn all those matches?" I pointed at the cross with my lips.

"Nooo...." she says and goes to the freezer and gets a popsicle out.

"What kind of bible school is that? When I was a kid we got to burn the matches? Why you eating a popsicle? Didn't they even give you a popsicle?" I ask her and she laughs at me.

"Nooo, they gave us snow cones. I'm gonna go play outside, you ask too many questions," she says haughtily and slams out the back door.

I look in on the boys, now laying on the sectional watching TV, enjoying the last of the summer before school starts again. Sapa is lying in a sun ray. This time of the day when the sun is heading west, it turns everything on the reservation golden and few of the rays get through my trees. Sapa always seems to find them. It is as if he knows what part of the house to be in at just the right time. If only I could feel as content as my cat. I don't know why I am trying to have a relationship. I have everything I need in my life.

I turn the radio up a little as they play one of my favorite pow wow songs, *"Highway 18"* by the Crazy Horse Singers. I feel fine right now. Not drunk, not hopeless, not sober, not hung over, just a mellow buzz. This is the feeling I like. This is what I try to maintain and not step over that thin line of being drunk.

The pow wow song ends and a slow rock song starts playing. It is a really good song. I keep making earrings as I listen to the song, the voice.

"Mom, who sings this song? It is bad ass," I look at her, as she looks up at the ceiling.

"Van Morrison! Tupelo Honey!" she points a finger at me and screams as if she is going to win a prize.

I turn it up. Mom pretends to sing along but she only mumbles words she doesn't really know, trying to make it sound like she is singing. The song is really relaxing, despite my mom's mumbling. I think I can add it to my fifty favorite songs list. That list has been growing and changing since I was about twelve years old.

I love nice, lazy, peaceful afternoons on the rez, but sometimes they made me nervous. As if the peaceful day was simmering away and ready to come to a boiling point.

I hear a car pull up and peek out. It is my Uncle Shayne; my boys go running out to beg him to play horseshoes. I see him pull the set of horseshoes out of his trunk in an old milk crate. My uncle practically lives out of his car; everything he owns is in the trunk. Sometimes he sleeps in it, other times he pitches one of the tents he carries with him. He keeps it real clean and working. He is a rez mechanic. He doesn't have a job or a home, but he is never broke because someone always needs his help.

He comes in, sits down and pulls out a small paper bag with two giant golden Old English Malt Liquor cans in it and puts it on the table. He snaps open one of the cans and takes a long drink out of it. Then he puts it down.

"So what's up?" he asks.

I look at him, his ponytail, and his tattoos from all those years on the inside along with the hard lines etched in his face. He had a teardrop tattoo. Worry lines cross his forehead, even when he was relaxed—all those years of waiting to go home, probably. He wrote to all of us all the time. We hardly wrote back, but he seemed happy to get any letter. Grandma Pacific wrote to him more than anyone.

"Just finishing up some stuff we want to sell tomorrow. The boys harass you for your horseshoes?" I ask him.

"Yah, shit, better find them a set. No such thing as a rez boy who don't like horseshoes. Anyways, I saw their dad Dave up in Whiteclay. He said to remind you they start football practice this weekend." Uncle Shayne gets up and starts the stove on low under the soup to warm it up again.

"Oh, right!" I say with a quill in my mouth. I take the quill out and wrap it around the rawhide. "I guess I know where my last paycheck is going, since school starts the week after next."

Jasmine comes in the kitchen and starts bothering her Grandpa Shayne. He makes them both bowls of soup and they take them into the living room. I can hear the horseshoes clanking outside along with the familiar ring of the boys' laughter. Still nice and calm out. Maybe I don't have to worry about anything. Maybe there is such a thing as a relaxing night at home, in my life... on the rez.

When Uncle Shayne finishes his supper, he helps my mom and me. As we finish earrings and bracelets, he takes our unfinished ones and puts holes in them, adds ear hooks and clasps. When we finally finish, there are fourteen bracelets and six pairs of earrings. My mom puts them in Ziploc bags and hangs them on the wall. Uncle Shayne starts cleaning off the table. He clears it of all the bits of rawhide, quills, leather, broken ear hooks and dumps it all in the trash as I put the quills on the back porch on top of the freezer to dry.

I look out back and there are dark clouds rolling in fast. Crap, I forgot mom hung clothes out on the line earlier. I go get an empty laundry basket from the washer and run out to get the clothes. The boys are still playing horseshoes, oblivious to the approaching storm. It is still hot out—the wind is hot as if someone opened the oven door.

"You boys better get inside, it's going to rain soon," I tell them, throwing the clothespins in the ancient pillowcase that hangs on the line and houses them.

"Awww," they say in unison. Just as they say it, lightning hits close by and thunder cracks the universe.

One of them screams, "Jesus" and they both run in.

I guess they could have helped me, but just left me for dead. The treetops are swaying and dancing in this hot wind. My hair is trying to escape from the bun I have it in. The hot wind is trying to wreak havoc, but the rain comes hard and fast. I stand there and enjoy the fat cold raindrops for a minute and smell the wet earth and concrete before another clap of thunder sends me running with damp clothes and I am soaked. That rain came down quick.

As soon as I run inside, I leave the clothes on the back porch so my mom won't scold me for leaving them outside long enough to catch a storm. I walk in the kitchen all wet. Thunder booms so loud it shakes the house and the lights go out. Someone lets out a girly scream and the lights come back on. Everyone starts laughing and blaming each other for screaming.

"If it wasn't me or Grandma that screamed, or mom because we are all in the kitchen, it had to be someone in the living room," Jasmine points at her brothers and Grandpa Shayne.

In turn the twins both point at their Grandpa.

"Hell, naw," he says laughing, going back in the kitchen. "It was one of those *tay tay* boys." My uncle uses the slang word for mama's boys.

The boys start fighting and blaming each other, to the point where they start hitting each other. Then it escalates to wrestling in the living room. Lightning goes off again and Uncle Shayne yelps like a Chihuahua, then quickly tries to turn it into a warhoop.

"Hey!" I holler. "Knock that crap off! Don't make me come in there."

Everyone sits down to play Crazy Eight. Except me. I pull some beads out and start looking for something to bead, some unfinished project or some earring I only made one side to. I tend to do that. I find nothing so I put my beads back in all the boxes of chaos that no one understands except me.

"Hey!" Uncle Shayne says, as he deals cards, "You in?"

I shake my head no.

"As if!" my mom says and all my kids laugh.

"She is too big of a poor sport!" Creighton hollers.

"Shhh, you don't need to scream," I tell him.

"Oh yeah," my Uncle Shayne says, smiling. "I remember one time George sunk her last battle ship and she beat him with the game."

"Yeah," Craig said. "She used to accuse me and Creight of cheating at Candyland and we were only four years old."

Everyone laughs. I say nothing and continue to organize my beads.

It is a joke with my family how I cannot handle playing board games. I can handle it. I think it is just the fact that I win so much, everyone has to cheat when I play; therefore when I catch them, then I am called a poor sport. Plus everyone gangs up on me.

"How the hell does someone cheat at Candyland?" Uncle Shayne asks as he laughs. Their game is already going.

"It's possible," I finally speak up to defend myself. "When the boys would get one purple square they would jump two, when they got two they would jump three or four and they helped each other out, only to take me down. They were four years old, but they cheated only because their dad taught them. And they all did it to take me down."

Everyone laughs. I am enjoying my family time, even if they are laughing at me.

"Listen, whether you are four years old or forty, it is cheating. And I was trying to teach these boys morals... how else are they supposed to get ahead in the world?" I try to make my point.

"Shit, just let them marry white women," my uncle says and laughs.

Jasmine calls last card and instantly get accused of cheating.

"Nervy!" Then my mom says, "How is marrying white women supposed to get them ahead in the world? Don't listen to your uncle, boys. He is full of crap." She lays down a two, to which the next person lays down a two.

It goes on until Jasmine has to draw eight cards and about starts crying.

"You know the whole white privilege thing," Uncle Shayne says. He is looking at his cards and doesn't see my mom glaring at him.

I want to tell her white privilege never stopped her from being with a white guy but I keep my mouth shut.

"Listen, other than white privilege, at least you know a white woman won't break these guys noses someday, or their windshield. Indian women are mean. Plus they might break their hearts," he is shaking his head as he whistles and lays down his last card, simultaneously pissing everyone off.

Creighton shuffles and deals the seven-card round.

"Not all Indian women are mean," I say.

"That is like saying water ain't wet, or Indians aren't keen on getting diabetes. True story, Sis. Indian women are mean and vindictive," Uncle says and whistles again, as if he has a good hand.

I shake my head, "That's only because we have to put up with Indian men."

I see the text going off on my phone. It's Ricky. *Almost there. Let's cruise a bit.*

I grab my purse to check my makeup. Man, am I buzzing.

"Well, there are two things you boys cannot trust in this world: women and a fart. However both can be relieving," Uncle Shayne says. All my kids giggle. I shake my head and head to the bathroom to pee and freshen up.

I think about the times in my life I have been mean. To men, I have. I had my share of taking a bat to a car window, once or maybe twice, if you count my brother's cop car. I have popped some tires with a steak knife. I chased the boys' dad around at one point in time like no other men existed. Until I realized there were plenty of other fine Indian men around. But that was my late teens and twenties. For Gods sakes, all I wore was hoop earrings and my hair in a high bun back then. I even used black eyeliner for lip liner. What the hell did I know? At least I had the sense to never shave my eyebrows off and draw them on to the point where they no longer even resembled eyebrows. I barely even pluck the suckers because it hurts so much. *Damn, Boogie. What good is a gay friend if they can't do your brows?*

I hear a horn honking. I come out after spraying on some kind of fruity body spray.

"I'll be back," I tell everyone.

They are in such a heated game, no one pays attention. I walk out the back door and Ricky is in his rusty brown Ford truck. I hate the thing. I nicknamed it Clank Clank. However, Clank Clank was legit enough to leave the rez and pick up my washer and dryer from the nearby border town of Hay Springs, so no complaining. I put my Yankees hoody on and watched the gentle rain.

"What's up?" I smile and get in. Ricky is smiling and his smile always makes me smile. Even when he smiles like he is up to no good. Some Tool is playing from his dashboard and I turn it up. He hands me a Budweiser. I open it—it is a tall boy so I am assuming we are sharing. We cruise without talking because the music is too loud. Both windows are also open, whipping my hair around. Great. All that combing to look good is out the window. I hand the beer to Ricky, he takes a long drink and hands it back.

We go north of town, past the Catholic high school he attended and past one of their graveyards. We even pass the secret baby graveyard no one cares for... the church won't acknowledge it because it is a part of their shameful history. It is where they supposedly buried babies of former students impregnated by male staff back when the boarding school first started forcing kids from their homes to assimilate them to be more like white people. However, no one ever says how those babies died, no one acknowledges them, and some people tie tobacco ties on the unkempt graveyards of unmarked baby graves.

Up on the hill, past the baby graveyard, is a hill that has been called "Beer Can Hill" since who knows when. This is where Ricky pulls up. His truck is a trooper in the slightly grayish mud.

"Wow, I haven't been up here for a long time." That is all I say. Because I don't know what we are doing here. Journey starts playing one of their *nana nana* songs on the radio and I am about to ask him what we are doing up here when I see the storm has left to the east and the rain is reduced to a mere sprinkle. Not only that, but to the west of us, nature has taken over the horizon.

There are all the fire colors of the sunset. Above that are magnificent shades of fuchsia, pinks, violets and a dark purple. I say nothing but watch the sun sink and look behind to the East. There is a double rainbow. I am almost out of breath.

"Holay," I say. "What the hell was that?" I mean I am sure I have seen something like that. I ain't no spring chicken, I have seen sunsets before. I look at Ricky. He drinks the beer up and throws it out the window.

"Really?" I exclaim. "After seeing that, you are going to litter?"

"What the hell, Sis. Get out and look at how old those cans are laying around. Your grandma probably threw some up here. It **is** called Beer Can Hill."

I get out and look. The hill is shining silver from all the old cans. I won't admit it looks kind of glittery. And pretty. I turn to watch the last of the sunset. I hear Nirvana's cover of *Lake of Fire* playing. Perfect song. I hear a familiar click. I turn and see Ricky holding his phone up.

"Gross, Ricky! What the fuck!" I hate having my picture taken, especially with my hoody up like I am some punk, and he is laughing. I go to grab his phone away and we somewhat struggle between us. Finally he has me in a bear hug. So I grab his phone and take our pic together.

When we both look at it—there it is. We are happy, smiling, hugging. Although it looks like we are hugging in the picture, it is sort of some kind of submission hold over the camera. I still take horrible pictures. I still look huge, but we look good together. Plus the sun is coloring the sky behind us in colors Crayola would love to market, except they will never capture a Rez sky at sunset.

We laugh at our picture, although I secretly love it. We almost look like a couple.

We jump back in Clank Clank and head on back down the hill. I scoot over on the seat until I am sitting right next to Ricky. Even that feels like a big step—and also like I am being nervy. That was a big moment for us on Beer Can Hill, but we still didn't kiss. In fact, we hardly ever kissed, now that I think about it. I am wondering if that is even the kind of thing I want to be a part of. Kisses are always crucial to a relationship—well, at least until you meet that guy who thinks slobbering while kissing is sexy.

As we pull into town Ricky pulls into Hooky's to get some snacks, he says. Ricky is a big boy so I know he likes to eat. Shoot, I am a big girl and can throw down just like him, too. In fact, I cooked many a meal for him. Hooky's is on the east edge of Pine Ridge, and has been there since I was a kid. A somewhat dusty convenience store that only has one way in and out because of shoplifting, it surely would violate every fire code in any city because of all its blockades. It also sold fresh lemons as the only produce because kids in the hood pour Kool Aid on lemons and eat them. The store sold all kinds of bar food and munchies. It was the best. As he is shopping, I am wondering if that was romance we just experienced. Then I laugh. I think if it was: would I have to ask myself that question?

Ricky comes out of Hooky's with his arms loaded. He also has three slushies for the kids. Jesus, I didn't even ask him.

He hand the drinks over to me through my window. There is four altogether. One is just ice.

"This guy!" I tell him. "Not that much, you high?"

"Shey, I don't even smoke no more," he says as he turns the key and fires up Clank Clank.

"I know, but those were some good ol' days when we did, huh?" I say.

He just smiles at me. I realize at that moment, even though we went through some bullshit as friends, I was so happy to have him back in my life. I always miss him when he isn't there, a phone call or text away. We pull in to my house and Ricky parks on the street since Shayne's car and my car are in the somewhat of a driveway.

I walk in the back door with the slushies and ice water. The kids bombard me. Ricky walks in after me with the bag of munchies. The boys grab the Hot Cheetos and run with it because they know Jasmine will eat them all.

"Hey!" she screams after them. Damn, she has my mom's voice. I shudder. She looks further in the bag and finds a pickle and a small bag of sunflower seeds and heads to the living room, satisfied. Rez snacks.

Ricky pulls a small paper bag out of nowhere and hands it to me. It is some peppermint schnapps. He knows I love me some peppermint schnapps.

"Yay! No wonder you got the ice water," I exclaim.

He knows I love peppermint schnapps. This reminds me of one New Year's Eve wandering the small border town of Rushville, going from bar to bar and house party to house party as if we knew people. We kissed at midnight that year, but that was it. One magical kiss, I thought, anyway. He was back with Lola a couple days later. I was a little bit heartbroken but not enough to dwell on it or admit it.

"What we playing?" Ricky asks. He sits down and waits to be dealt in.

"We were going to play spades but with three of us we can play rummy now," my mom says.

"Oh, yeah. Poor sport status over here, enit?" Ricky points at me with his lips.

I roll my eyes and look for an old shot glass I bought at a rummage sale. I know I have one. I find it—it is from Atlantic City, New Jersey. Somewhere I have never been but someone went there, bought this shot glass and only cared about it enough to sell it for a quarter. Now it is mine and I probably put more use to it than they ever did. If this shot glass could talk, it would probably sing all the old country songs and heard us cry, too. I have a weird fetish for tourist things. All the things people buy: ashtrays, thimbles, spoons, snow globes, etc. They traveled to these places, made memories there, and bought all these things that I ended up with. Maybe it's because I never leave the reservation, except to go shopping.

I finish cleaning the shot glass out and they go back to a competitive game of rummy. I fill the shot glass up, take a shot and chase it with ice water. I fill it up again and pass it to each person. Only Ricky and I are chasing the shot with ice water. My mom and Uncle Shayne are hard-core suckers. After a couple rounds of shots, I decide to trace and cut some patterns out of rawhide for earrings —trying to come up with new patterns. I'm in a pretty happy place, at home with my family and my best friend, laughter going around and the smell of rain is still in the air. It is peaceful.

Craig comes in and asks Ricky to show him how to set up the ranking of players for his fantasy football team and I stop tracing. I listen. *Oh no, he didn't.*

Ricky comes back from the boys' room beaming. I am shaking my head as I narrow my eyes. Unbelievable. Of all the dirty, low down things. Now he is acting like a woman.

"I forgot to tell you, you won't have help in this year's draft because I invited each of the twins to manage their own teams," he laughs.

"Alright, fine," I say and pour another shot. After I chase it, I start in on him. "I can't believe you would do this to me? I feel cheated. In fact I think it is cheating. I would never sneak around and pull that crap on you."

Ricky laughs, "What I do? I thought your boys would like to play fantasy football instead of letting you get the glory for the moves they'd be making in your name."

"Cheater!" I say and do another shot before I pass the bottle on.

"Poor sport status, again. I think you using your boys was cheating," he replies.

My mom is laughing and Uncle Shayne is shaking his head. Apparently everyone is agreeing with Ricky.

"How do you think she beat the whole league two years ago?" Craig says, smiling and looking evil himself. "I'm just wondering how you knew our email addresses."

"Oh, that was easy," Ricky says. "I figured your mom probably sends out the same cheesy jokes to you in email, too, so I looked and sure enough, she did." Ricky's still laughing.

I had enough of the teasing and needed to go bathroom. When I finish, I check on Jasmine. She is in my little room that she mostly shares with me. She is playing with her Barbie's and this huge homemade townhouse I made out of produce boxes and cut-outs from magazines. It's the same as my Barbie townhouse when I was a kid, except my Barbie's were Indians from the moccasin factory that used to be in town. My Grandma Pacific used to get cases of them to take home. We would all help her put them together and she would get paid $50 for a box of 100 Native dolls with leather clothing we glued on and beads we sewed on here and there. She gave it up when she realized she made more money doing her porcupine quillwork.

Jasmine told me she thought it was cool my Barbie's were Indians. I told her it wasn't because their legs and arms didn't bend, I just wanted a blond-haired, blue-eyed real Barbie.

I turn to look in on the boys. They have the bigger room, and since our living room is so small, they keep the second-hand computer in their room. They also have a small twin bed and a set of bunk beds. Sometimes, Jasmine will sleep on the top bunk. Most times, she sleeps with me. The boys are busy helping each other fix their fantasy football team.

"Boo!" I say.

"Out!" Creighton says. "No pout babies allowed!" He gets up and closes the door in my face.

Whatever, I think to myself and turn back to the kitchen.

When I get back and gossip is at full swing, talking about who was just indicted, who cheated on who. Indictments are like a seasonal thing on our Rez. There is always some big drug bust going down. People knew who was involved but not really to the extent that the government made it sound. Indictments for embezzlement, indictments for abuse—I suppose all of it goes hand in hand with the poverty—so when it happens, it is no longer a shock. I can imagine if this kind of thing happened in a white town constantly, would it be so common that after a while, and the gossip was even boring? The most shocking news wasn't the embezzling, the drug rings, the rapes. It was when they sent an 82-year-old woman to prison for selling bootleg DVD's, which is exactly what the hot topic was when I walked in the room. Most of the crimes committed on our reservation that people get sent to prison for, are done for the sake of someone taking care of their family. Not including the violent crimes, although sometimes, that might be the case. Like my Uncle Shayne, he went to prison for defending and protecting me.

I sit back down to join the gossip. My mom has turned off the TV and the radio station is playing classic country. All the kids are pre-occupied. Ricky and I are drinking the schnapps and my mom and uncle switched back to beer. Freddy Fender is singing about tear drops when we hear glass shattering outside my house. My Rez chick ears tell me it is a windshield.

As we run outside, I hear Lola's shrill nasal voice calling me a whore. I see my mom telling the boys to keep Jasmine inside. As we all go outside, I see Ricky's windows are all smashed out. Well, his front and back—we had rolled down the door windows. She hits the back of my Uncle Shayne's car window and it shatters.

"What the fuck you think you are doing, you fucking bitch?" I run towards her and Ricky grabs me.

"Sis, let me handle this. I'll pay for his window. She's drunk and I don't know where my kids are. She had them last," he whispers in my ear as his arms are around me. I suppose it looks like he is hugging me, but he is holding me back. She's a bony little bitch. I will take that damn bat away from her and break out the windows to her brand new sports car.

"Get her fuckin' ugly ass out of here!" I holler at him. "I don't need your fuckin' drama, either!" I push him away. He backs off from me, looking at me and turns to walk towards her.

Lola yells, "Sis, you fucking whore! Get your own man instead of stealing mine all the time!" She just screams at me.

"Put that fucking bat down and talk to me, or shall I take it away from you, then we talk, bitch?" I walk towards her and my Uncle Shayne grabs me by my arms then holds me.

"Let me go, Uncle, look what she did to your fuckin car!" I try to wriggle away.

"Stay out of it, Sis," Shayne says.

She lets out an animal-like growl that turns into a scream and runs towards me with the bat. I try to get away from my uncle's hold. Ricky grabs her and holds her as he takes the bat away and throws it. I see the hickeys on her neck that he says he left her for. That scandalous bitch.

"You say you are his friend, I knew the whole time you two were fucking around! I knew it! I'm his babies' mama. You are nothing but a home wrecking whore!" Lola is snarling and spitting and thrashing in Ricky's arms. She is a mess.

I quit thrashing so I wouldn't look as stupid as she does. I watch her thrash, and my uncle lets me go. Her hair is everywhere, out of its tight bun. One of her drawn on eyebrows is missing, her lipstick is smeared, and she has slobber all over her face. She does not look like the pow wow princess Ricky fell in love with.

I wanted to beat her up. I don't know if I even could, honestly, but the schnapps made me feel like I could. And at the same time, I felt sorry for her. How do I know if Ricky isn't lying to her to come and see me? How do I know he isn't lying to me about her? I don't. Although—Ricky and I were friends a long time ago when she'd accused us of seeing each other. We really were. This time she has a right to be mad, if they are not really broken up.

"Ricky, get her out of here. I called the cops," my mom says calmly. I know she is lying. Ricky walks her to her car and talks softly to her. She looks at me and smiles as if she won. Lola is nodding and looking at me victoriously. They hug and she kisses him—maybe he kisses her. I am confused. She gets in the passenger side. He walks back to us.

"I have to take her back. She is too drunk to drive. She left the kids with no babysitter and you know our oldest Cheyenne is only 8. I have to go," he said apologetically.

"Go, then," I say and turn to walk in my house. I don't look back but I hear him telling my uncle he will be back after his truck and he will bring cash to give my uncle for his back window. I walk in the house dejected.

This is the bullshit I usually avoid. This is what sucks about being a single chick on the Rez. I am single by choice, not because I am waiting for a man. I feel like kicking myself. As if Ricky and I ever had a chance. What was I thinking, letting him fool me with sunsets and rainbows and shit. God, I am dumb.

I sit at the table and pour a shot, drink it then do another before I realize I have no more ice water to chase it with. I grab my mom's beer to chase it with and it is warm. I gag. I drink and drink and laugh and laugh with my mom and uncle. I won't let Ricky ruin my night. Pretty soon, I notice it is midnight.

"Shit, I better go bed," I tell them. "I have those appointments tomorrow."

"It's OK I spend the night, Sis?" my uncle asks.

"Hell yeah, Uncs. I owe you my life, move in if you ever want," I hug him from behind and kiss his cheek. I give my mom a hug. I pass the schnapps to both of them on the table. I walk to my room.

I lay by Jasmine and go to sleep to the sound of those two listening to The Eagles and laughing. In the back of my mind, I push the thought of Ricky away. I'm not his woman, or his babies' mama, I am only his friend.

That is the way it is.

[seven]

Wednesday

I wake up on my own the next morning at 7:37 a.m. still buzzed up. I look at my digital clock and roll on my back. I walk out to the kitchen and see an ashtray full of cigarettes. My Uncle Shayne already took off on a hustle. Christ, I was drunk —smoking and letting them smoke in the house. I dump the dirty ashtray and grab the shot glass off the table. Nice thing about having my mom around, those were the only dirty dishes. She cleaned everything before she went to bed, except the table had sticky rings on it from the schnapps and shot glass, and some of the rings were dark gray from the cigarette ashes that must have flicked and floated that way. I grab the spray bottle of Windex and spray the table down. God, I love the smell of Windex.

I open all the windows that are not open and fill the mop bucket with hot water and Pine Sol. I don't even know if I am going to mop, I just like the smell. I find three beers I must have stashed the night before. I kind of remember stashing them. I place them in the freezer and start cleaning. When I finish, I drink some ice water. Instantly, I feel buzzed even more. It's as if the ice water reactivated the drunk cells to wake up and party again.

I find Ricky's phone as I clean. I notice he put the picture of us up on Beer Can Hill as his wallpaper. I smile. We look good together. But I am not Lola, I tell myself.

I think of my boys' dad. One time Dave gave me a Black Hills gold heart necklace with my birthstone on it for Christmas. I found it because I was snoopy. I was always that way all my life. Grandma Pacific said it was because I lost my belly button. I even unwrapped any Christmas presents that were labeled to me under the tree before Christmas every year. I had no patience and had to know. So the necklace made me giddy and love Dave even more. I started looking for more presents for me. I was pregnant with the twins then. Finally in the trunk of our car, I found the same kind of box. I squealed and opened it. I expected to see matching earrings. I didn't.

It was the same necklace with a different birthstone. I felt sick.

I looked at the month of the birthstone and quickly eliminated any of the women in his family before I jumped to conclusions. No one fit it. Then I thought of who I had been suspicious of lately.

I was hyperventilating as I walked in our trailer. Dave was sleeping on our bed. I laced up my shoes and jumped on the bed. I braced myself so I wouldn't fall, being that I was big and pregnant. I started kicking him while he slept. He woke up real pissed off.

"Oh, what the fuck did I do? Ow, what the fuck! fuck!" He is screaming as I kick. I cried and fell beside him. I showed him

the necklace and he tried to say it is for his mom, his sister, anyone. Finally I promised him I won't be mad if he tells me the truth. He named the girl I was suspicious of. I howled and started throwing everything I could at him until he left. Soon as he leaves, I called Zona.

We pulled into Hooky's where Dave's other woman was a cashier. I walk in to buy a bottle of water. Zona and I are talking the whole time. Zona was talking loudly about how she hated home wreckers especially when the man has a family. I nodded and agreed. I am trying to hide my sniffles. I want to say something to her but Zona planned it out—just nod, agree with me and buy whatever you're buying. I got this, she said. Soon as I closed my hand over the cold change she gently placed there, Zona reached over the counter and popped her in the nose hard. She fell into the candy and we walked out. Her co-workers ran to her side. She knew why; she knew what she did wrong, and what he did was wrong. She never pressed charges but she sported two black eyes for two weeks after.

I look at the picture of me and Ricky in front of the sunset. I try to decide if Ricky's giving me all the laughs he ever had, along with his uncertainty about us. Was this the same as Dave giving me a necklace that was never meant to be anything special? How do I know what is even real anymore? I can't tell with Rez boys.

I go into the boys' room and plug Ricky's phone into the computer while the boys sleep. Quietly, with a few clicks of the mouse, I save the pictures Ricky took. We look even better on the computer.

I think I better save these pictures because you never know—someday maybe we won't even know each other anymore like we do now. I realized that last night. I can never come between

Ricky and Lola. They have kids together. This could be the end of our almost twenty-year friendship.

I put Ricky's phone on my bedside table to charge. I have to go to take a shower and get ready for another day.

When I come out all fresh, clean, and brand new, my mom is trying to make coffee and her hand is shaking. Looks like me, I think.

"Mom, there are three beers in the freezer." I tell her as I am brushing my hair. She playfully punches me in the arm, but it kind of hurts for being playful. It kind of makes me want to playfully punch her back.

"Eeez, you stasher!" she says and beelines for the freezer. She snaps that first can open and I swear I am thirsty all of a sudden. I feel like I need it or I will be sick, again.

"Ow," I say rubbing my arm. "I didn't mean to stash. It's probably genetic. Soon as I get drunk, I remember you stashing beer all over the house. Childhood memories."

I watch her open a can and flip me off as she drinks it. It looks so good, and when she passes it to me, I help her drink it up. There is no hope, I swear.

She holds the can up to me. "Breakfast of champions," she says and tips it.

"Champions of what?" I remark dryly, "The race to cirrhosis?"

She laughs her raspy laugh as if it was really funny. I want to throw up. I said it sarcastically and she laughs. I go ignore her and wonder if those dying in hospitals of cirrhosis would think that it's funny. In a matter of minutes we guzzle a whole 24-ounce can of Budweiser. In a matter of minutes I feel better, but I feel bloated.

I go to the bathroom and throw up cold beer. I sit on the bathtub and cry as I run the sink water. I feel like shit. I feel like dying. I feel like I am stupid. I just want to go back to bed but something is making me go out and face the world to try and make it better for my kids. Beer has no part of that. I lean over the toilet and throw up until I taste the peppermint from the night before. I am still dry heaving and done throwing up cold beer foam.

Finally I get up, brush my teeth, comb my hair, and wash my face. I put on a pair of jeans, a lavender polo, and my favorite sandals. No flip flops. I am trying to be official today.

When I go back out, my mom made scrambled eggs, fried bologna, warmed the skillet bread up from the night before, plus there is a plate of thick slices of commodity cheese. Despite the fact that my jeans are tighter than they ever been, my love handles are prominent, and the old Indian trick of sucking in my gut no longer works. I sit and eat.

My mom sets a jar of hot banana peppers in front of me and a strong cup of coffee. I eat and drink until I feel better about life. Maybe it is unhealthy but it was a perfect breakfast on the rez.

I watch all three of my kids lumber in because they smelled breakfast. I hope they don't think cooking breakfast is an everyday thing. It is either when I am in a good mood or their grandmother or one of their uncles are around.

Craig goes straight for the coffee and pours a cup with a bunch of commodity evaporated milk. He has been loving coffee since he was four, like me. Creighton squirts mustard all over his eggs and bologna until it sounds like a fart.

"Ew, poop!" Jasmine laughs. "Whoever eats mustard on their eggs and bologna is gross!" Then she proceeds to squirt a big pile of ketchup on hers.

"You're both sick," Craig says as he blows and sips on his coffee like an old man, leaning against the counter.

"Your mama has some appointments then we are going to find Mark to sell all the bracelets and earrings we made. Who wants to come?" their grandma asks them.

No one says anything.

"No one?" I ask. "Fine, I will find a babysitter."

"Whatever! We're twelve years old," Creighton says.

I look at Jasmine but she is swirling her bologna in the ketchup. "Not even you, Jazz?"

"Sometimes it's boring sitting in the car," she says.

"Really? When I was a kid, I sat in the car outside the bars for hours. In fact, all I was raised on was chips," I tell them this and my mom smacks me on the back of the head.

"Shush, let's go, they will be alright. We'll have Misun come check on them later." Ha, my mom must be feeling guilty.

"Can we go to Uncle Misun's?" Creighton asks. "I want to go swimming."

"Let me call him in an hour or two," I tell them and put on my shades. Everyone's satisfied with that and we leave. I look over at my mom. She has a long pair of beaded earrings on, her jean vest and shades. She looks all "AIM-ster."

"You have any earrings I can borrow?" I ask her. I only ask her because I know she carries all her Native jewelry in an old ass Ziploc in her purse. She looks at my shirt and pulls her Ziploc bag out. After shuffling through all her earrings, she pulls out a pair of about three-inch-long purple beaded earrings with faded silver bugle beads on them.

I put them on and she takes the ponytail holder out of my hair. She pulls my hair down and smoothed it out.

"Hey, woman. It is hot out. Hello?" I say to her trying to get the ponytail holder back so I can put my hair back in the high ponytail.

"No! What is wrong with you Lakota women these days? Always putting your hair up on your head like your some kinda gangster or Mexicans. Wearing big gold hoops in your ears. You're Lakota, be proud of your hair, even in the heat." She sounds like Grandma Pacific so much, I get scared. I don't even do a "once over" in the mirror.

We walk out in the bright sunlight and it is already hot out. I am already sweating and my hair is down. I see all the broken glass in my driveway and get mad all over again. That bitch. Both of them. Lola and Ricky.

"You want me to drive?" my mom asks.

I hand her the keys and go around to the passenger side and wait for her to open my door. As soon as I get in, I'll roll down the window because not only has the air conditioning probably not worked since 1987, the door also hasn't opened since Madonna was a virgin. Being that this was a 1980 Ford LTD, I wait for my mom to reach over that huge front seat, shimmy part of the way and open the door for me.

Our first stop was Social Services, which was right outside of town to the east. I had to get help. My quillwork would not help now that the season was about over. My mom pulls into the farthest parking spot. That was so typical of her.

"Take your time, don't worry about me. I have reading material and refreshment." She opens her purse and pulls out a beer, puts it in a koozie she had in her purse also and unfolds an old ass National Enquirer Grandma Pacific left at my house.

I roll my eyes and get out. I open the door to Social Services and I am not the only one there. A guy, sitting in the waiting area, is filling out paperwork. I walk to the front desk with the intention to proudly announce I am ten minutes early for my appointment. The girl at the front is someone I went to high school with but we were not friends. I mean, we never hung out.

But not for any reason, we just hung out in different crowds. She came through my line plenty of times at the grocery store. Once in a while we made small talk—that was about it.

"Hi, I'm early," I say and smile at her. She looks at me with the eyes of a dead fish. She ignores me. So I stand there. I read signs about how to be a good parent, according to white people. I look around. Maybe I wasn't supposed to come stand in this line. I have been here before to sign up for food stamps but I never observed any rules. I look all over. I see her texting on her phone. Now, I am getting offended. I clear my throat.

"Um, I have an appointment in like seven minutes. Do I just take a seat?" I ask her. She again looks at me with dead fish eyes under her bangs. Oh my God, I am freaking out. Am I doing something wrong? Finally, I just start to walk down the first hallway filled with offices and peek in the offices of some fat Nebraska-born social workers. She comes running after me. She shoves a clipboard full of green paperwork at me and a pen with a plastic spoon taped on the end. She leads me back to the sitting area.

"Bring that back when you are done," she says.

I say nothing. I take a seat.

I start to fill out the paperwork. It is all confusing. I answer it the best I could. Except the parts that ask about my sex life with the children's fathers. They have the nerve to ask when we did it and how many times? I try to think of an answer. How do I tell a social worker we did it all the time? That I can't count?

Finally I write, "Every day, all the time, any time, everywhere." *Fuck them, so nosy.* Old farmer bitches who never get laid—that is probably what they want to hear.

I giggle and finish the rest of it to the best of my ability. The guy sitting across from me laughs, too. I look at him and smile. I forget I am sweaty, my hair is down, and probably all funny from my window being down and my mom going over 45mph in my 1980 LTD. I take my paperwork back up to Dead Fish Eyes and sit back down.

The rez boy and I smile at each other a few more times before he asks my name.

"Sincere," I say.

"Yeah?" Then he says, "I am sincere."

I laugh and look sideways. "No, I am Sincere, that is my name."

"No, for reals?" he asks. He smiles again and he is cute— maybe about five years younger than me but cute. He has long hair pulled back in a ponytail, a small mole on his chin, a mouth full of white teeth and shoulders like a trooper.

"What is your name?" I ask.

"Clyde," he says. "Clyde Lost Heart."

He offers his hand and we shake a gentle handshake.

"Sincere Strongheart," I say.

"That's your real name?" he asks.

"Yes, why?" I let out a dumb giggle.

"It don't sound real," he answers.

I am trying to think of how to be clever, or something to say, or how to flirt. I look up at him and he laughs. I laugh, too. They call his name and he disappears. I stop sucking in my gut and try to sit in a relaxing way in the hard plastic round chair. I cross my legs. I uncross them. I sit sideways. I sit all kinds of ways. Finally I sit like a man watching baseball with my legs sprawled in front of me. Only thing was, my hands were not in my pants. They were behind my head with my fingers clenched. If Grandma Pacific could only see me now, being so unladylike.

Finally, they call my name. I am told by Fish Eyes to take a right down the hall and then a left and another left. I do, and I look up.

There is a lady sitting there, sweating despite the air conditioning in here is blasting. It could have to do with her tight powder blue polyester suit, or maybe the flowered polyester shirt with the huge mess of knots tied at her neck out of the same material. I wonder who designed shirts that tied a huge bundle, bow-tie sort of thing made of the same material at the neck. Clearly, they will never own up to that.

She stood up and let out a big sigh.

"Hello, Sincere is it? Have a seat please." She sits back down and the girth of her thighs pull her pants way up so I see her ankle length nylons, all brown against her white skin. Clearly, she was from Nebraska. Most of the social workers on the reservation were. All their cars in the parking lot have license plates from Nebraska. Funny, they judge us, but have no jobs there, so they work on our reservation and determine whether they can help us or not.

Wow, Sis, judge not! I think. What the hell—she could be a sweet old lady who bakes great brownies and here I was judging her for judging me, which she didn't even do yet.

She was studying my application as if she ate a lemon. Reading it, marking it, muttering, "Mmhmm" to herself.

I will not take offense, she could be happy to get someone in who worked so long.

She looks up at me suspiciously. "Ms. Strongheart, it is Ms., right? I mean, I am assuming you are not married."

Well, so much for her being non-judgmental. The bitch probably don't even bake brownies but I bet she eats the hell out of them.

"I need to know why you quit your job," she peers at me over her thick tri-focal glasses.

"Well, I uh, I had been there for twelve years. I felt like, it was, um, a dead end job. I felt as if it would go nowhere. I still was never full-time and only had a few raises... in, um, all the twelve years," I stammer out then cough.

"Wrong move, wrong move," she clicks her tongue. "In a place like Pine Ridge, you have to count your blessings—not push them away." She is breathing hard as if she took a flight of five steps.

I stare at the wood paneling on the wall. I see a pattern that looks like Elton John in his big pink sunglasses, when he sings *Rocket Man*. She gulps her coffee from a mug that says "World's Greatest Grandma" and I wonder if she bought it for herself at a yard sale. She lets out a small burp and it smells like Steak-Um's. I swear I am going to puke cold beer foam all over her desk.

"I just thought, well, that there had to be more opportunities out there for me, other than, you know, the store," I say. "Is there?" I ask her meekly.

I notice she also smells like chicken soup. I wonder if she has food in her drawer. She is looking at me, shaking her head.

"As you know, Pine Ridge is a place with few opportunities; your choices are limited," she tells me.

"Where do you live?" I ask her.

"I live in Gordon," she answers, still looking over paperwork.

"So why don't you work in Gordon?" I ask her and I knew it was the wrong move. I am past pissed. Maybe I walked in here past pissed. Shoot, what do I know, maybe I was born past pissed. Maybe I am past pissed aggressive. (Nice, I will have to market that term.)

"Well, I grew up in Gordon, but there is little work for my field. The calling was here in Pine Ridge," she says, with her bottom lip sticking out, scanning my paperwork.

"So basically, because there was no opportunity in Gordon for your job, you drive here every day to a place of no opportunity to take one of the few jobs that one of my people can use."

It's not a question. I just had to say it. So I state it. I don't ask.

"By quitting your job, you immediately disqualified your family for emergency assistance. You will still receive your food stamps but you will be sanctioned 10% for non-cooperation. Your medical assistance is immediately expired until further notice and/or cooperation." She proudly stamps a big fat red "Case Denied" stamp with the date under it on my application.

"What the hell? I came in here looking for help. Instead you made things worse for me. Is that your job?" I ask.

I am getting angry to the point of tears.

She looks at me with indifference. I know she could care less but she acted as if I just asked for money out of her own pocket.

"What if I sign up for college?" I ask. "Is there any kind of help if I sign up for college?" I ask this desperately. I know I was being a smart ass with her, I realize it. She also showed her power as a social worker by denying me everything and making my situation worse.

She puts her arms behind her head and leans back, as if to show power in the form of her arm pit stains. The cubicles fills with the smell of raw onions. "What would you go to college for?"

"I'm not sure. I don't know, but it is something I have always thought of, especially lately," I say this while trying not to breathe.

"You have to have a plan. You have to know what you want to go to college for. We need to know that and that it is something you are serious about," she tells me. "There is some assistance for single parents going to college, and we have a separate application for that. I suggest you think long and hard about this and stop by the tribal college. Talk to a counselor there." She is shuffling through some files in a drawer behind her.

"This is a one page application, fill out both sides. It must be accompanied by a written essay—showing us why you want to enter this program, why you think you need to change your life, and why you are ready."

I nod. She is talking as if I am four-years-old, but she also can approve me for this program so I leave my smart-ass mouth shut from now on.

"How many words?" I ask her as I take the application.

"It is unlimited. The longer it is the better your chances." She goes back to looking on her desk.

"Thank you," I say humbly and walk out of her office. I look around for the cute boy named Clyde again. He's gone.

I walk outside to the car, feeling defeated but hopeful. Maybe that is the purpose of social services, to make you feel that way. I walk towards my car; mom is flipping through her National Enquirer and listening to the radio. I reach in the window and open my door.

"What's up?" she asks.

"I was denied help for quitting my job and had my food stamps sanctioned." I am immediately all sweaty, red-faced, and no longer look professional.

"Those motherfuckers," she said. "Check out these movie stars and all their cellulite." She shows me a picture of what she said. As if they were not human, too.

"Well your Grandma called and wants me to go to the store and get her some of those orange marshmallow peanuts and coffee and bobby pins. Did you need anything from the store?" she asks.

"A bottle of water," I tell her. "Take me to the tribal college. I want to see if it is possible to go. Go run around for Grandma and pick me up when you're done. Oh, and tell Grandma to quit using bobby pins, that is so gross. Q-tips are better for her."

My mom laughs, "She is old, set in her ways, and has been using bobby pins since she was in boarding schools. Maybe they made them use them. I don't know."

We drive into town and through the four-way. I start feeling a paranoia coming on with all the change. Maybe I shouldn't have quit my job. What the hell was I thinking? Now, my life has to take a new direction. Now I have no choice but to make it better, because it can't get worse. It just can't. I have kids.

My mom pulls into the tribal college center main campus located on the west side of town. I have never been here before except to sell earrings on the college employees paydays and I never went in. Mark usually did.

"I'll be here when you are done, and good luck," mom says and pulls away. I remember a time when I couldn't trust her with my car. I watch her drive away and am thankful she has had her head on straight lately. I turn to walk in the college center and wonder for the 15th time, *what am I doing?*

I am thankful as always for the blast of air conditioning when I walk in. I know I am sweating a hangover. Again.

I walk in the admissions office and no one is in there. But someone is around here because probably the second or third pot of coffee is brewing somewhere. Indians love their coffee. You can walk into any tribal program office at any time of the day and smell fresh coffee. I start reading notices and signs when an older lady walks in and right past me. She starts straightening stuff out on her desk when I clear my throat and she jumps.

"I'm sorry," I say and kind of laugh a little bit.

"No, no, you scared me. I didn't even see you," she laughs along with me. "Maybe I won't need a cup of coffee now."

We both laugh at that. She has that older Indian lady perm of tight curls and glasses. Her eyes are kind and she smells like Avon's Imari perfume.

"Is it too late to register for classes?" I ask.

"No, not at all. Which program were you interested in?"

"I'm not sure. Do I have to know before I register?" I ask her. I am very nervous and she can see it.

"No, not at all," and she pats my back and leads me out of the office. When we walk in the hallway, she hands me an application, a pen, and some other information on the college. "Why don't you walk down and look in the classrooms. There should be an advisor in each one from the different programs. Maybe they can help you either decide a program, just start with your basics, or determine if you really want to go."

"Thank you," I tell her. Then I walk down the shiny linoleum towards what could very well be a better future for me and my children. I peek in one room, looks like science or math. No one is in there and I walk away. I peek in the room the nursing program has set up, there are a quite a few students milling around. I am not nurse material, so I turn around and walk into the next room.

There is a sign that says Social Work/Human Services program. I already detest the sign because I can't imagine why anyone would want to go to school to be a social worker, but nobody is in the room. There are pictures set up of people helping other people, serving food, handing out turkey dinners, etc. As if. They just cut my food budget by 10 percent because I had the audacity to quit a dead end job. (*But you were drinking*, a little voice says in the back of my head. I brush it aside.)

At least no one is in the room, I can sit and fill out my paperwork quietly. I'll just take basics. I sit for ten minutes filling out paperwork and am almost done when I hear someone sing song a "good morning" to me.

I turn around and say, "Good morning" to a tall, fluffy white guy with fluffy white hair. His movements and voice set my gay-dar off.

"Are you here to register with our Human Services program?" he asks me.

I shake my head. "Um, no, actually the room was empty. So I was just registering. I'm still undecided," I tell him.

"OK, that's fine," he says and busies himself with shuffling papers. "So you don't see yourself as a social worker?"

I want to say **Hell No**, but I just shake my head.

"May I ask why?" he asks, not looking at me, just stapling papers together.

"I don't know," I tell him. "It's just something I never thought I would pursue." I pause and look at him, as he is finally looking at me. "Ever," I add.

He puts down his paperwork and walks over to sit across from me at the table. I smell coffee and patchouli on him. He puts his chin in his hands and I feel nervous because I am feeling like he is going to get real personal here.

"What is your opinion of social workers?" I avert my eyes away from him and look at my hands. Why did I pick this room?

"Be honest," he says. "You won't hurt my feelings."

"I just don't like them," I tell him.

"Why? Because they seem like these evil people who take kids out of homes?" he asks.

"Well, there is that. And..." I feel as if he is testing me. "I don't have time to list all the reasons."

"Fine, give me your main reason, just one." He leans back in his chair as if I am going to tell him a story.

And I guess I kind of do tell him a story.

I take a deep breath.

"I just came from Social Services. I just quit my job, my dead end job and I needed emergency assistance. The lady working there was rude. She had nothing nice to say and made me feel as if I was asking for her money, from her pocket. She treated me horribly. I feel like I have no dignity already, asking for help and they just made me feel like a beggar. Even the receptionist," I blink back my tears.

"Ah," he sits up straight. "You my dear are only dealing with those on the front lines. They become jaded from the job. They still should never treat people the way that they do but it happens more often than not, sadly. Social work is a whole plethora of services. We help the disabled, the elderly, those with addictions and so on. It is about caring for the needs of the people. That is what it is about. I bet you didn't even know your own people, the Lakota, were like social workers. You had different societies that took care of the needs of the people. Societies that helped the elderly, societies that fed maybe those with no men in the family. Your people had no poor people, no jails, and no starving people. If one starved, everyone starved, but that was never the case. I teach about how Lakota people had it right before the settlers did. The Lakota had it better than any social service program that is out there today. Now, tell me this, if you could change something about social workers, what would it be?"

"I think they should have some empathy, not treat people like shit. Just because someone is signing up for help doesn't mean they are out to cheat the system," I say, not even caring if I cursed. I was actually interested in this conversation.

"And how can this change, do you think? Is it possible?" he asks.

"By not hiring insensitive people. By creating programs that really help people and give them hope. There is really little hope here, and why take away that little bit of hope and make them feel defeated before they are given a chance. How is anyone supposed to help themselves when they feel defeated?"

I look at him and realize I ranted. "Sorry for the rant. I just get too fired up when I am treated as if I am stupid, and that just happened today, just now," I tell him.

"That's fine. I needed to hear that. You have both passion and compassion, something that should be required of all social workers, in my humble opinion. I think you would make a wonderful social worker. I could see you in the future writing grants to create programs for your people." He is looking in the far off future and making me see what is possible.

"How do I sign up?" I ask him.

He starts to get together a package for me. "We have a scholarship program for those who are willing to stay on the reservation and work. It is too late for this semester but you could sign up and try for the spring semester in January. It is a full scholarship with living expenses. Of course, you do have to write an essay covering why you think you deserve the scholarship, also comparing your life now to where you would like to see it in the future. I would like to say it should be between 500 to 1000 words, but you may write it as long as you would like."

I sit and fill out the rest of the application, everything except the scholarship application. I also change my original application to Human Services and sign up for the spring semester instead of now. That way, I won't be rushing around last minute.

I also know it will be a few rough months to January classes, but I have my art work to fall back on. If I play my cards right, I can use the same essay for both the scholarship application and the social services program application. Killing two birds with one stone.

I got up to shake his hand and tell him I will be back next week to hand in the application and essay.

I walk out of the college center feeling better than when I walked out of the Social Services building this last time. The air conditioning stays inside with the building so I am instantly hot in the bright sunlight. I hear my mom fire up The Beast before I see it. She is, of course, in the farthest parking space.

"Well, it must have went well. This time you have some pep in your step. Last time you were all sour grapes leaving the Social Services building," she says.

I didn't think she noticed but I guess moms know their kids best.

"I think I may have found my calling in life," I say all dramatic as I collapse in the front seat. "In fact, maybe the planets are aligned."

"Silly rabbit," she taps me on the head with her rolled up magazine. "Let's go to your house, I need to pee. Plus, I found Mark, he went over there to shower and change his clothes. He says he will sell our quillwork."

"He better not use my toothbrush again, that sick ass. I need to change my clothes anyway," I say as we head in the direction of my house.

"What's wrong with your clothes now?" My mom hits the green light at the four-way, which is cool because she has to pull into the turning lane and there is a cop in the other lane. By the time she pulls up to turn, he is long gone.

"These jeans are too tight. I just want my comfy yoga pants," I tell her as we pull into my driveway.

"Since when did you ever do yoga?" She laughs at me. We walk in the back door.

"I could do yoga if I wanted to," I retort.

Again she laughs. I hear Mark laughing even harder in the bathroom.

"You, yoga?" He comes out brushing his teeth **with** my toothbrush. He realizes that I see my toothbrush and runs back in the bathroom.

"Geez, Mark. Next time you go to jail, do yourself a favor. Keep the free toothbrush!" I yell through the closed door.

I peek out the front door because I saw my twins out there.

"What you guys doing?" I ask them. They look excited. "Is it football practice already?"

"Yes! I'm going to knock Creighton out, watch!" Craig says.

"Where's your sister?" I notice I don't hear her.

"Misun came and picked her up, she took clothes but we told her she has to ask you to spend the night. I guess Cante is having a going away party," Creighton says. "And shut up boy, I'll knock the snot out of you."

They start roughhousing when their grandma comes out and threatens them to go cheer for them at football practice.

"Jesus, Grandma, it's only practice! It's not even a game!" Craig says and we all laugh. She can be known for being loud at games, screaming until she loses her voice and war hooping and lee lee-ing.

"I'm just teasing," she says and both boys let out a sigh of relief.

Soon as Mark comes out of the bathroom, my mom beelines it there. I'm lucky that even though Dave and I had a stormy Rez drama, broken-windshield-type of relationship with cheating on both parts, we both grew up. We have grown past hating each other and started raising our twins together as responsible adults. That is not to say his wife Eva can handle our friendship as co-parents. And it is not to say, that my one year relationship with Will, his former best friend didn't cause drama in our friendship. It wasn't Dave being funny acting to his old buddy—it was Will who couldn't handle it. Some people are so immature. At any point, I am happy he is involved in their lives. Some men, many men, don't give a crap about their kids. Some women, too, for that matter.

I smell hamburgers frying. Geez, I love when Mark is around. We all go in to maul some burgers.

"Hope you don't mind. I fried some cheeseburgers real quick. I was feelin' kinda gaunt," Mark says, and he points with his lips to the oven. Everyone is clamoring around to make cheeseburgers. I add mustard and raw onions to mine. Since Mark is the salesman, I don't have to worry about whether I should or shouldn't eat raw onions.

Mark is telling Rosebud jokes to my mom and the boys. I laugh—they are funny but not that funny. He better not let our cousin Two Times hear them, his mom is from Rosebud.

"How do you know the toothbrush was invented in Rosebud?" Mark asks. "Because if it was invented anywhere else, it would be a teethbrush."

He laughs to reveal his missing teeth.

"Geez, Mark, you're the one with missing teeth," I tell him.

"Oh yeah, do you want to be?" He shakes his fist at me.

"Whatev. Let's go get this done. My palms are itching. I know I have money coming," I tell him.

Mark and I only fought a few times for real. The last time was violent. We were drinking whiskey at the Dam and he started choking me. I got away and hit him with a two by four. I never fought Misun. I usually fight with Gary and Frieda. Gary always wins, but Frieda only beat me up once. Misty is lucky she moved away; I would have beat her up a few times. Not that I am tough, it is just how we are, we fight, we get over it, and we all eventually talk again.

In Boogie's family they will hold a grudge for years just for an argument or over a block of cheese. I have no idea how they resolve anything. We have our outbursts of violence but we don't lose time as a family together. I guess every family is dysfunctional in some sort of way.

I lock the house up and put the key in the tomato pot. Well, it was supposed to be tomatoes. I always forget to water them, but they still tried to grow. Now they were all shriveled and the plant was droopy. The tomatoes even had the nerve to turn red. Poor little wrinkled things.

"Damn, Sis, do you ever water this plant?" Mark touched the dry cracked soil. "Looks like the damn badlands here."

I laugh, "I forgot about it. I'm not a green thumb. It did OK for about three weeks to a month, though."

"Shoot Sis, I would say you have a black thumb. You didn't honor them as you should honor the plant people, didn't you know, they are always standing in prayer? That is why they are tougher than us, because they always stand in prayer." He looks at me seriously.

"Really?" I ask him. I have no idea what is coming next but I am glad he is in the storytelling mood. That is where he needs to be to go street bang some art.

"Oh, yeah! If you listen closely to the plant people, they will talk to you," Mark says. "They will tell you what you need to do.

They have a stronger connection with the spirit world than we do, because all they do is provide food and oxygen for us and stand and pray. We don't give back to them, we pollute their world." He leans down close to my poor withered tomato plant and pretends to listen.

"Well, what is my tomato plant saying?" I ask him. I am smiling because whether he is joking or serious, he is one funny fucker. He was exactly like this as a child, too.

"Shhhh," he hushed me and has his hand to his ear, as if he is listening. "This plant is a boy plant. He is saying 'Please help me.... just pull me up by the roots and let me die!'" Mark says this in a wheezy voices and makes coughing noises. I push the back of his head and laugh. What a nutcase.

We walk around some bushes to the driveway and I hear my mom telling Dave that she wished he were still her son-in-law, and the boys are loading up in his truck.

"Nervy, mom! Azzz if!" I say.

Dave laughs and starts his truck. "Yeah, Sis wishes that, too." He starts backing out and I flip him off. He wished!

"Ooh, you're lucky you're in your car," I yell as he backs out.

I haven't wished that for years. I left him and his cheating ways behind long ago. And I know he didn't change because he always tried to cheat on his wife... with me. Well, after I ended my affair with him. (Once a dog...)

"Who's driving?" Mark asks.

"I can," I volunteer since I'm sober, although I am starting to hang over. The cheeseburger helped.

"Wait, is George working today?" I ask, looking in the rearview mirror at Mark.

"I don't know," he says.

"Oh well, anyway I'm sober but we need to find a driver. I'll need a beer soon," I say as I start the car.

"Where to first?" I ask Mark.

"The store," he says.

I pull into the shopping center. We cruise behind cars looking for license plates that aren't South Dakota.

"Nevada!" mom says.

Just our luck. There's an empty spot by the S.U.V. We wait. Finally, we see a gang of women coming out of the store. They all look like some sort of southwest blend of Indian—all wearing turquoise jewelry and long skirts.

Mark's standing by the car. "Excuse me ladies," I hear him say and then they all walk to the rear of the S.U.V. They all talk for a while then Mark comes running over to us.

"They're all from Arizona, just one lives in Vegas. Anyway, they're all sisters and daughters. Well, one lady said she'd give you $250 for everything. That's somewhere about $14-$15 each, maybe more. I told them I thought it would be okay. What do you say?"

"Shit yeah!" mom says.

"Of course," I say at the same time. *Get it all over with at once. Quick. No piddling around while my brother shit-talked.*

"Hunnert and twenty five each?" mom asked.

"Yah. What about Mark?" I ask.

"Fifteen each?" She waits for me to agree. I nod. Mark just made $30 for ten minutes of shit-talking. He stays outside talking to them while one of them runs in, I'm assuming, to the ATM.

An older lady comes out with a bunch of twenties in her hand. She hands them over to Mark. He talks a couple more minutes then all the women explode with laughter. Mark's a flirt. I don't even want to know what story he told.

"I told them you was in labor," he says when he jumps in.

"Fuck you," I say and mom laughs.

"Not you, I told them my mom was in labor." Now I laugh and my mom shakes her fist at him.

I give him thirty and mom a hundred, and tell her we have to split a twenty.

"See? Now aren't you glad I made you quill," Mom slaps me with her money.

"Yeah, yeah." I was especially glad because pretty soon tourist season would be over.

"I'm done for the day. Is anyone coming over to my house or do you all have plans?" I ask.

"Take me to Clay," Mark says.

"Me, too. But on the way back, I want to pick up Snitzy," Mom says.

"Gross," I tell her.

"Mind your own beeswax," she says.

"I do or else I'd knock Snitzy out. And don't think he is coming over to my house," I tell her this as I pass the dump.

She ignores me.

We pull into Whiteclay. We all walk in the Last Bar. My mom buys her beer. I buy a twelve-pack of Budweiser. Mark buys his six cans and a pack of cheap cigarettes. That should make him Mister Popularity for a while.

"Sincere!" someone is yelling. It's Mason, the white boy. "Sincerely, that's you."

Be cool, girl. I tell myself. *You're 32 not 14.*

"It's me," I say, hoping it sounds charming. "What you doing here?"

He was stocking the cooler.

"This is my uncle's bar. Sometimes I help him out when he's shorthanded." He smiles at me. "So, how you been? See the rest of the Series?"

"Yah, I know my grandma's a Red Sox fan. What counted was the one I watched at the bar because I won the bet." I gave him a nervous smile.

"Sup man," Mark puts his hand out to Mase. I notice his chest is puffed out.

"Hey, what's up, my name's Mason." He shakes my brother's hand.

"Sorry," I say. "This is my brother Mark and my mom, Velma."

My mom shakes his hand. "Are you Shorty's boy?"

"Yeah," Mason says. "That's my pops."

"You mean from Dad's Bar and Grill?" Mark asks.

"I thought so," my mom tells him. "You look like him."

I don't think he looks like his dad at all.

"Yeah, I should have known you were Sincere's mom, she looks like you," Mason tells her.

I do not look like my mother at all either.

Mark un-puffs his chest. "Kola, Kola," he shakes Mason's hand again and pats him on the back. "You don't have to call her Sincere, we call her Sis."

"Well, Sincere is her name and I think it is a nice name," Mason says and he goes back to stocking.

I think I love him.

My mom and Mark tell Mase to say hi to his dad and start walking out. I grab my twelver and pickle.

"Sincere," he says.

"Huh?" (*Geez, I could have said, "What." Huh sounds like low intelligence.*)

"You watching the Yankees game tonight?" he asks.

"I didn't know there was one on, but yah, more than likely," I tell him. I notice how nervous I am around him when I'm sober.

I realize my hair is still out and I have my mom's long beaded shoulder duster earrings on.

"I'm going fishing after this out at Denby. Maybe when I'm done, I'll stop in and check the score." He smiles at me.

Oh boy. "You don't even know where I live!" I say.

"Well, this is the part you tell me," he chuckles.

"Oh, um, well I live by a church. Wait, I'll just write my number down and call me, and I'll direct you," I tell him.

I find a pen and receipt in my purse. I write my number on the receipt and hand it over.

"Alright, I'll be calling you Sincere," he smiles again and stuffs the receipt in his pocket.

Holy crap! That boy makes me so nervous. I feel like a virgin bride about to meet her betrothed. I walk back outside. Damn, it's hot out. Mark's standing at the passenger door talking to my mom.

"Here comes Pocahontas now," he teases me.

"Shut up, Mark." I open the trunk to the Beast and put my twelve-pack in. "Mom, put your beer in here. I don't want to get stopped."

She hustles out of the front seat with her box of beer. I stand holding the trunk open for her and dial Frieda's cell with the other hand.

"*Tanksi*, do you know anybody who has any cheese for sale?" I ask her. Tanksi means little sister.

"Um, hold on." I could hear people in the background. I hoped my nephew and niece are okay.

"Ten dollars?" she asks.

"How about six cans of malt?" I ask. (That's nine dollars.)

"How about six cans and four quarter cigs?" Freida barters.

"Okay, better have it, too!" and I hang up.

Mark used up my box of cheese on the cheeseburgers. I would pay for the "golden brick" though. I'm lucky someone had one. The commod gods were watching out for me today.

I pull in the grocery store next. I have to buy dish soap and something for dinner. I buy stuff for pork chili. That should go good with cheese. I also buy dish soap, cat food and laundry soap. I still didn't need to buy toilet paper because of the toilet paper we scored from the parade, but I buy a four-pack anyway. I buy some bologna and bread, chips, and that cheap kool-aid stuff sold in a gallon jug.

I will take that stuff over to James and Wiconi. I know how Frieda is—I wished she would take better care of them. I throw in some Ramen noodles, too.

When I come out, my mom's flirting with the Eggman. Yuck. Eggman is an old white guy. He's about 94-years-old, I swear. He always has a Pall Mall, non-filter stuck in his lips but he never lights it. He sold eggs even back when my grandma was in her heyday, dollar a dozen. But I'll pay the extra 49 cents at the store.

"What about you, girlie?" he says through his cigarette. "Dollar a dozen."

"No," I tell him. "I only cook and eat powdered eggs."

"Farm fresh," he says.

"Last time there was a bloody eye looking thing in the yolk. No, thanks," I tell him. I slam my trunk and get in.

"Impossible," he says.

"Possible," I say and start the car.

My mom laughs and waves.

I cruise on into Pine Ridge. A cop has someone pulled over on the side of the road. I'm glad it's not George. He would surely pull me over. I take a right at the edge of town in Crazy Horse Housing. Our tribe has three main cluster housing projects in town. Snitzy lives in one of these houses with his mom. The dude's like 50-some odd years and still lives with his mom.

What a prize.

I have to yield for every speed bump, child, and dog. Speed bumps were added for the protection of children who are always in the streets. Since the speed bumps were added, the population of dogs increased. So the position of dog catcher was added. How's that for creating jobs...

We pull into Snitzy's house, or his mom's house. He comes out with two shopping bags full of tomatoes. He gives one to me and one to mom. I love tomatoes fresh from the garden. I start thinking what I can make with them.

"Mom sends you guys these. Her garden grew too many this year," he says.

"Good. I'm scoring all kinds of ways today. Eggs from the Eggman. Tomatoes from Auntie," my mom laughs. "Must be my lucky day."

She's getting on my last nerve. She needs to go home now. I hate how she calls her auntie and snags her son. I know they have to be fourth or fifth cousins. Disgusting.

I pull into her trailer and see that Shyla's back.

"Tell Shy to come over later if she wants. Just me and the kids will be home," I tell her as she gets out. I wave to her. Glad to be rid of her and glad Snitzy's out of my car. Phew, he had a stench.

Finally, I pull into the house. I feel like I got a lot accomplished today. I'm proud of myself. I feel finally like I have a future, instead of just passing day by day... merely existing and drinking. I go inside of the house, nobody's home but Sapa. He meows hello and rubs against my leg. Nothing makes him as happy as hearing the crinkle of a shopping bag.

When he sees me pull out a can of cat food, he meows louder and faster. I pop open the can and put it on the floor. "Here you go fat boy." He meows back and starts chowing.

"Did you just call me fat girl, huh?" I nudge him with my foot, but he ignores me. I turn the TV on. I turn it to Sports Center and start putting the groceries away. I call Misun to check on Jasmine.

"Hey bro, how's Jazzy?" I ask as I put stuff in the fridge.

"She's good. She wants to spend the night?" It sounded like a madhouse behind him.

"That's fine." I put the new dish soap bottle by the sink and grab the old one. The old one I added water to so many times to keep diluting it and make it last. It was mostly water. I do that with shampoo, conditioner and laundry soap. It's an old Indian trick. If an Indian woman's worth is making a dollar stretch, then I'm the shit.

"Wiconi and James are here. I was just going to take them home and stop by to get Jazz some clothes," he says.

"Oh shit," I realized I forgot Frieda. "Stop by first. I'll ride with you over there. She has some cheese for me."

"Give me half the cheese," Misun demands.

"How about a quarter of it?"

"Deal. Be there in a few."

I realize he's moving next week. I'm really going to miss him. So is Jasmine. By the time Misun pulls up, I have a little overnight sack for Jasmine packed. I also have the groceries bagged up for Wiconi and James. The beer and cigs are in the car.

"Hi babies," I say to my nephew and niece. I hand them the food.

"Hi auntie," they both say. "Remember, this food is yours. Not any of your mom's friends, just yours."

"OK," they both say.

When we pull in, Frieda's standing at the door with the box of cheese.

"She must not want us to go in," I say. "Bullshit."

Misun puts the car in park and jumps out.

I take her the beer and the four cigs are in my hand.

"I need to use your bathroom," Misun says.

Frieda doesn't say anything. I grab the cheese from her and go in. Frieda's on again-off again punk ass boyfriend, Joe, is there.

"I bought **the kids** some food," I tell her, so Joe's fat ass heard me emphasize kids.

"Why? I'm making soup and bread." She acts offended. It does smell good. Indians will make soup when it's 104 degrees out. I'm a Rez chick, I love my soup. I see her dough rising. I love to eat raw dough. I go in the kitchen to swipe a piece, when I see Misun's ex is sitting in there. I'm so pissed. Every time I see Tiff, I see red. I grab a cup and take a drink of water to calm down.

No wonder Frieda stood in the doorway. I turn and Tiff's looking at me. She looks away real fast.

"You know your girls are moving out of state next week," I tell her.

"Frieda told me." She's looking at the tabletop.

I walk over to her. "My brother does everything he can to give them a good life. I used to feel bad for them because they didn't have a mom. But now, I think it's a blessing. I wouldn't want any of them thinking that women are supposed to act like whores."

She's still looking at the table. Frieda's gone in the bedroom with her kids. I know she doesn't want them to hear what I had to say.

I palm her forehead so her head bounces off the wall. Then I turn and walk out. Misun's coming around the corner.

"Let's go, bro." I cut him off and hustle him out.

When we get in his blazer, he turns to me, "Whadju do?"

"Nothing."

"Lies! You look guilty."

"I bounced Tiff's head off the wall, that's all," I say.

"Oh, OK," he shrugs.

Misun used to chase Tiff when she whored around. He slapped her up once, not as many times as she beat him though. After that, he realized she wasn't going to change. He wasn't going to chase her and he didn't want to be the jealous boyfriend anymore. He was heartbroken for a long time. Now his head and heart are in the right place, but I am sure he is still healing.

Now all these young girls are all over him. I think he slept with most of the ones we worked with, but he doesn't want a relationship yet —all because of his girls. He once told me a woman has to be good enough for not just him, but his girls, also.

I jump out at home. "Hold on, I'll bring your cheese out."

"I'll get it later, just bring her clothes out." First time I see him turn commod cheese down but I bet they have a bunch already. His grandparents always support local schemers.

The twins are inside packing a duffel bag. I go grab a change of Jasmine's clothes and some pajamas. After I come back in, I look at the boys.

"Where the hell do you think you're going?" I ask.

"Dad and Eva are taking us camping," Creighton says. "We'll be back Sunday."

"Camping where?" Nice to know this was planned.

"In the Black Hills." Craig comes running out with a can of OFF!

I want to take it back but I can stay inside. Plus, I only want Eva to buy her own just to be spiteful, but what the hell, I didn't want my own sons to get bit up.

"Well, have fun, I guess..." I'm pouting. I'm going to be home alone.

"With the bugs and the rain and, and, gathering firewood, and don't forget the Blair Witch," I say.

"HA! Mom's jealous," Craig laughs.

"So!" I tell him.

A horn honks outside. I peek out. It's Dave, their dad, my ex. A man I once kicked the crap out of and threatened to pull a Lorena Bobbit on with a corn cob knife. I walk outside with them, only because Eva hates to see me and Dave talk. And I'm evil.

I ask him what campground. He tells me it's the one we camped at when I was pregnant with the twins. Craig asks about it. I tell him it was lightening all night and their dad was scared.

We all laugh. I give the twins hugs and walk away. I turn to wave and Dave is looking at me <u>that</u> <u>way</u>. Whatever. He has such a wondering eye—he must like his women psychotic. If Dave and I had stayed together, like everyone predicted we would've, one of us would be dead or missing teeth.

I walk in the back yard and pick up a little. The lawn has been mowed, so really, there's nothing to do. I wander into my house. I had planned on making pork chili and bread, but I'm home alone.

Maybe I'll call Boogie. Maybe not.

There's nothing wrong with being alone. I remember there's still a couple of cheese burgers Mark made earlier. I grab a beer and jump online. I'll check email and send one to Ricky.

"I have your phone. If I am not here, it's on the stand by the bed charging. – S." I have no idea what else to say. He probably woke up at Lola's—again.

I open Microsoft Word to start my essay. I can't think of anything so I open the beer and pull up a playlist. Dwight Yoakam and Sheryl Crowe start singing, *"Baby Don't Go."* I sip my beer and play Spider Solitaire until I can think of something to write. The song is over, I still didn't write anything. I guzzle the rest of my beer and let the song list continue. *"Santeria"* by Sublime plays.

I walk around the house. Sapa's outside chasing grasshoppers. The sun didn't set yet but began its westward descent. Somebody was mowing their lawn and someone else was having a barbecue. Somewhere, maybe a street over, someone was burning trash. These were all the smells of summer on my reservation.

I grab another beer, pour it in a cup, and go to the front porch. *I wish I had a cigarette,* I think as I sit down. I don't smoke but once in a while I like to smoke just one. I think about everything I did today, all I accomplished. Even though I'm 32, I really do have time to get a degree. I always worked my dead end job because I didn't like the way I was treated earlier. If everyone that tried to get help was treated the way I was treated, what would that do to their spirit?

What makes a person that has to ask for help even want to try to do better, when they are treated so demeaning? How, when someone was not even raised on this reservation, do they know the trials and tribulations one goes through to survive?

I want a cigarette even more. I change to my cut-offs and flip flops because two beers in makes the pants tighter.

"Nam! Wilberta!" I holler over the fence.

Nam appears at the doorway, squinty eyed and scratching his belly. "Yah?"

"Give you two beers for a couple of cigs?" I hold the beers up.

"Yah shit, they're rollies, though, that okay?" He raises an eyebrow. I nod. He pulls a bag of tobacco out of his pocket and starts rolling me a couple of "rollie" cigarettes.

"Where's Wilberta?" I ask. "Passed out." He licks the rolling paper. "She's damn lucky she passed out, too. I'm not in the mood to slap her up."

"Geez, why?" I ask him.

"That bitch act like she was gonna hit me because we ran out of beer."

"Damn." He hands me the two cigarettes, I hand him the beer. I walk back to the house. If this is how an empty nest feels then I definitely need to have more kids.

Maybe.

Maybe not.

My cell phone vibrates in my bra as I walk in the house.

"*Taku*," I say.

"Huh?" It's Mason.

"*Taku* means 'what,'" I tell him.

"Oh, well that's a rude way to answer the phone," he teases me.

"Well, you should have been a Yankee's fan. I'm just teasing. I didn't look at the caller I.D. By the way, speaking of the Yankees..." I say.

"*Taku?*" when he says it, it makes me giggle.

"There is no Yankee game on."

"Huh? I swear there is." He acts innocent.

"I checked the guide. No Yankee game."

"Okay, I'm at the stoplight, which way do I go?" Mason asks.

Oh dear, stoplights! I run in the house and look in the mirror. I spray perfume on and put some lipgloss on.

"North, second right, wait first right," I direct him as I throw the rollie cigarettes down on my dresser.

"OK, how far?" he asks.

I see the headlights coming toward me. I go out the front gate to the driveway.

He says, "There's a cute little Indian girl coming towards me."

"Ha!" I close my phone as he closes his and pulls up. He's smiling at me as we walk towards each other. He gives me a hug. Oh, he gives wonderful hugs.

"What's up, little Indian girl?"

I laugh. "Whatever! Want to sit outside for a while or go in?"

He takes his shades off. He's wearing a Red Sox hat.

"Yuck," I say.

"What?" He plays dumb.

"The hat."

"Isn't it the shit? I have a cousin in Boston. It's really from Fenway," he tells me.

"Whatever! He probably bought it at a convenience store and made you feel good by saying it's from Fenway," I tease him.

"Well, as long as it's from Boston," he says.

We walk in the house anyway. I give him the remote, he starts flipping through the stations.

"You want a beer?" I ask. When he nods I grab a couple of beers from the fridge for both of us.

"You know what?" he laughs. "I thought you had the MLB package. The Cubs are playing though."

"OK. And I wished I got the MLB package. Not available on the rez." I open the beer and take a drink. When he looks at me I automatically suck in my gut. That's an instant reaction for me when I'm amongst cute guys.

He takes a drink, too. His beer gut is adorable, only guys can get away with that.

"Hey, how did your fishing go?" I ask.

"Good. I mean not great, but I got two big catfish. Can I gut them here or not?" He raises his eyebrows.

"Um, outside at the picnic table?" I ask if that's alright with him.

"Shit, we might as well cook them here," he says. "Or not?"

"That's fine, if you want to cook. I don't know how to cook catfish," I tell him.

"Fine, I'll teach you. Hey, I got a six pack of Bud bottles in the truck and some whiskey. I'll bring them in, too, OK?" This time he doesn't say "or not" nor does he ask. It's more of a statement. I kind of like that "take charge" attitude.

I decide the two old cheeseburgers out of the fridge I'll give to Nam and Wilberta. I turn and Mason has his fish in a bucket, a pint of Crown and a six-pack of Bud bottles. He opens the whiskey.

"One shot before we go outside." He takes a guzzle and passes me the bottle.

"No chaser? Damn, boy." I take a shot, make an ugly face and grab a cup to get some water. *Uff.*

"Jesus, that was not smooth, sure that's Crown?"

Mason laughs and takes another shot. "One more," he says.

I listen and take one more shot. Then I grab the cutting board. It's the only thing he requested. We walk to the middle of the yard to the picnic table under the tree. I sit on the table.

Mason stands up and pulls out a hunting knife. I look away. I don't do "blood and guts."

"You have a cooking pit out here?" he asks.

I look at it—it's just a hole in the ground, really. I take a drink of the beer and nod. "Yah, my brother Mark just dug it the other day when we had a cookout."

I don't know where he got the grill part from though. I suspected it was the other piece from my oven. I made a mental note to check the oven. I realized I forgot the burgers for Nam and Wilberta. "I forgot something inside, you want anything?" I ask.

"Music? And where's your woodpile?" He's scaling the fish.

"By that broke-down shed." I point with my lips. I go in, grab the burgers, turn the country playlist on with a speaker out the window, and grab two Bud bottles. I turn off the TV. When I go out, Nam is talking to Mason. They must already know each other.

"Just the guy I wanted to see. Mark made too many burgers earlier." I hand Nam the plate. I hand Mason a bottle of beer. Some Tom Petty is playing, *"You Don't Know How It Feels."*

"You're not going to really cook those out here are you?" I ask.

"Naw, I'll cook them inside, but can we build a fire later, alright?" he asks.

"That should be fine, with all my trees around the house, no one should bother us," I tell him.

"Well I better get back, thanks for the burgers Sis, and Mason, tell your pops I said hi, OK?" Nam takes off to go feed his woman and says, "Thanks for the beer, again."

We both say you're welcome. I look at Mase and laugh, "Did you give him some beer, too?"

He nods, "Yes, ma'am. It was a damaged case I meant to throw out at the dump. A can busted inside so it was almost a full case. He took it home to his wife as soon as I told him."

Mase is pulling the dead catfish innards out and throwing them at my cat. I grab his beer and put it up to his lips. While he takes a drink our eyes meet. Josh Turner's *"Your Man"* is playing and my insides are melting. We hold each other's stare for a few seconds as I pull the bottle away and wipe a drop of beer from his bottom lip. Then I hear the insides of the catfish squish in his hand and come back to reality, and I laugh as I put the beer bottle down. We both laugh.

"Gross, that cat better not think he is going to kiss me up later," I say as I take a drink of my bottle of bud. Damn, it tasted good. Mason is looking at me smiling.

"Can I have a kiss?" He is looking at me still smiling.

I am nervous as hell but I lean over and kiss him gently on the lips and close my eyes. I open my eyes as I pull away and his eyes were open the whole time. We smile at each other.

Finally, I let him finish gutting the fish and we talk. We talk about our childhoods, about what we thought we were going to be when we grew up, opposed to now. We talked about books. I was very happy to learn he liked to read and even read some of the same books as I did. And he read Gibran's The Prophet. I was always too nervous around him to talk this much, but amazingly, we were getting along great.

When he finished we moved inside. He washed up at the sink and asked me for certain ingredients as I pulled them out of cupboards. I didn't even know I had cornmeal, tons of it from commods. I don't get commodities, but I always know people who get too much. As he puts the catfish on to sizzle in the frying pan, I get a bag of salad open so I can slice some tomatoes into it—garden fresh tomatoes.

Mason grabs me around the waist. I immediately suck my gut in. I feel like he is smelling my hair. I am nervous, yet feeling so good.

"Let's do another shot," he says in my ear. I notice he didn't ask.

I turn towards him and he doesn't move away. He grabs the bottle from behind me on the counter and we each take a shot while we are standing real close. We don't say anything just continue to look at each other as Johnny Cash and June Carter sing "*Jackson*" in the background. Finally he goes to flip the fish over and I exhale and turn back to the salad. Wow, I never thought he would be standing in my kitchen, cooking for me. Shit, I should take a pic and send it to Zona. I call his name and aim my phone at him, he smiles while he is cooking.

I type, "Look who is in my kitchen cooking for me!!! Let's see how I repay him!"

After I hit send, I noticed I sent it to Ricky. He is in my phone as Homeboy and Zona is in my phone as Ho. Immediately, I panic. Then I remember I have Ricky's phone. I will just have to remember to erase it later. I excuse myself to go pee, after I am done, I email Ricky again.

"Don't pick up your phone until tomorrow, I am not home. – S"

S is for scandalous, I think as I went to join Mason. He has the light by the table off and about five candles from around the house lit on the table. Along with our plates, two ice cold bottle of beer and a plastic lemon full of lemon juice, for the fish I am presuming. I am also presuming he found that in the fridge since I know he didn't bring it. Embarrassing he saw the inside of the fridge. It was getting bare after the pow wow and having so much company. We don't say a word as we eat. And it is perfect and delicious. I've never had a candlelight dinner and maybe it was just at my kitchen table but it was so perfect. We look at each other while we eat and smile every now and then.

Finally I finish. Almost. But I was full. I push my plate away.

"That was wonderful. So who caught those fish for you?" I smile coyly at him.

"Hey, little girl, this boy can fish," he points at himself as he pulls a paper towel off the rack and hands it to me. He grabs one for himself and wipes his face. We clear the plates off and wash them. But we blow the candles out and leave them and the beer bottles on the table.

"Let's go build that fire." He nods his head towards the backyard. If he was an Indian, he would've pointed with his lips. He grabs two cans of my beer out of the fridge since we drank his six-pack up and his bottle of crown. I grab a blanket off my bed and when I get outside, his fire is very small. My cell phone rings in my bra. He shakes his head at me as I pull it out.

"*Taku*?" I say.

"Sis?"

"Yes?" I answer her.

"Oh, what you doing?" Shyla sounded like she needed a favor. Then I remembered I told our mom to tell her to come over because I would be home alone. Dammit.

"Just visiting a *friend* in the backyard, chillin' by the fire." I emphasize the word friend so maybe she knows it isn't Boogie or Zona.

"Which *friend*?" she asks.

"Chee, nosey. None of your business. Why?" I ask her.

"Because mom said just you and the kids would be home and I wanted to come over and use the internet at your house."

"Yeah, you can. There are no kids here. Boys are camping with their dad, Jasmine is at Misun's. I can't come get you though, I've been drinking," I tell her.

I notice Mason has that fire roaring now.

"OK, well I have a ride. I was just wondering if I can bring a friend over. We can sleep in the twins room and not bother you."

"Who?"

"Chee, nosey. It's none of your business." Shy says, then she answers, "Don't worry, it's not a dude. Just one of my besties."

I was going to ask her how many best friends she has but instead I just let it go and tell her "fine" but they have to stay out of our way.

"You won't even know we are there, for real," Shyla lets out a small giggle of excitement. I don't blame her anyway, for not wanting to be around mom. She probably had a wicked party going.

"That was my sister. She's coming over to use the computer and bringing a friend, but they promised to stay put in that other room," I say looking at him.

I kind of blush then, because I didn't want him to assume that I was hinting that he spend the night or see my room even. Geez, good thing it is dark enough so he can't see me blush. He's wrapped up in the blanket I brought out. Nervy, I was the one in cut offs, and my legs were cold.

I stand by the fire a little bit to warm up, plus I just made myself all nervous and uncomfortable around him again.

"So what is your deal, anyway Sincere?" He asks me and the reflection of the flames dance on his face.

"What do you mean?" I laugh. "Do I have a *deal?*"

"Well, you giggle around and talk shit with me all the time, then when I try to respond, you freeze up and run away. Half the time, I thought you couldn't stand me, then my dad told me what you said to him and that confused the crap out of me. I never got to know you. I feel like I am starting to—now you are standing over by the fire, as if you don't know me. Come here, tell me **who you are?**"

"Wow, who I am. I don't know, a mom, I guess." I walk towards him and see his bottle of Crown. I open it and take a swig. The food must have mellowed me out enough that my confidence from earlier left me. He opens a can of Budweiser for me. We exchange the bottle for the can. He takes a shot and then pulls me into his arms. "I guess I don't really understand the question. No one ever asked me who I was." I snuggle up against him. He has the best hugs.

"Well do you think you will ever leave the reservation? Or do something else?" he asks.

At first I was a little offended. Then I realized he was being honest, not an asshole.

"Truthfully, I never gave much thought to life off the rez. I moved from my mom's house to my first boyfriend's parent's basement when I was still in high school. I thought I was going somewhere then. We ended up moving into his family trailer after high school, having twins, and a horrible relationship. We are friends today but that took work. Then I fell for Jasmine's dad, thinking he was going to take me away from here—well, that went to hell quickly. He is who knows where. I guess if I do leave, maybe I would like to come back to try and make it a better place. My life consists of being here and the border towns. Do you know I have only been through the Black Hills once in my life? One time and it stormed so bad we only camped out two times. Seriously, that is my land and I never got to enjoy it. And I wonder how many people on this reservation are so poor, they never get to enjoy those Hills. Me and my best friend in high school used to dream of moving away to New

York City and working as waitresses while we aspired dreams of being a painter and a dancer." I smile at him.

"You wanted to be a dancer?" he asks.

"No a painter, I used to be good at it. Oil," I tell him. "She wanted to be a dancer."

"What happened to those dreams?" He offers me the whiskey again.

"Life," I tell him, as I take a shot and hand it back. "She married my brother. I started shacking up. Life just happened. What about you, what was your dream again? A race car driver?"

I see Shyla and her friend walk up the driveway. They each have a backpack. I wave at them.

Mason laughs at me. "Well, I wanted to be a racecar driver when I was six. But after I grew up a little and started helping my uncle out with his hobby of fixing cars, I wanted to go to school to be a mechanic. Don't laugh."

"I wasn't going to laugh. So what happened to your dream?" I lean into him. He tightens his arms around my waist.

"Nothing major, just life I guess. I got this girl pregnant in high school, married her. Dad had a heart attack so I started helping with the bar. It was easier, I guess, than leaving the old hometown. I ain't complaining, the bar is good business. I can afford to vacation once a year, anywhere I want to go."

"Where do you go?" I ask, instantly I imagined walking on an exotic beach with him.

He laughs, "Usually to the Black Hills to fish, or other fishing and camping spots. Sometimes I hit up a NASCAR race with a buddy, but most of them are married now. It has been awhile."

There went my exotic beach. I laugh with him. "You married?"

"No, been divorced for four years. She moved to California, my son comes to spend summers with us. I never had any more kids. I never really had another serious relationship. Just kind of played the field."

Like me, I thought. I didn't want him to know that, though. Exactly how much I played the field. Most guys are offended by girls who choose that lifestyle.

He takes a drink of the whiskey, then gives me the bottle. It's almost empty—this is probably our second to last round of shots.

"I still work on cars, as a hobby. I have a few cars. But I am usually so busy with the restaurant, and I am the only one here. All my brothers and sisters moved away from Po Dunk. I'm the dumb one who stayed."

"Don't say that, maybe your heart was the only one in the right place. Besides, Po Dunk isn't so bad, around the holidays Christmas music plays, and I have no idea where from," I tell him.

He throws his head back and laughs, "You are too cute, Sincere. Dance with me."

I kind of like how he states his questions. He isn't asking me. The next song that plays is *"I just got started loving you"* by James Otto.

"Perfect," he whispers.

I have my head on his chest, his arms are around my waist, and my arms are around his neck. I turn my head sideways and smell him. I close my eyes and use my senses to remember this moment. I hear the song, the crackling of the fire. I smell the wood smoke and his cologne. I feel the sway of us dancing, the warmth of the blanket, and the security of his arms. *This had to be one of the best moments of my life*, I think.

Damn close, anyways.

The song ends and I hear a car take off out front. Mason hands me the whiskey bottle. We drink the last shots. I need to pee and see if my sister left.

"I have to go in for a minute, check on my sister," I tell him. He gives me the empty beer cans and whiskey bottle. I am so thankful he did that and didn't assume he could just throw them on the ground because this is the reservation. *Yes!* I think to myself as I walk away.

I walk in and open the door to the boys' room. Shyla is leaning on her friend. I do a double take because I thought it was a boy but I saw her boobs. Shy jumps.

"Sorry, I heard a car and thought you left," I tell her.

Her face is beet red. "No, that was your friend, that one dude."

I raise one eyebrow at her. "Ricky? I told him you was out back with your boyfriend."

"Holy fuck, that isn't my boyfriend!" I tell her. "What did Ricky say?"

"Well, I assumed he was because you guys were kissing and hugging when I pulled up. Ricky looked out the window. Started cussing, grabbed his phone from your room and left."

"What song was playing when he looked out?" I ask her. My heart was beating as if I was a straight up hooch. I know I did nothing wrong. I am almost sure of it. I mean it was a kiss and a dance. Maybe we were kind of grinding on each other but nobody could see through that blanket.

"That one by James Otto," she says and starts ignoring me.

"Did he say anything else?" I ask.

"He just asked who that dude was. I told him some white guy that I didn't know." She was so involved in whatever they were doing she has no idea that she just snitched on me.

Being with Mason was so comfortable. Ricky didn't even cross my mind, except when I accidentally sent him the picture of Mason. Shit, it was the picture I didn't get to delete. Fuck. Well, he didn't see us kiss. And officially I didn't do anything wrong. I mean, he left me to take off with Lola yesterday. Officially, I was still in the clear, the dance was innocent.

I grab two more beers and go back outside. Mason is walking back from the shed. I guess he peed, too. He is folding the blanket up and I feel kind of sad. He must be going home. Next he uses dirt to put the fire out. I kind of get in pout mode but remember, I have no reason to be pouting. For Pete's sake I was supposed to be with Ricky.

"Let's go," he says.

I follow him but instead of turning towards his truck, he goes in the back door.

"I thought you were going home?" I asked him.

"Sincere, would you let me drive after drinking that whiskey?"

I shake my head. He grabs the beers and puts them back in the fridge. Then he pulls me into his arms again and kisses me better than before.

Fireworks.

And we kiss.

But kissing doesn't make me a whore, nor does it mean I have done Ricky wrong, well maybe a little wrong, but not that bad.

After a couple minutes we break apart.

"I am on the rez, kissing Sincere," he smiles at me.

"I am finally kissing Mase," I say.

I grab his hand and lead him to my room.

Now, I have officially crossed that line.

If I am not a whore, I am a bad, bad person.

[eight]

Thursday

I wake up Thursday morning to a note on my night stand.
"Today's delivery day, had to meet the beer trucks early.
Call me, let's do something later. – Mase"

And then he drew a heart by his name. I smile and get up. I stretch and smile at last night's memory.

Shyla must have stayed up all night. The door is closed in the other bedroom. I use the bathroom, splash water on my face and walk into the kitchen. There's another note.

"Coffee ready to go, just turn it on – M"

This guy! And he drew another heart. My heart was skipping a beat. Well, it always does around him, but he was in my house! He cooked for me! Kissed me! Danced with me! We had awesome sex!

How sweet. I turn on the coffee maker and ignore the shake in my hand. The coffeemaker groans. I have to try to stay sober today. Just for me and my promise to myself to turn my life around. I call Dave's cell phone. Eva answers.

"Are the boys up?" I ask.

"No, I mean yah. They went fishing." Then she hangs up.

Bitch. I think. Then I backtrack. *No, she isn't being a bitch.* She is camping with a bunch of dudes. She is busy cooking and washing dishes by hand. I need to quit being negative. It is an evil trap to allow yourself to hate people, and she probably did hate me but I am going to make it a point to quit making her jealous just because.

It's not like Dave and I would ever get back together anyway. I call Misun.

"Sister, I was just going to call you!"

"Really? Well, you know my psychic powers."

I tease him as I pour a cup of black coffee.

"Well anyway, Sarah, that young chick is borrowing her mom's van. We're going to go to Augustora Dam and Cascades. Want to go?" He sounds happy. I should lay off on that Sarah chick, too, while I am in this new mindset. Besides, two more weeks and he's gone. I still can't imagine him moving away.

"No, I'm good. I have too much to do."

I feed Sapa some dry cat food to his dismay. Fatboy has no choice, canned food and fish guts were a treat.

"What you going to do? You ain't got a job anymore?" In the background, I could hear one of the girls ask if he put M&M's in the pancakes. He spoils his girls so much—they better find men that praise them.

"I know, but I still need to make money." I look hopelessly at my beads and quills in the hutch. I know it's impossible with my shaking. I need to detox.

"Hooker," he laughs.

"Shit! Whatever! That's your ex!" I say. I sit at the table and see the candles Mason gathered from around the house on the table still. I smile.

"No hookers make money. That bitch gives it away," he laughs.

"No shit. Anyway, just call me on your way back. If Jazz needs something, tell her or you know where the key is. If I'm not here."

We chat a little more and say our byes. I feel almost as if he's the only normal one in the family. Then I wonder if I'm normal to him. Ha!

I have twelve dollars left from yesterday. Groceries are way expensive on the reservation. They know almost everyone and their mama get EBT so they price gouge even more on EBT day. Right now I don't need groceries. I still have everything to make pork chili, which I will probably make Sunday when the twins get back, or maybe tomorrow.

I jump in my car to go to White Clay. I can't fool myself. I need a beer. I grab my keys and jump in the Beast. As I drive through my hometown, I notice a new sign going up. "HOPE RECOVERY CENTER." I dial the number on the sign. A lady answers.

I ask her when they're open and what services they offer. She tells me inpatient–outpatient treatment and as soon as they find facilitators. AA meetings and NA meetings. I ask how one signs up for treatment. She tells me to write an essay no less than 250 words as to why I want to go to treatment and come in first thing Monday morning to complete and alcohol and drug evaluation.

She tells me, "Congratulations for choosing sobriety," and I hang up. Now I feel guilty I keep on going south towards Whiteclay.

Oh well, this means I have the weekend to detox. I had all week to drink. This is the last time today. Honest. And another essay.

This is like killing three birds—one stone. Soon I'll have killed a whole flock. I will just have to find a way to convince them why I need to change. Now for sure I have to get on that essay. I cruise south to White Clay and notice I need some gas. $6 for gas and $6 for four big cans of Malt.

Halfway to Whiteclay, there's the cops by the dump and BIA (Bureau of Indian Affairs) Criminal Investigators. If the BIA cops hadn't been there, I would've been scared to drive through but they're all busy. Seeing that many tribal and federal cops in one place means one thing—a dead body.

I drive on by. It should be safe to buy beer and drive back. As I drive through town, there are people standing in groups all over, probably gossiping about what happened. I'm sure I'll hear it. I pull up to the pump at Last Bar and tell the guy out front to put in $5.00.

Mark hits my passenger window and I scream.

"Sis!" he says when I reach and open the door for him.

I hand him the money. "$5.00 gas, four big cans of Old E, and sunflower seeds," I bark at him before he gossips.

Before he comes back out, two guys already told me the story. Hit and run, happened sometime early in the morning by a white guy. He ran over someone that was released from jail. Since we have a brand new jail on the reservation, people have to walk the two miles it is into town at all hours. None have been killed as of yet though—well, until today. All of a sudden, I got a funny feeling. Key words: *white guy, this morning.* Shit.

Mark comes back to the car, "Let me go with you."

I look at my four beers and scowl. "Geez, fuck! OK! This is all I got though."

"Don't worry Sister, where there's a will there's a way," he says.

"That's only when it's a will to drink. I swear on one thing, the easiest thing to do here is drink! I get sick of it," I tell him.

"If you're sick of it, why do you do it?" Mark asks. "Why did you buy those four beers?"

We drive by the apparent crime scene. I spit my sunflower seeds out my window.

"What makes you sick will make you better," I tell him.

Mark about breaks his head watching the cops.

"Quit!" I yell at him. "You look all suspect."

"Just trying to see if I can see anything," he sulks. "Can I open a beer?"

I nod at him. "I'll take a cruise. Let's kill it before we get home. I'm too sick," I tell him.

"So what do you think about that white guy killing a skin?" He snaps the can.

"I don't know," I say. "Could just be a rumor for all we know."

I still have that funny feeling in my tummy. I have to call Mason when I get home. take a cruise out towards Slim Buttes, which is west of town. We pass the beer back and forth for a bit.

"Do you know who Chief American Horse is?" Mark asks.

"I think I may have seen a black and white picture of him on someone's wall somewhere," I tell him as I spit seeds.

"He died out here. They killed his whole tiospaye. His whole family," he tells me. He isn't even all dramatic about it like he usually is. He is very somber.

"Who did?" I ask him. I pull into an approach on the side of the road. I take a drink of the beer and look at him.

"The government," Mark says.

"Why?" I ask. I feel a story coming.

"Because he had that flag," Mark said matter-of-factly, like I was supposed to know.

I sigh, "OK what flag? I'm not going to guess."

"The 7th Calvary flag. The one they took from the Battle of Greasy Grass or as white people call it The Battle of Little Bighorn or as Custer calls it, they-can-kiss-my-white-ass-bye-battle." Then he laughs so hard he coughs. I smile and hand him the beer.

"So this American Horse guy..."

"Chief!" He barks.

"OK, so Chief American Horse and his *whole* family were killed because of that flag?" I ask him again.

"Uh-huh," he nods, "Over that way." He points to the northwest with his lips.

"Don't point with your lips, it's not nice," I tell him.

"You do it, too, Sis! It's an Indian thang. So shush," he says.

I don't admit or deny it.

"So what happened to the flag?" I ask.

He shrugs. "I don't know. It might be at the Smithsonian. See, the government needed that flag back. A Calvary isn't supposed to exist once it's defeated and has no flag. That's why they massacred all those people out at Wounded Knee. The government wasn't worried about no ghost dance, it was revenge for Greasy Grass. The bastards couldn't stand that they were out-strategized and whipped. So they killed all those women, babies, men, and elders. But yah, that 7th Calvary shouldn't exist, man."

I look at him for a minute after he's done telling me this. I think I make him nervous.

"How come I don't know this? I'm older than you? Where did you learn this?" I ask.

"From books! From people! I'm not just a drunk Sis, I think!" he tells me, taking a drink of the beer.

"I know but—I never knew the history. I'm older than you." I'm kind of pouting at myself. "What people?" I ask him.

"Mostly the elders I drink with. They learned from their elders. One lady, I know her grandma was shot. She was like 10-12 years old. She came down with Chief Spotted Elk's people. Most everyone knows him by Chief Big Foot, the guy in the snowbank frozen? Anyway, this little girl got shot running away but she had a bullet in her leg for all of her life. This lady said her grandma would always show them, and tell them in Lakota, '*Remember this is what the government did to me? And they killed my family.*' See Sis, this is where this comes from," as he holds up the beer can.

"The government did us so wrong, they screwed our people over for years. Putting them on reservations, breaking treaties, putting kids in Catholic schools only to physically, mentally, and emotionally abuse them. Not to mention the sexual abuse, just to mess them up even more, they just screwed us, literally. Then gave us blankets with small pox, foods rations that our bodies can't handle, like the commods now all processed and we wonder why diabetes is rampant. We went from a diet of buffalo meat, berries, timpsilas, whatever, to a diet of bleached flour and what not. Our bodies still haven't adjusted—generations later. They screwed us—we drink. That's why it's hard to be sober and drug free. Too much anger in us. Historical trauma, it's called. Sometimes, I wonder if that anger is embedded in our DNA. That's why so many kolas are locked up. Who knows? Then again could just be they're locked up cuz us Lakotas are some crazy motherfuckers." Mark looks out the window.

I laugh and hand him the beer back. He starts in again. "Take Uncle Shayne, when he was locked up, he was in the penn with some Seminole skin from Florida. Uncle Shayne said these guys, black guys, are all impressed because he's from the people that whipped Custer. They're all impressed that our tribe whipped the government's ass here in America. So this Seminole skin says, 'That ain't shit, my people, we so badass, we are still officially at war with America.' So Uncle Shayne asks, 'What war? Where is it being fought?' The dude says 'Well, we're not fighting it, it's on paper. We haven't signed it and sold out.' So Uncle Shayne calls him a pussy ass Indian. Told him if they're so bad ass, because they think not signing a paper is a war, might as well end it and sign it. Save face, because that's not war. Then Uncle blasts him and kicks the shit out of him. The whole time hollering, 'Remember me, I'm Oglala Lakota!' He got locked up in the hole for 60 days for that. See, that's the kind of crazy ass anger we have. We don't need to be drinking to be crazy, but at the same time we suffer. What to do, enit?"

"What does "suffer" mean to you, Mark?" I ask. I think this is good material for my essay.

"Suffer—is when something is taken away from you. You can see it, know it was once yours and can be yours, but you suffer because it's not."

I nod and start up the car. He takes the last drink as we head back to town. When we pull into my driveway, my mom's screaming so loud in my house, I look to make sure the neighborhood isn't watching.

When I walk or run in behind Mark, mom's sobbing, standing in the kitchen. Shyla's standing in the living room.

Both of their hair is all over. Shyla has a scratched face and mom's nose is bleeding.

"Jesus Christ!" What the fuck?!" I ask.

"It's her!" They both scream and point at each other.

"She's a narrow-minded bitch!" Shyla says.

"Don't call my mom a bitch!" Mark tells her.

"She's a dyke, a dirty dyke!" Mom hollers and points at Shyla. She has a hickey that wasn't there last night.

"Hey, don't call my sister a – a what?!" Mark says.

I almost laugh.

Mark turns and looks at her, "You a dyke?"

Shy glares at him, "I don't like that word but yes, OK. I'm a dyke. I'm a lesbian. I'm gay. I like girls."

"Fucking disgusting," Mom spits.

"Mom...shh," I say. I don't know how to handle this situation. I'm in shock.

"Call the cops!" Mom says.

I kind of giggle, despite the situation.

"And tell them what—your daughter's gay?" Mark asks.

Shyla's too mad to think it's funny, "Yeah and tell them her son's in the closet."

"Now, now, we're talking about you, Shy. And no one's calling the cops. Don't get testy," Mark says. "Let me take Mom outside for a minute."

He puts his arm around her and leads her out. I'm staring at him as he walks out. It all adds up. Why he has one kid, why he don't or won't marry Arlene, why he is so articulate. My brother was gay that whole time, and my sister, too! Jesus, my head must be in the sand. I'm the oldest sister. I'm supposed to know these things. And I was bitching about having no gays in our immediate family. Now the gay floodgates have opened.

Shyla's friend *or girlfriend*, I guess, kisses her. I'm not sure I'm comfortable with that *yet*. I look away.

"We're going to go," Shyla said. "Let Mom cry it out, she can't change me."

"How long have you known?" I ask.

"All my life," Shy says.

After she combs her hair and washes her face, someone in a white car picks them up.

Drama, I swear, right when I don't want it. And I woke up with the intention of staying sober. There's one intention that did a quick 180, I think, as I walk to the car to get the other three beers. I see that my "brand new gay" brother has grabbed them already. I'm not mad at him for being *like that* but I'm hurt that he never told me.

I walk up, they each opened a can. Nervy.

"Here," Mark says. "Take one for yourself."

"How nice of you!" I said sarcastically.

"Why not share? Three beers—three of us. Makes sense," he shrugs.

"Yeah," I say. "I wouldn't want to catch anything from anyone... like being gay. Seems to be spreading like wildfire," I say as I tap my can.

Where did my enthusiasm for being super positive go? Now I am taking it out on Mark.

He avoids my eye contact. I don't blame him.

"Mom has money, she'll buy you more. Won't you ol' girl?" He pats her back and she nods and sniffles. I want to tell her to get over it.

"Soon as I finish this, we'll go. I need to calm down. Christ, no more drama today. I hope," I snap my can and take a drink.

"Hey Sister," Mark says.

"*Taku?*"

"How come Indians don't kiss?"

I shrug as I take a drink of my beer.

"Because when the guy goes to kiss his ol' lady, she looks behind her and says, 'who you pointing at?'"

I laugh and spit beer.

"That's you." I point my lips at him.

He rolls his eyes.

We continue to drink the beers by the clothesline. I need to go inside and pee. I grab my phone off the counter, my purse and for some reason I look in the fridge. Oh yeah, me and Mase didn't hardly even touch my twelve-pack. I pull it out and count, I have eight cold beers.

"Ready to roll, mama?"

She nods.

We get in the Beast to go. I make Mark drive, not to be mean or selfish, but in case we get stopped, I don't want a D.U.I. OK, that is mean and selfish. My cell phone rings. It's Boogie.

"Where you at?" What you doing?" he asks.

"In the Beast, going to Clay," I tell him.

"No, Rushville!" my mom says.

"Rushville?" Mark and I both look at her.

She shows us a hundred dollar bill.

"Rushville," I say.

"Who has money?" Boogie asks.

"My mom," I tell him.

"How much?" he asks. I look at her in the back seat.

"Guess," I tell Boogie.

"Fifty?"

"More." I don't want her to know we're talking about her.

"Hundred?" Boogie sounds anxious.

"Yup." I don't think she caught on.

"I have twenty, can I come?" he asks.

"Hold on," I cover the phone. "Shall we get Boogie?"

My mom nods. She's acting too much like a drama queen. As if Shyla said she was knocked up or something and she's traumatized.

"We'll be right there." I hang up the phone.

Mark whips it and does a U-turn." A siren goes off and lights flash. We instantly all freeze as he stops the car.

"Fuck," he says.

It's George. Hopefully he isn't after me, that bitch.

"Jesus Christ! What!" Mark hollers at him.

"Shit, calm down." George laughs. "Sup Sis?"

I give him the peace sign.

"Do you know where Uncle Shayne is? Or have you see Two Times?" George asks us.

"No, man," Mark says and puts his seat belt on. A little too late for that.

"Hey mom," George peeks in the back.

"Don't bother her, she's had an ordeal," Mark tells him. "Put your seat belts on in front of the cop, you guys," Mark sings songs.

I don't know if Mark is acting gayer or if it's my mind playing tricks on me. *Didn't I ever notice this?*

"Why, what's wrong with mom?" George questioned.

"Shyla's gay." Mark says as he turns up Carly Simon's *"You're so Vain."*

I decide my mind's not playing tricks on me, he *is* acting gayer.

"Little Shyla? Gay?" George says. "I don't believe it."

"Well, don't. I don't have time, we're going to Rushville then we'll be at Sister's," Mark said. "Don't be mean to us, OK, we have to take care of mom right now. But we love you bro."

He pulls out and goes towards Boogie's. Mark pulls up and hits the horn. It doesn't work. Sometimes it does, sometimes it doesn't. A horn on the rez is a vital part of the car. You're basically screwed if you don't have a horn. Since no one knocks, a horn is how you call someone out of their house. Seems rude, but that's how it is on the Rez. Plus, with dogs and crusty kids running wild in the streets, you need a horn to herd them out of the way. It's like a third world country minus the chickens and cattle roaming the streets, too. They would've been soup. I guess that's why there is none. I get out and knock on the door.

Boogie's grandma opens it. "What do you want, a dimer?" she hollers.

"Hey! Shh!" Boogie's grandpa leads her away.

"Let's go," Boogie runs up the steps.

I'm still laughing. "Wait, your grandma is getting me a dime-bag," I laugh again.

"Shit," he pushes me out the door.

We jump in. We only stop to gas up again, and Burt gives me that look. I do not reciprocate. My mom must want liquor so we are planning a trip to Rushville. Cripes, you would think something was wrong with Shyla. It's not as if mom doesn't have gay friends. I mean, she loves Boogie. Boogie's in the back with my mom. They talk. Mark drives and I doze off. When I wake up we're at the 7-mile turn. I look in the mirror at myself. Jesus Christ on a cross! I look in my purse. I only brought eye liner, powder concealer and lip gloss, so I put it on and hand comb my hair. Finally I take it out of the bun it is in, it's still wet. I decide to try to wear my hair down more often. Like my mom told me to.

"Let's go to the bar!" Boogie says.

I shake my head no. I wanted to call Mase since I heard about the accident. (White guy—hit and run, the words keep going through my head) But my rez phone don't work in Nebraska.

We pull into Dad's Bar and Grill, it's the only place open until 5 p.m., then the other two bars open.

I can smell the skillet as soon as we walk in. White people are sitting at the tables finishing their lunches. They all look up to see who came in. Mark puffs out his chest.

"Damn *wasicus* have to stare. Raised on cow's milk, so they stand around and stare like cows," Mark says.

Mark's one of those types that will find racism in a can of corn. I know it exists but if you look hard enough, you'll find it. I know these people look up every time that door opens so I don't see racism. However, should one of these hayseeds pause in the middle of their Thursday Special of the two-piece chicken meal and stare, then yeah, that is rude. And if you get caught staring... stop.

I feel someone staring at me just because I'm having these thoughts. I look towards the kitchen at the back of the bar. It's Mason at a table. I smile and he smiles. He's busy clearing tables.

"Behave Pocahontas!" Mark nudges me.

I turn to Boogie. "Did you know Mark's in the closet?" I want him to get off the subject of teasing me about a white guy.

"Whatever," Boogie says. "He busted the doors on that down years ago."

They both laugh. My eyes grow wide. Where have I been?

"Oh shit. Don't tell me you two..." I start.

Mark hits me, "We're gay and related, not hillbillies. By the way, Shyla's gay, too," Mark tells Boogie.

"Old news," Boogie dismissed with a wave of his hand. I think he's bullshitting.

"How did you know?" I ask him.

"She asked me about it when she was fourteen. How it felt to come out and just general advice..." He tells us, looking around the room for someone to serve us drinks. Mason's at the till, his dad, Shorty, is flipping burgers and his mom, Barb, is gossiping at another table. It's fine with me mom's in the restroom and she's paying.

"And she asked you because you're a lesbian?" Mark teases Boogie, who snaps his eyes at Mark. I laugh.

Finally, Mason comes to our table. He tousles my hair. "Did I leave my watch on your night stand?" he asks all innocently. He's chewing gum and melting my heart at the same time.

Mark and Boogie look at me, but they don't say anything. They make me nervous and they make me wish he was an Indian.

"I-I-I don't know. I'll look when I get back," I stammer.

"No biggie," he says. "I'll probably be down this weekend to get it. Maybe even tonight. You guys want something to drink?" Mason hands us menus.

"A pitcher please?" Mark says, "and four glasses."

When Mason walks away, I blush.

"And I was supposedly keeping secrets, Pocahontas," Mark smirks at me.

"No, it's not like that," I start to say.

"Lies," Mark exclaims.

It's my turn to stare at white people. "OK then. It is like that, but so what?" I finally say. I can't deny it.

"He's white, that's what," Marks tells me.

"What about Rick?" Boogie asks. Mark raises his eyebrows. They are both anxious to hear about my life. Man, they need to get laid.

"I don't know. I don't know anything, OK? I just know that I'm happy, OK? Sssh," I point with my lips because he's coming back with our pitcher.

"Tab?" Mason asks.

"Yes," my mom says. She reaches in her "Indian purse," her bra and pulls out the hundred dollar bill. "Just hang onto this until we're done."

I wonder who she robbed. I thought she broke it. Boogie must have put in the gas and bought the beers in Clay. When Mason walks away, I think that I'm going to marry him and work here. I'll be gossiping and waiting tables and...

"Sis!" Boogie says.

"Huh?" I say. He startles me.

"I said what about Rick? Wasn't you on cloud nine over him the other day? What's this? Cloud two?"

My mom's talking to Mark but his nosy ass is listening to Boogie and me while nodding at her. *Fake sympathizer, that's what he is.*

"Well, maybe this is cloud two, Boog. I don't know. Nothing's written in stone with him," I point my lips at Mason. "Ricky involves a lot of baby mama drama. I'm not up for that."

"Bow to the white man," Mark mutters under his breath. I flip him off.

"I think Mason's gay," Boogie says all <u>queer-like</u>.

I scowl at him, "Shut the hell up! You wish! Not everyone's gay, Boogie."

"No, just a good third of your family," Boogie said flippantly like a little bitch.

"Mom, buy us shots?" I ask her sweetly while I kick Boogie under the table.

"Only if it's tequila," she says.

"Ugh, god, no," I groan.

"Shut up. Beggars can't be choosers," Boogie says and kicks me back.

"Mase!" I yell.

When he gets to our table, my mom orders an appetizer sampler platter and a round of Jose shots. Mason raises an eyebrow at me, and I shake my head. Last time I drank tequila, I told his dad I loved his son.

He brings back four shots, we do them real quick and then everyone splits up. I am thankful my shot was whiskey and not tequila. My mom goes to get quarters for the juke box. Boogie and Mark go to play pool. Mason sits to talk to me.

"So how you feeling?" I ask.

"I'm OK. I swear I was still buzzed. I snuck a couple of red beers earlier. I'm good now." He smiles at me and leans back in the chair drumming his fingers on the table. "So Sincere, how are *you* feeling? Are you sore?"

My eyes got big—I'm in the middle of drinking my beer. I want to choke. I could feel the blush rising in my cheeks. As if I'm a virgin... what the hell? My hips and legs are a little sore, but AZZIF I would admit that.

"Aww, did I embarrass you?" he teases.

"No," I look at my mom. She plays some Alan Jackson, *"Too much of a good thing is a good thing."* What an appropriate song for the moment.

"How was your trip back?" I ask him.

"I came back through Gordon, I had to pick up a delivery for my mom, remember?" he says.

I sigh with relief.

He smiles again, "What?"

"Nothing."

"Did you think I killed that person?" he asks. "I heard about it."

"No," I tell him, even though I did. *Even though I stressed about it all morning.*

"I wouldn't do that, Sincere," he's looking at me, but I can't look up.

"I know," I say and look at the table. "Thanks for putting Crown in my shot glass. I can't handle tequila," I nod.

"You're welcome. How long you guys here?" he asks me.

I shrug my shoulders. "It's kind of up to them." I point at Boogie, Mark, and my mom with... my pointer finger. Something I hadn't done in years. It seemed rude to point. It is. Now I know why we Indians point with our lips! What a revelation!

Calm down, keep your silly thoughts to yourself. Act cool. I think.

His mom and dad are going out the door. He waves at them and his dad winks at us—embarrassing.

"Do a shot with me, Sincere?" He gives me a slow smile, his perfect smile. His dimples.

"With that smile, OK. Has to be whiskey. Don't ever pour me a tequila shot in your life," I tease him as I jump off the bar stool and we walk to the bar.

"Yes ma'am." He goes behind the bar and pours us each a shot. After we do the shot, he pours another pitcher for me to take to my mom and everyone, on the house.

"Here," I put the pitcher down. "On the house, he said."

"Hell, if it's like that tell him he can have you," Boogie says just to make them all laugh. Nice to know all these hostile Indians are so quick to sell me out like that. I thump Boogie in the back of the head.

I go back to the bar to sit down. There are a couple of other customers that came in. I have my glass of beer while Mason laughs, jokes, and gossips with them.

The bell rings on the glass door. An old man with a walker comes in. It takes him about three minutes flat to get to the bar. After he settles himself by me, Mason comes over.

"Wheat beer, Glen?" he asks.

"Yeah, yeah, yeah. You know the deal. Every day I come in here for the same damn thing. One wheat beer. One." He holds his bony finger up. "And this young yay hoo has to ask me every day if that's what I want. You tell me whose mind is slipping, eh?"

He's asking me. Oh dear and I thought he was just rumbling.

"My mind is slipping, Glen," Mason walks over to him with his wheat beer.

"Did you hear about that hit and run on the reservation today?" Glen says.

My ears perk up, "Yeah, what of it?" Mason hands me a bottle of Bud. He leans on the counter with his elbows.

"They found out who it was that did it, or his wife turned him in—it was the Undertaker's boy, you know they live on the back road between Chadron and Pine Ridge. Seaver. That's his name."

"Vern?" Mason questions.

"Yeah, yeah, it was him. Killed a homeless guy, I guess. Went home. Wife turned him in, blood all over the grill," he says.

Now I get that heavy feeling in my stomach again as I think of Zona. I wondered where she was. I get up to pee. "Be right back."

I go tell Boogie what I just heard. "I hope she wasn't with him. That girl—men will be her downfall."

"Men will be everyone's downfall, except Shyla's," my mom says.

Pointing With Lips

I walk away. She's still playing out her shock and shame. I fix my hair and make-up in the bathroom—which means I wiped any smudgy part of eyeliner under my eyes, put on lip-gloss, and patted my hair down with water. I guess I'm not as high maintenance as I want to be. By the time I walk out, the other customers have left except for my people and Glen.

"Hey, Pocahontas!" Mark yells. "One more shot, then we're casing up and going."

Ayez, I didn't want to go.

"Okay," I walk over to Mason. "Pour three tequilas and one Crown Royal, again."

"My dad just called. He wants me to work for him tonight. So I guess I'll come get you tomorrow. We'll go to the movies or something, huh?" He hands over the three shots. I take them over to the table.

"Hold on. I'll go get the lemons," I tell them. Boogie makes a crack about me being employee of the month to make them all laugh.

I pretend I'm doing a shot of tequila with the lemon and salt but its whiskey. What they don't know won't hurt them. The door opens. We all turn our heads as if we are the white people they all had a problem with a half hour ago for turning their heads. And it's Ricky. And he's drunk, you could tell by his appearance.

"Oh fuck," I say.

"Uh-Oh," Boogie and Mark say together.

"Go take him outside, Mark. Hurry, you owe me," I whisper.

"Leave him, I'm bored. I need drama," Boogie says.

I push Mark, "Now."

Marks walks over to Ricky.

Ricky looks all wild around the bar. His eyes still adjusting from the brightness outside. Mark walks him outside.

I walk over to Mason who's cleaning glasses behind the bar. I hear the bell as my mom, Boogie and Glen walk out.

"Was that your man?" Mase asks me.

"No," I say, then, "kind of or he wanted to be, but he has a girlfriend. He's been my friend for about twenty years."

He's wiping his hand on a towel hanging from his pocket.

"I can't explain, without making me sound bad. He was or is my best friend. We're always there for each other, but we decided to try to be more than friends... like a few days ago. During Oglala Nation Fair. To me, it's not the same. I mean, I used to be all there for him, wait for him, then he would get back with Lola, his woman. He acted like we wasn't even friends. Now I think, you know, it's better if we're friends! It's almost like too much effort is put into trying to be a *couple*, like *romantically*. We're better friends. And truthfully, he's probably going to get back together with Lola, or I think he did the other night. I don't know, you don't have to believe me, but I hope you do. So there," I exhale.

"You're cute, all you had to say was no."

I smile at him.

"Well I guess I need to go get rid of him and go home. I'll call you?" I ask.

"Sure, anytime. I'll be down probably tomorrow." He was standing with his hands behind his head. Then I tiptoe and kiss him. It was supposed to be just a peck, but it turned into a toe curler. A kiss that made fireworks go off and it wasn't even the Fourth of July.

I haven't been involved in many great romances in my life. I mean they were more measured in high speed car chases, bruises and broken hearts. But if a man kissing you involves toes curling and fireworks, I think it's worth hanging on, right?

Well I was thinking so as I walk out with a smile on my face. I drop the smile when I see Ricky standing with Mark and Boogie. Shit.

I honestly don't mean to be scandalous. Scandal just follows me, sometimes. I walk over to the three amigos.

"Get away, Sis! I can't deal with you right now. Just get the fuck away." Ricky's passing a jug around with Mark and Boogie. I hear either Boogie or Mark mutter something about sellout and traitor. God, what racists. I go stand by my mom. I am not about to try to deal with all three of them. I look in the bar and see Mason smiling at me. So now I know they all saw my toe curling kiss. Oops.

"They want to go to Gordon to the bar, and I want to go back to Pine Ridge," Mom says it like she's pissed.

"Let them go. Ricky always has money," I tell her.

"Then who's driving us?" she asked.

"I will," I tell her. I wasn't sure about that, but if Mark and Boogie wanted to bail with Ricky and make me the villain then fuck them. I will get us home on the back roads.

Mom goes over to talk to them. I see her give Mark a twenty. I know how they are—they were going to sympathize with Ricky and make him buy drinks.

I really, really felt bad. I honestly have to believe that this never would've worked out. How many times before did he go back to Lola? Besides, I could still be mad about Lola breaking my Uncles' back window. I try to find reason to justify myself.

They leave down the road. Ricky flips me off and I smile and wave. I can play this part. I have always been there for him, through every relationship he has ever had. All of a sudden he wants **me** to be one of the women he screws over.

My mom's sitting in the car, sipping beer out of a big plastic cup. I look in at her, "Be right out, okay?"

She sighs. She has her AIM shades on again. She fake sniffles. I don't know how long I can put up with this drama queen act either, but oh, well.

I run back in. Mase is sitting at the bar with a remote in his hand, flipping channels. He smiles at me lazily. I am sure he watched everything that went down. I was embarrassed but he seemed to understand—or at least tried to.

"Can you call me in 20-30 minutes, when my phone gets service?" I ask him.

"Why, what's up?" He looks at me.

"Um, Boogie and Mark took Ricky to Gordon to the bar. I have to drive me and my mom back," I tell him.

Mase tries to convince me to wait until closing but there is no way I can put up with my mom that long.

"Yeah, I suppose I can call you," he walks me to the door. This time it's just a peck, not a toe curler. But the hug, the hug is warm and promising like all his other hugs.

I get in the car. I'm nervous, because I'm so buzzed. My mom has me stop at the liquor store. I go in with her. She gets a case of beer and a half a gallon of whiskey. Whew. Afterwards we go across to the convenience store and she buys a large soda and pays for gas. I pump the gas and tell her I'm taking the back roads back into town. She shrugs and agrees. I hope she's not brooding over Shyla still because I will get pissed. There are many other things Shyla could be doing.

I turn north of town on a dirt road. Waylon Jennings was playing.

"Mom," I say.

She's making a mix. "What?"

"Don't be mad at Shyla, please?" I plead with her. We pass through corn fields. She finishes making her drink and takes a sip.

"I'm getting over it, Sincere. I just thought she would be normal." She hands me the drink.

"What's normal?" I ask. "I'm not normal, because I'm a single, sometimes scandalous, and an alcoholic mom. Right?"

"Sometimes you're scandalous? How?" She looks out the window.

"It's the Rez, mom. As long as you're a single mom, you're sometimes scandalous," I tell her, believing it myself. "You should know that."

"If you say so. I was never sometimes scandalous," she laughs.

"Shit, you were scandalous **all the time**, that's why," I laugh back at her. She doesn't say anything because she knows it's true.

We enter a valley. The sand hills of Nebraska are pretty. When George and I were kids, our dad used to take us fossil hunting and we'd find sea shell fossils in these hills.

"Come and get your love" by Redbone plays.

"These guys are skins," she tells me. "Redbone."

"Really?"

"Yah." She's singing the song. When it's over she tries to give me a drink but I decline. I have enough problems, thankfully though, it looked like George was done with harassing me. As we get near the highway, I turn onto it and drive until I hit the road to the Nebraska side of the dam. There's a back road there all the way into Pine Ridge.

"Mom, do you think Indians drink because of all the anger in us?" I ask.

"Probably," she says.

She's not good for conversation. I wish Mark was here.

I take a right at the Dam and slowly make my way over the rutted road to the west side of the dam.

"Well, when did you start drinking? Or when did you drink so much that you knew there was no turning back?" I ask her.

I pull up by the Walls, a fishing spot on the west side. We get out and walk to lean on the front of the car. We are high on cliffs that overlook the Dam. There's hardly any trees up here, mostly dried up weeds and old cow patties. Some trash flies here and there because no one respects the Earth. I always wonder how we went from living with so much honor to total lack of respect for anything. I look at the mixed drink. I know that's what it is. When alcohol was introduced to us, it took us down. It defeated us more than any cavalry ever could. The government probably loved it.

"I started drinking really bad after your sister Rita died."

"I was two, right?"

She nods.

"I thought I had a normal life. Your dad married me, and we tried real hard to have a happy family. He worked. I stayed home and had babies, three in a row—George, then you, then Rita. One morning, when she was three months old I woke up to nurse her and she was cold and blue in her crib. I flipped out crying. I thought if I checked on her sooner, you know, or if she nursed. When Charlie came in to check it out, he said I was crying, holding her, trying to make her nurse. After that we both fell off the wagon. Your Grandma Pacific and Grandpa Ray had you guys all the time. That's how your dad ended up doing time. Some guy was paying attention to me at a party, they fought. Your dad nearly killed him, he beat him so bad. After he went to prison, I just kept meeting all the jealous ones, abusive and jealous." She stares off at the water, as if she is looking for some porthole to take her back, let her start over.

"All Lakota men are jealous. All of them," I tell her.

"Well, the women are, too," she says.

"I know but to me it's an ugly feeling. Like why do people *want* to be jealous? I know a girl who, I swear, gets jealous when the sun shines on her man. In the grocery store, he looks at the ceiling or floor all the time." I laugh. It's not funny, it's pathetic.

"He should slap her up one time," she laughs.

I didn't. There is never a need for abuse and it goes both ways on the rez.

"Well, he did. He went to jail, she bailed him out. He used to work for us at the store, but she would rather work and make him stay home. It's pathetic, like I said. Jealousy is the backbone of their relationship."

"Yeah, but what would we do without our Lakota men?" Mom asks, looking off in the distance for dramatic effect. She's such a drama queen.

I don't say anything. I think I just quit a Lakota man for a white man. Not just any white man, a border town white man. That will piss people off. Like Lakota men have been doing that for years but no one cares or says anything when they come back from somewhere with some white woman with a funky name like White Dove in tow. But if an Indian woman does it, then it's scandalous.

"Do you think, as Lakota people, we suffer every day?" I ask her.

She nods. "Yes, we make ourselves suffer though." She holds up the mixed drink indicating that that was why we suffer.

"Mark said what suffering means to him is knowing something belongs to you but you can't have it. What do you think of that?" I ask her.

"I think that about sums it up. What I think, I always felt. What belonged to me was normalcy. Is that a word?" She looks at me. I shrug my shoulders.

"I think so." I stare off into space now. "If it is a word, it's what I want, too. Seems like every time I reach to try to be normal, as soon as I touch it, I do something to screw it all up."

"Well my girl, you're not the only one like that. You're not alone, remember that. The people we think are normal are probably not normal. I'm so gone, I don't even know if happy is really a thing, except maybe what I look for in a beer can."

I'm still looking off in the distance. "Let's go. This talk is depressing. I want to find my happy, dammit."

She holds her drink up to show me, that's where her happy is. She takes a long drink and hands me the cup. I take a drink of happy.

We get in the car and head to town. I'm really buzzin' now. Ha! I like how people can't say they're drunk, they're just buzzed, and really buzzed. We carefully make our way through town and to my house. When I get in the house the phone is ringing. It's Mason.

"Oh shit you're home, your cell phone is shut off, I think," he says.

"Really?" I look at my cell. "Oh the battery is dead. Sorry, we just got here. We sat at the Dam for a bit."

"Well, I was worried, we're pretty busy so I won't come down for sure until tomorrow. No closing early tonight."

"That sounds terrific," I tell him, then I realize how drunk I am. Who the hell says terrific? Definitely not a Rez chick.

"Well, I'll call you later after closing, okay?"

"Sure thing. I'll be here, sweetie." I'm still drunk talking. *Shut up, I tell myself. Making a fool.* He just laughs at me.

"You're drunk. Stay home, OK? Later, Sincere. I'll be thinking about you."

"Bye." I hang up the phone.

My mom's trying to figure out how to work the radio, but she keeps swaying. Damn, we barely put a dent in that bottle of Lord Calvert, and we were drunk.

"I'll play some music on the computer, mom," I tell her.

"I wanna hear some Patsy Cline," she slurs.

"Christ, OK. Who broke your heart?" I ask.

I put on *"Walking after Midnight."* Probably her least depressing song.

"Shyla broke my heart," she says, and she immediately goes into depressed mode.

"Mom, stop. Shyla's okay. Her head's on straight. Just understand her, OK? She is her own person and she is who she is," I tell her.

"I know," she says and sniffles with no tears. Drama queen status.

"Tony the Tiger!" I exclaim.

She wipes her non-existent tears.

"Who the fuck is Tony the Tiger?" she questions.

"You know, the Frosted Flakes guy," I answer.

"What about him?"

"He's the one who says terrific," I tell her.

"No, he says Grrrreat!" My mom laughs hard.

Oh, now I feel drunk and dumb.

I get my shot glass out and we do shots like we have business. My cell phone beeps when it gets enough of a charge, telling me there's a message. I drunkenly dial the messages. It's Misun wondering where everyone is. He wasn't back from their day out yet but call him. Yeah, I'll get right on that, I think.

There's a knock on the back door. Mom turns the radio off. We freeze. Someone starts coming in the back door, we take off for the back rooms. I hide under the bunk beds. I don't know where she's hiding but I can hear her breathing. The back door opens, I hear footsteps. Someone's in the kitchen. Shit, we left the jug of whiskey on the table.

"Police!" I hear someone say. "Come out with your hands up or I'll drink your whiskey up!" I recognize Uncle Shayne's laugh and crawl out from my hiding spot.

When I walk out, he's laughing. "Shit <u>Leksi</u>. You scared the hell outta me," I said.

"Who's here with you?" he asked me. He was sober.

"Mom. The boys are camping, Jazz is with Misun," I tell him.

"Where's your mom?" He asks me and taps it on the table twice.

"I'm in here!" I hear a muffled yell.

"Oh shit, I think she might be under my bed. The frame's broke. You need to lift it up to get her out," I tell him. He goes into my room and frees her.

When they come out, my mom's laughing and telling him how fast we hid. We all take seats at the table. Uncle Shayne pours a shot and drinks it.

"We have a problem, ladies," he says.

Crap, I don't like the sound of this. I thought today's drama was over.

"George is in jail. Two Times is in the hospital."

"What?" We **both** yell at the same time.

"George caught Two Times and Kris in bed. They fought. George beat him with his cop club and a dead porcupine. He was in uniform, but off-duty. Two Times is bad off, I was with him in the emergency room. George is in jail. Right now, he's in protective custody. He can't have any visits. I hate to say this, but it might go federal." He pours another shot.

"What about his job?" my mom asked.

"Once a tribal cop is arrested, he can't be a cop anymore." He lights a cigarette. "I'm sure he's fired. I stayed with Two Times but they ended up flying him to Rapid."

"Rapid!" My mom gasped.

"It's not life threatening, his knee is busted up pretty bad. His knee cap, that is. Plus he needs surgery to remove the porcupine quills." He puffs on the cigarette until my mom takes it out of his hand and starts smoking it.

"So what do we do? What can we do? What the fuck is up with the porcupine quills?" I ask him.

"Nothing. I tried, believe me. I tried. George, we have to wait on his charges. Two Times is going through surgery on his leg, his mom's with him. There's nothing we can do. I guess when they were fighting, George had a dead porcupine in the back of his unit, was probably gonna give it to you Sister, but instead he beat Two Times with it." He lights another cig.

"We can drink, that's all we can do," mom sighs, as if we weren't going to.

"Or we could find Kris and beat the shit out of that bitch," I said. I was pissed. That bitch isn't worth one brother losing a job and the other brother being hospitalized.

"Sheesh! One of us is already in jail. Behave. We'll see what happens tomorrow," my uncle scolds me.

In my drunk mind, I still want to beat her up. What the hell was she doing with Two Times—she knows he is like our brother. Now she caused a big family feud.

But I listen to them. We drink from the half a gallon. I guess I tried to play it off as my way of handling the bad news about my brother. Although, anything could've happened, like a tree falling over and I would've still drank. I wasn't foolin' anyone by saying I was drinking for any old whichever reason. I was drinking because I had a problem. The only time I can seem to admit it is when I'm hung-over.

"Sis!" my mom says. "Are you trying to pass out?"

"Not even! I'm spacing out. I mean I'm thinking. What?" I'm drunk, I feel like I'm whirly.

"Uncle Shayne wants to cruise. He's sober, he can drive," she tells me.

"Oh kay-ay," I hiccup. Shit, I hate hiccups. I can't get rid of them. Only with George. We're not real-real close but we know each other and we know how to get rid of each other's hiccups. We suction our palms on the other's ears while they drink a cup of water. Sure fire and foolproof. I tried it with other people, didn't work. Only with my brother George. I hiccup again.

"Get a jacket. The window's still broke. Sun's going down," she tells me. I find a hoody in the bottom of the hall closet. I kind of stumble when I get it. Whoa! Drunk again. All of a sudden we're in his car. It is cold, I'm not sure where we are... everything is a haze, a blur, then a blank spot.

And then when I come to I'm handcuffed. I'm in the back of a cop car with my mom.

"What's up, Mom?" I ask.

"What do you mean—what's up?" She's pissed.

"We going to jail?" I ask.

"Duh," she says. "Thanks to you."

"What I do?" I was spinning.

"You can't act right, that's what," she said.

"Where's Uncle Shayne?"

"He left when you started fighting Kris."

"Where?" I ask. I'm still drunk, but I'm not blank anymore.

"At her and George's house. You jumped out at the stop sign and ran over there."

"Why didn't you stop me?" I ask her.

"I tried. She called the cops on us." She rolls her eyes at me.

"I'm sorry," I whimper.

She just grunts at me.

We pull into the cop garage. The cops let us out and takes off the handcuffs. We walk into the booking area—this wasn't my first time in jail. Probably not even the third time. It was, however, my first time in the new facility.

"Have a seat please." The cop points with his lips to a couple of plastic seats on the right. As I go to sit down, I see George in a cell block behind where the chairs are. Protective Custody Block, the sign says.

"Mom, it's George?"

She looks towards him. He comes up to the window and motions, "What's up?"

"We're going to jail," I say. He reads my lips and rolls his eyes.

He puts up the number four and says, "What?"

"I tried to beat up Kris," I mouth the words dramatically.

"She did beat up Kris." Mom points to me with her lips.

"I did?" I ask.

"Yes, you did. Now get away from the window and get over here."

The cop calls me over. George gives me a peace sign. I give him a peace sign back. The cop motions me to the desk and fills out my paperwork. The C.O. is an old schoolmate. He shakes his head at me.

"No good, Sis," he says.

I look at the paperwork: Assault, Disorderly Conduct, and Liquor Violation. I think that's $135, if my memory and addition capabilities serve me correct.

"Look, my file says I'm 5'4"!" I exclaim all proud. I had been 5'1" since 7th grade.

"Since when?" Tanner, the C.O., teases. "C'mon Sis, we'll PBT you after 8 hours. If you blow zeroes, we switch you over to female housing. Your bond is $135."

I walk in the drunk tank—only one other lady is in there, passed out. I feel lucky but I remember it is still early. Lucky there's only one in here. When they open the door to let my mom in, I ask the time then I hiccup. Damn hiccups!

"You're booked in at 9 p.m. PBT at 5 a.m., Sis. Sleep tight."

"Good night," I sing song.

"Fine mess you got us into," Mom says.

"Sorry." I'm so drunk still. I start drinking water so I can pee it out of my system.

"Why you in here, Mom?" I ask.

"Liquor Vio," she says. "I can probably get a T.R. bond, but you—you're stuck here until court on Monday."

"That's right, no court on Friday." Damn, I feel dumb.

Mason was supposed to come see me tomorrow.

Misun's supposed to drop Jasmine off tomorrow, and here I am in the drunk tank—with extra charges, to boot. I beat Kris up and don't remember. My old best-friend. My sister-in-law. The mother of my niece and nephew. *Shit.* What about Two Times... in the hospital. George... no longer a cop and in jail, could face federal charges.

I know she was my sister-in-law, mother of my brother's children, my old best friend, but I had to beat her up. She was probably one of those women who felt unloved by her husband. Her husband who works long hours, cheats on her, his job required him to stay fit, while she felt she was growing old. Maybe Two Times made her feel young, pretty, alive again.

But I still had to beat her up, just because.

It's an unwritten oath in *tiwahe* (Family). You defend your own. You will do anything you can to protect them. Whether it be fighting for their well-being or their honor. That's how Lakotas are. My Uncle Shayne taught me that at age nine. You do what you can for you family. Kris caused a fight between two brothers. My brother lost his job, quite possibly his freedom, for the sake of being Lakota and the sake of family—I had to defend him. Plus he's the only one in the world that knows how to get rid of my hiccups.

I am trying to justify my evilness, my role as a villain once again. My mom tries to go to sleep right away on the bench.

"Mom, scoot over, it's cold," I nudge her with my elbow.

"No," she says, defiantly.

"Stay up. Talk to me," I tell her.

"No. Eight hours is a long time—sleep," she closes her eyes.

I lay beside her, trying to warm up. It's so cold in here. The bench is hard. The lady laying on the other side of the cell smells like a garbage can. I had flip flops on, so I'm barefoot. I make a mental note to always wear socks when I drink, so when I go to jail my feet stay warm. Then I laugh at myself for planning my next trip to jail, as if... I close my eyes and try to sleep.

I don't think I slept, but they opened the door and it woke me up. They pushed a young girl in. She was crying.

"What time is it?" I ask her.

"Ten o'clock," she whimpers.

"Fuck! That's all?" I close my eyes again but she whimpers harder. Pretty soon it's a wail.

"Fuck!" I mutter and get up. I go take a drink of water from the toilet/sink combo. I drink water until I almost gag, then I pee, wash my hands and sit on the bench. I yawn, but I know I'm still drunk. I can't sleep. The young girl's sitting on the opposite bench crying. *Oh boy.*

"You know this is the drunk tank?" I glare at her.

She nods.

"You'll probably get released in eight hours on a T.R. bond. That's a 'temporary release' bond." I just want her to shut up.

That sets off another crying tangent. I groan.

My mom sits up, "Shut the fuck up and do your eight hours! I'm doing mine!" Then she lays back down and almost immediately starts snoring.

I laugh, "Yeah, you heard her."

She tries to quit crying and starts sniffling. That's better at least. I lean against the corner of the room on the bench. I close my eyes. I hear the girl pacing then she furiously starts pressing the button with a speaker by the door.

"Can I help you?" a correctional officer says.

"What are my charges?" she cries.

"Liquor Violation," he answers her. She whimpers and sniffles. "What about my boyfriend? His name is Jackson?"

"He's got a liquor violation, disorderly conduct, and driving under the influence," the speaker says.

"Is he getting out?" she asks.

"No, go to bed," he says. She starts crying again. Her face is all scrunched up and tears flowing down.

"You better quit crying, or one of these chicks here will get up and blast you," I yawn, then go to take another drink of water.

She sniffles, "M-my boyfriend's in j-jail."

"I heard," I tell her. "Consider yourself lucky he's in jail. At least he ain't cheating on you."

She cries harder.

Now I'm pissed, "No matter how much you cry, you're still going to be in jail. Now shut the fuck up!"

She whimpers. I pace. I think about my life. Fun stuff.

Finally after what feels like a whole day, she passes out. She's young, like 18 maybe, barely disqualifies for the juvenile detention center. Her hair is tangled and her socks are dirty. Ick, I smell feet. I hate people.

I see them pat searching two more young girls. They come in giggling and loud.

"Our gig is up," one of them said and they both laugh harder.

Two young boys walk by the drunk tank and throw signs up to the girls. They throw gang signs back and giggle. Kids are so dumb. They try to use inner-city accents and identify with another culture. It irks me and I'm thankful my sons are not into being a "gangster."

"I wonder what our charges are?" one of them says. The other one starts pushing the button.

"What are our charges?" she asks.

"Serious," the C.O. replies. They both giggle.

"Serious, like how?" The shorter one asks.

"Serious, like you're going to do time for this," he says. "Extortion, possession of a controlled substance, liquor violation, and possession with intent. Now shut up."

"Damn," I said, "That *is* some time." They both turn around like they just now noticed me.

"How much?" The tall, thin faced one asks.

"Six months, at least," I tell her.

I have no idea but I am tired of their damn giggling, too. Neither of them are laughing now. They both look worried.

"What did you guys do?" I ask.

"Well, we always had this scheme. We find out which old ladies are close to their dogs, then we take the dogs. Whoever gives a reward, you know. That's our beer and partying money. But this time we got caught. We hit the same lady up that we hit up last week. We couldn't remember who we sent to the door. So we sent our homeboy, Tailbone. And she caught us. Tailbone was the one who returned the dog last week. She made us wait, said her son was bringing *over* the reward money. The cops come. Tailbone kept a copy of every "Lost Dog" poster made in the cubby hole. So we got caught. The drugs, all I knew about was the weed. Someone had meth."

"Damn, you guys stole dogs from grandmas?" I ask them. They both nod, their eyes big.

"That's fucked. You're both fucked." I glare at them. I don't know about any law for dognapping on the Rez but I will put the fear of God and Uncis (grandmas) everywhere into them.

"How much time is that?" The short one asks.

"A lot. I'm not sure how much, but I do know that you two are definitely going to hell."

They both start crying.

I start pacing the cell again. I am the villain.

"If you're going to cry, cry quietly!" I whisper loudly, then I kick my mom with my toes. "This woman here just went on a wild rampage, putting people in the hospital after she drank a fifth of tequila, because someone stole her poodle, Bubbies."

They move to the other side of the cell, away from my mom. I smile as I pace. They're crying quietly now.

"We didn't steal no Bubbies, did we?" The tall one keeps wiping her eyes and sniffling.

"No," the short one says. "No Bubbies." And she lets out a muffled cry.

I keep pacing until they pass out by each other. I see some guys come in the jail. I point to my wrist at one of them. He shows me a one and a five three times, 1:15 a.m. I nod thanks. Over halfway over. I sit on the bench that my mom is lying on. She stretched out so now I can't lay by her. I can only sit. Another lady comes in. She's drunk as hell. She says something to me that I don't understand one bit and laughs. Then she lays on the floor by the toilet and passes right out. Damn. Someone should've told me that was the soft spot in here.

Finally, I sleep.

"There you are! Bitch! Where was you two when I needed you?!" I dream Frieda's yelling at me. It better be a dream, I think as I open my eyes. It's not. She's standing there in one of her skank outfits looking like a... skank.

"What the fuck?" I open my eyes. Still in the drunk tank, now my little sister has made an appearance. I rub my eyes, then yawn. I blink and look at her.

"What?" I say.

"You." She points her finger in my face. I bat it away. "You weren't home. And she wasn't home either!" She points at mom. The drunk tank starts waking up to Frieda's little dramatic performance.

"So!" I tell her. "What?"

"You were in here, all this time? I needed you! Both of you! D.S.S. took my kids because you two weren't home!" She spits.

"So it's our fault?" I stand up to her. I don't care how tall she is. "Fuck you!"

"You girls behave! Frieda, when did they take them? Why?" Mom gets up.

"About an hour or two ago. Cops broke in my back door. Everyone went to jail. They drove me around to look for someone to take my kids. But every member of my family is out of town, in jail, or in the hospital! Now I lost them and it's my family's fault! Bastards!" She cries.

"Calm down," my mom says. "Wait, who's in the hospital? Two Times?"

"Mark," she's still crying. "He, Boogie, and Sis' boyfriend got in a wreck. They're all in the hospital."

"Oh, fuck." I start pacing again. "How are they?" I ask her.

"Why should I care?" Freida yells. "My life is ruined! They took my kids away! And it's your fault!" She points her finger at me *again*. That's it, I can only take so much fingers being pointed in my face.

"Fuck you, Frieda," I say as calmly as I can.

"Fuck you, Sis. I'm sick of you acting like you're better than me. You're just a whore, too!" she yells.

I smile, despite my anger.

"That means then that you admit you're a whore! Congratulations," I tell her. Mom's trying to stand between us. "Now try to admit that you, **YOU** alone lost your kids, you stupid bitch!"

She socks me one in the face and stuns me. I'm bleeding. I'm in shock, she never fights me. She's usually scared of me. I get over the shock quick and start choking her. The C.O.'s run in quick.

"Ladies! You want to get mace in the face?" Tanner yells.

"Put her in protective custody!" I yell, "Before I kill her."

"I'll kill you first!" Freida yells back.

"You both better be quiet! Before you both get more charges!" Tanner yells. He's holding me back—another C.O. is holding Frieda back.

"Who started it?" Tanner asks our cellmates. Everyone except my mom points at Frieda.

"Bitches!" she yells. "Jealous bitches—hating cuz your men loooove me." They drag her off to a single cell in the same segregation cell block as George. I put toilet paper on my bloody nose.

"Stupid bitch," I say. My adrenaline is all rushing now. I hit the button.

"What?" Tanner says.

"What time is it?" I ask.

I, at least, want to be switched over to housing.

"4:00 a.m. Sis, one hour to go."

Fuck. I pace. Fuckin' Frieda loses her kids, too. *Stupid. Stupid.* She's going to have to go to parenting classes to get them back. Maybe this is what she needs. It's always Misun and I coming to the rescue. And now Mark, Boogie, and Ricky are in the hospital?

Christ!

This is God telling me to quit drinking. Seriously. I know it is.

I felt it was when I made the appointment for a drug and alcohol evaluation. Now I know it. It's like doomsday.

When that sun comes up, it's a brand new day and I will be sober. For real. I'm not just saying that because I'm in the drunk tank. For real... this time.

By the time the C.O. comes to PBT my mom and I, I'm on the seventh year of my ten-year plan. I feel good about life because according to the seven years of the ten-year plan, I have a four year degree. I have another daughter and am happily married to Mason. Even my cat, Sapa, proves he's not gay by giving me grand kittens. We both blow .000.

Thank God. Somehow.

Brand new day.

"Normally, we switch you over to the female inmate housing, but bond's been posted for both of you," the C.O. tells us.

"Who?" I can't imagine.

"They're waiting for you outside," she says.

They do our paperwork to process us out. We get our shoes and property back. George is waving at us. Mom blows him a kiss. She asks about him and Frieda. wave, much as I hate him, I love him.

"They both have holds on them until court on Monday, can't do anything until then." She gives us the papers to sign. She escorts us out the front of the jail, the opposite way we came in. We both walk outside. The sun is almost peeking over the Eastern horizon. I blink. Shyla's sitting in George's car. We walk up to her.

"I got mom out, all I had was 35 bucks. We need to talk, Mom. Sis, that guy got you out." She says and points with her lips down the parking lot.

It's Mason.

It's a brand new day.

[nine]

Friday

I smile at Mason and get in the passenger side of his truck. He is sitting there smiling at me and I know I look like crap. My hair is probably a mess. I have my hoody and flip flops back. I have my hood pulled over my hair. I can't even say its bed head; I slept on a bench, I have bench head.

"Thanks, you didn't have to do that you know," I smile at him and hope he don't want a kiss.

"Well good morning to you, too." He leans over to kiss me. I put my cheek out for him to kiss. Lord knows if I kiss him, he will never want to see me again.

"Please, I need to brush my teeth and I know I smell like the drunk tank. Who told you I was in there... and stuff?" I ask him as he starts the truck to back out. It sucks to see him look so good in this early morning sun. Even the sunrise looks great. Everything looks beautiful except me. I feel like crap. I better quit thinking like that. I will be trying to cry. He has an Audioslave CD in and "*Doesn't Remind Me*" started playing.

"Nobody. I couldn't get ahold of you. So I called the jail. They said to have a money order for $135 by 5 am. So here I am." He's driving me back to my house.

He has his Red Sox hat on, despite it being Boston, he looks cute. I almost forget he actually likes the Cubs—lately he has been big on Boston.

"You going fishing?" I ask him.

He nods, "Yup, soon as I dump you off."

"Did you hear about Boogie, Mark, and uh, Ricky."

"Yeah, Shyla told me. Your sister's pretty nice." He looks at me. "I knew she was your sister. I could see the resemblance." He stops at the stop light.

"I shouldn't have let them go," I tell him.

"Well, they did it on their own, it's not your fault. They're all OK, I guess. Just broken up. That one—Ricky—broke his neck. Cops are trying to figure out which one was driving. Besides, if you was with them, you'd be in the hospital." The light turns green and two minutes later he pulls into my driveway.

"Wanna come in? I'll make you some coffee?" I ask him.

"Yeah, sure." He nods and turns off the truck. He has a thermos for more coffee.

I go in and start coffee right away. He sits on the couch with the remote. I jump in the shower right away. After washing the drunk tank residue off with hot water, I brush my teeth, and put on fresh clothes. I grab his watch and the lotion.

I sit by him as he's watching Sports Center. I tell him about yesterday and what happened with everyone as I lotion up.

I tell him about my adventure in the drunk tank and my ten-year plan. I omit the part about the marriage to him. I tell him I am tired of this lifestyle. I tell him about the crying girl, the dog thieves, and about my brother George and my sister Frieda hitting me.

He laughs about the dognappers.

"So," I tell him. "Today is a brand new day."

"Well, then Miss Sincere, can I kiss you now?" he asks.

I nod. We kiss right there on my couch. Toe curler, again. I am starting to wonder if we are both good kissers or if it is just him, or just me. Maybe we both are mediocre and make each other great.

"My last paycheck is today," I suddenly remembered. Man, this week went by fast. "I can pay you back!"

"That's okay," he tells me. "You can pay me when you get back on your feet, and if you try to ditch, I know where you live," he winks. Gross, I don't like winks. But he is so damn cute.

He finishes his coffee.

"You coming back?" I ask, then stand up and stretch.

"Yeah. I don't have to work today, but I have to run some errands. You cooking something up tonight?" He takes his coffee mug to the sink.

"Yah, I was going to make pork chili and fry bread," I say.

"Damn, I'll get some movies and be back."

I have my arms around him; he smells good, like Irish Spring soap and coffee and spearmint gum. I could inhale him all day.

"OK, it will probably just be me and Jasmine home. Shyla said she's with her cousins and Misun and his girlfriend are in Hot Springs, still. They went swimming at one place, got a room and are going swimming at another place before they come back."

"Sounds good. Hey, Sincere," Mase pauses, "everything that happened yesterday is not your fault. You can't fix everything. Maybe fighting Kris and going to jail *is* your fault. Sometimes, though, you have to let things happen. Even if it is to your family. I mean, it's good to take up for them, but you can't control everything, you know? You only need to worry about you and your kids. I'm not preaching but take care of yourself, OK?" He's looking at me.

I nod and blink back tears. *How many times has my dad told me the same thing?* I think.

"Don't be blaming yourself, it will eat at your heart and you have a good heart."

I just nod. His arms are around me and it feels good. I find myself not wanting him to go, but we both have things to do.

"I love-" he pauses and looks at me. For once he looks nervous.

"I could love you, you know." We both laugh.

"Yeah, well, I could love you, too!" I look down, blushing. *Why does he make me feel all of twelve years old?*

"I'll be back." He kisses me, touches my nose with his finger and jumps in his truck. I wave until he's gone. *This boy makes me giddy.*

My cell phone rings and it's Misun. I lean against "The Beast" and tell him everything. I tell him about my war wounds, a bruise from Frieda on my left cheek (wait till she gets out), and scratches from Kris, probably a handful of hair was missing, too.

We talk about Mark, George, and Shyla's coming out. I ask what happened to them yesterday and he tells me they'll be back this afternoon. They decided to get a room after touring the Black Hills. We talk about if I get the opportunity to go to treatment.

"Pork chili tonight," I tell him.

"Alright, we'll be over. I love you, Sis. And I think Mason is right, when he told you to quit trying to take care of all of us. I mean not to say mind your own business, but let Frieda learn, let George deal with his charges and wife, let Mark—," he pauses and laughs, "Let Mark be Mark. Let Ricky go, don't feel guilty for liking the white boy. I always thought Ricky strung you along. Let Shyla and mom come to terms with her sexuality. And let me go away to school. Do you for a while. You have to love and take care of yourself, OK? Do it for your kids." And with that he hangs up.

I am sort of crying. He is right, I have to quit running around thinking I am making things better for everyone when I can't even make it better for myself. Now that I have some alone time, I think I will go write that essay for treatment, school, help, a step forward.

As I walk towards the house, I notice my trunk is open. I lift it to close it tight and I see mom's beer in there. We didn't drink any of it. Wow. My heart starts beating fast. I touch it. It stayed cold. I take it inside and put it on the counter. *I can call her and have her come get it,* I think as I stare at it. And stare at it. *Or I can pour it out and not tell her.* She's probably having a heart to heart talk with Shyla, I think as I dial her number. Her voicemail picks up. Must be having that talk.

"Hey, mom! I noticed you left some of your beers over here. Stop by when you get this message and pick them up." I hang up and look at them. I ignore the fact that I said, "some of your beers..." I know deep down I said that because my mom has no idea we didn't drink the beers.

Today's a brand new day. I have to start my essay. If I want to get help, I have to write it. Misun suggested treatment first and school next semester. He offered to watch my kids and start a semester late himself. That sounded good to me.

I need to change.

I need **a** change.

No more suffering.

Like Mark said, suffering is what you know can be yours, you can see it, but can't touch it.

That's us Lakota for the past hundred or so years. Suffering because we were made to suffer at first. Then suffering because we made ourselves suffer.

I grab a beer and take it to the sink to pour it out. I open it, my hand shakes as I pour it out. I pour half of it out.

Then, I take a drink.

"Just to get rid of the shaking," I say aloud to myself. I drink the rest of the can. I throw it at the wall and scream. I throw a few more cans around the house while screaming. I hear something break. I hear cans spraying open. I sit on the floor and cry. *I fucking hate this addiction.* I sob. Then I remember Misun telling me to love myself. I remember Mason telling to take care of myself. I remember my mom saying I have the strength inside me to pull myself out of this. I remember my kids. *I can do this.* I have to. For them and for me.

I have to at least start my essay. I grab another can and go to the computer. I play James Otto's *"Just got started loving you."* Not only does it remind me of Mason and our dance, it reminds me of myself. I feel like I just got started loving myself.

I open the beer, take a drink. I am still sniffling and wiping tears as I open up Microsoft Word.

The cursor blinks at me. I think of what to write. I think of what I want them to know. Maybe I want them to see me. Why I want a better life. I want them to know what it is like for me, and the struggle I have with addiction. I am still crying and wiping tears. I will show them a week in the life of a Rez chick. This Rez chick. I wipe my tears, take another drink and I start typing.

"The pow wow grounds on my reservation are always dusty. Actually, the whole town is dusty..."

ABOUT THE AUTHOR

Dana Lone Hill was born and raised on the Pine Ridge Reservation. Dana started writing at the age of 4 and was published for her poetry at the age of 8. However she went on to drop out of high school with a 3.83 GPA, drop out of college twice, and quit the education classes she was taking while in prison.

Dana never looked back, never let her past hold her back despite her hardships. She had a firm belief that when bad things happen, they can be turned into good things if you look at them in the right light and from the right angle. She has only moved forward with this belief and is hoping her book is well-loved. She would not change one step she ever took on this beautiful planet because every one of those steps made her who she is.

She is the mother of four children, Ty, Jalen, Stephon and Justice. She has one cat, Mischa. She currently lives off the reservation and has taken on the role of the highly criticized "urban Indian" but still dreams of being home on the rez. She is

Dana Lone Hill

a freelance writer for The Guardian, Lakota Country Times, The Intersection of Madness and Reality, LA Progressive and has a blog at www.justarezchick.wordpress.com.

She enjoys beading, quilling, painting, writing, watching the New York Yankees and chick flicks. You can follow her @JustARezChick

ACKNOWLEDGMENTS

There was a long journey to get right here and have this book be published. And many people have believed in me and supported me along the way. So many people to thank that I may as well get started.

First I want to thank Tunkasila, our Grandfather (Creator) for having my back and guiding me along this journey and blessing me with everything in my life.

I want to thank my children. They are my life. I have not always been there for all four of them but they have always been in my heart and the only reason at all I pushed forward and moved on. Ty, you were my first baby and you changed my life for the better. Jalen, your strong personality showed me that every single child from birth is an individual. Stephon, you old soul, you showed me how much love I have in my heart just by being my son. Justice, my sweet daughter, only daughter, you are every bit the little woman I had hoped you would be and that is stronger than me. I love you all so much.

To my parents:

Mom—My whole life I owe to you for having me and raising me when you were only a 17 year old girl. You proved that courage is not a choice, it is essential when you are a mother, a Lakota woman, you proved this time and time again. You showed me over and over to love life and take chances, travel, see the world. Every opportunity I have ever received, you told me to reach for it. I love you and thank you for showing me that I am a strong Lakota woman.

Dad—I will never forget your words to me. Every single one of them. If it wasn't for you, I wouldn't have been able to handle some of the crap I went through. I always remember you telling me, no matter who I face in life or what I face, I have my ancestors behind me. And I will never forget you telling me how strong my heart is. And I know you were also always behind me with your prayers.

To my siblings: Wow, there are so many of you.

Travis—I love you, always. We been through so much together and in my heart I know we're going to be together at the end too because that is how it always was. Me and you.

Jesse—My first brat ever, carried you on my hip until you got too big. But you still act like a brat to me.

Jaida—My sista, you are so beautiful and creative and I always knew you would see the world.

Jaron—My baby brother, I could never be mad at you and still can't haha, you came into my life right before my sons did and I can't imagine life without you.

Jenna—My brattiest sibling ever, I love our fights because deep down we have a strong love but I still know more than you, haha.

Jonna—My baby sister, I knew I was going to spoil you the minute I saw you. I love you for your laughter.

Kayla—I regret missing years growing up not knowing you and sharing our dreams but I am thankful we know each other now and I love you just as much.

Wakiya—Wow, I have so many words. You were taken from us so young by the Department of Social Services that it was always a pain in my heart knowing you were out there somewhere. I want you to know, I deserve no credit for finding you. There was a strong force behind that and it was the prayers you told me that you said every night for 21 years for

God to guide your family to find you. You believed in those prayers strongly and that is how we came to be family again.

Shannon—My little sister, I am thankful to have met you and hope to still spend time with you again someday. I love you whereever you are.

I love all of you.

To all my stepsisters—Leticia, Tashina, Zanita, and Siyota, a whole gang of strong Lakota women, I love you.

To my hunka brothers—Q, Tobe, Phil, and Dirty, Dirty Steve I love you guys!

To all my aunties and uncles, thank you for all the stories, this book would not be possible without you. To my cousins, nieces and nephews, I love you all.

To my cellmates in cell block 17 at PCJ, you were with me from the beginning of this book and to the end. Only one of you read it but you all had a hand in it and you all lent your ear when I would read you parts of it. To my little cousin X, there is no part two! And thank you for being my first editor. All you girls, X, Billie, Nelly, Doreen, Alicia, and Delonnie— thank you.

To the girls I met in that journey—Keebs, Dani, Susan, Nicole, and Kujo—you were the for real ones with me. So I will mention you here and I want you to know there is not a day that goes by where you are not in my thoughts. D-UNIT!

To two of my forever friends, Aimy and Sox, without either of you this would never have been possible.

And lastly, those who helped with the book along the way:

to Trace DeMeyer—not only for your work with Native adoptions and kids lost in adoption and your tireless work helping people find their way home, find who they are, I mostly want to thank you for believing in me and being the first one to give me a chance in helping me to be published. I am forever grateful.

To Kim Pittman, my cover designer, thank you for stepping in when I needed you! You are an angel!

Tatiana—a/k/a Tatty Pants, thank you for training me in my writing. I know I have a long way to go but I can see how I am way better because of you.

To my best of friends—Lisa Brewer, Myk Hall, Priscilla Magouirk, Gaylen Ducker, Joyce Courtney, Jacklyn Coats, Gregory Marto, Jon Eagle, Jenny Williams, Joette Lee, Dorian New Holy, and Tom Goings—thank you all for believing in me.

To my 360 friends: Joe Carroll, Big Ned, Ant, Karin, Janet, Michelle, Catina, Mamesta, Daisy, Al, Billy Johnson, Lauri, Mizz Teaque, Lionel, Jenny, Rala, Tigga, Rippa, Nina, Eddie Blue Eyes and Adeeb, thank you all for your support, critiques, and love along the way. And Sara, you deserve your own thank you even if you never see it. I love you all. And I love you Big Ned for saying you predicted this shit, my bbff foreva, brutha from anotha mutha.

To those who passed waiting for my book to be done, Michelle Cooper, Scott Peters (Atarishark), Mike Shain, Grandma Erna, and Aunt Nellie—I wished I would have hurried but I hope somehow you are still proud of me.

To all the Native brothers and sisters on the inside! Remember who you are and where you come from, and there is always more than where you are now. It is not rock bottom, it is a springboard so jump!

Lastly, to all the music that motivated me along the way while writing and to the New York Yankees (and Derek Jeter), you will always be a part of my life.

To baseball, you were my first and will be my last love, always.

First & last

Dana Dane

Dana's Blog: www.justarezchick.wordpress.com
On Twitter: @JustARezChick
On Facebook: https://www.facebook.com/Pointingwithlips

All PHOTOS BY AUTHOR, USED WITH PERMISSION
POINTING WITH LIPS © 2014 was published by Blue Hand
Books, a collective of Native American authors who guide and
assist other Native writers to publish their paperbacks and
ebooks using Amazon's Create Space and KDP. They are based
in western Massachusetts. Visit their website at
www.bluehandbooks.org.
Like them on Facebook:
https://www.facebook.com/bluehandbooks

Dana Lone Hill

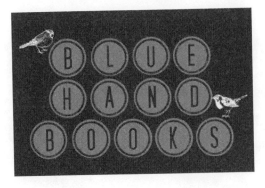

BLUE HAND BOOKS
442 Main St. #1061
Greenfield, MA 01301
(413) 258-0115
www.bluehandbooks.org

Made in the USA
Charleston, SC
02 July 2014